A MATT McCALL NOVEL

DEATH ANGEL

C.C. RISENHOOVER

CONTRARY CREEK

Contrary Creek Publishers

Also by C.C. Risenhoover

DEAD EVEN
BLOOD BATH
CHILD STALKER
LETHAL RAGE
TRESTLES OVER DARKNESS
WHITE HEAT
WINE, MURDER & BLUEBERRY SUNDAES
MURDER AT THE FINAL FOUR
SATAN'S MARK
HAPPY BIRTHDAY JESUS
LARRY HAGMAN

Copyright © 2001 by C.C. Risenhoover

All rights reserved. No part of this book may be reproduced in any form or by any electronic or mechanical means, including information storage and retrieval systems, without permission in writing from the publisher, except by a reviewer, who may quote brief passages in a review.

Printed in the United States of America

FIRST EDITION

Library of Congress Cataloging-in-Publication Data

Risenhoover, C.C.
    Death Angel / C.C. Risenhoover. – 1st ed.
    p. cm.
    ISBN 1-930899-01-7
    LCCN 00-107529

AUTHOR'S NOTE

The individual characters who appear in this book are wholly fictional. Any apparent resemblance of a character to any person alive or dead is purely coincidental.

DESIGN BY JEFF STANTON

Published by Contrary Creek Publishers

For my children and their spouses

Paul, Elizabeth and Bob, Tim and Karen,
Brandy and Chris, Jeff, Justin and Robyn

And my grandchildren

Blaire, Will, Graham, Sophia and Jason

ONE

Scott Tyler was a strong man, but there was no way he could stop the tears from welling up in his eyes. His only son was lying on the hospital bed; life support systems attached to his body, his vital signs monitored by strange blipping patterns on a screen. Tyler thought the machines, which were emitting rhythmic sounds, would cause his brain to explode.

What had started as an enjoyable evening had deteriorated into a nightmare. He had nothing to hold to except hope for a miracle, and Tyler had seen and experienced too much terror and destruction in his life to have much faith in miracles.

But such hope was all that was left.

That and prayer.

He had tried to pray for Andy, but the words had stuck in his mind and throat. Prayer, for him, was a last resort. He did not pray when things were good, so why would God listen when things were bad?

DEATH ANGEL

Across the room that seemed to be a haze of white, chrome and vinyl, Tyler's eyes focused on his wife's tear-stained face. Only Heather was not his wife anymore, something he had difficulty accepting. They had been divorced for several years. She now belonged to Bob Mack, who had an arm around her and was whispering sympathetic words into her ear. Tyler figured he should be the one where Bob Mack was, but that was all in a past he could not accept or forget.

Even in his grief, watching his son battle the Death Angel, Tyler could not help but feel both love and antagonism toward Heather. When he had finally realized he loved her, had given up his drinking and womanizing, she hadn't been there for him. She had overlooked his infidelity for years, but had finally had enough.

Heather surprised him when she filed for divorce, and surprised him even more when she married Bob Mack a couple of years later. Mack was ten years older than she was and owner of the town's largest restaurant, small potatoes by big city standards. But Mack was well off, certainly one of the wealthier people in Putnam, Texas.

Why, Tyler wondered, when his only son's life was on the line, did his brain whirl with thoughts of Heather and Bob Mack? It was, perhaps, because he felt both anger and envy toward Mack for the role he had played in Andy's life. Mack had been there for Andy when he had not.

Watching his son fight for his life, Tyler was overwhelmed by a flood of guilt. This would not have happened if Andy had not been following in his footsteps, if the people in town had not always likened the boy to his father.

Tyler, when a teenager, had been a star football player. All he knew was that something in him lived to play the game with reckless abandon. Andy had been a mirror image of him, which was why he was battling for his life.

His mind could not help but go back to the past, when he, not Andy, was wearing pads and a helmet.

● ● ●

September was always hot and humid in Putnam, Texas. Situated in the woodlands of East Texas, the small town was about an hour and a half drive from the Gulf Coast. The breeze that most often came from the Gulf and filtered through the trees was sticky, like hot taffy. The

One

humidity was like sweat.

There were two sawmills within the city limits. They were the town's major employers. There was a paper mill thirty-five miles to the south and another fifty miles to the west. The highways into and out of the town were usually clogged with log trucks and pulpwood trucks on weekdays.

Putnam was the county seat. A red rock courthouse was set in the middle of the city square. It had a four-faced clock on top. None of the faces kept the right time, but most people didn't pay much attention to the courthouse clock anyway. They set their watches by the sawmill whistles. The whistles signaled employees when it was time to be up and getting ready for work, when it was time to start work, when it was time for lunch, when it was time to go back to work, and when it was time to end the workday.

The two men who blew the whistles for their respective sawmills were the only ones in town who could be counted on to have the correct time. Or, what passed for the correct time.

The only thing in Putnam more important than sawmill whistles, church and school bells, was Friday night football. That's how Scott Tyler remembered the town in the early seventies, back when he was a star running back for the high-school team.

He had been a star all right, a powerful runner who enjoyed crashing into tacklers, who dished out more punishment than he took in slashing his way to touchdown after touchdown. He had been arrogant, too, an All-State selection who thought he was All-World.

The world had been his oyster then. The scholarship offers had rolled in. He blessed the University of Texas with his presence, but he found college ball a lot different from high school ball. A lot of Scott Tylers were in the college ranks, an entire team of them at the University of Texas, all fast and tough and anxious to prove their mettle.

He had taken a beating in college ball. There were a lot of fast, mobile linebackers and defensive backs who enjoyed nothing more than slamming their shoulder pads into the knees of a guy who thought he was tough enough to run over them.

But Tyler excelled as a college running back because he had a spirit that would not quit. He refused to accept defeat on any level.

DEATH ANGEL

A lot of people thought he should have gone into pro ball, but Tyler had a different dream. He wanted to be a combat pilot, so after college joined the Marine Corps.

After getting his wings, he married Heather. She was five years younger and, in his opinion, the most beautiful girl in the world. Many in Putnam shared that opinion.

The problem was that there was no war and no combat, not exactly an ideal situation for a pilot who dreamed of becoming an ace. So Tyler had gotten out of the Marine Corps and been recruited by a government agency to fly arms to rebels in Central America. His plane was shot down and he was captured.

For nearly a year he was a prisoner, caged and tortured. But he didn't break. There was no way they were going to break him, no matter what they did.

He was prepared to die, thought he would never again see Heather. But then an elite counter-intelligence unit rescued him. For Tyler it meant a trip home.

The problem was that he didn't want to go home. All he could think about was crawling back in the cockpit of an aircraft, and inflicting as much pain as possible on those who had captured him. He was desperate for revenge, to beat those whom he thought had beaten him. He didn't understand the kind of game that was being played in Central America, didn't really care. He just wanted his pound of flesh.

The agency that hired him no longer wanted him, so he was forced to go back to Putnam where he became vice president in his father-in-law's bank. He received accolades from the townspeople. They were always patting him on the back and recalling the good old days, the days when he was a star running back and Putnam was one of the state's high school football powers. Andy was born, and then people talked about how it would be the same again when he grew up, how another Tyler would restore Putnam to its football prominence of old.

For Tyler, having a son and being a bank VP was not enough. He felt empty, depressed and alone. He started drinking and womanizing, making moves on every good-looking and eligible woman in the county. And he made moves on some that were not so eligible, primarily some of the young and tantalizing married women in Putnam's coun-

One

try club set. Some even claimed they were Heather's friends.

It had been a slide from there. He lost his wife and job, which he figured he did not deserve anyway. It had been there because he was married to Heather.

Battling alcoholism and life-threatening depression, Tyler had felt the need to get away from Putnam, to find a place where he could regroup. His parents, of course, lived in the town and were supportive. Only he was too self-centered to see them in that role. He didn't think that they could understand what he was going through. He didn't understand it himself.

So he left.

Instead of trying to find a job in Beaumont, Houston or Dallas, he decided to go to San Antonio. There was a guy there he wanted to see – the man who had led the unit that rescued him from the prison camp.

It took a few years, but he got himself straightened out. He went back to Putnam, opened an insurance agency and did pretty well. Putnam people had not forgotten his football days. He felt he had to be there for Andy's years in high school.

The days, if not the lonely nights, were kind to him. He and Andy hunted and fished together, and he encouraged his son's athletic endeavors. He was proud of the boy, encouraging, but never pressuring him to play any sport. He did not want to live vicariously though Andy. He had seen enough fathers foul up their sons in that way.

Tyler had not remarried. He had dated a number of women, but found none to compare with Heather. Comparisons were always the problem. He figured he was destined for a lifetime of regret for having lost her.

Sharing time with Andy was what he lived for, to be there when the boy needed him, and to get out of the way when he did not. Their relationship was not just that of father and son, but one of friendship. Tyler was feeling good about making up for the lost years.

Then came the game against Lufkin.

Tyler had always worried about the way Andy had played the game with such abandon. Tyler had played the same way. But there was a difference. Tyler was a block and Andy was a chip off it. Tyler had been six-foot two inches tall and weighed two hundred pounds in high

DEATH ANGEL

school. Andy was five-eleven and weighed one hundred sixty.

But like him, Andy was a reckless, slashing running back whose elusiveness would have worked in his favor if he had used it. But instead of trying to avoid contact, Andy seemed instead to look for it. He exhibited a fierce determination to win and be the best, something Tyler understood quite well.

It might have been understandable, Tyler thought, if Andy had been hurt in a head-on collision with a big linebacker. But he had simply been running a pass pattern on the first play after the kickoff and had collapsed in a heap. No one had touched him.

A private aircraft flew Andy to Methodist Hospital in Houston, where doctors worked through the night and early morning hours to keep him alive. Now he was on life support, constantly monitored. And it was obvious things were not going well.

TWO

In another part of the world, Matt McCall was crouched behind what was left of a wall of a building that had caught more than its share of rocket hits. The building was basically gutted, rubble everywhere. But he had been told that one of the lesser-known terrorist groups would be bringing a recently captured American diplomat there. And they would be turning their captive over to a similar group, who would then take him to another country friendly to their alleged cause.

McCall was in the company of three members of the Mossad, Israel's answer to the CIA. The difference in the organizations, McCall figured, was that the Israeli government gave the Mossad more latitude in taking care of business than American government officials wanted to give the CIA.

They had staked out the bombed hulk of the structure for more than four hours. It was deathly quiet, and he was beginning to wonder if their source had provided them the wrong information. He doubt-

DEATH ANGEL

ed it. The Mossad was very thorough.

Then he heard the ominous sound of vehicles coming toward them. There was no need to signal his companions. All knew their roles.

McCall could see the street that led up to and past the building. And though the sounds of the vehicles kept get closer, he could see no lights. There was no light anywhere, except from a quarter moon and the stars.

Finally, he was able to make out the approaching vehicles. There was an old Jeep in the lead, an even older troop carrier following close behind. The slow-moving vehicles came to a screeching halt, probably caused by worn brake shoes.

The two men in the Jeep got out, came around to one side and leaned up against the vehicle. Two other men got out of the front seat of the truck and joined them. They all lit cigarettes and started talking, a conversation McCall couldn't make out. What he could make out was that all were armed with Uzis.

He wondered whether or not this was the group holding the prisoner, or the group to whom the captive American diplomat would be transferred. If they were the ones holding the man, then he would be in the back of the truck. If so, was he tied up or was someone guarding him?

The only way to be sure, McCall knew, was to wait for the other group. Their arrival, of course, would put him and his three companions at a numerical disadvantage. However, the four of them knew going in that they would probably be outnumbered. They were counting on surprise as an ally. McCall figured they would have to move swiftly, decisively, to keep the terrorists from executing the diplomat on the spot. It was a dangerous game, but one McCall knew well. He had played it throughout the world.

About ten minutes passed before McCall heard the motors of other vehicles moving in their direction. His eyes scanned the darkness, looking for some sign of movement from the direction of the sounds.

Suddenly two Jeeps followed by a truck rumbled down the narrow street. They were brought to a halt facing the vehicles that had arrived earlier.

Each Jeep had a driver and passenger. The four got out of the

Two

Jeeps and joined the quartet that was smoking. Two men got out of the truck and also joined them. Cigarettes were passed around and pleasantries exchanged.

A sense of uneasiness gripped McCall's mind. *Where in the dickens is their prisoner?* he asked himself. Something wasn't right. Were the early arrivals waiting for someone else?

Ten to four and maybe more coming, he thought. He had faced greater numerical odds on many occasions, but he was too smart to relish such situations. A smart man wanted the odds in his favor.

Suddenly, automatic weapons fire opened to the rear of his position. Turning, he saw one of his companions crumple.

Trap! his mind screamed.

Quickly looking back toward the vehicles, he saw armed men scrambling out of the trucks. Those who had been talking and smoking were taking cover behind the vehicles. Bullets were ricocheting off the building and the surrounding rubble. His two surviving companions joined him and they exchanged knowing glances. There was no need for conversation. Each understood their circumstances.

They were surrounded.

McCall knew his Mossad counterparts would not be taken alive, not by the kind of rabble that was attacking them. He felt the same way. Better to die here, he thought, than to be threatened and tortured…to rot in some cell where the rodents have more ability to reason than your captors.

"Let's take as many of them with us as we can," McCall said, realizing as he said it that he didn't have to articulate what his two companions were already thinking.

They had the high ground and good cover. McCall figured it would have been an edge, if they hadn't been outnumbered fifty to three. The slight edge was blunted by the darkness. If their enemy was brave enough to launch an all-out attack, there was little doubt that they would be quickly overrun.

McCall's experience, however, was that the kind of people shooting at them were brave only when shooting women and children in the back. They tended to cower when an opponent had a gun and didn't have his back turned to them. So he figured the darkness really benefited him and his cohorts.

DEATH ANGEL

It was hard to talk above the din of battle, bullets hitting all around them, but McCall managed to say to his companions, "Hang tough here. I'm going to crawl back to the rear and see if I can make how many there are behind us."

The building and rubble gave McCall adequate cover, though there was the danger of a stray bullet. The terrorist group seemed to be shooting without really targeting, just squeezing off rounds for no apparent reason. *Come daylight they'll be able to do a better job of zeroing in on us,* he thought. That's why he was determined to use the darkness to make some kind of effort to escape.

McCall found two of the enemy crouching behind a pile of debris, rising periodically to squeeze off bursts of Uzi fire in the general direction of his companions. They seemed to be in some kind of rhythm, rising simultaneously. With his nine-millimeter Browning, he tattooed both between the eyes.

Two men to his left saw the pistol flashes and saw their comrades fall. They fired wildly in his direction. But McCall was gone, like a ghost.

The two who had seen the deaths of their fellow terrorists started calling out warnings to the others. The fear in their babble brought a smile to McCall's face. The yelling and responses enabled him to pinpoint their positions.

He decided it was time to play a game of terrorize the terrorists.

One of McCall's more deadly assets was his ability to become like a chameleon, whether in the jungle, desert or a city. With all the rubble and debris in his present location, it was easy to blend in. He was also fortunate enough to get an unexpected assist from nature. Dark clouds began to roll in, extinguishing what little light the moon and stars had provided. It became pitch black, the darkness broken only by erratic bursts of gunfire. *Allah just did you boys in,* he thought.

His companions were not returning fire, content to let the terrorists wonder if they occupied the same position as they had earlier. McCall took his big Bowie knife from its scabbard and crawled toward some voices. *The idiots can't keep their mouths shut,* he thought.

The terrorists, he figured, would be bunching up. Two, three maybe even four or more in a group. He knew how the cowardly bunch operated. He planned to terrorize them by penetrating their lit-

Two

tle groups, cutting the throat of one in each group, and then disappearing into the darkness. McCall knew that discovery of their dead comrades, knowing death had been close enough to breathe on them, would unnerve and panic the others.

So he began his grim task. He found a group of five men and arbitrarily chose the one in the center for extinction. Although the five were fairly close together, none were aware that he was in the midst of them. The razor-sharp blade was thrust and withdrawn before the man could cry out.

He had penetrated another group of four, taken one of them out, before those in the first group discovered the body of their dead comrade. They cried out and the second group soon joined them. Those left alive raked the area with erratic automatic weapons fire. But they were shooting at ghosts.

McCall knew the terrorists would now be clustering even closer together, which enabled him to execute the second phase of his plan. He moved swiftly, yet stealthily, rigging grenades with trip wires. There was no way, he realized, that he could get them all, but he could kill, maim and cripple a few. Maybe that would save some unarmed men, women and children from death.

He completed rigging the grenades, then tossed one into the tight knot of terrorists. The night exploded with the screams of those who survived its impact. There was genuine panic as other terrorists began to change positions. This set off other grenades, the explosions in chorus with screams of pain and more erratic automatic weapons fire.

McCall made his way back to his companions who, with all the action behind them, had no longer been able to hold their fire. They had opened up on the men and vehicles below and in front of them. "What in the heck did you do, McCall?" one asked.

"The same thing you would have done. I think we can slip out the back way now."

The two shook their heads. "No...you go," the one said. "They killed Isaac. We're going to get our revenge."

Israeli sense of honor, McCall thought. Yet, he subscribed to that same code of honor. He would insist on avenging his friend, too. "How many grenades you guys have?"

"I've got six," the other man said.

DEATH ANGEL

"Me, too," the one said.

"I used all mine. How about each of you giving me two."

"This is no longer your fight," the one said.

McCall laughed. "It's a good morning to die."

The terrorists in front of them had no idea they were about to be attacked.

THREE

It was mid-morning on Saturday and Tyler hadn't had a wink of sleep since getting up at six a.m. on Friday. He was not tired, though. There was too much nervous energy flowing through his body, too much fear.

A nurse suggested he and others continue their vigil in the visitors' waiting room. Tyler fed a machine some coins and got a cup of black coffee. It tasted awful, which he somehow appreciated. It made him aware that not all his senses were numb.

He felt very much alone. He wanted to talk to Heather, but it didn't seem like an opportune time. Bob Mack tolerated him and that was about it. He knew Mack didn't like the idea they lived in the same town. He was jealous of Heather, which Tyler could understand. He figured he looked a lot better than Mack.

At noon, the doctors took Andy back to the operating room. At twelve thirty-seven a doctor came out and told them he was dead.

Scott Tyler was not a man who cried, but the doctor's words

DEATH ANGEL

brought a torrent of tears and sobbing despair. After suffering through the lost years, the last few had been centered in his son. Without Andy, he really didn't have a life.

Blinded by his own grief, Tyler was unaware of how Heather was taking the news. He was unable to comprehend that anyone other than himself felt remorse. He just knew his strong legs were ready to buckle and his chest felt like it was about to explode.

● ● ●

Death had been the natural order of things in Central America. He had seen a number of people die in the prison camp, the result of inhumane treatment and anger on the part of their captors. That's all that one could expect from an irrational and bloodthirsty enemy.

Death was also the natural order of things for the old. But the death of one so young, who had so much to live for, caused him to mentally curse God for allowing it to happen.

Then, just as suddenly as the anger toward God gripped his mind, it dissipated. God, he knew, wasn't responsible. God gave human beings the freedom to make choices. Their choices determined the way they lived and died. *If Andy hadn't followed in my footsteps, he would be alive*, Tyler thought.

Mentally, he started blaming himself because Andy had tried to be like him. He wondered whether he had put pressure on his son to be like him.

But why? Why had Andy fallen unconscious to the ground after running a simple pass pattern? He hadn't been touched on the opening kickoff. He had been the decoy on a fake reverse. There had also been no contact in pre-game warm-ups. So what had caused Andy to lose consciousness?

"We want to do an autopsy," the doctor said.

Heather objected, but it was not a request. Texas law required it. The doctor didn't want to sign the death certificate without being certain of what killed his patient. Tyler figured the doctor already knew a lot more than he had told them.

It was hard for Tyler to think about Andy being cut up, but he, too, wanted to know what killed his son. Heat prostration seemed the most logical reason, though the night had been mild for mid-September. Tyler remembered August practices in Texas heat where he

Three

had often felt like he was dying, but later they seemed mild in comparison to the prison camp.

The doctor was sympathetic, suggested they go to a nearby hotel and check with him the following day. "I know you're anxious to get your boy home," he said.

"Don't you know what killed Andy?" Bob Mack asked.

"We think we do," the surgeon said, "but we want to do an autopsy to verify it."

"What do you think?" Tyler asked.

"I'd rather wait for the autopsy results," the doctor said.

They didn't press the issue. Mack asked, "You need a ride to the hotel, Scott?"

Tyler gave him a blank look, then answered, "Yeah...I guess I do." He had been on the plane that brought Andy to Houston, but so had Mack and Heather. He wondered how they could offer him a ride. They hadn't rented a car. They had come to the hospital in the ambulance.

There were a lot of people in the visitors waiting area, people from Putnam who had driven to Houston to show their support for Andy and his parents. They had all been a blur to Tyler, not really a part of what was happening. Now they were all hugging him, trying to console him, but his emotions were both numb and raw from the hurt. There was nothing any of them could do, he thought.

Heather's parents were there. Tyler's folks had not made the trip, though he knew they were just as concerned. They had loved Andy as much as they loved him.

Jack Gregg, Heather's father, handed Tyler a plastic sack and said, "I picked up some shaving stuff for you...toothpaste, toothbrush, underwear. I know you didn't have time to go by your house and get anything."

Tyler nodded appreciation and noted his former father-in-law's eyes were red from crying. In the midst of his and Heather's problems, and even after their split, Jack Gregg had never wavered in his fondness for Tyler. He had fought the divorce, had always maintained that in time his son-in-law would straighten himself out. It had been Tyler's decision to leave his position at the bank, not Gregg's.

"We're going to stay over, too," Gregg said. "Bob offered you a

DEATH ANGEL

ride with us, didn't he?"

"Yeah...he did," Tyler replied. Bob and Heather Mack were riding in Jack Gregg's car.

Suddenly Louise Gregg, his former mother-in-law, was there pulling Tyler close, hugging him. Through eyes awash with tears, he saw her tear-streaked face. Andy had been her pride and joy, the son she had never been able to give her husband. And she felt about Tyler as her husband did.

Somehow, Tyler made it through all the expressions of sympathy, the hugging and hand clasping. It was like a dream in black and white. He moved through it like a zombie.

The dreamlike state continued. He was surprised to find himself in the front seat of Gregg's Lincoln Town Car and sensed more than felt its forward motion. He did not even realize it had stopped until he was standing at the hotel registration desk clutching the sack his former father-in-law had given him. Bob Mack, Heather and Louise, he decided, must have been in the back seat of the car. It was another unimportant detail that impinged on his cloudy brain.

He was not sure how he got checked in, was just suddenly in a room, a king-sized bed as its centerpiece and rays from an early afternoon sun filling the place with light. He closed the drapes to shut out the light, then stood in the darkness and sobbed uncontrollably. He didn't know how long he cried, but eventually his entire body seemed devoid of all fluids. The inner parts of his body meshed into a giant sinewy knot, raw and bleeding.

He had never known such hurt and pain.

Still in a trance, he got the shower going and scrubbed himself with soap. The hot water should have felt good to his body, but in his emotional state, he had difficulty feeling anything other than the pain of Andy's death.

He used the toilet articles Jack Gregg had given him, put on the clean underwear and redressed in the clothes he had worn to the ball game. They were casual, a soft yellow oxford shirt, light green sweater, pleated jeans and loafers.

Still operating in zombie fashion, he turned on the TV. There was a ball game. He immediately shut the set off. The game was a grim reminder of Andy's last conscious moments.

Three

He picked up the telephone and dialed. "*San Antonio Tribune*," a female voice answered.

"Matt McCall...I want to speak to Matt McCall."

There was another buzzing type ring and a male voice answered, "Yeah..."

"Matt...Is that you?"

"Sorry...he's not here. You want to leave a message?"

"Is he working today?"

The voice laughed. "Probably, but not here. You want to leave a message?"

"No...no thanks."

Tyler knew the *San Antonio Tribune* number by heart. He also knew Matt McCall's home number, which he dialed next. After a couple of rings a voice said, "This is Matt McCall. At the sound of the tone leave your name and number and I'll get back to you."

He put the phone back in its cradle. Where was McCall? Maybe he was at his cabin by the river near Wimberly. Or, maybe he was at his ranch west of San Antonio. He tried the telephone at both places. At Wimberly he got another recorded message. The housekeeper at the ranch said she had no idea as to McCall's whereabouts.

It was a nice fall day so he figured McCall might be fishing, floating the river in a canoe. They had spent many pleasant days together, floating rivers and fishing. Or maybe he was with Celeste, Tyler thought. He called her number and got another recorded message.

He contemplated calling the San Antonio Police Department, to ask Detective Lieutenant Bill Haloran if he knew McCall's whereabouts. He decided against calling Haloran. McCall and the detective were close friends. Tyler appreciated that when in San Antonio he had been included in their friendship. He didn't have friends like them in Putnam, no one, really, with whom he could talk.

Tyler had been an extrovert when growing up in Putnam. But after returning to his hometown from the prison camp, after he started sucking down alcohol and chasing women, he had become increasingly introverted, also more and more paranoid.

When he finally lost it all, went to San Antonio and looked McCall up, he found no sympathy from the man who led the unit that rescued him from the prison camp. McCall would not let him wallow

DEATH ANGEL

in self-pity.

"Don't blame what happened for making you an idiot," McCall had said. Thinking about his words, Tyler could not help but have a smile tug at the corners of his mouth. With what had happened to Andy, he didn't feel like smiling. But thinking about McCall and some of his outlandish comments caused a ripple of warmth to skid over the icy pains of grief.

That's why he wanted to reach McCall. In this dark hour, he needed the warmth of a friend who could be genuinely supportive and would understand and share the grief, but who would also offer some positive direction. McCall had been that friend when he was a slave to alcohol, when his entire world was in shambles.

Now it was in shambles again.

He knew his parents and the Greggs were there for him, that they would do their best for him. But with Heather in another man's arms, Andy had been the only reality from his past that he really cared about. He cared about his parents, of course, but his love for them was different from the love he had for Andy. With him gone, he now wondered if life was worth living.

Tyler was an intelligent man. He subconsciously knew his grief would lessen at some point, that he would be able to go on with his life. He just questioned whether he wanted to or not. What was left to live for? His son was dead and he would never again know the love of the only woman he had ever really cared about.

As his feelings of loss intensified, his depression grew. It was gnawing at his internal organs and his mind. The ringing of the telephone startled him. "Scott, I know you don't feel like eating," Jack Gregg said from the other end of the line, "none of us do. But you need to eat something. We're going to try. How about joining us?"

Gregg was right, he didn't feel like eating. But when he did, it would not be with Bob Mack at the same table. "Thanks, Jack, but I think I'll pass."

"Can we bring you something?"

"No...I'll just have room service send something up."

Tyler was restless, unable to sleep, seeking relief from the demons plaguing his mind. Without realizing why, he left the room and ended up in the hotel bar. It was like many other bars he had been in, dark

Three

and a bit depressing in spite of all the mirrors. He wondered why anyone would want to watch himself drink.

He ordered a scotch and water, then sat there looking at it, remembering how he had almost drowned himself in a grave of alcohol. He looked at the drink for a long time, realizing that if he took one sip he wouldn't be able to stop.

What the heck, he thought. He dismounted the barstool and put a five by the glass. "Something wrong with your drink?" the bartender asked.

"Yeah...everything."

He realized there was no place where he could escape, so he just went back to his room.

FOUR

When Andy Tyler was finally pronounced dead, the one who secretly liked to call himself the Death Angel breathed a sigh of relief. *The kid,* he thought, *must have had a strong heart.* He had figured on him lasting just an hour or two, four at the most. So when Andy Tyler hadn't died right away, he had worried that the youngster might come out of his coma and say things that were better left unsaid.

There was still the father to worry about. What, if anything, had the kid said to him? Death Angel had survived in the shadow world for many years because he had always tied up loose ends, had never left anything to chance.

When he had first gotten into the business, he had loved the dog eat dog world of drug dealing in the big city. But he was too smart to allow such excitement to be his motivation. The only intelligent motivation, he believed, was money and power. There was more security, more opportunity in small town America. It enabled him to have the

Four

best of both worlds. So he had moved his operation to Putnam.

In Putnam, he could still keep his finger on the pulse of big city drug dealing, but with less threat to himself. He had plenty of people willing to take risks for the kind of money he paid them. Why should he, if he used the brain God gave him, take any?

A kid like Andy Tyler could have blown the entire deal, if he had been allowed to live. He knew that there were always going to be nuisances like Andy. It was best to nip any threat like him in the bud.

Now the question was, *Is Scott Tyler a threat?* If there was even a hint that he might be, he had to be stopped, too. Death Angel had the ears of the right people. It wouldn't take him long to make his determination.

But if there was any doubt, Scott Tyler had to die.

FIVE

McCall couldn't shake the feeling that what he was experiencing was déjà vu. How many times over the years had be played out the string? Like a cat, how many lives did he have left? He was pretty sure he had passed the proverbial nine several years earlier.

"You guys want me to go up the middle...y'all flank them?"

The talker of his two companions asked, "Are you sure you want to do this, McCall? You don't owe us anything. You didn't owe Isaac anything."

"Maybe it wasn't you guys, but the Mossad has pulled me out of a lot of tight spots before. Besides, every time I kill one of these clowns I'm probably saving a lot of mothers and babies they're planning to blow up."

The other of his companions said, "I'll take the right. I guess you'll take the left, Josh. And if we don't make it...well, McCall, you're one American I'm proud to die with."

Five

McCall laughed. "I don't like that kind of talk, Caleb. Tell you what...I'll give you clowns five minutes to get in position, then I'm going straight up the middle. Wait until I open up before you hit them."

"What about the ones behind us?" Josh asked.

"I think they're a little disoriented," McCall replied. "I took a pound of flesh back there. Let's not get greedy."

Pitch darkness continued to be their ally. McCall knew the men in front of them had heard the screams of their dying comrades, that they were a bit edgy. That seemed obvious because of their bursts of erratic and undisciplined gunfire. *Give these fools automatic weapons and they're just naturally going to have to shoot them*, McCall thought. But stray bullets, he knew, could make a man just as dead as aimed ones.

"Sorry, McCall...that we got you into this mess," Josh said.

"Hey, there was no way you could know. There's a leak somewhere. I'm counting on one of you guys getting back and fixing it."

"It'll get fixed," Caleb said. "You can count on that. Whoever sold us out...he's a dead man."

The trio moved out, more like an advancing, victorious army than three men terribly outnumbered and outgunned. McCall felt more confident, however, fighting alongside Josh and Caleb than he would have if all those they were going against were backing him. There was, he believed, a mentality of bravery among the Israelis that was missing in most warriors. It was an intangible thing he had witnessed over several years of work with the Mossad and the Israeli military.

The terrorists, obviously, were not expecting a frontal attack. They were content to use the vehicles and rubble for cover, to wait for the light of day when they could more easily pinpoint their targets.

McCall moved close.

Very close.

He could hear the enemy jabbering to each other. He had determined earlier that the attackers were an undisciplined lot, certainly not the kind who had been trained in some elite terrorist school. Probably one or two had been. Now those one or two were trying to lead a ragtag band of clowns who didn't know anything about how to fight as a unit.

DEATH ANGEL

The truth is, they don't know how to fight at all, he thought. What worried him was that some idiot like one of these, some simpleton with the mentality of a fruit fly, would get lucky and kill him. He figured that with his training he deserved better. If he had to die, he wanted it to be at the hands of the best.

He waited until one of his adversaries lit a cigarette, then shot the match out. The bullet caught the man in the mouth and created panic among his comrades. That intensified, because a grenade followed the bullet, its fragments killing or wounding several.

By then, Caleb and Josh were coming in from the flanks, their Uzis spitting out deadly venom. A Jeep caught fire and exploded, lighting up the darkness. The singing of bullets was everywhere. Men were screaming, crying out in pain.

For McCall, it was like the memory of so many firefights, though that was all just flashing through his subconscious. There was no time for thinking, just for reacting to the danger around him.

A grenade exploded, and then a truck began to flame. Its bed must have been filled with munitions, because there were multiple explosions and the night was filled with tracers, reminiscent of a Fourth of July fireworks display.

McCall used every clip for his Uzi, then started picking targets more carefully for his nine-millimeter pistol. Josh and Caleb were wreaking equal havoc.

Then, like a well-trained relay team, they came together on the far side of the action. It was as if they shared a sixth sense about when it was time to leave the scene of battle. They disappeared into the darkness, hearing the confused terrorists still firing wildly at nothing in the darkness.

SIX

At eleven fifteen Sunday morning, Tyler, Bob and Heather Mack, and Jack and Louise Gregg met with the doctor who had been in charge of Andy's care.

"I know you're anxious to know what killed Andy," the physician said, "but right now we just don't know for sure. Tests are being run, but it's going to be a week or ten days before we know the results. Even then, we're not sure we can tell you exactly why Andy died. Forensic medicine...contrary to what you see and hear on TV...is not an exact science."

Tyler said, "But you do have some suspicions?" He did not bother to search the faces of the others in the room to determine if they wanted answers as much as he did. He did not care if they wanted them or not.

"Yes, we have some suspicions, Mr. Tyler, but I don't like to deal in speculation. I'd prefer to wait for the complete reports."

"You must think there's something peculiar about Andy's death,

DEATH ANGEL

or you would have just signed the death certificate," Tyler said. "Isn't that right? I mean...if it had been a heart attack, heat stroke, something like that?"

The doctor didn't want to answer, but Tyler had him in a corner. "Yes...there are some things I'm not satisfied with. But I need to wait for the results of the test to be sure."

"Doctor, my kid's dead and I don't know why. I don't want to listen to a lot of bull about waiting for tests. You know something you're not telling."

The doctor shrugged. "Like I said, I can't tell you anything definite at this point."

Tyler was sitting in a chair across the desk from where the physician was seated, but suddenly, like an enraged bull, he lunged across the desk and grasped the collar of the doctor's white smock.

He would have dragged him across the desk if Jack Gregg and Bob Mack had not restrained him.

Ashen-faced, the doctor slumped back in his chair. The pipe that had been in his mouth was on the floor, its tobacco strewn across the surface of the desk. "He's distraught," Gregg said, feeling the need to explain Tyler's action.

"I understand," the physician said.

Tyler, now like a limp rag, slumped in his chair. The color was gone from his face and he started sobbing uncontrollably. His breakdown caused Heather and her mother to follow suit.

"This is a difficult time for all of us," Gregg said. "Scott's normally not a violent man."

"I understand," the doctor said again.

Gregg said, "You will be in touch with us...soon?"

"As soon as possible."

SEVEN

There was a fall storm the day Andy Tyler was buried. Thunder rumbled across the wooded hills and lightning bolts carved jagged streaks of blue-white light across the sky. Then the rains came, a torrent of wetness from dark and ominous clouds. It was the kind of storm that usually accompanied the annual hurricanes that play tag with the Texas coast.

In spite of the weather the First Baptist Church, with the largest sanctuary in the town, was packed. Kids from the high school turned out in force, as did their parents. The entire funeral service ripped at the emotions, from the baleful music to the tearful sermon delivered by the church's pastor.

It was the church where Andy had been a member and the church where he had been baptized. It was the church of the Greggs, of Tyler's parents, and had been Heather's until she married Bob Mack. There had been a time when it was Tyler's church, too, but he had drifted away from it. After returning to Putnam, he had not felt com-

DEATH ANGEL

fortable in religious surroundings.

Though the church's pastor used a lot of scripture in his remarks, the message was set in the context of Andy's character. He was, in the minister's words, a model teenager, an honor student, regular in church attendance. From the preacher's perspective he had no faults, which made his death all that more difficult to explain.

Dazed, but in control of his emotions, Scott Tyler sat with family members and half-listened to the minister's words. Claps of thunder seemed to shake the building, as if God was angry at what was taking place.

Then it was all over and people were filing by Andy's open casket, taking a last look at the youth whose body seemed very insignificant in contrast to the high ceiling and tall stained glass windows. The sobs of those who passed, especially Andy's young friends, was lost in the cavernous bulk of the building.

Two of the last to pass the casket, before family members, were Matt McCall and Bill Haloran. Neither had known Andy. They had come to Putnam because of Scott Tyler, because he was a friend and they wanted to do what they could to help him through a difficult and trying time.

After all the normal ritual had taken place at the church, the funeral party got into their cars and followed the long, black hearse carrying Andy's body, and the black limousines carrying family members. The downpour of the cool fall rain, along with the thunder and lightning, caused a number of those who attended the church service to pass up the graveside ceremony. Still, the long line of cars on the way to the cemetery seemed endless, all moving at a respectful crawl.

There was a tent at the cemetery, open on three sides, to protect the grave and family members. But there was no way to completely escape the driving rain, which swirled and blew across the mourners from every direction.

McCall and Haloran stood in the rain with the others at the graveside. They had bought cheap raincoats and an umbrella at a local department store earlier that morning, but the newly purchased gear did little to protect them from the swirling deluge.

The casket and flowers on top and around it took a beating from the rain. The minister made his remarks mercifully short and to the

Seven

point. In comparison to what had gone on in the church the committal service was almost like an afterthought.

After shaking hands with family members, McCall and Haloran made their way back to the reporter's car, trying to avoid as much mud as possible. Once inside the dryness of the vehicle, McCall cranked the Cadillac's powerful engine, then drove it back to the motel where they had rented rooms.

"What are we talking about in terms of time?" Haloran asked.

"I want to dry out...change clothes," McCall replied. "Let's say thirty minutes."

They were to be involved in the continuation of the death ritual. They had been invited to the home of Jack and Louise Gregg, where more sympathy would be offered to Andy's survivors, and where people would stand around eating and making conversation. McCall hated such rituals, but felt they had to be there for Scott Tyler.

McCall had only learned of Andy's death the previous day. Tyler had been trying to get in touch with him, but he had been doing his freelance thing for the Agency. Haloran told him about the death when he got back to San Antonio. They had driven to Putnam, but had arrived too late to get in touch with Tyler. So they had seen him only briefly at the funeral service.

Haloran told McCall that Tyler was suspicious about Andy's death, but both figured such was to be expected from a grief-stricken father. After all, each year thousands of young men put on football gear and each year a few died. Usually, the causes of their deaths were easily explained.

McCall, however, was not one to dismiss suspicion lightly. His investigative mind never allowed him to think of any unusual death as normal. He was ready to listen to Tyler's suspicions, and he was ready to do whatever was necessary to clear up the matter for his friend.

Inside his motel room, McCall felt the need for a hot shower. He had taken one earlier, but there was something about the day that called for another. Besides, he always felt he could think better after a hot shower. Or, if the situation merited, a cold one.

With the shower curtain drawn, hot rivulets of water cascading over his body, he soaped himself and thought about the movie *Psycho*. Crazy as it was, motels did that to him. He half-expected someone with

DEATH ANGEL

a big kitchen knife to fling open the curtain.

Crazier still, there were times when he hoped it would happen. He figured he would snatch the knife away from the would-be assassin and use it on him.

In fact, it had happened once before. On that occasion, however, McCall had been ready and waiting for the psychopathic killer to make a move.

To some degree, McCall thought of himself as bulletproof, though such feelings varied with his many moods. Most of the time he figured he could handle any situation and that no one was capable of killing him. Part of the feeling, perhaps, came as a result of all the people who had tried. Scars from wounds marked his body. His life had been one narrow escape after another. And those who had marked him for death – those who had made him walk with the Death Angel – had usually bought the farm.

As McCall rinsed the soap off his body and toweled himself dry, he thought about his friendship with Scott Tyler. McCall, seemingly easy going and laid back, was not quick to call a person friend. He was selective, almost to the point of being a snob. But for those whom he called friend, he was willing to risk his life.

Friendship with Scott Tyler had not been an immediate thing. When rescued from the prison camp Tyler was battered and dazed by months of torture, the result of being unwilling to submit to the demands of his captors. Tyler would not give them the confession they wanted, no matter what they did to him.

McCall appreciated a man like that, one who preferred death to dishonor. Still, when Tyler made overtures of friendship shortly after the rescue, McCall dismissed it as gratitude that would fade away like smoke from a battle that had been decided. It was later, when Tyler needed his help again, that his friendship for the former Marine pilot was solidified. That friendship came to include Bill Haloran, McCall's most trusted confidant.

The tailored dark blue suit McCall had worn to the funeral was replaced with dark gray slacks, a light gray shirt, a gray and green striped tie, a medium gray jacket and black slip-on shoes. Tall, handsome and rugged looking, he was meticulous about the way he dressed and rarely bought anything off the rack. He had expensive tastes not

# Seven

only in clothes and cars, but in just about everything, along with an obsession for cleanliness. Part of his psyche, possibly, was the result of his days behind enemy lines in Vietnam, when cleanliness and clean clothing were only a memory and not as important as staying alive.

Haloran was just the opposite. He had worn an old off-the-rack dark blue suit to the funeral and never worried whether anything matched. He was losing the battle to an oversized gut and was unconcerned about a healthy diet and exercise. His clothes were generally too tight or too loose, and always out of style.

When McCall stepped out of his motel room, umbrella in hand, he was surprised. It had stopped raining. The sun was shining brightly. There was not a dark cloud in the sky.

He knocked on the door to Haloran's room. The detective emerged and said, "I'll be danged...can you believe this weather?"

"Yeah...I believe it. This is Texas. If you don't like the weather, hang around a few minutes...it'll change."

The Gregg house was one of those big white jobs with columns in front. It looked like a southern plantation residence, with massive grounds and large trees. When McCall saw it, he was glad he was not the one who had to mow the yard. He figured it was the most expensive real estate in Putnam, which was what he expected of the banker. There was another bank in town, Tyler had told him, which had been started by dissidents. But the assets of Gregg's bank made the other seem as an illegitimate child left out of its father's will.

Walking up the sidewalk to the front door, McCall decided the only thing missing were red-coated, black-faced ceramic horse handlers on opposite sides of the steps. The big house was not all that old, but reeked of Old South gentility.

"Tough looking house," Haloran said.

McCall laughed. "Probably a tough owner to boot."

He pressed the doorbell, chimes sounded, and a nice looking black woman opened the door. "Matt McCall and Bill Haloran...I believe we're expected."

"Yes sir," the woman said in a thick voice. "Just follow me, please."

She led them down a large hallway and past stairs, to a large living area off the kitchen. A couple of dozen people were there, in pairs

DEATH ANGEL

and groups. Some were standing, others sitting on the expensive furniture. Most were eating off paper plates around a massive table loaded with all kinds of food. Haloran wasted no time filling a plate. McCall passed. Funerals did not make him hungry.

"Mr. McCall...I'm Jack Gregg. Scott has told me a lot about you."

The man who stood before him, his hand extended, was tall and imposing. His hair was bluish gray, which accentuated his piercing blue eyes. McCall shook his hand and said, "Scott's told me quite a bit about you, too."

Gregg smiled. "I hope it was all good."

"It came from Scott, so you know it was. He admires and respects you."

A woman, who looked as though she belonged in the house, joined them and the banker said, "This is my wife...Louise."

McCall took her hand and she said, "We're so grateful to you, Mr. McCall...for rescuing Scott from that awful prison camp."

It was not something McCall wanted to talk about. Fortunately, Haloran showed up with a plate of food and introductions had to be made. "I don't see Scott," McCall said.

Gregg's face clouded, sorrowfully. "He went for a walk. He wants to see you, but he's not in the mood to be around people."

"Where did he go?"

"There's a trail out back...leads through the woods and down to a creek. It's where Scott and Heather used to take walks."

McCall noted the hurt in Louise Gregg's eyes at the mention of her daughter and Scott. Tyler had told him Heather's parents had been upset by the divorce, that both were opposed to it.

About that time, Bob Mack and Heather joined them. Again, there were introductions. McCall could feel Heather's eyes studying him. He knew Tyler had told her a lot about him. "I'm glad you came," she said. "Scott needs some friends."

"I figure a lot of these people are his friends," McCall said.

"None that he wants to associate with," she said.

Her father frowned. "That's not true."

"Oh, daddy...you know Scott doesn't gave a hoot about anyone in this town, not even his own parents. He just tolerates the people

Seven

here. Now Mr. McCall and Mr. Haloran...he thinks they're wonderful."

A half-smile crossed McCall's face. "I am, but he's wrong about Bill."

Neither McCall nor Haloran liked what she had said, nor the way she had said it. But the reporter figured it was best to pass it off as a joke. After all, the woman was supposed to be in mourning. Otherwise, her comment would have drawn his sarcastic wit.

He quickly changed the flow of conversation and, after a few minutes, Mack and Heather drifted off to visit with some of the other mourners. Only Mack did not seem all that mournful to McCall. That evaluation, he thought, might have been because he did not like the man. He also figured the dislike might be because Mack had married his friend's wife.

McCall was quick to judge, sometimes too quick. But there was something about Mack, he thought, that just didn't fit with what he had seen of Putnam society. He was big, slick and smooth talking, as out of place as an illegal alien at an Immigration Department banquet.

East Texas could definitely be foreign to those who did not understand its people. He figured Mack didn't.

Heather, McCall thought, was a real beauty, even surpassing the glowing verbal pictures Tyler had painted for him. She was tall, with a flowing mane of auburn hair that dipped past her shoulders. She had been wearing a hat and her hair had been up for the funeral service, but now her hair glistened when the light bounced off it.

He thought that most soft women with brown eyes had eyes that were equally soft, like those belonging to Louise Gregg. But Heather's brown eyes were fiery. And while she looked soft, McCall's assessment of her was that she was not. She was cool, aloof and had a toughness about her that might have been caused by sleepless nights waiting for Tyler to come home from his womanizing and boozing. He suspected, however, that Heather had always exhibited a fiery coldness.

The conversation with the Greggs, though brief, started dragging. "If it's okay with you, I think we'll go see if we can find Scott," McCall said.

"He shouldn't be hard to find," Gregg said.

"The trail will be muddy, though, and I'm sure he'll be back in a

DEATH ANGEL

few minutes. He knows you were coming. But if you want to go...just go out the back door. The trail starts between the two big oaks."

They had only reached the sprawling back porch when they saw Tyler emerge from the trees. He waved a greeting and they waved back, then awaited his arrival. McCall had seen Tyler's tortured face after his captors had battered it, and when he was a slave to alcohol. On those occasions, there had still been life in his eyes. Now there was none. He looked as though he had aged twenty years.

"Let's go somewhere where we can talk," Tyler said, "somewhere away from here."

McCall shrugged. "Wherever you say."

"The Putnam Café. It's downtown...quiet. Won't be more than three or four people there."

They didn't go back in the house. Haloran rode with Tyler in his pickup truck and McCall followed in the Cadillac. Parking was a snap, only a few cars were in front of the café.

The occupancy of the establishment was what Tyler had estimated, three customers and a waitress. All offered him heartfelt sympathies. After such courtesies were exhausted, they found a table out of earshot of the other customers. The table was old and wooden, covered with a red vinyl cloth. The chairs were equally old and uncomfortable.

The café, in an aging brick building that had seen better days, had a high ceiling that was dirty with soot and grime, along with a wooden floor that had been mopped with harsh detergents. Other than the ceiling and the blades on the ceiling fan, the place looked clean. McCall figured the place would be tough to keep warm in winter.

"What kind of beer you got?" Haloran asked the waitress.

"Root beer," she said.

"Then I guess I'll have coffee. What kind of pie you got?"

"Apple, lemon and coconut."

"Homemade?"

"Yeah."

"Then bring me a piece of apple with a scoop of ice cream on top...if you guarantee the pie's homemade."

"I guarantee it."

Haloran's order brought a faint smile to Tyler's mouth. He, along with McCall, ordered only coffee. He knew it bugged McCall for a

Seven

restaurant to advertise anything as being homemade, which was why Haloran had engaged in the homemade pie dialogue with the waitress.

They sat quietly until the waitress brought the pie and coffee, then each doctored it to individual taste. "I guess you know Bill and I don't know what to say," McCall said. "What can you say about something like this?"

"You guys just being here...it means a lot."

McCall studied Tyler's eyes and saw the pain there. Medication could help some pain, but not Tyler's kind. "Being here's the least we could do."

Tyler sighed. "Nothing's going to bring Andy back, but I could handle it better if I knew why he died. Something's not right and I can't get any answers."

Haloran said, "On the phone you told me they did an autopsy. You'll know more when you get the results."

"Don't you think a week or ten days is a long time to wait for results?"

The detective shrugged. "Not necessarily...not if they're being thorough. Some of the tests...they take time."

"It just doesn't make sense," Tyler said, ignoring Haloran's explanation. "And why wouldn't the doctor give me the preliminary report? He knows something he don't want to tell...I don't know what."

"Tell you what, Bill and I can check into this thing for you," McCall said. "We'll get in touch with the right people and get them moving."

"I'd sure appreciate it. I really would."

They sat quietly for a few moments, sipping their coffee. Then McCall asked, "When was the last time you talked to Andy?"

"Thursday night. He came by my place and we talked about going fishing on Saturday. He said he had heard the bass were really hitting at Toledo Bend. He was supposed to have a date after the game Friday night, then he was going to come by my place and spend the night so we could get an early start."

Toledo Bend was a sprawling two hundred thousand surface acres reservoir northeast of Putnam. Fed by the Sabine River and numerous creeks, it was a maze of vegetation, standing and fallen timber, which provided great cover for freshwater game fish. McCall and

DEATH ANGEL

Haloran had fished the lake a number of times.

"Did he seem nervous or upset about anything?" McCall asked.

"He was nervous about the game, but it was a good kind a nervous. You played, Matt...you know what I mean. But upset...no. Andy was a happy-go-lucky kid. He was serious about the way he performed on the football field and in the classroom, but he enjoyed life...especially hunting and fishing. He didn't like living in Bob Mack's house...wanted to move in with me. We talked about it, but I told him it would hurt his mother too much."

Haloran said, "From what I heard today, I'd say he was a pretty good student."

"Honor student," Tyler said, proudly. He always had nothing but A's on his report card."

"Any girl problems you know of?" McCall asked.

"He was going steady with a girl named Melanie Richards and they were getting along fine. He would've told me if they weren't. These kinds of questions...I guess you're wondering about Andy's emotional state. But I don't see how that could a had anything to do with his death?"

"Probably didn't," McCall said. "But until we find out why he died, we just have to feel our way along in the dark. Why don't you just give us a rundown on what happened on the football field last Friday night...everything you can remember right up until the time Andy died."

Recalling his son's death was an emotional struggle for Tyler, but he managed to choke out the bitter memories. McCall and Haloran interrupted him occasionally for more details. For all it was a difficult and unpleasant conversation.

Later in the afternoon McCall and Haloran left for San Antonio, both worried about Scott Tyler's mental condition.

EIGHT

McCall liked East Texas, but enjoyed it most when the leaves on the hardwood trees turned to soft hues of red, orange and yellow. September was still too early for the woodlands to be painted any color other than green.

The way some people perceived Texas, some that had never seen its varying terrain, amused McCall. They thought of it as flat, a place with nothing other than cows, cactus, oil wells and cowboys, an idea perpetuated by watching too many TV episodes of *Dallas*. The eastern part was timber country. Other portions of the state boasted mountains, hills and beaches. There was lots of farming, manufacturing and high technology, and more surface acres of water than any state other than Alaska.

Setting the speedometer of the Cadillac on seventy, watching a brilliant orange sun setting, its rays playing off the wetness of the tall timber, McCall said, "There is something wrong. You agree, Bill?"

"You talking about the delay in the autopsy report...fact they must be running lots of tests?"

"Yeah...the doctor could have signed the death certificate. He could have called it a heat stroke or heart attack...something like that."

Haloran mused, "But something wasn't right?"

"Yeah...and they could have done an autopsy at the hospital instead of sending the body to the Harris County medical examiner."

"I know what you're thinking...and for Scott's sake I hope you're wrong."

"Do you have to be back tomorrow?"

"Not necessarily. I could call in...take another day off. What's on your mind?"

"Well, we could go through Houston...spend the night there, spend tomorrow asking a few questions."

"We did tell Scott we'd look into the matter," the detective said. "I just hope we don't find something that's going to make it worse for him."

"Not knowing...that's what's bugging Scott. He's a strong man. He can probably handle more than we're giving him credit for."

"I don't know about that, McCall. Andy's death may be the straw that broke the camel's back."

"I don't think so. He could have used Andy's death to start drinking again."

"May still happen. Wouldn't surprise me if he crawled into a bottle."

"I can't see it. He's made it this far. He'll make it the rest of the way."

Haloran chuckled. "I thought you were a cynic."

McCall smiled. "About most things...yeah. But a man who went through what Scott did in that prison camp...well, he's not the kind of man who'll go all the way over the edge. He almost did it with his drinking and womanizing, but before it happened he straightened himself out."

"With a lot of help from you."

"I didn't do much."

"Bull. What I'm saying is that if our worst suspicions about Andy's death are right...then that could push him all the way."

They made only one stop before reaching Houston, to gas up the

Eight

car and get Styrofoam cups filled with bad coffee. Traffic entering the city was intense, causing McCall to say, "I thought this place was in some sort of recession. All I see is construction and more cars in front of us than they've got in the whole state of Maine."

"What's Maine got to do with anything?"

"Your problem, clown, is that you don't recognize a great statement when you hear it."

"If that was a great statement, I guess you're right."

They were both anxious to do a mood shift, away from the gloom of Andy Tyler's funeral and from thoughts of what they might learn from the medical examiner. Contrary to his earlier statement about Scott Tyler's strength, McCall worried that he might be on the verge of falling apart.

"You hungry?" McCall asked after they had checked into a hotel and were on the elevator.

Haloran feigned dismay. "I was born hungry."

"Let's freshen up first...then go eat."

"Just knock on my door when you're ready. I don't need that much freshening up."

McCall grinned. "Believe me...you need it."

"Jerk."

Theirs had been an unusual friendship from the beginning. Haloran had been warned about the moody, sometimes volatile newsman who did not play by the rules. Yet McCall, he believed, had always been straight with him. Maybe, he thought, it was because he wanted to believe. There was much about McCall he did not know – much he did not want to know. He just knew that in a showdown life and death situation there was no one he would rather have backing him.

Sometimes it bothered him that McCall knew everything about him, that he knew almost nothing about the reporter. McCall's past was shrouded in mystery, subject to a lot of speculation. Haloran had come into contact with people from McCall's past that made him think that his friend had once been a high level CIA operative, that he might still be connected in some way. But none of that came from McCall.

There were numerous questions about McCall's financial independence, something that bothered power brokers in San Antonio and beyond. That independence also bothered some editors at the *Tribune*.

DEATH ANGEL

Because he had won a Pulitzer and numerous other awards, the paper's top management allowed him to operate as a loose cannon. He chased only the stories that interested him, many of which caused some conflict with Haloran's bosses. That did not particularly bother the detective. What sorely tested their friendship was McCall's tendency to play vigilante. If the law moved too slowly, or not at all, the reporter was not averse to initiating his own special brand of justice. Haloran had never known another man so obsessed with justice.

Haloran was lying on the bed, thinking about how he had been party to some of McCall's vigilantism, when the reporter knocked. The detective opened the door and was greeted with, "We have a guest for dinner."

"Who?"

"Dr. Oliver Stanton...the guy who was in charge of the hospital team that tried to save Andy Tyler's life."

"How in the heck did you get him to have dinner with us?"

"I asked him."

On the elevator Haloran persisted. "Dang it, McCall, isn't Stanton the guy who wouldn't talk to Scott? And you just call him up and he drops everything to go to dinner with us. It doesn't make sense."

"Well, I wouldn't just say I called up. It took more than one call...some to people other than Dr. Stanton."

The detective sighed. "I wish I had your contacts."

"No you don't. They take more from you than they ever give."

Haloran had backed up McCall when the reporter was searching out and administering justice to Middle East terrorists, a group who killed American Jewish children as a means of acquiring the release of so-called political prisoners in Israel. Because of the atrocities these terrorists committed, the detective had turned his head while McCall exacted justice. He had met some of McCall's contacts during the process, cold men who wore dark suits and seemed sure of their right to judge others. Haloran had been forced to admit that sometimes their way was the only way.

"Okay, big shot," the detective asked, "what's on the menu tonight?"

"We're going to eat here at the hotel. I'm sure they have a good steak."

Eight

"With the price of the rooms they ought to throw in a steak or two. A room for a night costs more than my grocery bill for a week."

McCall laughed. "Loosen up, Bill...you only live once."

"If I had to pay these prices all the time it would be a short life. With savings and retirement, I figure I could live about two weeks."

The hotel was nice, though a bit ostentatious. Like many similar edifices, an attempt to create an atmosphere of old world charm had come at considerable expense. The attempt had failed, but most people did not know the difference so management had no qualms about charging exorbitant prices.

The dining room was the last stop up for the elevator. The restaurant provided a semi-panoramic view of the city. McCall could understand a view of the ocean, scenic woodlands or mountains. He had difficulty understanding why anyone would think diners would want to watch traffic congestion while they ate.

A hostess seated them next to a long stretch of windows that spanned the room. McCall asked her to be on the lookout for Dr. Stanton.

"Forget the cost of the room," Haloran said while looking at the menu. "The cost of a steak here is more than my house payment."

McCall, who was picking up the tab for all of the detective's expenses, laughed. "Don't worry about it."

"I'd just as soon you give me the money for the steak and let me go buy a box of KFC to eat in my room."

"Then you wouldn't get to meet Dr. Stanton."

"That probably wouldn't ruin my day."

"Relax...enjoy yourself. How about a drink?"

"It'll take several to make me forget these prices."

"Then have several...as long as it's tea or coffee."

"Maybe I'll go all out and have a Diet Coke," the detective said.

Haloran was gulping his second Diet Coke and McCall was on his first cup of coffee when Stanton arrived. After the amenities, the doctor seated himself in one of the plush chairs that went with the table. He noticed what his dinner companions were drinking and ordered a Coke.

"Well, Mr. McCall you..."

"Drop that Mr. stuff. You can call me Matt, or McCall...either

DEATH ANGEL

one."

The doctor smiled. "Okay, Matt...as I was going to say, you have some powerful friends. I don't get many calls from Washington."

"If you're lucky you don't get any. But we do need your help. I can understand your reluctance to talk to us before you talk to Andy Tyler's folks, but it might be best if we know first."

"I'm not qualified to be the judge of that," the doctor said.

"Look, the medical examiner's report is going to the police before it goes to the family...right?"

"I'm sure the proper authorities will see it."

"And I assume you're going to work with us or you wouldn't be here."

Stanton sighed. "I understand you led a team that rescued Mr. Tyler from a prison camp...in one of those places we're not supposed to be."

"He tell you that?"

"No, the man from Washington did. And I'd already heard about you when I was doing my military stint...some of the stuff your group did."

Haloran was all ears. "What did you hear?"

"Never mind," McCall said.

"I came here because they told me you aren't one of those journalists who kisses up to liberal politicians," Stanton said.

"I don't kiss up to so-called conservative ones, either."

"The Tyler kid...what I suspected, it's going to come out. I knew right away...and I think Scott Tyler knew I knew. I thought he was going to kill me when I didn't tell him."

McCall figured the doctor might be a tough man to kill. He was a muscular guy, an inch or two short of six-feet and weighed about two hundred pounds. He looked fit. McCall figured him for a man who worked out with something heavier than a golf club.

"Morphine poisoning," Stanton said. "That's what I suspected. God knows, I saw enough boys in Vietnam overdose on drugs. The kid's skin color tipped me off. That's why I insisted on the autopsy. Not that I had a choice about the matter."

An overdose of cocaine or heroin caused morphine poisoning. The doctor's diagnosis confirmed McCall's and Haloran's worst fears

Eight

about Andy's death. Their suspicions had been aroused when Tyler had told them about the length of time that the doctor had predicted before all the tests would be completed. McCall figured Tyler was knowledgeable enough to suspect the reason for the delay, but that he would also refuse to admit his son was a doper.

"Did you find tracks...needle marks?" Haloran asked.

"That's the strange part," Stanton replied. "What the kid took, he ingested orally."

"Whoa," McCall said. "That's more than a bit unusual. What do you think he ingested?"

"A mixture of crack and Novocain."

McCall shook his head in resignation. "Then we're talking about intentional poisoning...suicide or murder."

The cocktail waitress brought more drinks, interrupting their conversation. The waiter followed close behind her, so they ordered. All chose ribeyes.

Haloran waited until the waiter was out of earshot. "Know what I noticed on the menu? They didn't have pie. I don't have a lot of respect for a restaurant that doesn't serve pie."

McCall laughed. "I think you can get by on cheesecake or chocolate mousse."

"Maybe...but it won't be the same as homemade pie."

"I doubt you've ever had homemade pie," McCall said. "But to a more serious matter, I assume, doctor, that you don't think Andy Tyler was a doper."

"I saw no evidence of it in my examination. The coroner's office hasn't either."

"Is the coroner's report complete?" Haloran asked.

"Not yet. Results of a few tests haven't come in, but we know enough to be comfortable with what killed the boy."

"The quantity of crack and Novocain that he ingested...how much are we talking about?" McCall asked.

"More than enough to kill anyone. The amount would have put most people in a coma almost immediately. The kid was healthy...an athlete. His body was able to fight it for a period of time."

"How long?" Haloran asked.

The doctor shrugged. "It's hard to say. It could have been no more than an hour, or several hours."

McCall said, "Then he could have ingested it at the pre-game meal, or maybe even at lunch."

"For all I know," Stanton said, "it might have been in his breakfast orange juice. But I really don't think his system could have handled it that long."

Haloran looked at McCall and asked, "Are we talking suicide here, McCall?"

"I doubt it. Be a strange way to commit suicide. I think somebody killed Andy Tyler. It might have been accidental...some kid spiking his food or drink to see how it affected him. The Novocain, though...I don't understand why one of his classmates would have Novocain. I can understand the crack, but why mix it with Novocain?"

The doctor said, "We're not completely sure it was crack and Novocain, just ninety-nine percent sure."

"That's probably as close as you're going to get," Haloran said.

McCall sighed. "That's for sure. When are you going to tell the family?"

"All the tests will be in within three or four days. But you know the report has to go to Putnam's law enforcement people as well as the family."

"Yeah...and I bet the police department in Putnam is a real winner," McCall said, sarcastically.

"Some of the small towns have pretty good people," Haloran said.

"Yeah...they do. I'm being a little judgmental without giving them a chance."

Haloran laughed. "There's no such thing, McCall."

"As what?"

"As you being a *little* judgmental."

McCall ignored his attempted humor and asked the doctor, "You have any objection if I talk to Scott Tyler first? He's kind of on the edge. I'm not sure how he's going to take the news about what caused Andy's death."

"I'd welcome your intervention. I just have to ask that you not tell him anything until the report is complete."

"You have my word on that."

Eight

The conversation and meal lasted a good two hours. There was considerable speculation as to how the substance that ended Andy Tyler's life had gotten into his system. And the more McCall talked to Stanton, the more he appreciated the doctor and his caring attitude. He believed that with most doctors greed was an overriding factor – most could not even spell compassion. He was not ready to change his mind about most, just figured Stanton was an exception to the rule.

After the doctor left, McCall and Haloran went to the hotel bar for a Coke. It was quiet there, soft music provided by an elderly black man who, obviously, had a love affair going with the piano. It was the kind of music McCall appreciated.

Haloran sipped his Coke, then asked, "How you going to handle this thing with Scott? I think it's good you're the one who's telling him, but I wouldn't want to be in your shoes."

"I don't envy me either, but he's a friend. If I hadn't volunteered to do it, you would have."

"I guess so."

"I'm going to call Scott tomorrow and ask him to come spend some time at the ranch. It's away from everything. It'll give him a chance to get himself together."

McCall's ranch was west of San Antonio, a thousand acres of isolation. He had built a huge log house on it that was, for all intents and purposes, a showplace. The logs had been imported from Wisconsin and the house was furnished with fine antiques. Only a few people, Haloran being one of them, had ever been a guest there. It was one of McCall's two hideaways.

"You going to stay there with him?" Haloran asked.

"Yeah...I think so."

"I'd like to be there, too."

"You know you're welcome."

"I'm not like you, McCall...I can't just take off whenever I choose."

McCall did have a pretty free rein at the *Tribune*. When he was working on a big story it was a twenty-four hours a day thing, and he always put in more than forty hours a week. But he usually called his own shots in terms of time and stories. He had earned that right, though it irritated a few editors.

DEATH ANGEL

Haloran continued, "I'll talk to the chief...see if I can get a few more days off. I've got the time coming, and it would probably be best if we both saw Scott through this thing."

"I can use all the help I can get," McCall said.

It was almost midnight when they got to their rooms. As exhausting as the day had been, McCall could not sleep. He soaked his body in a tub of hot water, hoping it would help. Still, sleep would not come. Nor did watching an inane TV show help relax his mind.

His mind was racing with memories, of how Scott Tyler had looked when he pulled him out of the prison camp. He had been battered, had gone through hell, but his eyes had some spark. Even when he was having his bout with alcohol it was there. The man was no coward, he knew, and when a man had an ounce of courage, he could build on it. He was hoping Tyler could reach down inside himself and grab more than an ounce of the stuff.

He worried because when he had last looked in Tyler's eyes there was only the dullness of resignation. The fight was gone. He was just hoping it had been doused by grief, that it could be rekindled.

He was not sure how he would handle telling Tyler about what had killed Andy. He figured it wouldn't hurt to make him angry with the person responsible. That, he thought, should bring the fire back to his eyes.

Maybe some kid fooling around with crack was responsible for Andy's death. Maybe it was just an accident. There were a lot of maybes. Still, the deeper recesses of his mind told him it was murder. Something told him it was cold, calculated murder.

But why?

Why, he asked himself, *would someone want to kill the kid?* It didn't make any sense, but drug use didn't make any sense either. He felt little or no compassion for users. *Drugs*, he thought, *are a crutch for a crippled mind.*

While his compassion level was almost nonexistent for users, McCall had a genuine animosity toward dealers and governments that tolerated them. He wanted economic sanctions against those countries, absentee trials and death sentences for drug lords whose governments winked at their activities. He wanted the U.S. military and the CIA involved in the war on drugs, the latter to carry out any death sentences

Eight

that might be imposed. He wanted the military to protect the nation's borders, public executions for drug dealers and severe penalties for users.

His was not a popular view with liberal politicians, nor with most of his colleagues at the newspaper, but he was of the school who thought the only way to stop the disease was to make the cost too high for sellers and users.

The fact that many of those with whom he came in contact disagreed with his views did not bother McCall, nor did he feel compelled to try to make them see things his way. He approved of and respected people who could think for themselves, even if they did not agree with him, but did not have much use for those who blindly followed without knowing why.

He definitely was not a follower, a man who floated downstream just because it was the safest and most accepted pattern of behavior. He thought for himself, which meant he often had to go against the grain or swim upstream.

Finally, at about two o'clock in the morning, he fell into a fitful slumber and a struggle against strange dreams that came and went in his subconscious. He was relieved to be up at six o'clock and in the shower. By six-thirty, he was ready for the day, feeling strong and refreshed.

At seven o'clock, he met Haloran in the hotel coffee shop. He thought the detective looked refreshed, except for his clothes. They always looked tired.

After relishing a sip of coffee, Haloran asked, "Think we ought a see anybody else here in Houston?"

"Naw...not really. Doc Stanton will keep in touch, let us know what's going on."

"After getting Scott to the ranch and telling him the bad news...what then?"

"You already know I'll be going back to Putnam...to see if I can get a lead on who gave the kid the drugs."

"Yeah...I knew that. I'll be there with you as much as I can. If I'm not, you'll get your tail in a sling with the Putnam police."

McCall grinned, poured part of a package of Equal in a fresh cup of coffee, stirred and asked, "How come you think I can't do anything

DEATH ANGEL

without getting in trouble?"

"It's your history, big shot."

"Just thought I'd ask."

By eight o'clock, McCall had the Cadillac negotiating Houston traffic en route to the interstate and San Antonio.

NINE

Scott Tyler had at first resisted McCall's invitation to the ranch, saying he needed to stay in Putnam to await results of Andy's autopsy. He relented after McCall told him he had talked to Stanton and that the doctor would call the ranch.

Before Tyler arrived in San Antonio, McCall had dinner and went to a movie with Celeste Grigg. It was not enough, but it was getting to the point where no amount of time alone with Celeste was enough. She wanted it that way, thrived on him wanting to be with her all the time. She was ready for marriage and a family. He was not.

Celeste had been quite open in declaring her love for him and he had suspicions that he loved her, though he had difficulty defining the term. His reservations about commitment were, in part, based on Cele's death. He knew he was on a guilt trip, but it was hard to get off the train.

Cele had, a few years earlier, been the woman he was sure he

DEATH ANGEL

would marry. But a maniac had killed her while trying to exterminate McCall.

After Cele's death, Celeste had been there for him. Early on, he had accepted her friendship, but it took a considerable amount of time before he accepted her love. Now he felt comfortable with her, like with no other woman. Still, there was a nagging reluctance on his part to make their relationship permanent. He fought it and sometimes made stupid mistakes because of it.

McCall worried because numerous people he had loved and cared about had come to a violent end. Cele had died because she was in his condo when a bomb meant for him had exploded. The same maniacal killer had tried to get him with a car bomb. Instead, a young Hispanic reporter and friend had been killed. Even Bill Haloran had taken bullets that McCall believed he should have taken himself.

There had been others, too, especially in Vietnam. Every original member of the Special Operations unit he had led was dead. Some had died when he was not with them, but that made him feel guilty for not being there. He was tormented that so many associated with him had died.

Through circumstance, fate, whatever one wanted to call it, McCall had led a violent life. Now he was feeling some pangs of remorse for even Andy Tyler's death, wondering if by simply knowing Scott Tyler he had brought the Death Angel into his life. It was not intelligent thinking, but McCall tended to blame himself for much that went wrong in the lives of his friends.

As for Celeste, she was truly the most beautiful woman McCall had ever known. Her personality and warmth were as beautiful as her face and body. She had perfect white teeth, long blonde hair, sparkling blue eyes, a sensuous mouth and a body that evoked envy in most women and a stupefied interest from almost all men. Her legs were tan, silky and exciting, the kind that would have been insured for a million dollars if she had been a movie star. She was rare in that while she used makeup she did not need it. The purpose of makeup, McCall thought, was for women to try to look like Celeste did naturally.

She was no bimbo, either. She was smart and mentally tough, necessary attributes in handling McCall.

"How many days are you going to be on the ranch with Scott?"

Nine

They were sitting on the couch at her place. He was cradling her in one arm, had a caffeine-free Diet Coke in his free hand. She had a glass of iced tea. They were listening to a Roberta Flack CD on the stereo.

"Probably three...four days," he replied. "I'm not sure."

"You're taking a lot on yourself...being a father figure for someone your own age."

He laughed. "Father figure?" Where'd you come up with that?"

"Surely you know it. For as long as I've known Scott Tyler he's been dependent on you...like a child. Or maybe he's like a dope addict and you're his fix."

"Well, Dr. Grigg...I didn't know you were an expert when it came to the human psyche."

Celeste was a legal secretary, but was close to graduating from law school. "I'm no expert, but I know enough to believe Scott's dependence on you is a little unhealthy."

"Good grief, Celeste...the man's been through hell. I've helped him out a few times, but he's not dependent on me."

"Don't get teed off at me, Matt McCall. I'm not telling you anything you don't know. Scott's been clinging to you ever since you hauled him out of that prison camp."

McCall had never told her about the prison camp. Tyler had. Scott liked Celeste and she liked him. She just thought he ought to start dealing with his problems without McCall's help. She was also fearful something might happen to him and McCall would blame himself for it. She had lived with that enough.

"After he got out of the prison camp I didn't see him for a long time."

"Yes...and look what happened during those years. He became a drunk, lost the only woman he'll probably ever love, lost his job, his self-respect...everything. He let you put him back together. I like Scott...a lot. But he's weak...fragile. And he thinks if anything goes wrong you can fix it. That's what he thinks now. But you might not be able to fix things for him now, Matt. The death of his son...it's too much to ask of you."

McCall knew her concern was for him, that she feared he might be affected in a negative way if he could not help Tyler. "What do you want me to do, Celeste...just walk away?"

"No...I just want you to be careful, to realize you're not God. And make Scott realize it, too."

"Bill's worried about the same thing, more or less."

"And you're not?"

"Of course I am. But I give Scott credit for being a lot stronger than you and Bill do."

"I love you, Matt McCall, and I don't want you blaming yourself if the pieces of Scott's life don't fit together anymore."

There was considerable difference in their ages, but McCall thought she sometimes looked at things in a more mature way than he did. He was an admitted cynic who viewed life analytically, but there were occasions when his emotions stepped in front of his reason.

The next day he had his usually run-ins with Katie Hussey and Turner Sipe. She was the *Tribune* metro editor, Sipe the city editor. They both hated him. And McCall thought a monkey had more journalism knowledge than the two combined. He figured neither would know a good story if it jumped up and grabbed either of them by their throat.

Katie and Sipe were forever complaining about him to another of his least favorite people, managing editor Ed Parkham. Their regular meetings to cuss and discuss him were generally in Parkham's office, which McCall had bugged with state-of-the-art equipment. A couple of copy editors monitored the trio's meetings, so everyone on the news side of the paper knew what they were planning. The three were continually baffled that the staff was able to predict their every move.

The trio detested McCall and devoted a considerable amount of time conspiring against him. They pretended to be unaware that most of the news staff was firmly on McCall's side.

Reporters and other editors applauded McCall's independence and envied him because they were not so lucky. Most of them were just living from paycheck to paycheck and desperately needed their jobs.

Katie, a cup of coffee in one hand, pulled a chair up close to McCall's desk and sat. She had been standing for a couple of minutes talking to him. "There's a really good story out there, McCall...just waiting to be written."

McCall, also enjoying a cup of coffee, leaned back in his chair

Nine

and put his feet on the desk. "Lots of good stories out there, Katie...all waiting to be written. But the one you're suggesting isn't one of them."

Her face flushed crimson. It always did when he shot her down. "Why don't you just come out and say it, McCall? You don't like Congressman Bob Bright so you don't want to do a story about him...no matter how many good things he does for this area."

"Okay...I don't like the jerk. He's a buffoon. And I'm not going to do a story about him. If you want a puff piece, just let the congressman's flak write it."

Katie had a mean mouth and McCall liked to watch it twitch when she was angry. He checked out her bleached hair and red face and decided she was a rather colorful character. Her body had not been computer designed. She was shaped like a horizontal box with ankles a bit too thick for her stumpy legs. But, despite her appearance, she was Parkham's number one squeeze. McCall figured they were meant for each other because Parkham was no prize either.

"Bob Bright's a good man...and the only reason you don't want to do the story is because I thought of it."

McCall laughed. "I hope you don't blow a fuse...doing that kind of thinking. And you're right, I don't want to do the story because you thought of it."

Agreeing, he knew, would irritate her even more. Her suggesting a story on Bright, though, had nothing to do with his reluctance.

Her anger intensified. "Whether you like me or not, McCall, I'd think you'd care enough about our profession to want to report the news."

He laughed again and sipped his coffee. "First, don't refer to it as our profession. Your profession and mine...they're not the same. And what you're advocating is a puff piece about a politician you like...a liberal jerk who kisses up to this country's enemies and to any group who'll throw him their votes. You know I don't like politicians in any shape, color, size or ideology, so bug off and have somebody else do your dirty work."

Her eyes turned venomous and her mouth weaseled. "The congressman liked the stories you did on the Brown Berets," she said, reluctantly.

The Brown Berets was a Mexican organization. McCall was one

DEATH ANGEL

of the few Anglos its leadership trusted. "So that's it. The good congressman suggested I write a story about him. Ever occur to you why he wants me to write it?"

She did not respond so he answered for her. "The man wants the Mexican vote, a large bloc of which is controlled by the Brown Berets. He thinks if I write something complimentary about him the Brown Berets will trust him. I couldn't write something complimentary about the toad because that's the same as attacking people I like...in this case, the Mexicans. I'll be glad to do a story on how Bob Bright became a millionaire on a congressman's salary. I'd be glad to do that piece about a lot of the clowns in government. But I'm not writing a puff piece for you or anybody else, Katie."

She said nothing, just got up, anger in her face, and walked away. McCall watched as she moved away and thought, Some women shouldn't wear tight skirts.

Many labeled McCall a male chauvinist, some basing that opinion on his dislike for Katie. It was true he had some old-fashioned ideas about women. He tended to put those he cared about on a pedestal.

Katie, on the other hand, represented everything he detested. She had been a no-talent society writer who, through kissing up to the right people, became metro editor. McCall figured that even if he drank and were in a drunken stupor, he would pass on having any kind of relationship with Katie, but some of the powers at the paper were not so choosy.

Ed Parkham, for example.

He was a real paleface, a soft man with ghost-like qualities. Even the top of his head, seriously lacking hair, was pale. In his late forties, Parkham wore black horn-rimmed glasses that served as a foreground for deep-set and pale blue eyes. He had almost colorless eyebrows, a pug nose and oversized mouth.

While Parkham, McCall knew, disliked him, as much as Katie and Sipe did, he needed him. His reputation and stories won awards, something Parkham used to prove to top management his worth as a managing editor.

His other adversary at the paper, Turner Sipe, was as much of a kiss-up as Katie. A former do-nothing reporter, he had kissed up to Parkam enough to become city editor. He was overweight, in his fifties,

Nine

and had done nothing to distinguish himself in his forgettable career. He had overcome his minimal writing and editing talent by being a good ol' boy.

Really a bunch of winners, McCall thought. He wished he had time to nail Congressman Bright, just to irritate Katie more, but other things were more important at the moment. There was Scott Tyler to think about, dealing with his grief and trying to find the person responsible for his son's death.

TEN

Scott Tyler showed up in San Antonio about mid-afternoon. About an hour later, he and McCall were en route to the ranch. Tyler seemed subdued, his mental state, McCall surmised, regressing. He was hoping a few days at the ranch would help, but figured Tyler's condition would worsen when he found out the results of the autopsy.

It was dark when they pulled up to the house. Gathering storm clouds blocked any light the moon might have offered. The porch light was on, as were lights inside the house. Rosita, who with her husband took care of the place for McCall, had turned them on. They lived in a small cabin about fifty yards from the big log structure.

Rosita greeted them and announced supper was ready. McCall had never asked her to cook, but she always insisted on taking care of him and his guests. "You didn't have to cook, Rosita. We could have stirred up some groceries."

She smiled. "You know I like to cook for you, Señor McCall. You

Ten

don't come to the ranch often enough. And it's been a long time since you were here, Señor Tyler."

"How many times have I told you, Rosita," Tyler said, forcing a weak smile, "to call me Scott?"

"You might as well give up, Scott. I've been trying to get Rosita to call me by my first name for as long as I've known her. She's a hardheaded woman. Sorry, I guess hardheaded woman is redundant."

Rosita's smile widened and she went back to the kitchen.

"You're lucky to have people like Rosita and Juan taking care of the place for you," Tyler said.

"Don't I know it. I wasn't comfortable about leaving the place until they agreed to go to work for me...to watch over everything. But hey...you need to get settled in. Just take the guest room you've always used."

"Wish Bill could have come with us."

"He'll be on out," McCall said, "if that clunker of a car he drives doesn't blow up on him."

While Tyler was taking his gear to the specified room, McCall went to the refrigerator in the kitchen and poured himself a glass of buttermilk. He didn't drink anything stronger than coffee. And sometimes he even rejected coffee for weeks at a time. He was one of those people who refused to be dependent on anything.

Though he was not able to spend as much time as he would have liked at the ranch, McCall loved the place. The big house was set right in the middle of the one thousand fenced acres, land that was primarily inhabited by deer, quail, coyotes, rabbits, armadillos and rattlesnakes. A small stream ran across the land. An earthen dam had been built across the stream to make a lake of some twenty surface acres. It was about fifty yards east of the main house and was well stocked with bass, crappie and channel catfish.

With more than three thousand square feet of living space, the log house had four bedrooms, three full baths and two fireplaces. One fireplace was in the den and the other separated the kitchen-breakfast room from a paneled study that had floor to ceiling bookshelves that were full to overflowing. Indeed, the number of books on the shelves and stacked on the floor of the room tended to overwhelm visitors. It was obvious the man who owned the house had a love affair with the

DEATH ANGEL

printed word.

The large study was furnished with a massive roll top desk that had made the journey from the nineteenth century. The top was rolled back and an old manual typewriter was setting on it.

There was an uncomfortable looking dark-stained oak swivel chair that belonged to the desk and a couple of small oak tables that each held a lamp and stacks of papers and books. There were also three large filing cabinets, a radio/CD player and a blue leather reclining chair that lingered under the shadow of a floor-base reading lamp.

Wall space that was not occupied by bookshelves and windows was covered with pictures and other memorabilia. It was a comfortable-looking room, definitely a man's room, and it showed evidence of being the most lived-in room in the house.

Both fireplaces also showed use, though fires in them during winter were more for atmosphere than warmth. The house was centrally heated and air-conditioned, power provided by large windmills that sent electricity to a large series of batteries.

Every room had a ceiling fan. Water for the house came from a deep well.

McCall took his drink to the kitchen. The odors wafting from the kitchen were tantalizing and made him aware he was hungry. "What's for supper?"

"I'm frying quail, making jalapeño pinto beans, salad and flour tortillas. Better enjoy. It's the last of the quail."

"Hope there's enough for your friend, Señor Haloran."

Rosita smiled. "I planned for him. I'm cooking eighteen quail."

McCall laughed. "Well, that ought to be a good appetizer for him. He'll probably eat a half dozen peanut butter and jelly sandwiches after supper."

"He has mucho appetite," she said, laughing. Then, just as quickly, there was a mood swing. "Señor Tyler...is he going to be all right?"

"That's a tough question, Rosita...one I can't answer."

"Sad...sad about what happened to Señor Tyler's son."

Tyler had not come out of his room so McCall took his drink to the study, stretched out in the recliner and read. About fifteen minutes later Bill Haloran showed up. "This is wonderful," he said on seeing and smelling what Rosita was cooking. "I was afraid I was going to have

Ten

to eat McCall's cooking."

They all gathered around the antique table in the breakfast area, which was actually just an extension of the large kitchen. McCall had insisted Rosita and Juan eat with them, something he always did. When they had first entered his employ they had been timid and reluctant, but now they were comfortable with McCall and his friends.

Juan was a slightly built man, just over five and a half feet tall. He was two or three inches taller than Rosita. Despite his size, McCall always marveled at his strength. Though getting on in years he was always working. He was like a windup toy that had a backup battery pack.

When Juan showed up for supper, it was apparent that he had recently taken a shower. His hair was still wet and slicked back, and he was wearing a freshly starched and ironed plaid shirt and jeans. His boots were polished to a mirror shine.

Four of those at the table ate heartily. Tyler picked at his food. McCall and Haloran considered quail the food of the gods. The detective, who had been introduced to the delicacy by McCall, claimed he could eat quail every day. "You'd probably get tired of it eventually," McCall said.

As important as the food to McCall was the coffee Rosita made. She boiled it in a big blue coffeepot that seemed to be permanently parked on the cookstove. There was, to him, nothing like boiled coffee. Its flavor was superior to every other method of making it.

Between bites Haloran said, "Be okay with me if you cook quail again tomorrow, Rosita."

She laughed. "That's all of them...no more."

"Don't worry, Bill, we'll fill the freezer again when the season starts," McCall said, "It's not that far off. By the way, how are the dogs doing, Juan?"

"Fine, Señor McCall...probably a little too fat."

"When quail season starts...we'll work the fat off them."

McCall owned two fine pointers and kept them at the ranch. Juan had built the dog runs and housing for them. The two animals were tested veterans that knew how to avoid the fangs of rattlesnakes, a vital attribute in the area they hunted.

Haloran asked, "How about dove tomorrow?"

DEATH ANGEL

"Maybe," McCall replied. "That is...if Scott can help me knock down a few. I've seen you shoot, and if we're depending on you to put meat on the table we might all go hungry."

Tyler managed a smile and Haloran said, "I ain't that bad of a shot, McCall. If you didn't always take the best shotgun..."

"Whoa there, Bill. I always let you have any shotgun you choose." McCall had a fine collection of firearms, including more than a dozen shotguns.

"I never know which one to pick," Haloran said.

"Not my fault. You always pick a pretty one and don't pay any attention to whether it's an improved cylinder or full choke. To be a cop, you know less about guns than anybody I know."

Arguments between McCall and Haloran about the detective's shooting problems were commonplace. Tyler, Juan and Rosita had heard them often enough. Tyler usually did a little agitating, but not this time. It was further evidence of the depressed state he was in.

After dinner, Juan went to take care of chores, Rosita washed the dishes and cleaned up the kitchen, and McCall, Haloran and Tyler returned to the den where a fire was blazing in the fireplace. It was a cool night, but not really cold enough for a fire. The flames just provided a mood for the setting.

Haloran and Tyler settled in on a big leather couch and McCall slouched in a favorite chair, also soft leather. No one bothered to turn on a lamp because the glow from the fireplace was more than adequate. McCall had poured another glass of buttermilk, Haloran was nursing a root beer and Tyler had a mug of Rosita's boiled coffee.

Haloran asked, "What's the schedule tomorrow?"

"Whatever you guys want to do," McCall replied. "I figured we might do a little fishing in the morning...dove hunting in the afternoon. That okay with you, Scott?"

Tyler's mind seemed to be in the twilight zone. "Oh...uhh...whatever you want to do."

"It's kind of important to us to do what you want to do, Scott."

"Sorry, guys...I guess I'm not good company."

"You're not company here," McCall said. "You're family. So you let us know when we're invading your privacy or space."

Tyler sighed. "Don't get the idea I don't appreciate what you guys

Ten

are trying to do. It's just that...well, if you don't mind I think I'll go to bed."

Haloran grumbled. "You mean I have to sit up and talk to this joker by myself?"

Tyler smiled, weakly. "Afraid so, Bill. But you can handle him."

"I can handle lots of stuff...but it don't mean I want to."

When Tyler left, Haloran shook his head in resignation. "Not good, McCall...not good at all. He's about as close to the edge as a man ought to be."

"Hate to say it, but you're right. Well, all we can do is be here if he needs us."

"He needs us now but doesn't know it."

"I disagree with you there. He knows it."

They played checkers until midnight. Both went to bed with unanswered questions about Tyler's mental condition.

• • •

Morning broke cool and clear over the ranch, the sun painting an orange glow on the eastern horizon. There was something about the place that spoke of a better time, a time when people did not cluster in one small area to breathe pollutants from cars, industry and themselves.

The only alarm clock McCall needed were the scents wafting through the house. McCall knew the wonderful bouquet was an aromatic mixture of fresh boiled coffee, fried eggs, deer sausage and homemade biscuits. Bleary-eyed, he made a beeline for the coffeepot, poured himself a cup and doctored it with Equal.

Rosita laughed and said, "You stayed up too late, Señor McCall."

He grinned. "Don't start preaching at me."

"Somebody needs to. You need a good woman...like Señorita Celeste."

This time he laughed. "I don't need marriage counseling, either."

"She's right, you know." The words came from Scott Tyler, dressed in a robe and house shoes. "You're a fool if you don't marry Celeste."

"Celeste isn't that stupid."

"Oh, yes she is," Haloran said. "She ought to be smarter, but she ain't." He had not bothered to wear a robe, just boxer shorts and a T-shirt.

DEATH ANGEL

Anxious to change the subject, McCall said, "Dang it, Bill...don't you know that running around like that you're about to cause me to exceed my gag index?"

Rosita laughed. "Señor McCall...you should be ashamed."

"For what...for telling the truth? The man comes to breakfast half-naked...and you see the shape he's in."

She shook her head in resignation and Haloran said, "Whether I'm half-naked or not depends on how you look at it, McCall. I consider myself half-dressed."

Even Tyler managed a chuckle at the absurdity of the conversation, which fueled McCall's and Haloran's desire to keep it going. The banter continued until Rosita got breakfast on the table and Juan magically appeared.

"Thought I'd go out and catch a few bass this morning," McCall said, spearing a piece of sausage with his fork. "You want any fish, Rosita?"

"I'd rather have catfish."

"And I'd just as soon fish for catfish," Haloran said. "McCall, you and Scott catch the bass and I'll get Rosita a mess of catfish."

"Some reason you're kissing up to Rosita?" McCall asked.

"Well, I was hoping she would make some peach cobbler for supper."

Rosita laughed. "I would have made you a peach cobbler, Señor Haloran, even if you were not going to catch me some catfish."

Juan said, "Everyone be careful today. The snakes are bad...blind and mean."

"Rattlesnakes are cantankerous enough even when they're not shedding," McCall said. "But don't worry about us, Juan. We're all pretty skittish when it comes to snakes."

After breakfast, they all took care of their morning rituals. Because they would be going dove hunting in the afternoon McCall, Haloran and Tyler dressed in camouflage clothing. The afternoon's attire would also call for snake leggings with their boots, but such protection was not necessary for fishing the lake. It was easy enough to see snakes around the lake or in the water. Juan kept the grounds around the lake clear of hiding places for reptiles.

Haloran found a familiar spot on the bank and settled down in a

Ten

lawn chair, Juan in another beside him. Juan had thrown some soured maize in the water to attract catfish. The two men put blood bait on treble hooks attached to their lines and cast out about fifteen or twenty feet from the bank. Attached above each hook was a small sinker, and about three feet above the hook was a bobber. Both were using six-foot light-action rods and ultra-light spinning reels.

The detective had also brought a cooler full of iced-down cold drinks to keep him company. Not that Juan wasn't good company, but Haloran always liked to have a can of pop nearby.

McCall and Tyler, after chasing off a couple of water moccasins, launched themselves into the lake in a flat-bottomed aluminum boat. It was a sixteen-foot DuraCraft painted a dull green. McCall sat in front and sculled the craft with a short paddle.

Tyler chose a rod and reel and topwater lure to begin the day's fishing. McCall's choice was a fly rod with a popping bug.

Good-natured banter began immediately when Juan hooked a nice five-pound channel catfish and battled it to shore. "You going to help Juan or sit on your rear and drink RC Cola all day," McCall yelled to Haloran.

The detective shouted back. "You probably hadn't noticed, big shot, but I don't have one in my hand. And I don't see you helping out."

No sooner were the words out of Haloran's mouth than McCall set the hook on a nice bass. He fought the fish to the boat, hoisted it aboard, removed the hook and returned it to the water.

"Make a note of that," the reporter called out. "Juan, show Bill your fish again so he'll know why we're here."

Juan, however, didn't have time. He had already hooked another catfish. "Juan's got the best hole," Haloran complained. The two were fishing within a couple of feet of each other.

That's the way the morning went. They all caught large numbers of fish, with McCall and Haloran spending considerable time ragging each other. Tyler didn't seem to be enjoying the fishing that much. He caught his share of bass, but did so quietly and methodically.

About eleven-thirty, they called it quits. Juan took the fish that were to be cleaned to wherever he performed the task. McCall, Haloran and Tyler went to the house, cleaned up, then went out on the front

DEATH ANGEL

porch to relax. On the long porch that stretched across and around two sides of the house there were several chairs, three of which were rockers, and a porch swing. They all chose a rocker. McCall and Tyler each had a mug filled with coffee. Haloran was sampling another RC Cola.

"I wish Andy could have seen this place," Tyler said. "He loved fishing and hunting."

Neither McCall nor Haloran responded immediately. Then McCall said, "From all you've told me, he must have been a heckuva good kid. Sorry I never met him."

"Yeah...you would have liked Andy. And he would have liked you. I just wish both of you had met him before..." Scott Tyler's sentence tanked in midstream, as if a large force had stopped his thought process.

"You said the doctor would contact me here...as soon as he knew something more about the autopsy?"

"Yeah. He'll let you know as soon as soon as the results of all the tests are in."

"It's not fair...Andy dying like that."

"No...it wasn't," McCall said. "But there's not a lot of fairness in the world, Scott."

Haloran mumbled, "Amen to that."

"I guess I could come up with something trite like, I know what you're going through," McCall said. "But the truth is...I don't. I've never had a son to lose. From what you've told me, though, the two of you shared something special. He's gone, but your love for Andy hasn't died. Probably the greatest memorial you could give him would be to live your life to the fullest, to never forget him, to keep his memory alive."

Tyler looked at McCall without saying anything, a lot of hurt in his eyes. Both McCall and Haloran were grateful that Rosita came out on the porch about that time and announced that lunch was ready.

They lunched on tacos and refried beans, then spent a couple of hours shooting skeet and trap. It was a warm-up for their scheduled late afternoon dove hunt. McCall didn't care about shooting skeet and trap, but Haloran thought it might help him later score a little more consistently on doves.

The detective had always had his share of trouble hitting doves.

Ten

The maximum speed of the bird was said to be thirty-seven miles an hour, but they are real acrobats in flight. Wind could also give a dove a boost, and there were very few days in Texas when the wind wasn't blowing.

McCall kept a couple more World War Two-vintage Jeeps at the ranch. The two had not been perfectly restored, as had the one he had driven there. They used the dull green vehicles to drive to a stock tank where doves usually came to drink in late afternoon.

The land McCall had purchased was rough, covered with mesquite trees and a few scrub oaks. There were ravines, rocks, flatlands and hills, grassy terrain and barren spots. It had at one time been part of a working cattle ranch, which accounted for a number of stock tanks nestled in drainage areas. And, contrary to its perceived horticultural status, even the sparse clumps of grass were richer in nutrients than some of the lush greenery in other parts of the state.

Juan wanted to raise cattle, a project that didn't interest McCall in the least. But to keep Juan happy, he had bought a hundred head of prime beef that had the run of the land.

For McCall the place was simply a getaway, an isolated area where he could fish, hunt, read and write in peace. And where he could forget, at least for a short time, some of the things he had been called on to do in his life. He had been well paid for what some termed his secret life, but it had taken a tremendous physical and mental toll on him.

McCall drove one vehicle with Tyler as his passenger. Juan and Haloran were in the other. As they drove, they encountered several deer. The place was a Mecca for alleged big bucks, but McCall had no interest in deer hunting.

The ranch was in a part of Texas that had more deer than it had when Indians ruled the land. The result was natural and predictable. The modern whitetail deer didn't get as large as did whitetails in other parts of the country – places where there is more to eat and fewer deer. McCall allowed Juan and a few others to harvest deer from his land, but specified that they kill does. If deer were to be killed, he preferred that they be harvested for food, not for a trophy rack or head to be displayed on a wall.

They arrived at the stock tank and McCall immediately arranged the obligatory rattlesnake hunt. The four men killed ten rattlers, all of

DEATH ANGEL

which had their breed's nasty temper and willingness to sink their fangs into anything that moved. Juan skinned the snakes. The hides brought a good price for use in making belts and hatbands.

"Juan can have the hides and the money," McCall said. "I don't want any snake's skin around my head or my waist."

The stock tank was a glaze of murky water, surrounded by land that was cracking in the Texas heat. In order to accommodate the dove population, Juan had planted a couple of acres of maize and sunflowers, favorite food for doves. For the migratory fliers it was like finding a McDonald's or a Burger King in the middle of nowhere.

McCall and Tyler found cover and relief from the sun on one side of the tank, Haloran and Juan on the other side. McCall and Tyler were below an embankment of the pond, in a depressed area, so they posed no danger to the other hunters.

The birds began their acrobatic maneuvers over and around the stock tank about four-thirty. Amidst the barking and flak of the shotguns, the darting and swirling gray doves put on an aerial show that would have been the envy of the U.S. Air Force's Blue Angels. By five-thirty, however, the hunters had forty doves, the legal limit, and were ready to call it quits for the day.

Back at the house, McCall helped Juan clean the birds. They actually just breasted them and fed the rest to the catfish in the lake. The meat was turned over to Rosita to cook for supper.

On the big porch waiting supper, McCall relaxed in a rocking chair and nursed a tall glass of buttermilk. Haloran was drinking a root beer, Tyler a tall glass of lemonade. The trio had spent many similar evenings on the porch, watching the bright orange ball setting in the west. There had been tension during those evenings, too, because that had been a period in which McCall was trying to dry Tyler out. And even after McCall thought he had succeeded in getting Tyler to give up the bottle, there had been the tension of wondering if he would stay clean.

It seemed that Tyler's presence always meant tension or some crisis to be resolved.

Tyler had proved himself capable of beating the bottle, had returned to Putnam to resume his life. After that he had telephoned McCall and Haloran occasionally, but they had not seen him. He had

Ten

immersed his life in that of his son, to try to make up for the lost years when he had put up a wall of alcohol and women between Andy and himself.

In a way, Andy had been a crutch.

Now Scott Tyler was back with McCall and Haloran, as lost as before but now in a black fog that might not lift. McCall and Haloran had once mended a broken man, but now Tyler was broken in ways that would be harder, if not impossible, to fix. All they could do was try.

ELEVEN

The second day at the ranch was almost a duplicate of the first. The only thing that really changed was the menu.

"A few more days of this and I'm going to get fat," Haloran said.

McCall laughed. "You're already fat."

On the morning of the third day, they had walked down to the lake when the helicopter appeared. It was black and ominous looking, and seemed to come out of nowhere. It stalked the house for a minute or two, then set down in a clearing beside it.

Two men emerged from the helicopter. One was Dr. Oliver Stanton. The other was Arnold, chief aide to the Ol' Man, the individual who was the real head of the Central Intelligence Agency. The man Arnold worked for was the Agency's power -- not the political appointee who was forced to endure the slings and arrows of liberal legislators and an ill-informed press.

Stanton looked casual enough in slacks, a sport shirt and light-

Eleven

weight zip-up jacket. Arnold, in his usual dark blue tailored suit, looked completely out of place.

McCall had mounted his crew in the Jeeps at the first sight of the chopper. They drove swiftly from the lake and back to the ranch house. After greeting the new arrivals, McCall suggested coffee on the front porch. Rosita had a pot boiling.

Haloran had met Arnold. Tyler had not. The detective was a bit puzzled that Arnold was involving himself in the death of a high-school football player, but decided it was just a matter of McCall calling in some markers. Just as strange, he thought, was a busy doctor taking time to come to the reporter's ranch to talk to a bereaved father.

Tyler didn't bother to ask who Arnold was, or why he was there. His mind was on what Dr. Stanton had to report. "Beautiful place you have here, Mr. McCall," the doctor said, taking a chair and cradling a mug of coffee in his hand.

"Thanks. You'll have to come out sometime and do a little fishing and hunting."

"I'd like that."

Arnold smiled, wryly. "You never invite me out."

McCall laughed. "That's because you depress me."

"I know someone who depresses you more." His reference was to the Ol' Man, who wanted McCall back in the Agency full-time, body and soul.

"You're right, Arnold. You don't depress me as much as that old buzzard does."

Arnold laughed. "I'll tell him you send your warmest regards."

McCall shrugged. "Yeah...you do that. But we're not here to exchange pleasantries. I'm sure Scott's anxious to hear what you have to say, doctor."

Stanton cleared his throat, sipped some coffee from the mug and said, "This isn't easy, Mr. Tyler. Your son...Andy...he died of morphine poisoning."

Tyler came up out of his chair, his face flushed. "That's a dang lie."

"Easy," McCall said. "Listen to what the doctor says. He's not accusing Andy of anything."

"That's right," Stanton said. "There's no indication Andy was a

DEATH ANGEL

doper or anything like that. But he ingested a mixture of crack and Novocain. That's what killed him."

Tyler sank back in his chair, his face in his hands. McCall said, "What I believe the doctor's saying, Scott, is that someone did an experiment on Andy. This mixture's strange as heck, even stranger that it was ingested. Someone must have put it in Andy's orange juice...food. Why, I don't know. Maybe some kid did it as a joke. Whatever, the perpetrator should pay for what he did."

"The information's been turned over to the authorities in Putnam," the doctor said. "I'm sure the police are looking into it."

Tyler was mute and immobile. There were no tears in his eyes. They had all been spilled. There was nothing in his eyes but emptiness.

Stanton handed Tyler a copy of the autopsy report. He glanced at it, then handed it to McCall without a word. Then he got up from his chair and walked into the house. McCall gave a movement of the head as a signal to Haloran, who followed him inside. With the gravity of the information Tyler had been asked to accept, the reporter did not want him to be alone.

There was a moment of silence on the porch, broken when Arnold said, "I don't guess I have to ask what you're going to do, do I, McCall?"

"Probably not."

"What do you mean?" Stanton asked.

"I mean McCall will turn that little town upside down until he finds out who killed the kid."

The doctor said, "I'd figure the local law could handle it."

Arnold chuckled, grimly. "I doubt they'll move fast enough for our friend here. That is...if they move at all."

"They'll probably want to call it a suicide," McCall said.

"It could be," Stanton said.

"It's possible, but I doubt it. From what Scott's told me, Andy wasn't the type. Things were going too well for him."

Stanton said, "You probably can't count on an honest evaluation from a grieving father."

"You're right," McCall said, "but I'm basing my opinion on the boy probably being a lot like his father...and his mother. I only met her at the funeral, but she's the kind who looks you in the eye and says what

Eleven

she thinks. And I know Scott's character. He's been to hell and back."

Arnold shrugged. "The offspring of some pretty strong people haven't been able to handle life."

"Hey...I've been wrong before, but don't think I am this time," McCall said. "And you don't really believe he committed suicide, do you, doctor?"

Stanton shook his head. "There are certainly easier and more common ways to poison oneself."

"I'll turn over every rock in Putnam to find out what happened to the kid," McCall said. "I owe it to Scott."

Arnold grunted. "That's bull. With all you've already done for Scott Tyler, you don't owe him a thing. You just can't stand not knowing the truth. It drives you crazy. That's why you and the Ol' Man go at it tooth and toenail. You never can be sure when he's telling the truth."

McCall glanced at Stanton and asked, "Does the Doc here know the Ol' Man?"

"Not yet," Arnold replied. "I just met Dr. Stanton myself, but I think we can use him."

McCall warned, "Pay attention, Doc. The key word is use."

Stanton laughed. "There's already been more cloak and dagger than I'm used to...the call from Washington, coming here by helicopter."

"By the way," McCall said to Arnold, "you could have invited your pilot in for coffee...or to use the john."

"He's got coffee on board...and if he wants to go to the john he can use the bushes."

McCall smiled. "Hope he doesn't get bit by a rattlesnake."

"Rattlesnake?" Arnold questioned, nervously.

"Yeah...there are a lot of big ones out here. And they're real mean."

McCall talked to the doctor and Arnold for another fifteen minutes or so, then walked them back to the helicopter. He was dreading talking to Tyler, knew how painful it was going to be. He watched the helicopter disappear before going into the house.

The reporter appreciated Arnold's willingness to help out in the investigation of Andy's death. It, obviously, was not the kind of thing

DEATH ANGEL

the Agency involved itself in, but he was able to count on Arnold for help with just about any project. He knew why, of course. The Ol' Man was willing to give favors so he could ask them. And the favors he asked always made the Death Angel McCall's partner.

He found Haloran in the kitchen with Rosita, drinking a cup of coffee and finishing off a bowl of peach cobbler. "Where's Scott?" he asked.

"He's in his bedroom...with the door closed," the detective replied.

"He doesn't have a gun in there, does he?"

"Not that I know of, McCall. But if the man wants to kill himself, we're not going to be able to keep him from doing it by keeping him away from guns. Besides, you said Scott could handle anything."

"Just about anything," McCall said.

"You know what I think?" the detective asked.

"No...and I'm not sure I want to."

"I'm going to tell you anyway."

"Now why doesn't that surprise me?"

Haloran laughed. "You wouldn't like me if I didn't speak my piece."

"You're making an assumption."

"Regardless, I'm going to tell you what I think. That is...you've got a lot more confidence in Scott than I do. He's going to turn this whole mess over to you cause he thinks you can fix it. Whether you like it or not, you've become his mama and daddy."

McCall didn't like what he was hearing. It was what Celeste had said about Tyler, about the man's dependence on him. "You're full of it."

"Am I?"

McCall didn't answer, just smiled and poured himself a cup of coffee. He wondered, *Is that my motivation? Do I want to be a father figure to Scott?* He was more inclined to think that his motivation was that of one man trying to help another who was in need, just helping a friend.

"What's the schedule?" Haloran asked.

McCall shrugged. "Guess we'll have to check with Scott. I don't know what he wants to do. I don't think he's particularly enjoyed him-

Eleven

self here."

"I don't think he can enjoy himself anywhere right now," Haloran said.

Tyler did not join them for lunch, but about two o'clock came out of his room and got a cup of coffee. He stood around in the kitchen for a while, talking to Rosita about nothing in particular. She was a good listener.

A while later he walked down to the lake with McCall. It was there that he asked, "You going to help me, Matt?"

"Help you do what?"

"Find Andy's killer."

"That's something you don't even have to ask. But if we find him, what then?"

"I don't know."

McCall appreciated an honest answer. Though he was not averse to taking the law into his own hands, he didn't want Tyler doing it. He figured there was a good possibility that the killer was one of Andy's classmates. He couldn't begin to predict how Tyler would handle that.

"You want to stay here a few more days?" McCall asked.

"No...I want to get on back home. This thing with Andy...it's unfinished business. I don't think I'm going to be able to rest until it's taken care of."

"We can leave in thirty minutes or so if you like. It'll be a couple of days before I get to Putnam...few things I need to clean up in San Antonio."

"I understand."

"Well, understand this, too. I don't want you doing anything until I get there. Let's give the local authorities a chance to handle this thing."

Tyler nodded agreement, but McCall was pretty sure he hadn't really heard what was said. They went back to the house, packed and were soon on the road to San Antonio.

TWELVE

McCall figured it would take him three days to take care of business in San Antonio before going to Putnam. His estimate was pretty much on target, but on the second day he got the shocking news that Scott Tyler was dead.

"The police are calling it suicide," Jack Gregg told him by telephone, "but it doesn't make sense to me. Maybe Andy's death was just the straw that broke the camel's back...I don't know."

"How?" McCall asked.

"He hanged himself."

"No way. If Scott was going to kill himself, he wouldn't have done it that way."

"I don't know," Gregg said. "He was distraught...so I just don't know."

"I do," McCall said. "I was supposed to be there in a couple of days to help him look into Andy's death. He wanted answers, and I was going to do my best to help him find them."

Twelve

"Well, I guess it's pretty much the end of the road now."

"Wrong," McCall said, angrily. "Now I know I'm looking for a murderer...and there aren't enough trees in East Texas for him to hide behind."

"You really believe someone killed him, huh?"

"Yeah...and Andy, too."

"But why?"

"I can't answer that right now."

"The police here are calling Andy's death a suicide, too."

"They're probably too busy trying to catch someone speeding to worry about murder."

Gregg said his purpose in calling was also to ask McCall to be a pallbearer for Tyler, and that he planned to call Haloran, too. McCall said he would talk with Haloran and that they would both be at the funeral.

McCall was at the *Tribune*, working on a piece about a Vietnamese gang in San Antonio. He added a last paragraph to the story, then telephoned Haloran. "Meet me at the diner in ten minutes," he said.

"Has it ever occurred to you that I have a real job?"

"It's Scott...he's dead."

"Oh, no."

Ten minutes later the detective was scooting into a booth that McCall had commandeered a couple of minutes earlier. The waitress showed up simultaneously with two cups of coffee.

"So...how did he die?" Haloran asked.

"The police are calling it suicide. He allegedly hanged himself."

"Maybe it wasn't alleged. Maybe the man did hang himself."

"You know better."

"No I don't. You're not being objective about it, but...what else is new?"

McCall dumped a little more than half a package of Equal in his coffee, stirred and said, "I know Scott wouldn't have taken himself out by hanging."

"How do you know?"

"He told me."

"He what?"

DEATH ANGEL

"I never told you about it, but we discussed suicide on a number of occasions. It was back when he was on the sauce and really depressed. I didn't tell you at the time because it was just talk...but Scott had it all planned if things got too bad."

"Bullet in the head...what?" Haloran asked.

"He was going to drown himself."

"That's just as bizarre as hanging."

"To you...maybe, but not to Scott. You know he had a bit of flair for the dramatic...and he liked to plan everything down to the last detail."

"Yeah...but drowning?"

"He told me about an old swimming hole on a creek that runs through Putnam...a place where he had a lot of good times with friends when he was growing up. It was a special place...a special time. So that's where he wanted to die if he was going to make the choice."

Haloran sipped his coffee, pondering what he had heard, then said, "The man was even weirder than I thought."

"I sort of understand his way of thinking."

"I know you do, which, I might add, worries the dickens out of me. But has it ever occurred to you that Scott was so messed up in the head that he just didn't bother to follow through on his original plan...if he even remembered it?"

McCall shrugged. "It occurred to me, but I don't believe it. If Scott were going to kill himself, he would have done it according to plan. It's the way he was made."

"No...that's the way you're made. I'm not so sure about Scott."

The waitress brought the coffeepot over and McCall quipped, "You're looking good, Mary Lou. New hair-do...what?"

Mary Lou, a well-built woman in her thirties, blushed and said, "No, I ain't had no new hair-do."

"You could have fooled me. It seems to me that you used to be a brunette."

"You're crazy...you know that? I ought to pour this pot of coffee in your lap."

"Whoa, let's not get irritable here," McCall said.

"Do it and I'll give you a nice tip," Haloran said.

Mary Lou, laughing and shaking her head in resignation, took

Twelve

her coffeepot elsewhere.

Haloran was pleased to see McCall loosening up, being more like his old self. The exchange with the waitress was the first humor he had witnessed in the reporter since he had learned of Andy Tyler's death.

He was quite surprised that McCall seemed so calm about Scott Tyler's demise, though he figured there was a lot of turmoil raging inside him. Maybe, he thought, and feeling guilty for thinking it, Scott's death had taken the monkey off McCall's back. Maybe, subconsciously, he was glad that he didn't have to carry the guy's burdens any longer.

"Celeste going to the funeral?" Haloran asked.

"Probably."

"Should I take my own car?"

"I'd like for you to drive Celeste's car down...then ride back with her."

"You going to stay?"

"Might as well stay a few days...shake a few bushes while I'm in the area."

"Better be careful," Haloran said. "People in East Texas don't cotton to strangers messing in their business."

"I don't know anyplace where people cotton to it," McCall said. "But if you're talking about the local law, I don't care how they feel."

"You might ought to. Some pretty nasty old boys are wearing badges and toting guns in that part of the world."

"Thanks for the warning, but someone has to stand up for Scott and his kid. I figure if I don't do it, they'll both just be buried and forgotten."

"Just don't go taking names and kicking butt before checking things out."

"You talk like I'm a loose cannon."

"Ain't you?"

McCall left Mary Lou a nice tip, paid the bill and went back to the *Tribune*. There he noticed a flurry of activity around managing editor Ed Parkham's office. It took him only a few seconds to see and understand the focus of so much ado about nothing.

Congressman Bob Bright was visiting.

McCall, who thought every politician was a jerk, was certainly

DEATH ANGEL

not one of Bright's supporters. He didn't trust the man at all.

He took note of metro editor Katie Hussey's big smile, and her attempt to be the center of the congressman's attention. City editor Turner Sipe, of course, was kissing up, and Parkham was trying to look knowledgeable. It was a real stretch.

The scenario might have amused McCall if it hadn't made him so nauseous. Things got more sickening when they brought Bright over to his desk. Parkham said, "McCall, I believe you know Congressman Bright."

McCall shook Bright's extended hand, looked straight in the man's eyes and said, "Depends on what you mean by know, Ed. I'm not sure any of us really knows a politician."

The congressman was tall and had been muscular, but age had taken its toll. Still, it was easy enough to see he was very fit for a man in his sixties. His voice flowed like his mane of white hair, and he had white bushy eyebrows that accentuated the slits he called eyes. The nose was Roman and he had, McCall thought, a suspicious looking mouth. Of course, that might have been because the reporter was suspicious of anything that came out of a politician's mouth.

Bright laughed, nervously, and said, "How are you, Matt? You know I'm a big fan of your work."

"With the three people you're with here, that gives me a twenty-five percent rating."

Sipe, a grin on his face, said, "McCall's a big kidder, congressman."

"That's right, Turnip...a real ha ha," the reporter said. He always called Sipe "Turnip" when he wanted to make him mad, which is why he called him "Turnip" all the time.

Bright chuckled, again nervously. "You underestimate yourself, Matt...you have a lot of fans."

"I agree," McCall said, "just not many around the desk right now. You and me...that's about it."

Ignoring his sarcasm, Parkham said, "We were just thinking that while Congressman Bright is here in the city, you might want to interview him."

McCall knew it was Katie's work. She was trying to put him in a position where he couldn't refuse. He was tempted to tell the quartet

Twelve

where they could go, but decided to surprise Katie with his congeniality. "Nothing would please me more. And you guys might want to stick around. You might be able to add something to the interview."

Obviously, Katie and Sipe were shocked. Parkham said, "You can use my office if you like. It's more comfortable in there."

"Whatever is most comfortable for the congressman."

He noted that Katie was twitching uncomfortably at his willingness to be cooperative. He was pretty sure she was wondering when lightning was going to strike her, or when she was going to wake from a dream.

They adjourned to Parkham's office and he sent a copy boy to get coffee for the group. Reggie Smith, Bright's publicity flak, was waiting in the office. He was a black man who had once posed as a journalist for the *Trib*, a testimony to Affirmative Action. Smith thought his color qualified him for any position he wanted in a system that had discriminated against his ancestors.

Now on the government dole, Reggie was in hog heaven and dressed for his role, from the silk suit to the reptilian shoes. He was a good-looking fellow, tall and muscular, but with an almost feminine voice.

"Mind if I use a tape recorder?" McCall asked, setting his pint-sized machine on Parkham's desk.

Bright smiled. "Well, I sure can't complain about a quote that's on tape, can I?"

"You can, but you shouldn't," McCall replied. "We've got a file on your background, so I won't waste time with that. What do you say about getting right into the meat of current issues."

"Suits me."

"Okay...in the past we had a lot of problems with bank failures...savings and loan failures. What do you think about someone asking a bank for a loan at an interest rate well below what it normally charges its best customers, not wanting to make payments on the principal for six years, not having anything for security and using the money for any purpose he pleases?"

Bright laughed. "A banker making that kind a loan would be pretty stupid."

"Really? You've supported that type loan in the past."

DEATH ANGEL

"Where did you get that kind of information?" Bright asked, defensively.

"You deny you've supported loans like that?"

"Of course I deny it."

"Funny...you boys in Washington are always voting those kind of loans to countries you know are going to default. But what do you care? You just put the burden of repaying them on American taxpayers."

Katie, uncomfortable with the line of questioning, said, "I don't think this is the kind of thing we had in mind."

"Of course it isn't," McCall said. "You want a puff piece that'll help the congressman get votes."

Sipe was frustrated by what was taking place, but didn't know what to do. Parkham seemed to be willing to let things run their course.

"I think we're getting off the track here," Bright said. "We ought to be talking about what I've done for this area."

McCall laughed. "You mean trading your vote to get federal money in here? Frankly, I think most taxpayers are fed up with pork barrel projects."

Flushed, Bright said, "I've supported legislation that brought jobs and federal money to this area."

"At what cost?" McCall asked. "And anyone elected would do the same thing. You congressmen trade votes to feather your own nests. You have perks that are the envy of kings...and most of you retire as millionaires. Too bad you can't manage the nation's finances as well as you manage your own."

The congressman rose to his feet, Reggie following suit. "I think this is getting a bit out of hand. It's obvious you..."

McCall interrupted. "Sorry, Bob, but politicians don't impress me. If the President came into the newsroom I wouldn't go across the room to meet him. If he came over to my desk and wasn't trying to con me into doing something, I'd be courteous. But I'd be cautious because I'd figure he wanted something."

"You're very much a cynic, Mr. McCall," Bright said.

"Thank you. I wear my cynicism proudly. But the truth is, I'm really just another American who's tired of being lied to by a bunch of hypocrites who claim to be working in the nation's interest."

"Clark Ramsey told me you're more interested in making news

Twelve

than reporting it," Bright said.

The reference was to the county district attorney, a man who despised McCall as much as the reporter despised him. "Is Clark an expert on news now?" McCall asked. "He's going to have to create a lot of phony news to get people to vote him in as governor."

Haughtily, Bright said, "I think Clark would make a fine governor."

"I agree that he would be as fine a governor as you are a congressman."

Bright frowned, along with the others in the room. It was a large room that was getting very small. "I'm sure you meant that in a derogatory way," the congressman said.

"I leave it for your interpretation...something I learned from politicians."

"Sorry you're more interested in attacking me than in getting a good story," Bright said.

"If you think I attacked you, then you don't know me. Talk to people who I've really attacked. You lead a pretty sheltered life, Bob...with Katie and Turnip here running interference for you."

Angrily, Katie said, "Come with me, congressman. I have other reporters who'll write a decent story."

McCall laughed. "Be sure to run it right next to all the tripe about the Royal Family."

When the room was clear of everyone except the reporter and Parkham, the managing editor said, "You can turn the simplest thing into a battle, McCall. And why that final dig about the Royal Family?"

"Because I'd like to get across to Katie and Turnip that a newspaper ought to print news, not make our readers think alleged English royalty is better than people in this country."

"I guess we have been running a lot of stuff about the Royal Family lately."

"Well, for your information, Ed, I'm going to be out of town for a few days."

"Anything you'd care to tell me about?"

"Place called Putnam...over in East Texas. I want to investigate a couple of murders over there."

"I don't recall anything coming in on the wire about any murders

DEATH ANGEL

over there."

"Police are calling them suicides. It was a kid and his father."

"How did it happen?"

"The kid...morphine poisoning. The father...hanging."

"And you're sure they were murdered?"

"Yeah...I'm sure."

Parkham liked the possibility. McCall was always looking beyond the obvious, always turning up something unique. It usually meant an exclusive series of stories and an award for the paper. He lived for awards.

"Be sure to let me know if we can help in any way," Parkham said.

McCall wasn't deceived by the man's friendliness. He knew Parkham, like Katie and Sipe, hated him. "Don't spend all the bail bond money," McCall said, laughing. "There's a pretty good possibility I'll have a run-in with the local police."

THIRTEEN

Haloran drove Celeste's new Saab convertible to Putnam the next day. She rode with McCall in his Cadillac. They arrived about six-thirty p.m. The funeral was scheduled for two the next afternoon.

They checked into the same motel the reporter and detective had stayed in on their previous trip. The place offered the best commercial overnight accommodations in the small town, which didn't mean it was endorsed by *Lifestyles of the Rich and Famous*. It simply meant the rooms were clean and the linens on the beds were changed daily.

After getting settled, they decided to check around for a good place to eat. Again, the term good was a matter of interpretation.

They found a place that specialized in barbecue, a large white frame building with hardwood floors and roughly hewed tables and chairs. Celeste thought the place was quaint, but McCall decided the proprietor got away with a lot in the name of being quaint.

Haloran ordered the combination pork ribs and beef dinner.

DEATH ANGEL

McCall and Celeste chose only the beef. They washed the meal down with old-fashioned bottles of red soda pop, which helped add to the aura of the place.

McCall was forced to admit the food was good, much better than he had anticipated. Especially good were the alleged homemade rolls, which were cooked on site. The place also had alleged homemade ice cream and peach cobbler.

The trio was very much aware that while they were eating they were being observed by two of the town's finest, who had also chosen to dine on barbecue. The uniforms worn by the twosome were typically blue, and the guns in their holsters looked oversized. They didn't look any different from cops in the big city.

The policemen, of course, weren't the only ones staring. So were the other restaurant patrons. People in Putnam watched strangers like they were new TV sitcoms.

The two uniforms finished eating first and walked up to their table. The taller of the two, a barrelchested man with sideburns reminiscent of the Elvis era, asked, "You folks here for the funeral?"

"That's right," Haloran replied.

"Sad thing...the boy and his daddy committing suicide," the speaker said.

"If they were suicides," McCall said.

Both officers stiffened. Then the speaker said, "Now...my guess is that you're Matt McCall."

"Good guess," the reporter said.

"We heard you was going to be coming down here questioning our findings on the deaths. You're going to find out we know what we're doing."

McCall smiled, wryly. "Then you've got nothing to worry about."

"Oh, we ain't worried," the speaker said. "It's you who ought to be worried. People around here don't take kindly to strangers messing in our business."

"I hope that isn't a threat."

The speaker laughed. "It ain't. Around here we don't have to threaten people, Mr. McCall. This ain't the city."

"It sure ain't, McCall said. "But since you boys know my name,

Thirteen

how about telling me yours?"

"I'm Sergeant Joe Cherry. My partner here's Officer Jim Burt."

Except for being three or four inches shorter, Burt was Cherry's clone. Both men were a bit nondescript, and both worked at trying to have menacing eyes. That kind of intimidation didn't work with McCall. They tried to lock eyes with him, couldn't handle his cold stare, so their eyes darted away in awkward confusion.

"Well, I'm sure glad you came by to make us feel welcome, Joe...Jim. This is Detective Bill Haloran from the San Antonio PD, and the lady's Celeste Grigg. We were all friends of Scott Tyler."

All nodded acknowledgment and McCall continued, "I do have a question for you, though. Who told you I'd be coming here nosing around?"

Burt looked at Cherry to answer and the sergeant obliged. "Can't tell you where it came from...but it's pretty common knowledge."

"That's good," McCall said. "I won't have to explain to folks why I'm hanging around after tomorrow."

Cherry warned, "If I was you...I wouldn't push things with folks around here."

"You're welcome to feel fortunate for not being me."

After the duo had left, Haloran said, "Nice to be so warmly welcomed."

Celeste said, "If those two are representative of the law here, I'm afraid you might be in for some problems."

McCall laughed. "Small towns have a lot to hide...more than just what happened to Scott and Andy. They're just afraid I'll turn over the wrong rock."

"Better listen to what Celeste is saying," Haloran said. "You're supposed to have that sixth sense...and if you really do, then you ought to realize this town could prove hazardous to your health."

"Dang it, Bill...you're like an old woman."

"No he's not," Celeste said. "And I'm no bimbo, either...and you'd better not treat me like one."

"Whoa," McCall said, laughing. "You know I don't feel that way about you. In fact, I kind of resent your even implying that I might."

"You'll have to excuse me, Matt. I'm a little sensitive right now...and worried about you. I was worried when Scott Tyler came

DEATH ANGEL

back into your life wanting you to mama him, and I'm worried now. When those cops were over here, the tension was so thick you could cut it with a knife."

She wasn't sure how he had taken what she had said about Tyler, but he didn't snap back at her. He was, in fact, strangely quiet. *He is,* she thought, *a hard man to read.*

"Yeah," Haloran said. "Don't you think it's strange, McCall, that the local police are already giving you warnings? To tell you the truth, the way those two acted makes my doubts about Scott being murdered disappear pretty fast."

Teasingly, McCall said, "I've always admired your perception, Bill. But that wasn't much of a warning. If you want to get my attention you have to slap me upside the head."

Haloran grunted. "That could happen, my friend."

"Bill, I just wish you could stay here with Matt," Celeste said.

"I would if I could, but I've got a real job...not like McCall here. But I'll get back here as soon as I can."

"You two might want to include me in the conversation," McCall said. "And while I'd appreciate your help, Bill, I've been taking care of myself for a long time now."

Celeste smiled. "But not as well as I can."

The reporter laughed. "Now I can't argue with that."

Haloran had a couple of bowls of peach cobbler topped with ice cream. Celeste and McCall passed on dessert, but had coffee.

En route back to the motel in Celeste's car, McCall noticed they were being followed. "Looks like Sergeant Cherry and Officer Burt want to make sure we get to bed safely," he said.

Haloran looked out the rear window and waved at the police car, which accelerated quickly and roared past them. The two officers inside were staring straight ahead, as if they had important business elsewhere in Putnam.

"Weird," Celeste said.

Haloran agreed. "I can't believe they'd follow you on their own. Somebody ordered them to do it."

McCall laughed. "That's who I'd like to talk to. Maybe I'll start following Cherry and Burt...find out who winds them up."

Haloran grinned. "Bet they don't spot you as fast as you spotted

Thirteen

them."

"I wouldn't bet on it," Celeste said. "Matt's Cadillac isn't exactly inconspicuous."

"You're right," Haloran said, "even if it's not the only Cadillac in town."

"That's all good and logical but you two aren't thinking about another possibility," McCall said. "It could be that I want those two yo-yos to know I'm following them."

The detective shook his head in mock resignation. "You're right...I hadn't considered that. Just be sure to watch your rear, McCall. While you're looking up theirs, somebody might be flanking you."

"Your concern is duly noted, but I really didn't need the warning. Remember...I'm the one who thinks Scott was murdered. You two weren't ready to rule out suicide."

"Like Bill, those two cops made me rethink my position," Celeste said.

"While I'm here, I'm going to be looking into other things, too," the reporter said.

Haloran grunted. "Such as?"

McCall joked, "Well, if Elvis is still alive...there's a good chance he's holed up right here."

Celeste and Haloran laughed. She said, "Thanks for telling us why you're really here."

At the motel Haloran complained that he was tired and planned to let the television lull him to sleep. "Late-night television would put a shark to sleep," McCall said as he and Celeste walked along the thin carpet of the motel corridor.

He escorted her to her room, which was not one McCall would have chosen for a romantic evening. But Celeste could bring excitement to a concrete bunker. McCall thought she was the best evidence he knew that it was not where you were but who you were with that made the difference.

McCall flopped on the bed and asked, "Mind if I turn on the TV?"

"I mind, but go ahead."

Using the pillows on the bed they propped their backs up against the headboard and began watching an inane program. The telephone

DEATH ANGEL

rang and he answered, thinking it was probably Haloran.

"Matt McCall?"

"Yeah."

"A word to the wise. After the funeral...get out of town and stay out."

McCall laughed and the voice on the other end of the line hung up.

"Who was that?" Celeste asked.

"The welcome wagon."

FOURTEEN

The weather for Scott Tyler's funeral made it a sodden carbon copy of the day his son was buried. Rain fell in sheets, minimizing the meaning of the word downpour. Thunder rumbled through the timbered hills as if seeking a place to rest while jagged lightning bolts sparked amid the grayness of the day.

McCall liked rain. Storms, too. And he thought the day provided a perfect backdrop for what was going to be done. Rain was like tears and, ordinarily, he would have liked slow drizzle to symbolize the passing of a loved one. But with Scott and Andy, he thought the tears should be angry and unpredictable.

As was his custom, McCall awoke early. It was five o'clock when he showered. After other bathroom rituals, he put on casual attire. Since the funeral wasn't until two, there was no point dressing for it until after lunch. He figured Celeste was still asleep in her room, so went off on his own in search of coffee.

He used an umbrella to get to the motel office, which provided

DEATH ANGEL

free coffee for guests. He poured himself a cup, doctored it and then tested it. He grimaced at the taste, and then told himself he was going to have to give up coffee.

It wasn't a matter of the coffee being bad. It was, in fact, fresh and good. He just realized he was addicted to the stuff, that he drank entirely too much of it during the day. McCall didn't like to be addicted to anything, even ice cream.

The night clerk, still on duty, was a relatively young man with blond hair. McCall guessed him to be in his late twenties, though his hair was thinning and his face had a few premature wrinkles. Probably smokes and drinks too much coffee, McCall thought. "Good coffee," he said.

The clerk, faking being busy, looked up from some papers and said, "Just made it a few minutes ago."

"Live here long?"

"All my life."

McCall was leaning against the registration counter. The clerk came out from behind his desk and the counter, poured himself a cup of coffee and then returned to a position behind the counter. He was in the neighborhood of five-foot ten inches tall and weighed around a hundred and fifty pounds. His skin was pale.

"I'm Matt McCall."

"Name's Jay Sheldon, Mr. McCall. Pleased to meet you."

They shook hands and McCall said, "I'm here for Scott Tyler's funeral. Did you know Scott, Jay?"

"Oh yeah, I knew him. Everybody around here knew Scott. I bought my car insurance from him."

"Know anybody around here who would want to kill him?"

Sheldon looked shocked. "What?"

"Anyone you know of who would want to kill Scott? Did he have any enemies you know of?"

Sweat beaded on Sheldon's forehead, despite the coolness of the motel lobby. "I...I really don't know nothing about Mr. Tyler's personal business. I heard he committed suicide."

"Well, what you hear and what's true...that's two entirely different things. Scott was murdered...Andy, too. And I'm here to catch the maggot who killed them."

Fourteen

Sheldon coughed and mumbled, "The police here...they must not agree with you."

"There are quite a few people who don't agree with me...a lot of them don't because they've got something to hide."

"I...I'm not one to question the police. I think they do a good job."

"Doing what...catching out-of-towners speeding?"

"They catch people from around here, too," Sheldon replied, defensively. Then, realizing the ridiculous nature of his reply, he added, "I mean...they do a lot more than catch speeders."

McCall laughed. "Such as?"

"They do lots of stuff."

Sheldon, McCall figured, was one of those people who was torn between thinking he shouldn't talk to a stranger and wanting to blab all he knew. Working a graveyard shift at a motel did that to anyone. He was torn between his caution and his desire to keep contact with the day world and its denizens. The reporter figured when the clerk heard some gossip he absorbed it all. He would have laid money that Sheldon was also probably the most avid newspaper reader in the town. He was a man with a lot of free time.

"So, what does the local paper say about Scott's death?"

"Not much, except what the police say."

"And the police say Scott and Andy committed suicide?"

"That's right."

"Convenient," McCall said. He walked over to the coffeepot and got a refill. "Anyone around here question what the police say?"

Sheldon shrugged. "I don't know. Barry Travis...maybe. But he's always fussing with the police."

"Who's Barry Travis?"

"He's the county district attorney...only he's not a real Democrat. And this is a Democrat county."

McCall laughed. "So you think that's why he questions the police...because he's not a real Democrat?"

"He's a troublemaker...that's what he is."

McCall was quite familiar with yellow dog Democrat strongholds in East Texas. People in such counties would vote for a yellow dog before voting for a Republican. They were the flip side of Republicans

DEATH ANGEL

in places like Orange County, California."

"How did this Barry Travis get elected?" the reporter asked.

"He lied his way in...talking like he was a Democrat."

"Who appoints the police chief?"

"The mayor. Now he's a Democrat for sure."

McCall laughed again, then turned serious. "How bad is the drug problem around here?"

"Ain't one."

"Ain't one?"

"That's right. This town won't stand for drugs."

"Kind of like Muskogee, Oklahoma, huh?"

"What do you mean?"

"Never mind. You've been a big help, Jay. I'll be sure to tell the police how much."

He left the worried desk clerk and made his way back to the room through the blinding rain. He carried a couple of lidded Styrofoam cups of coffee with him, one of which was for Celeste. He knocked on her door, but there was no answer. He smiled and thought, *Now she's a woman who can sleep right through the smell of freshly brewed coffee.*

McCall went to his room, sat in the only comfortable chair there, sipped coffee and thought about his conversation with Jay Sheldon. The fidgety desk clerk hadn't asked McCall what he did for a living. *Probably because he already knows*, McCall thought. *The local cops probably drink coffee with Jay most every night.* McCall hadn't listed his occupation on the registration card.

Yeah, I imagine Sergeant Cherry and Officer Burt had some coffee with Jay last night.

He figured Jack Gregg might have mentioned to someone that he was coming to investigate murders, not suicides. Of course, word like that spread like wildfire in a small town. And he hadn't asked Gregg to keep his suspicions or intentions secret.

Knowing I'm here and why, maybe it'll make the killer nervous, make him make a mistake, he thought.

Obviously, word that a stranger was coming to investigate murders local authorities had concluded were suicides wouldn't sit too well with the local cops. McCall's experience had been that police, no mat-

Fourteen

ter where, didn't like their judgment questioned. *Heck, who does?* he thought.

McCall went back to Celeste's room and knocked on the door. "Who is it?," was her grumpy response.

He laughed and said, "It's me."

"Is that you, Matt?"

"You'd better hope it is. Open up, I've got a cup of coffee for you."

She opened the door and squinted at him. She was wearing a white terrycloth robe. "What time is it?"

"Time to get up," he said. "You don't want to spend the entire day in bed. We're burning daylight."

She yawned and said, "Napping would be a great way to spend a rainy day."

When they were inside the room she sat down on the bed and he took the lid off the cup of coffee and offered it. Her nose twitched. "I can't drink that right now."

"Fine...I'll drink it for you."

"You drink too much coffee."

"You don't complain about my other excesses."

"Yes, I do. You just never listen."

He laughed, sipped the coffee and then asked, "You hungry?"

"Starving."

"I'll give Bill a call...you shower and dress...and we'll see what delicacies this town has to offer."

It took three rings before Haloran's grumpy voice uttered a hello. "Up and at 'em, flatfoot."

"Why at this hour?" the detective said. "I was trying to get a little sleep."

"I'm taking Celeste to breakfast. You can sleep in if you like."

"Whoa now. Ain't you going to give me a chance to shower and shave?"

"Sure...you've got five minutes."

"Five minutes?"

"Okay...make it thirty."

Celeste complained that thirty minutes just wasn't enough time to get herself together. McCall couldn't understand it. She always

DEATH ANGEL

looked fantastic to him.

From the time McCall telephoned Haloran until Celeste was ready turned out to be forty minutes. Mother Nature was still drenching the area to the tune of rolling thunder and lightning, so they used umbrellas to get to Celeste's car.

McCall drove to the Elite Restaurant, touted to be the largest and finest eating establishment in East Texas. The place was owned by Bob Mack and was nicer than most places in San Antonio. Each table was covered with white linen and had a centerpiece of freshly cut flowers.

"From what I've seen of the rest of the town...surprising," Celeste said.

McCall and Haloran agreed. The building exterior was white colonial style with ample windows. The interior wall space was adorned with tasteful oil paintings. Rich mahogany furnishings were scattered about the spacious dining area, adding to the aura of elegance.

Chairs around the dining tables were posh and comfortable looking, the legs and wood trim a rich mahogany. The legs of the dining table indicated they were the same. Some wall space had been reserved for expensive beveled mirrors, and there was crystal everywhere. It accentuated the large crystal chandelier hanging from the center of the ceiling. Candleholders on the tables were also crystal, hosting long white candles.

There was nothing gaudy about the place. Rather, it looked like the work of a renowned decorator, and like something that would grace the pages of the *Architectural Digest*. Even the breakfast menu was elegant, which, when Haloran looked at it, drew a shocked response. "Dang, McCall...this place is more expensive than that hotel we stayed at in Houston."

McCall laughed. "Don't worry about it. Think of the atmosphere."

"You can't eat atmosphere. I can eat bacon and eggs off a paper plate in front of a 7-Eleven."

"Oh, Bill," Celeste said, "there's not a bit of romance in you. When you take your wife out to eat, you probably go to McDonald's."

"What's wrong with McDonald's?" the detective asked.

There were only a few customers in the restaurant. McCall attributed that to the weather, but the prices on the menu did seem a bit

Fourteen

exorbitant for a place like Putnam. Most small East Texas towns had a few wealthy people, but not enough to support a restaurant like the Elite.

"My name is Jane," the waitress said. "Are you ready to order?"

Like the other waitresses, all showing signs of boredom from the lack of business, she was wearing a long, old fashioned dress with a hem-line that touched the richly carpeted floor. The restaurant, McCall guessed, provided the dresses. They looked expensive.

"I'll have the Eggs Benedict," Celeste said. A china coffeepot was already on the table, along with crystal pitchers filled with orange juice and ice water. They had been placed there the moment they were seated by the hostess.

"I'll just have a couple of eggs over medium with a double order of bacon, biscuits and gravy," Haloran said. "You do have cream gravy, don't you?"

"I'm afraid not, sir. And we don't have biscuits, either."

Haloran grumbled, "No biscuits. What kind of bread do you have?"

"We bring you a large basket of croissants, bagels and blueberry muffins," she said.

"You'll survive for a day without biscuits and gravy," McCall said, laughing. "You'll have to forgive him, Jane. His cholesterol count just dropped below four hundred and it makes him grumpy. Mind telling us your last name?"

"Warrick."

She was a slim woman who, McCall figured was in her early thirties. She had dark brown hair, eyes to match, and a pretty face conditioned to show little expression. "Well, Jane Warrick, is it always this quiet in here?"

"We usually have more customers. It's the rain. Can I take your order, sir?"

"Just give me a couple of scrambled eggs and some crisp bacon. And give my regards to Bob Mack. Tell him Matt McCall is here."

"Mr. Mack isn't here," she said, icily. "He usually doesn't come in until the afternoon."

She left without further conversation. Haloran muttered, "Well, if she ain't little Miss Sunshine. The ol' Matt McCall charm didn't work with her."

"That's because I was a little handicapped," McCall said, jokingly. "With Celeste here, I couldn't use my best lines."

Celeste gave him a mock smile and kicked him.

"Darling...kicking my knee like that, you could put me out of commission."

"You're lucky I just kicked your knee."

The service was fast. They were drinking coffee from china cups when Jane Warrick brought their food on china plates. The silverware on the table was genuine.

Haloran picked up a croissant and eyed it suspiciously, as if he was deciding which end to eat first. "Wonder how these things are with gravy?"

"Try to act like you didn't just fall off the turnip truck," Celeste said.

Haloran grinned. "I know you make McCall take you to all those fancy restaurants in San Antonio, Missy, but him and me...we get the good stuff at the diner."

"Call me Missy again, Bill, and I'm going to dump this pot of hot coffee in your lap."

"She prefers Sweetie Pie," McCall said, smiling.

"There's enough hot coffee to go around, Matt," Celeste said, good-naturedly. "And yes, Bill, I know you and Matt are trying for some world record for chilidogs saturated in cheese at the diner, but..."

Haloran said, "Don't forget the chicken fried steak, Celeste. Get on us about that, too."

She feigned surprise. "Are you saying I get on your case, Bill?"

Haloran grinned. "I'm too smart to say that, Celeste. I'd like to hang around long enough to collect my pension."

The banter continued while they ate, then Celeste interjected a serious note when she asked, "Did Matt tell you he got a threatening phone call last night, Bill?"

"Is that right?"

McCall laughed. "More of an obscene call."

"It's really not funny," Celeste said. "I don't like the idea of you staying here and snooping around, especially when you can't count on any help from the police."

Fourteen

"I'm sure there are a few law-enforcement people around here who'll help me."

Haloran grunted. "I wouldn't count on it. And I'm with Celeste. I don't like the idea of you staying here alone."

"Don't worry. These folks will warm up to me in time."

The detective laughed. "Yeah...and the Dallas Cowboys will be calling me any day now to play quarterback."

They returned to the motel in what was now a slow and steady precipitation. McCall thought the rain had now become more appropriate for a funeral. Underneath her rain gear, which she removed on arrival, Celeste was wearing soft yellow slacks and a sweater that matched perfectly. But such perfection in dress was not surprising to McCall. She was always impeccable. From her toes to her head, everything had to be just right. Designer clothes were made for women like Celeste, though she would have been beautiful in rags.

En route back to the motel, McCall had announced he would be going to see Jack Gregg and Barry Travis, the county district attorney. "Want me to go with you?" Haloran had asked.

"No, why don't you and Celeste just stay at the motel and take it easy. We'll lunch about noon and then dress for the funeral."

Gregg's bank was just across the street from the county courthouse, a part of the general scheme of Main Street. It was larger and more impressive than the other storefronts. There was lots of marble and engraved lettering.

He guided the Seville into a parking space right in front of the bank, opened the car door and popped open an umbrella. He fed the parking meter and then found refuge from the pelting wetness under an awning that protected the sidewalk and stretched all the way down Main Street.

The bank lobby was like hundreds of others McCall had seen, only larger than he had expected. He walked the length of it; to where he calculated the bank's officers would be practicing their trade. There a secretary confronted him. The nameplate on her desk read, *Miss Stevens*.

She was a young woman, in her twenties, with a flowing mane of auburn hair and dark eyes that could devour a man. She was, he figured, the most beautiful woman in Putnam. But she would also have been close to the top of any such list in Dallas, Houston or San Antonio.

He introduced himself and her eyes flashed recognition. She smiled. "Mr. Gregg's having coffee at the drugstore next door. It's one of his morning rituals. I know he would like to see you."

"Thanks...Miss Stevens."

"Alicia...my name's Alicia."

McCall entered the drugstore and saw Jack Gregg sitting on a stool at the counter. He was talking to an elderly waitress behind it. Gregg turned toward McCall and flashed a smile. "Glad you're here. Didn't Mr. Haloran come?"

They shook hands and McCall said, "He's at the motel."

"Rosie," Gregg said, addressing the woman behind the counter, "would you please pour Mr. McCall a cup of coffee? Want anything else? Donuts?"

"No thanks...we had breakfast at the Elite."

Gregg smiled. "It's a little much, isn't it? For Putnam, I mean."

"Unusual...to say the least."

McCall had taken a stool next to Gregg, but when Rosie brought his coffee, the banker suggested they take a booth. There were four booths, only one occupied. Gregg picked the booth that offered the greatest privacy. No sooner had they seated themselves across from each other on the cold-looking red vinyl than Gregg said, "What you said on the telephone...I've been thinking about it."

McCall put sweetener in his coffee, stirred it and questioned, "And?"

"Maybe you're right. The more I think about it, the more trouble I have believing Scott committed suicide."

McCall took a sip of coffee and said, "The swimming hole...he told you about it, didn't he?"

"He told you?"

"Yeah."

"I wasn't sure."

"I doubt that he told many people."

Gregg shook his head in resignation. "I know this...when he told me, it scared the heck out of me. I thought he was on the verge of doing it."

Fourteen

"A lot of people are on the verge, but they snap out of it. With the hell Scott had been through...well..."

"Andy's death...maybe it was just too much of the hell you're talking about."

"That's what everyone wants to think...because it's comfortable. But I'm not buying it. When we rescued Scott from the prison camp, he didn't want to go home. He wanted to get back at the guys who tortured him. So Andy's death wiped him out...yeah. But he wanted vengeance. If he were going to do it...it would have been after he took care of those responsible. And then he would have done it just like he planned. He was programmed that way."

Gregg nodded agreement. "I think you can probably look at this thing more objectively than I can. I knew Scott longer, but you probably knew him better. You might have known him better than anyone here...better even than my daughter."

McCall smiled. "That part about being objective...I wish you'd mention it to Bill Haloran. He doesn't think I'm objective about anything."

They talked another fifteen minutes or so, until Gregg said he had to get back to the bank for a meeting. McCall accompanied him to the front door of the bank, then went across the street to the courthouse. The rain had turned to a fine mist.

Benches under big trees on the courthouse lawn were unoccupied. Elderly men who normally sat on the benches, whittled, chewed tobacco and stained the grass and sidewalk with their spit, had found other places to spend their time.

The county district attorney's office was on the second floor of the two-story building. It also had a basement where records were kept.

McCall hadn't bothered to tell Gregg that he was going to talk to Barry Travis. He wasn't sure why, except that when investigating a murder he treated everyone as a suspect. Of course, before he could get through Travis' outer office he was ready to pin Andy's and Scott's murders on the DA's secretary. She was one of those women who might have been going through menopause, though McCall thought it had probably been a lifelong condition with her.

With her hair pulled back in a bun, glasses resting on the tip of her pointed nose, the high collar of her dress snapped tightly around

DEATH ANGEL

her throat, she looked like a throwback to another century. McCall, however, figured she had been introduced to just enough of the women's lib movement to make her mean.

"I only need to see him for a minute."

"Everyone needs to see Mr. Travis for just a minute," she said, haughtily. "You'll have to make an appointment."

"He's here, isn't he?"

"Yes, but he's busy."

"That's a lot of bull. He's not too busy to spare me a couple of minutes."

Her face colored a nice beet red and she said, "I'm sorry...you can't see him."

"The heck you say." He walked to the door of Travis's office, opened it and went in, the dour secretary right on his heels. The man sitting behind the desk looked up, but before he could say anything McCall introduced himself.

"I tried to stop him, Mr. Travis," the secretary said, angrily. "Do you want me to call the police."

Travis laughed. "That won't be necessary, Thelma. Have a seat, Mr. McCall."

It was obvious that Thelma was a bit angry with the DA for not having him forcibly removed, so he couldn't resist a parting jab. "Tough luck, Thelma."

After she had turned on her heels and left, slamming the door behind her, Travis said, "You'll have to forgive Thelma. She's pretty protective of me."

The DA was wearing an inexpensive gray suit with a red and gray striped tie. McCall figured if the man were living in San Antonio, he and Bill Haloran would shop at the same stores. But while their choice of clothing was similar, there were definite differences in the two men.

Haloran, while on the heavy side, was a hard, tough man. Travis was heavy, too, but there was softness to him. He had boyish full cheeks, puffed lips, blue eyes and disheveled brown hair. McCall guessed him to be in his early forties and an inch or two short of six-feet.

"I'll bet you inherited the old biddy. I can't believe anyone would hire her."

Fourteen

Travis laughed. "You're right. She's been manning her post for thirty plus years."

McCall figured the furniture in the DA's office was older than the secretary, which made it antique. The chair he chose, however, was quite comfortable. The entire office looked comfortable, like sirens wouldn't go off if a man missed the brass spittoon and hit the wooden floor.

"The reason I'm here, Mr. Travis, is..."

"I know why you're here. And please, call me Barry. If you'd told Miss Turner your name, I'd probably have heard and come out and rescued you. I was planning to try to locate you...figured on making contact with you at the funeral."

McCall gave Travis a quizzical look. "You wanted to see me, huh?"

"Yes, I did. From what I've heard, you don't believe Scott Tyler committed suicide, do you?"

"I don't believe Andy committed suicide, either."

"Why do you think that?"

The reporter hesitated, then thought *What the heck?* He told Travis about Tyler's suicide plan, also his knowledge of the total man. It was the same stuff he and Jack Gregg had discussed.

"That's not much," Travis said.

"I don't need much. Call it a hunch if you will, but I knew the man...really knew what made him tick. Besides, I was told you didn't believe the deaths were suicides, either."

Travis laughed. "People around here always want to put me at odds with the police. Some people think I'm against everything the police say and do."

"Why's that?"

"I'm an outsider...and I don't always agree. That can be unhealthy around here. I came to Putnam seven years ago, started practicing law, decided to run for office and was lucky...or unlucky...enough to get elected. I really just knew Scott Tyler and Andy in passing."

"You do know Jack Gregg?"

"Sure...I know Jack," the DA said. "I have coffee with him over at the drugstore once in a while. And he financed my car. He finances cars for just about everybody in town."

DEATH ANGEL

"Did Jack tell you I was coming here to find Scott's killer?"

"No...don't think he did. That came to me in a roundabout way...not sure who told me. Scott told me you were coming here to help find Andy's killer. Anyway, I'd like to help you if I can."

"I take it the police aren't going to be much help?"

Travis laughed. "I sort of doubt it. What we have in Putnam is a serious case of small town partisan politics. I'm a Democrat, but because I disagree once in a while, I'm labeled a closet Republican. That doesn't set well with the mayor...and he's the one who appointed the police chief. The county sheriff, of course, was elected. He's a Democrat, too...real suspicious of me. To tell you the truth, I don't care much for either political party."

"That makes two of us," McCall said. "But don't you have some questions about Scott's and Andy's deaths."

"The problem is that I asked a couple of questions, which didn't have anything to do with the politics of the town. But anytime I ask a question, the police chief, sheriff and certain city leaders holler. The investigation into both deaths was inadequate because Dade Decker...he's the police chief...never wants any problems. He wants everything swept under the rug. And, Matt, I confess that I hadn't pushed for anything but suicide verdicts. I just wanted the paperwork in order, which it wasn't. And when I said something about it to Decker, all of a sudden he wanted a piece of me."

"So if I read you right," McCall said, "you have doubts that Scott's and Andy's deaths were murders."

"I don't know what to think. I know Scott was angry at Decker...that they had words."

"What about?"

"About Decker being so quick to rule Andy's death a suicide. When he talked to me he was mad about it. That's when Scott told me about you...said you would be coming here to take names and...well, I figured a Rambo clone was on the way."

"Scott tended to exaggerate my abilities," McCall said. "But I have to ask, Barry...are you going to help me?"

"I don't know, McCall. I'll back you in every way I can, but when it comes right down to it the best advice I can offer is to watch your back."

Fourteen

McCall liked the DA, figured he was probably a pretty good man, a guy who cared. He knew that if Travis helped him he would be walking on some dangerous turf, that he could hardly be counted on to come to his aid if he found himself in deep trouble.

The reporter jotted down a name and number on the back of one of his business cards, handed it to Travis and said, "If things go sour for me, call this number and ask for Arnold. Tell him what's going down and he'll take it from there. Don't call unless you think it's absolutely necessary."

The DA looked at the name and number, but knew not to question McCall about the request. "I won't," Travis said.

Next, McCall dropped by the local paper in hopes of finding a sympathetic ear. After a brief visit with the editor, he knew the paper practiced small town journalism at its worst, and he had witnessed some poor journalism in his day. The editor's idea of investigative reporting was finding out in advance what the menu would be for the next chamber of commerce banquet.

Back at the motel McCall dressed for the funeral. Then Celeste, Haloran and he went to the barbecue place where they had eaten the night before. "This," Haloran said, "is so much better than that Elite Restaurant. I'm a plain man and I like plain food."

McCall laughed. "I'm not going to argue...about you being plain, that is."

At the First Baptist Church Jack Gregg introduced McCall and Haloran to the other pallbearers. They were all local men, all in Gregg's age range. McCall studied their faces and made mental note of their names. He wondered if any of them could have been involved in Scott's or Andy's deaths.

Unlike the standing room only conditions for Andy's funeral, the church was simply full. But the ritualistic send-off for Scott was much the same, with the weather cooperating beautifully. Thunder boomed, lightning flashed, and the rains came down in torrents. And the minister's words about Scott were just as impassioned as they had been about Andy.

McCall felt as though suspects, who even included the church's pastor, surrounded him. As the minister droned on his eyes found the section holding the family members. He picked out Scott's mother and

DEATH ANGEL

father, who were seated with a number of people he guessed were aunts, uncles and cousins. He remembered some of the faces from Andy's funeral.

Louise Gregg was also sitting with the family, as was Heather Mack. *Thank goodness Bob Mack isn't here,* he thought. *That would be a little too much.*

After the pastor had concluded his remarks, the mourners passed in review, checking the contents of the open casket. Sure enough, a likeness of Scott Tyler was lying there, made cosmetically perfect by a mortician's skill.

McCall was a bit surprised by some of those checking out the body. There was Jay Sheldon, the motel clerk; Jane Warrick, the waitress from the Elite; Alicia Stevens, the bank secretary; Rosie, the counter person at the drugstore; and even Thelma Turner, the DA's secretary. He figured a funeral made Thelma's day.

DA Barry Travis was also on hand, but McCall saw no sign of Bob Mack. *Well, why should he come?* he thought. *There was no love lost between the two.* Had Mack come, he would have figured him for a hypocrite.

Late that afternoon the rain came to a halt, bringing about a dull sun that played hide-and-seek with scattered clouds. Celeste and Haloran headed back to San Antonio, but McCall wasn't going anywhere – not until he had some answers about Scott's and Andy's deaths.

FIFTEEN

While McCall was attending Scott Tyler's funeral, Congressman Bob Bright was meeting with one of the reporter's avowed enemies in San Antonio. Clark Ramsey, the county district attorney, hated McCall with a consuming passion.

Like Bright, Ramsey was a political animal and opportunist. He had designs on becoming governor of Texas, and many well-heeled and influential supporters thought that was only the first step. They envisioned their boy eventually getting to the White House.

Ramsey had the looks for the role. He was tall, imposing, built like a linebacker. His facial features were granite-like, as though they had been taken right off Mount Rushmore. His hair, gray at the temples, gave the illusion of being steely blue.

The DA had a look of strength about him, an aura of always being in control. His false modesty came across as the real thing. He reeked of sincerity, knew all the right people, pushed all the right buttons and was almost always in the right place at the right time. He

DEATH ANGEL

could turn almost any bad situation to his advantage.

The only one, seemingly, who could shove Ramsey over the edge, make him lose his composure, was Matt McCall. The reporter stayed on Ramsey's case like ugly on an ape, often pushing the DA to the breaking point. The DA was paranoid about McCall, who he figured he was watching his every move and waiting for him to crumble.

Ramsey was a wealthy man, the result of marrying a rich woman and of swindling an elderly woman and her son out of millions in real estate. McCall even suspected him of arranging their deaths. The DA was for the reporter a continuing investigation, one Ramsey feared might thwart his attempt for higher office.

McCall never claimed to be objective about anything, and certainly not about Ramsey. When the DA's picture perfect wife, daughter of one of the state's rich political strongmen, was murdered, the reporter did his best to pin the crime on Ramsey. But despite wanting to take his adversary down for the count, it was McCall's investigation that brought the real killer to justice.

During the course of his investigation, the reporter learned that even while his wife was alive Ramsey was having an affair with a young woman who was also later murdered. And the late Mrs. Ramsey was engaged in a little indiscretion of her own with the father of the DA's young mistress.

McCall had all kinds of stuff on Ramsey, a file that, if it were hay, would choke a horse. The DA worried about just how much McCall had on him; knew it was a bunch and that the reporter was just waiting for the opportune time to use it.

Ramsey, however, was an arrogant man, totally full of himself. He was conceited enough to believe that voters, whom he considered to have the mentality of sheep, would forgive all his so-called sins. After all, he was prepared to be their savior. He would promise them anything to be elected, just as he had done to gain his current office. And he was committed to the right political party.

So the DA fluctuated between thinking he was immune to the slings and arrows to believing McCall was persecuting him for no reason at all.

When Congressman Bob Bright wanted to see him about Matt McCall, Ramsey was not at all sure what direction the conversation

Fifteen

might take. Bright hadn't made the appointment, had left that up to one of his aides, so the DA was in the dark. He initially worried that McCall might have talked to Bright about him, that the reporter might have given the congressman disturbing stories that might cause the party to drop him as one of its bright and shining stars. After thinking about it, though, he decided McCall wouldn't give Bright anything. The congressman represented everything McCall hated.

Anytime McCall's name was mentioned, Ramsey started trying to justify his actions. Yet he was not willing to admit just how much the reporter affected his life. Nor was he willing to admit how much he feared McCall. He was always lying to himself, trying to cover that fear with false bravado.

"Good to see you, Bob," Ramsey said, shaking the congressman's hand and ushering him into his plush office. He had paid for his own furnishings, making his county-provided office as posh as his home.

"Hope this isn't an inconvenience, Clark, but I was in town and wanted to talk to you about a few matters."

"You're never an inconvenience. How about a cup of coffee?"

"That would be mighty nice...a little cream and a couple of spoons of sugar," Bright said, smiling. "Got to take care of the sugar people because they certainly take care of me."

Ramsey gave instructions to his secretary on the intercom, then said, "I understand you want to talk about Matt McCall. I guess you already know we're not on the best of terms."

"Yes...I know that. Too bad, really. We could use a man like McCall. But the truth is, he's dangerous...a real threat to this area getting the kind of government help it needs."

"I couldn't agree with you more," Ramsey said. "He's been a thorn in my side for some time. But I take it you've had a recent run-in with him?"

"You take it right, Clark. You know I need the Hispanic vote here...we all do. I had the idea that if I laid my program out to McCall, he would buy into it. But he wouldn't even listen...started hounding me about other stuff."

"I'm not surprised. The man is out of control. But why did you go to him anyway...he's not the paper's chief political reporter."

"Oh, I know that, Clark. But the Brown Berets trust him...the

DEATH ANGEL

entire Hispanic community for that matter. The spics love the kook. So do the nigger militants and the Ku Klux Klan. And I'll bet a million bucks the man is really a racist and bigot."

The secretary interrupted with their coffee. When she left the DA said, "Turner Sipe says he's asked some of those people why they like McCall. He says they tell him it's because McCall isn't patronizing...that he's always straight arrow with them."

"Sipe, huh? Isn't he a dip?"

Ramsey laughed. "Yes, but he's loyal to the party...and we can use him. He probably hates McCall as much as I do."

"This thing about McCall not being patronizing...if we weren't patronizing to some of these special interest groups the media would jump on us with both feet."

"You're right, Bob. You've got to promise the poor everything. It doesn't matter whether we give them anything or not. But we've got them convinced that we're the party of the poor. We've got most of the media convinced, too...except for people like McCall."

Bright laughed. "Kind of sad, isn't it...the kinds of stupidity we have to appeal to get elected. What's your impression of Katie Hussey?"

"She hates McCall. She and Turner have been a big help to me...to the party. They'd put McCall out if they could, but they don't have the power. Even Ed Parkham doesn't have the power to do much about McCall. Some of the people at the top...people who aren't with us...they love McCall."

"What about Ed Parkham?" the congressman asked. "How do you read him?"

"He blows with the wind. He'll side with McCall if he thinks it'll help feather his nest."

"Don't he and Katie have something going?"

"Yeah...I think so. But I don't think she has much control over him. She has moved up quite a bit at the paper because of her affair with Parkham."

Bright sighed. "Well, Katie and Turner...they gave me a copy of a scurrilous piece of tripe McCall wrote about me for Sunday's paper. I don't have to tell you it's not flattering. Katie says they can't stop it from appearing...and it's going to make me and the party look pretty bad."

"I'm real sorry, Bob. I wish there was something I could do."

Fifteen

"So do I. I know you've had problems with McCall...party leaders in the state have talked about it."

Fear rose in Ramsey's throat. "What do they...what do they say about my problems with McCall?"

Bright shrugged. "They're not happy with the situation. They want to support you, but they'd like to see McCall neutralized first. So would I. I think the party would be a lot more supportive of you if it weren't for McCall."

Downcast, Ramsey asked, "So what am I supposed to do? The man's on my case day in and day out."

"I'd do whatever was necessary," the congressman said, his eyes as cold as his voice. "Do you get my meaning?"

"Yes, Bob...I think I do."

Ramsey was glad he had just had his office checked for listening devices. He was paranoid about McCall putting bugs in his home and office, so had both checked regularly. He had never found anything, but it bothered him that the reporter always seemed to be able to predict what he was going to do. There was, he believed, a leak somewhere.

"There are rumors," Bright said, "that McCall is CIA connected. What do you think?"

Ramsey fidgeted before replying. "There was a time I thought they were just rumors, too. But I got caught up in a situation where I had to actually work with McCall in bringing some Middle East terrorists to justice. He had resources and friends...one I've never seen since...that make me wonder. Maybe there's something to it."

"Did you have him checked out?"

"Of course I did. But where McCall's concerned, records just seem to disappear."

"I know what you mean," Bright said. "I've done some checking of my own...come up with nothing. The CIA...nobody knows who really runs the agency. But the important thing, Clark, is to put McCall out of business. When that happens, I'm going to buy you the biggest steak in San Antonio."

"I'll sure look forward to eating it. This article he did...do you really think it's going to hurt you that much."

"Can't help. The good thing is that most niggers and Mexicans

DEATH ANGEL

don't bother to read. They just vote the party line. But the brown vote in Texas...it gets more important everyday. The man understands that has got a good chance to be governor."

Bright was dangling the carrot and Ramsey was anxious to chomp down on it. After Bright left his office, it was still on his mind. It seemed a shame that the only thing in his way was a reporter.

Bright's visit had made Ramsey feel warm and comfortable inside. It was nice to know he had a powerful ally like the congressman in his continuing fight against McCall. He appreciated the help of Katie Hussey, Turner Sipe and Police Chief Winston Fargo, but none of them were a Bob Bright.

It was time to take care of Matt McCall, once and for all, and the sooner the better. He couldn't get Bright's promise out of his mind, that with McCall out of the way he would soon be on his way to the governor's mansion.

SIXTEEN

McCall ran the bathtub full of hot water and broke out a carton of buttermilk that he had iced down earlier. He was anxious to soak his body in the tub and take some time to remember Scott. Then he would decide what course of action to take.

Sitting in the hot water, enjoying the buttermilk, he had opportunity to go over in his mind what he had learned so far. *Not much*, he thought. But it only took one slip of the tongue by someone and he would be able to establish a stranglehold that would eventually lead him to the truth.

There were a lot of bothersome things going on in his mind, like the way officers Cherry and Burt had talked to him. Well, actually just Cherry. Burt was the silent one. But it was obvious he was Cherry's shadow.

Then there was Jay Sheldon, the motel clerk, who seemed to know more than he was telling. And there was Bob Mack and his

DEATH ANGEL

restaurant, a place definitely a bit ostentatious for a town like Putnam. There was something funny, even phony, about the man who had married Scott's ex-wife. McCall wanted to be objective, but hadn't liked Mack from the moment he met him.

He also wanted to know more about Barry Travis. What he knew of the DA, he liked. A first impression, however, was not grounds for absolute trust. He had to know more.

After a couple of glasses of buttermilk, the water in the tub had cooled considerably. He got out of the tub, toweled himself off, then lay down on the bed and dozed off. It was about a quarter until seven when the telephone rang.

The voice on the other end of the line belonged to Alicia Stevens, the secretary he had met that morning at the bank. She suggested that if he hadn't eaten they might have dinner together. "I hope you won't think me too forward," she said, "but I might be able to fill you in on some things that would be helpful."

He couldn't understand why she would want to, and said so. "You didn't date Scott, did you?"

"No...I really didn't know him all that well. I probably knew Andy better."

"You didn't date him, did you?"

She laughed. "I'm not that young. Andy went steady with Melanie Richards. Her folks are friends of mine."

"I'm not trying to be difficult about having dinner with a beautiful woman," McCall said. "Your call just surprised me. Did Jack Gregg tell you where I was staying?"

"He didn't have to. There's only one decent motel in town."

McCall offered to pick Alicia up, but she suggested they meet at a place of his choosing. He suggested the Elite Restaurant at seven-thirty.

After hanging up the phone his suspicious mind pondered her call. There had been only their brief encounter at the bank, and he had seen her at the funeral. What was her real purpose in calling him? Had someone put her up to it?

You silly jerk, he thought. *The most beautiful woman in town offers to dine with you and you immediately think of her as some sort of Black Widow.* He was, however, too much of a cynic to take anything at face

Sixteen

value. There had to be some ulterior motive for Alicia's call.

He dressed in casual attire, sports coat and slacks, and put on a tie. He figured it might be required in the evening at the Elite. The pretentiousness of the Elite made him wish, momentarily, that he had suggested the barbecue joint for dinner. The Elite was, however, the best place for a quiet talk. And it was a pretty sure bet that Officers Cherry and Burt didn't dine there.

When McCall walked out of his room and toward his car, he sensed their presence before actually seeing them. He was walking past a stairwell when the big one tried to take his head off with a baseball bat. Quick as a cat, McCall ducked the swish of the bat. The barrel of it crashed against the stair railing.

The batter had no time to recock his arms. McCall buried the toe of his right shoe in the man's groin, planted two fingers of his right hand in the attacker's eyes, and then with his left hand wrested the bat from his adversary's grip.

By then the second man was rushing toward him, swinging his bat in wild fashion. McCall, with the deftness of a fencing expert, used the bat he had appropriated to block the blows of the new threat, while out of the corner of an eye he both saw and sensed a third danger coming from the rear.

Dodging a swing from the number two man, the reporter whirled and, with the heavy end of his bat, caught the third attacker flush on the jaw. The third man, holding a bat over his head in club fashion, seemed to momentarily freeze in midair, except for the teeth and blood that spurted out one side of his mouth. His head snapped backward as if connected to his body on a rubber band. His knees buckled and he fell face forward.

The attacker still on his feet hesitated when he saw his companions go down. Then he was forced to switch from offense to defense as McCall moved toward him, his bat slicing the night air with menacing sounds. It was too much for the attacker, who broke and ran.

"Forget this," McCall said aloud. He had his nine-millimeter automatic stuck in the back waistband of his slacks. He pulled the pistol and would have attempted to cripple the attacker, if the man hadn't disappeared around the corner of the building. It wouldn't have bothered him, of course, if he had missed a wounding shot and killed the lout.

He returned to the initial site of the attack to focus his attention on the other two men, but they had also made tracks. He figured the first guy had hauled off the other. All that was left was a lot of blood.

Not a complete loss, McCall thought. *I got myself a nice bat out of the deal.* It was a Louisville Slugger, a Don Mattingly model. It had a good feel to it, for smashing baseballs, heads or kneecaps.

He put the bat in his car and drove to the Elite, wondering why the commotion at the motel hadn't produced one single witness. No one stuck a head out of a room and no one came out of the motel office. At least, no one that he saw.

Had Alicia Stevens set him up? He didn't think so. Of course, anything was possible.

She was already at the Elite when he arrived, all cuddly looking and dressed like she had just stepped off the cover of *Vogue* magazine. If there was even more to this woman than met the eye, McCall decided, there was quite a package.

"It's nice to see you again," she said.

"Nice to see you, too...only I hadn't expected to see you this soon."

She laughed, showing perfect white teeth. "You probably think I'm terribly forward."

McCall shrugged. "I think all modern women are forward."

The hostess seated them, strangely enough at the same table where McCall had breakfasted that morning with Celeste and Haloran. And it was still Jane Warrick's table. "Would you like something from the bar?" she asked.

"I'll have a glass of white wine," Alicia said.

"A glass of cold milk," McCall said. "And do you work all the time Mrs. Warrick?"

"No," she said, curtly.

When the waitress was out of earshot McCall said, "She's got the personality of a cur dog with mange."

Alicia laughed. "You asked if I dated Scott Tyler. I didn't, but she did."

"You're kidding?"

"Don't you think she's pretty?"

Sixteen

"I guess. It's hard to tell with that personality."

"She's different than Heather...no doubt about that."

"Well, she's not as pretty...but neither of them will win any awards for personality."

Alicia laughed, then somberly said, "Jane's had a much rougher life than Heather. Heather's just a snob. Even though Scott ran around on her, she's never had it as tough as Jane."

"How's that?"

"Jane's husband was murdered," she whispered.

Why she suddenly whispered, instead of just speaking softly as she had been, McCall didn't know. The place didn't have any more customers than were there during the morning rainstorm.

His interest piqued, the reporter asked, "How? Why?"

"A drug deal...supposedly."

"Supposedly?"

"Jane's husband was a policeman...and he was supposedly dealing drugs. He was killed by another policeman."

"Let me guess who killed him. Was it Sergeant Joe Cherry?"

"That's right. But how did you know?"

"I'm psychic."

Jane Warrick appeared with their drinks before Alicia could respond. The waitress said, "I'll be back in a little while for your order."

She left and McCall asked, "How long ago did this happen...this killing of Jane's husband? And by the way, what was his name?"

"Dick," she replied. "And it happened about three years ago."

"Dick and Jane...appropriate. Any children?"

"Two...a girl eight and a boy ten. Jane and the kids live with her folks. If they didn't, she couldn't make it."

"Sounds as if she's got good reason not to be Miss Sunshine. She can't be getting wealthy here...not on tips."

"Bob Mack pays his employees well."

"Where does his money come from? I can't believe that many people in this town patronize the Elite."

"It's not how many...it's who."

"Okay...tell me who."

"I don't know their names. They're wealthy people from out of town...strangers."

DEATH ANGEL

"How do you know they're wealthy?"

"You're sure full of questions," she said, smiling.

He smiled back. "It's part of my charm."

"Well, I haven't seen the financial statements of Bob Mack's guests, but a lot of them drive fancy cars. Some of them have fancy airplanes that they land at the local airport."

"How often do these wealthy people show up?"

"I'd say once a month."

"Sounds almost like a board meeting, doesn't it?"

"But he has big parties here more often than that. There's just kind of a regular group from out of town at the big parties."

"You seem to know a lot about Bob Mack's business," he said.

She laughed. "It's a small town. Everyone knows."

"But you don't think Bob makes all his money from the restaurant, do you?"

"No...and neither does anyone else."

"So where does it come from?"

"I'm not sure."

"What are the rumors?"

"I'd rather not say."

Jane Warrick came and took their order. McCall asked, "Is Bob here tonight?"

"No...he's not here."

"When you see him, tell him Matt McCall asked about him...again."

When the waitress was out of earshot, McCall said, "Tell me about Dick Warrick's death...how it went down."

"I can only tell you what the newspaper said."

"That's fine. It's probably the official line. I met the editor of the paper today. He didn't impress me as the kind of guy who would go out of his way to investigate anything."

"The story is that Dick Warrick was peddling drugs to high-school kids. Joe Cherry caught him doing it and had to kill him."

"Where was he killed?"

"At the city park."

"When...what time of day?"

"After midnight."

Sixteen

"And I'm sure Officer Jim Burt was a witness."

She laughed, softly. "I'm beginning to believe you are psychic...or someone else has already told you this story."

"I've heard the story several times. The names and locations are always different."

"What do you mean?"

He shook his head in resignation. "Never mind. Did the paper mention why there was a shoot-out in the park."

"I didn't say there was one."

"I'd bet on it," McCall said. "At least, I'll bet that's what the official report said. Tell me if this isn't the way it went down. Dick Warrick was dealing drugs, the two officers caught him at it, he fired at them, they fired at him and the guy buying the drugs got away in his car. Cherry and Burt couldn't chase him because they were in a shoot-out with Warrick."

"If you're not psychic and didn't talk to anyone about this, you sure are a good guesser. But I didn't know you were here to look into Dick Warrick's death. I thought you were just interested in checking into Scott's and Andy's."

"Do you remember who told you I was going to be doing that?"

"I think Mr. Gregg might have mentioned it...but it's pretty well known all over town."

"Yeah...well, too many people know why I'm here and some of them don't like it."

She shrugged. "You know how small towns are."

"Big cities are the same. They're just a bunch of small towns jammed together. But I guess that's beside the point. I get the idea you think Dick Warrick was murdered."

"That's probably just because I'm prejudiced in my feelings toward Joe Cherry and Jim Burt. I don't like either of them."

"Either of them hit on you?"

"Cherry has...does. And he's married...has three kids."

"What else do you know about him?"

"Nothing, really. He came here a few years ago, but I don't know where he's from."

McCall laughed. "I wouldn't call Putnam a career move for a police officer."

DEATH ANGEL

She laughed, too. "I wouldn't call it a career move for anyone."

"That triggers my next question. Why are you here?"

"I'm a native."

"Not good enough. You're young, single, smart and pretty. Are you staying here because of some guy?"

"No guy...just my mother."

"Oh?"

"My father died my senior year of college and she was devastated by it. I guess I just got caught up in trying to help her put the pieces of her life back together."

"How long are we talking about?"

"He died a little over four years ago."

"And you dropped out of school?"

"No...I finished. I was in the last month of my senior year, so mother insisted I finish."

"Where did you go?"

"Lamar."

"And what did you major in?"

She smiled. "Communications. Doesn't everyone?"

He laughed. "It sure seems that way. So you were planning a career in journalism, huh?"

"You probably wouldn't think so. Like a lot of my classmates, my goal was to be a television anchor."

"You're right...I don't consider that journalism. But, you're still young. If your mother can't cut it alone, take her with you to one of the big markets and see what you can do."

"It's not that simple."

"Why not?"

"If you don't mind, Matt...I'd prefer to talk about something else."

Their dinner arrived. Everything they had ordered was prepared to perfection. McCall had eaten in a lot of fine restaurants and was baffled that the Elite ranked with the best. It didn't make sense.

They made lighthearted conversation during the meal. McCall began questioning Alicia again in earnest after the coffee arrived. "Can you think of anyone, Alicia, who doesn't want me looking into Scott's or Andy's deaths."

Sixteen

"Well, I can see where it might prove embarrassing to the police. It might even bother Bob and Heather Mack."

"Bob's understandable...but Heather? If Andy was murdered, don't you think she would want the killer to pay?"

Alicia sighed. "I don't know how to say this without it sounding wrong, but Heather is a pretty cold fish. I know she didn't like Scott living here...maybe couldn't get him out of her mind with him being so close. As for Andy, I'm not saying she didn't love him, but in a way, he was more her mother's son than her son. And I think Andy thought of Louise Gregg more as his mother than grandmother. I don't know if I ought to be saying these things."

"Hey, it's not going to go any further," McCall said.

"Well, I think Heather didn't mind having Andy as a son as long as he wasn't a problem, but when he died he became a problem. Do you understand what I'm trying to say?"

"Yeah...I think so. I've met a lot of people like Heather, too much in love with themselves to ever really love anyone else. I've been accused of being that way myself."

Alicia laughed. "Who accuses you...that beautiful woman who was at the funeral with you?"

He smiled. "She hasn't said it, but probably thinks it."

"Is she someone special to you?"

"Yeah. I'd have to say she's very special."

Alicia immediately sought to channel the conversation in a different direction. "About Heather...I think she's satisfied to let things stand as they are."

"You think she's willing to let Scott and Andy go on the books as suicides?"

"That's right."

"Would she be the type to hire muscle to scare me off?"

"Muscle?"

"Yeah, muscle. Three guys jumped me after I left my room to come here."

Her eyes showed surprise and her mouth quavered. She seemed visibly upset. "What...what happened?"

"Not much. The three guys who attacked me were armed with baseball bats and seemed to think my head was a baseball. Maybe they were just excited about the World Series."

"Three men with bats...how did you...?"

"Three losers. A couple probably needs medical attention. I'm going to check the local hospital when we're through here."

He decided that if she knew about the three assailants, she was a good actress. He was pretty sure she didn't know, but wasn't ready to totally clear her. McCall's mindset on an investigation such as this one had two settings – suspicious and very suspicious.

Alicia had, after all, made the dinner date with him and the three men had been waiting for him. Of course, they might have been waiting because they figured there was every possibility he would be going to dinner.

"I'll be glad to check the hospital with you," she said.

"Probably not a good idea. I think there will be some other people trying to tattoo my head before this thing is over."

"That's all the more reason for me to go along. They probably won't bother you if I'm with you."

He laughed. "You want me to hide behind your skirt. Oh, well, I guess a ride to the hospital will be safe enough."

McCall left a larger-than-normal tip for Jane Warrick. He hoped it would make her a little more approachable when he questioned her, which he figured was essential to the investigation.

The night air of Putnam was cool. The storms of the day had given way to a beautiful moonlit night. "What about your car?" he asked.

"I had mother drop me. I took a chance that you'd be enough of a gentleman to drive me home."

He laughed. "You took a heckuva chance."

They walked over to the Cadillac and he turned off its alarm system, then did a couple more checks before opening the passenger-side door. If anyone had tampered with the car, he would have known it. There had been a time when he hadn't been so careful. His carelessness had cost a young reporter his life.

As he goosed the accelerator and sped away from the restaurant, she said, "This is nice car, Matt. I know most newspaper reporters don't drive cars like this."

"TV anchors do. Only they usually drive something foreign."

Sixteen

Following her directions, he soon pulled up to the emergency room entrance of the hospital and parked next to a police car. They entered the reception area and approached a desk where an overweight woman in nurse's garb was typing on a form. The double doors behind the porky nurse opened and police officers Cherry and Burt emerged.

"Well, surprised to see you two boys here," McCall said.

Cherry asked, "You have a problem, Mr. McCall...accident or something?"

The reporter chuckled. "No...not yet. Just here to see if the hospital's admitted any accident victims earlier this evening."

"Ain't been none tonight," Cherry said. "Guess you're used to that kind of stuff in the city, but it's usually pretty quiet here. You doing okay, Alicia?"

"Fine," she said, her voice dripping with sarcasm.

"When I left my room earlier tonight," McCall said, "three guys were out in the parking lot whacking each other with baseball bats. I was sure a couple of them got hurt."

The reporter noticed that the fat woman at the desk was about to say something, but Burt stepped in front of her. She got the message. Her mouth clamped tight and she resumed her hunt-and-peck typing.

"Can't imagine three of our citizens beating each other with bats," Cherry said. "That's uncivilized...like something people living in Jasper, Newton or Kirbyville would do."

McCall was familiar with the three small towns near Putnam that Cherry referred to. He laughed. "Well, I don't know where they were from, but it looked to me like they were trying to commit suicide."

Cherry's eyes turned colder. "Is that some kind of shot?"

"I don't know what you mean," McCall deadpanned.

"Well, Mr. McCall," the police sergeant said, sarcastically, "you're out with the town's prettiest woman. Seems to me you could find something better to do than check our hospital for accident victims."

"Hey, this was her idea...not mine."

"That's right," Alicia said, again sarcastically. "I just love visiting hospitals."

Burt looked confused, but Cherry's face flushed crimson. "There ain't been no accident victims brought in tonight. So if that's the reason you're here, you're wasting your time."

DEATH ANGEL

McCall grinned. "Don't guess there's any need to check with the admitting clerk, is there? You've given me all the information I need."

"The admitting clerk's on a coffee break," Cherry said.

The reporter gave his best incredulous look. "You're kidding. Who's available to fill out the insurance forms if someone in critical condition is brought in?"

"Don't worry about it, Mr. McCall. It's covered."

McCall was sure it was, and that Cherry and Burt were not leaving the hospital before he did. It was easy enough to see the policemen were covering for the good ol' boys who had tried to crack his skull.

As the reporter and Alicia were leaving, Cherry asked, "How long you going to be in town, Mr. McCall?"

"Can't say. The place kind of grows on you. Everybody's so friendly."

Cherry warned, "Be careful, Mr. McCall. You too, Alicia."

In the Cadillac, the tape deck providing the soft and smooth lyrics of Roberta Flack, Alicia said, "Why is it that I get the distinct feeling Sergeant Cherry doesn't like you?"

"Gee, I don't know. I think I'm pretty lovable."

She laughed. "I've only known you a short time, but I figure if someone thinks they can scare you out of town...they're barking up the wrong tree."

Alicia's home was a large, rambling white frame house with a large covered porch. There was a porch swing, a couple of rocking chairs, and a veritable jungle of plants that hadn't given way to winter's chill. Putnam probably didn't get its yearly freeze until December.

The front yard was nicely appointed, with all shrubs and trees perfectly trimmed. Everything seemed to be in its place. It reminded McCall of his teen years, the homes of some of the girls he had dated. Alicia's mother had left the porch light on.

Alicia unlocked the front door, reached inside and turned off the porch light. Then she pressed against him and kissed him. "Am I going to see you again?" she asked.

"I think it's important for you to know that I see someone on a pretty regular basis."

"The woman who was here with you?"

"Yes."

Sixteen

"But you're not married to her."

"No...that's something I'm not sure about right now."

She smiled and kissed him again. "I'd like to see you while you're here. You don't have to give me any guarantees."

Back in the car, he worried about Alicia for a couple of reasons. First, she was a beautiful and desirable woman. Beautiful and desirable women had always been his most-significant weakness. Second, his commitment to Celeste was getting stronger every day. He was pretty sure it was love, but worried because death seemed to visit those he cared about much too often.

- - -

At the motel he secured the car and walked to the door of his room. He started to unlock it when the hair on the nape of his neck rose. Someone had entered the room, indeed might still be there. The clear piece of scotch tape he had attached to the bottom of the door had been broken. *They might have set some kind of trap for me*, he thought.

He took the pistol from the back waistband of his pants and with his left hand started to put the key in the door. *Watch it dip*, he thought. *The door might be rigged with an explosive charge.*

While trying to determine what course of action to take, a female voice from inside his room called out, "Is that you, Mr. McCall?"

He recognized the voice, but still cautious and gun at the ready he tested the door with his foot. He shoved it open, then stood clear with his gun pointed at the opening.

"You're certainly a careful man," the voice said.

McCall could see her now. He entered the room and, with the gun still at the ready position, checked the bathroom. Then he turned to his visitor and angrily said, "What are you doing here? You're lucky I didn't blow you away."

Heather Mack was propped up on the bed, a pillow behind her back. She was wearing tight black pants and heels, and a red sweater that accentuated her breasts. "Well excuse me," she said, testily.

"Before telling me why you're here...how did you get in?"

She smiled and held up a key. "Jay Sheldon will do anything for money."

"I knew that when I first met him. So...why are you here?"

DEATH ANGEL

"I needed to talk to you," she said, somberly. "About Andy's death...about Scott's death."

"Why me?"

"I want to know why you think they were murdered."

"As for Andy, I've never heard of anyone ingesting crack and Novocain to commit suicide. And Scott? Completely out of the question. Besides, he wouldn't have committed suicide while Andy's killer was running loose, especially since he knew I was coming here to help him find the murderer. He must have found out something in the meantime, which is why someone snuffed him."

She was a little teary. "I...I can't believe anyone would kill Andy."

He wanted to say, *Could you believe someone would kill Scott?* Instead, he said, "Maybe some kid was playing a joke for all I know, but if that's the case it was a bad one."

"You're bound and determined to look into this, aren't you?"

"I owe it to Scott."

"No you don't. You don't owe Scott Tyler a thing. From what I've heard he owed you a lot, but you don't owe him anything."

"You've got to understand the way I am, Mrs. Mack. I like to give Christmas presents, but I don't like to get them. In other words, I'm not one of those people who gives a gift with the idea of getting one in return. When it comes to doing favors for friends, it's not a tradeoff. Scott was my friend...and I owe it to him to finish what he started."

She said, softly, "When we were still married, I remember him talking about you a lot. I don't think there was anyone he admired and respected more. I was even jealous of you, thought he cared more about you than me."

Her admission bothered McCall. "If you knew how much that man loved you...you and Andy were his life."

"I certainly didn't see it. He was always drinking, running around on me."

"He made mistakes," McCall said. "Like most mistakes, he didn't realize them until it was too late. I think the people he worked for did a lot of damage to Scott...not letting him strafe the people who held him prisoner."

Heather smiled, weakly. "You have a violent nature, Mr. McCall...also great strength. I think people gravitate to you because of

Sixteen

your strength...because they believe you can fix things, make them right."

"I wouldn't know about that."

"I find that hard to believe."

"Believe whatever you like, Mrs. Mack."

"You can call me Heather."

"Fine. You can call me Matt, or whatever you like. I am curious, though. How's your husband going to feel about you being in my room?"

"He's in Dallas. And you're not going to tell, are you?"

"You think Jay Sheldon's going to keep his mouth shut?"

She smiled. "He had better. Daddy's bank owns Jay Sheldon."

"Has it ever occurred to you...coming here like this...paying Sheldon for a key to my room...he can own you? I'm talking serious blackmail here."

She frowned. "He wouldn't dare."

"I think you've misread Mr. Sheldon."

She shrugged. "Too late to worry about it now. And as long as I'm here, the least you can do is offer me a drink. After a couple of drinks I'll figure out something to tell Bob...if I have to."

"I've got buttermilk and Diet Coke," he said. "Take your pick."

"Buttermilk...yuck. You don't have anything stronger?"

"Nope. It's buttermilk, Diet Coke or water."

She sighed. "Diet Coke, I guess."

"I'll get some ice," McCall said, getting the plastic bucket provided by the motel. He took it to the ice machine several doors down from his room and filled it. When he returned, Heather was in the bathroom. He filled a couple of glasses with ice and poured the Diet Coke over it. He put her glass on the bedside table, took his and sat in a chair.

She took her glass, held it toward McCall and said, "Cheers."

He acknowledged the toast, sipped the Coke and thought, *She's beautiful.* But he didn't like her being in his room, didn't like her for putting him in what could be a terribly awkward situation. It had, he thought, been a weird day.

His mental computer flashed the day through his consciousness. That morning he and Celeste had breakfast at a restaurant that seemed

DEATH ANGEL

totally out of place in a town like Putnam. A waitress whose husband had been gunned down by Sergeant Joe Cherry had served them. And he had met Alicia Stevens and the country DA – a man who wasn't on the police department's Christmas card list.

That afternoon he had buried a friend and sent Bill Haloran and Celeste back to San Antonio.

The evening had started with a strange call from Alicia Stevens. Then there was baseball practice with three goons, dinner with Alicia, a visit to the hospital where Cherry and Burt were waiting, Alicia's invitation on the porch of her mother's home and now the ex-wife of the friend he helped bury was sitting in his bed.

McCall was rarely at a loss for words, but for a long time he and Heather didn't speak. They just sat quietly sipping their drinks. She broke the silence with, "I'm empty."

He got a can of Coke off the dresser and took it to her. As he was filling both glasses on the bedside table she reached up and pulled him down on the bed beside her. He put the bottle on the table and looked at her, not sure how he wanted the situation to play out. She seemed sure. She cradled the back of his neck in one of her hands and pulled him toward her until their lips met.

Her kiss was full of passion and it was hard for him to pull away from her, but he did. "That's as far as it's going to go," he said. "It shouldn't have gone this far."

"Why?" she asked, coyly. "I'm not asking for commitment."

"It might be better if you were."

"I figured you were as much a womanizer as Scott was."

"Well, you're wrong," he said.

"Are you some sort of Boy Scout?"

"I hope so."

"Do you have some sort of commitment to the woman you were with today?"

"Yeah...you could say that."

"I guess I should be a little embarrassed at coming on to you, but I'm not."

"You're a beautiful woman, Heather. Under different circumstances..."

"You don't have to explain...or apologize. I misread you...and I'm

Sixteen

sorry."

McCall sat down in the chair and sighed. "The thing I can't understand, Heather, is you with Bob Mack. You don't belong with a hood like that."

She shrugged. "I've never made the best of choices. I was wrong about Scott and now I'm stuck with Bob. So if we were talking baseball I'd be 'O' for two."

"With Scott it was a matter of circumstances."

"Oh, Matt...don't keep making excuses for him. You talk like those people who excuse killers because of the environment they were raised in. Those same people never explain why ninety-nine percent of the people in the same environment never commit crimes."

He didn't particularly like her analogy, primarily because she was right. She was using his kind of logic. "Well, I don't guess I know the entire story...only what Scott told me."

"No one other than me knows the entire story, Matt. It's not something I was all that anxious to share with friends and family."

McCall shrugged his shoulders in resignation. "I'm sure it was tough on you, Heather, but believe me...what Scott went through was no picnic."

"Scott was where he was because of the choices he made," she said. "He could have been with me, but chose to be elsewhere. And when he was here, he wasn't with me. He spent all his time chasing other women."

McCall understood. Heather had been a woman scorned. And because she was beautiful and desirable to other men, she had never comprehended or gotten over Scott ignoring her. Her fragile emotions and self-esteem had taken a battering.

"You're right, Heather, I can't apologize for what Scott did to you. I've got no right. But I can tell you that in the past few years he realized the error of his ways. He realized how much he loved you...what he had thrown away."

There was, McCall thought, a bit of mist in her eyes. But he couldn't be sure.

"There's nothing like a good case of hindsight," she said. "I know Scott loved our son, but I don't think he ever loved me."

"I think you're wrong."

DEATH ANGEL

"Would you feel terribly guilty if you made love to me?" she asked.

"Yeah...I would."

"Would you do just one thing for me?"

"I guess it depends on what you want me to do."

"I want you to hold me for a few minutes. Nothing else...just hold me."

Though the request was a bit unnerving, it was not one he could refuse. He held her in his arms, tenderly, for at least fifteen minutes, stroking her silky hair.

Later, as she got ready to leave, she said, "You're a strange man, Matt McCall. I see why people are drawn to you. You're so strong, so caring."

He laughed softly, uneasily. "You see something in me that a lot of people don't. I don't see it myself."

She smiled. "You just don't want to admit it. Scott must have drawn on your strength a lot in the past few years. I'd like the kind of friendship you and Scott had. I can see myself drawing on your strength as he did."

"If you ever need my help, Heather...it's yours for the asking."

"Thank you. I may need it...and soon."

SEVENTEEN

McCall's plan to sleep late was thwarted when, at six-thirty, he received a call from Celeste.

"Do you miss me?" she asked.

"Of course I do."

"Did you learn anything after we left yesterday?" Celeste asked.

"Quite a bit. One thing I learned is that my phone calls are being monitored."

"Oh...then you can't really talk."

"I can't talk about some things. I could say a lot of mushy stuff, though."

She laughed. "You're not the type."

McCall figured Jay Sheldon was listening in, reporting to whoever was willing to pay him a few bucks, which was a minor inconvenience. He would take care of it in time. *Jay's probably glad I'm in town*, he thought, *because he's making a few bucks off my visit.*

"I went back to the Elite last night...gathered a little information

DEATH ANGEL

about some of the players. I've got some names...people I can talk to."

"I was thinking about coming there this weekend," she said.

"Don't. There's no telling where this trail may lead. I may want you to come down here for several days later on. I'm more comfortable knowing you're safe."

"Has something happened?"

"Not really. I'm even thinking about trying out for the local baseball team."

She laughed. "Now what does that mean?"

"Nothing...really."

"What about Bill?"

"Tell him to hang loose there. I'll get in touch when I need him."

"When will I hear from you again?"

"I'll call this evening...about six-thirty. If I can find a secure phone."

"Do you think you're being a little paranoid?"

"No...but I can't discuss it now."

"I understand. I love you, Matt."

"Love you, too, Celeste."

After the call he lay in bed and pondered his feelings for Celeste. They were deep, strong, and the closest thing to love he had ever experienced. He had, he believed, loved Cele, who had died in an explosion meant for him. But his feelings for her had not been as strong as those he felt for Celeste. *So why can't I make a commitment?* he asked himself.

The way his mind was churning, it was pointless to stay in bed. He got up, showered, shaved, brushed his teeth and got ready for the day. It was a Thursday and he figured on talking to a lot of people before the day was over.

From his room he went to the coffee bar in the motel lobby and poured himself a cup. He took the Styrofoam cup to his car and for the next couple of hours drove around Putnam checking out the lay of the land. It was part of his training to give importance to where everything was located, routes in and out of town and the area's terrain.

The day was cool, crisp and clear, and he couldn't help but think Andy and Scott should have been there to enjoy it. Finding the person, or persons, who killed them, was uppermost in his mind.

When the time was right he drove downtown and parked in front

Seventeen

of the bank. He went to the drugstore, ordered coffee and a donut from Rosie, and asked about Jack Gregg. She checked the big clock on the wall behind the counter and said he would be showing up in about five minutes.

McCall took his coffee and donut to a booth. Jack Gregg showed up right on schedule, got coffee and a donut, then joined him in the booth. After the usual conversational amenities, the banker said, "Hard to believe Andy and Scott are gone. Andy's death...it nearly killed Louise. He was like a son to her."

"I'm sure his death was hard on Heather, too."

Gregg didn't acknowledge the reference to his daughter. "There's a game here tomorrow night. Louise and I haven't missed a home game in years, but emotionally I just don't see how we can handle going."

"I don't see why you have to."

"Well people kind of expect me to be there. I know just about everybody in town...know all their kids. They expect me to support the school...be there for everything. I don't guess you understand what it's like in a small town."

"I grew up in one." He could have added that there was just one bank in his hometown, that the local banker owned everybody. The way McCall remembered it, the man had financed everything from bicycles to cars to appliances to houses. He controlled everyone and was on the school board. For that matter, he was the school board. He wondered if Gregg was the same kind of banker.

"Is that right? Maybe Scott told me you were a small town boy. You know...Scott had coffee with me here nearly every morning. I really miss him and Andy."

McCall wanted to talk about Heather. She had seemed genuine, but he was suspicious of her, curious about her motives. Gregg's statement opened the door.

"Strange...the two of you maintaining a friendship after the divorce," McCall said.

Gregg shrugged with resignation and sipped his coffee. "I was always fond of Scott. Louise was too. We didn't want the divorce...wanted Heather to give Scott a chance to straighten out. Of course, when it came right down to it we had to be supportive of our daughter. But Scott was a good man. Some things happened in his life that caused him to get off track."

Rosie came over and refilled their cups, left, then McCall said, "I get the impression you don't have the same feelings for Heather's new husband that you had for Scott."

Gregg stiffened. "Bob's different...not from around here. I haven't known him as long as I knew Scott."

"Where's Mack from?"

"He came here from Dallas."

"Was he in the restaurant business there?"

"Yes...and he still has business interests there."

"The Elite is a first-rate restaurant."

Gregg smiled. "Yes, and I know what you're thinking. You're thinking it's out of place in Putnam."

McCall laughed. "You have to admit it's a little much for the area."

"Most everyone around here thinks that. It's not successful because of local people. Bob gets a lot of clientele from different cities."

"That's kind of strange, too, since Putnam doesn't exactly rank with Palm Springs."

"Don't ask me to explain the restaurant business. I guess it's just what Bob likes to do and he has the money to do it."

For the next few minutes, McCall grilled Gregg about Bob Mack, but the banker deftly sidestepped most of the questions. He did get the impression that Gregg wasn't enamored of his son-in-law. McCall had had a gut feeling about the Elite from the moment he walked into it, and it had only grown stronger. The Elite was a front to launder dirty money. Everything he knew and didn't know about Bob Mack increased that suspicion.

McCall left the drugstore and drove to a convenience store that had a pay phone in a booth outside it. He had seen it earlier that morning when driving around. He dialed a number in Dallas and the voice that answered belonged to Paul Bates, a television news reporter who had helped him chase some leads in the past.

McCall didn't care much for TV types, but Bates was different than most. He had been a TV news reporter for ten years or so, and had worked in several Texas markets and for a brief time in Washington, DC.

Seventeen

"Hey, pretty boy, I need some help."

"McCall...is that you, you silly toad?"

"Yeah, but I'm surprised you remember, Bates. I haven't talked to you in a coon's age."

"No one else calls me pretty boy."

"Must not be anybody there who knows you."

Bates laughed. "What do you want, McCall? I know this isn't a social call."

"Bates...do I have to want something every time I call?"

"You've never called when you didn't."

"Now you're trying to make me feel guilty."

"Guilt looks good on you."

One of the things McCall liked about Bates was that he didn't take himself too seriously. He was also as opinionated as McCall, and proud of it. His first wife had left him and his second wife had been killed. He had an eight-year-old daughter by his first wife.

"Okay, pretty boy, I do need some info on a guy named Bob Mack."

"Is that all you have...just a name? Why don't you try to make things easy on me, McCall."

"You'd complain if I made things too easy."

"Try me."

"He's supposed to be from Dallas...and he's supposed to still have business interests there. He's living in Putnam now...owns a restaurant here. Now find out what I need to know. Use some of those alleged investigative skills your station uses in the promos about you."

Bates grunted. "You're in Putnam? I wish I lived there. I'm tired of all this traffic and all the crooks in city government."

"Putnam doesn't have much traffic, but it has its share of scumbags. And what I'm asking you to do...it'll give you a break from covering the city council."

"Yeah, right. How soon do you need this information?"

"Yesterday."

"It figures. How do I get back to you?"

"You don't. I'll get back to you."

"Oh, is big brother listening?"

"More than one. I'll call you in the a.m. You're still working

DEATH ANGEL

nights, aren't you?"

"It's the only time any decent news happens."

"Bates, you wouldn't know decent news if it jumped up and bit you on the rear end."

The TV reporter uttered a few well-chosen hyphenated words, questioned McCall's lineage, and then the two men said their goodbyes. They had a good relationship, and after hanging up the phone McCall promised himself that he had get up to Dallas and see Bates more often.

He recalled the last time he had been with Bates. The TV journalist had told McCall more than he wanted to know about his ex. Her name was Diane. She was a fashion model who now lived in Houston and was married to a guy who had gotten her pregnant while she was still married to Bates. So Bates had a real hatred for Diane, but a tremendous love for his daughter. Sometimes Diane and her husband made it tough for Bates to see his daughter.

Bates was thirty-three, six-feet tall and weighed in at two hundred fifteen pounds. He was a jogger, but not a fanatic. McCall figured Bates did it for the same reason he did, to let off steam as well as keep his body in tune.

Bates liked fencing. That and jogging were his only sports interests. During one of their get-togethers he had told McCall fencing was similar to chess in civility and strategy, as well as being a good motor reflex activity. McCall had told him fencing was a sport for sissies.

The real tragedy in Bates' life had not been his divorce, but the highway murder of Theresa, his second wife. For a year and a half theirs had been a storybook marriage, but then one night a drunken state employee had snuffed out her life in a fiery crash on the double-decker interstate in Austin.

Bates had continued working in Austin long enough to see the drunk imprisoned, then had given in to his nightmares and moved to Dallas. McCall knew there wasn't enough action in the fast lane to keep Bates' mind off Theresa, but any assignment he dropped in his lap would help, especially one that got him out of the routine of TV news.

McCall next telephoned Alicia Stevens and asked if she would meet him for lunch. He didn't have to ask twice.

He then went to Putnam High School, figuring any lead on

Seventeen

Andy's death that he could find there would also bring him that much closer to Scott's killer. He started in the principal's office with the secretary, then talked to the principal. From what they said, Andy was nothing short of a saint. And no, there was no drug problem at Putnam High.

McCall had figured on being stonewalled by the school's administration. The principal, he understood, didn't want some big city reporter writing about Putnam kids using drugs. Putnam, after all, was a place where quality of life was stressed. It wasn't like a big city with mean streets or alleys where kids could be found shooting up and getting high twenty-four hours a day.

The principal didn't like it when he asked if the dosage of crack and Novocain Andy had ingested had fallen from the sky, or why late police officer Dick Warrick had been shot for allegedly dealing drugs. School administrators hated the truth, McCall knew, and trying to make them admit to the truth was just about impossible.

He cornered the head football coach at his office in the gym. The guy had a free period from the mentally exhausting task of being in charge of physical education and study hall. His name was Chuck Meyer. He was in his late forties and had heavy jowls and a five o'clock shadow that no amount of shaving could erase. He had a burr haircut and McCall suspected he used Grecian Formula 44. There was not a gray hair on his head.

"Bad...bad about Andy," Meyer said. "His dad, too."

"You think he committed suicide...that they committed suicide?"

"That's what the police say."

"Well, coach, the police make a mistake now and then. I imagine the clowns you have on the force here make a lot of them."

Meyer certainly wasn't going to support McCall's indictment of local law enforcement. He just sat there in his worn swivel chair, behind the gray metal desk, and waited for the reporter to continue.

"Was Andy despondent...anything like that?"

The coach rolled his tongue behind his lower lip and pondered the question, causing McCall to suspicion that the man often took a pinch of snuff between his cheek and gums. "Can't see why he would be. He was a starter...was probably going to have a heckuva season."

"I thought maybe you'd heard something...something that had

nothing to do with football."

"During the season I don't pay attention to anything but football...way I want my players thinking, too."

"That's well and good," McCall said, "but I imagine high-school kids think about other things, too."

"Like what?" Meyer asked. "The little jerks have it made. They're living off their folks, fooling around in school...so they don't have a thing to worry about except football. Of course, a lot of them have their mind on messing with some little girl."

The coach, McCall decided, had the sensitivity of a maggot. He had met a lot of guys like him, though; people whose entire lives evolved around a strangely shaped ball. There was no reason asking him about someone's mental state because he had a pep rally mentality.

"Did you know Scott very well?"

"Sure. Good man...not like some of the parents I have to deal with. He never pushed me to play Andy. I even saw Scott play when he was in college. Saw you, too. You were darn good."

McCall smiled. "That was too long ago for me to remember."

"Did you know Scott when he was at the University of Texas?"

"No...not really."

Meyer seemed disappointed with his answer. "Don't guess that's unusual...Texas and Baylor being rivals and all. I didn't get to go to one of the big schools...went to Sam Houston State. But hey, I hear you were the one that broke Scott out of that prison camp somewhere down in..."

"I didn't do it alone. I had a lot of help."

The coach didn't seem to hear. "I like all that war stuff. So do the kids. Sometimes before practice or games I show them a war movie...makes them mean. Hey, how about you talking to the boys today...tell them about killing gooks and stuff."

Disgusted, McCall said, "I'm afraid I'll have to pass. I have a lot of people to see today. I'm trying to find out who murdered Andy and Scott."

"Murdered?" The coach seemingly hadn't understood that McCall's questioning the suicide verdicts meant he was talking about murder.

"Yeah...murdered. Somebody snuffed Andy and Scott. And I'm

Seventeen

here to find out whom. I thought you might help."

Meyer crawfished. "Well now, I don't think it's my place to get involved in something like that."

"Guess not. Guess it's more important to let the guy who killed them run free. That way...maybe he can kill another kid."

"Uhhh...well, McCall, maybe you're being faked out. Maybe Andy did commit suicide and Scott wanted to go out the same way."

McCall rose from the hard wooden chair and his eyes took in all the inane slogans tacked to the office wall. "If he wanted to go out the same way, why didn't he ingest crack and Novocain? Why did he hang himself? I came here because I thought you might give a rip about Andy...that you wouldn't want his killer running around loose. But I see you don't want to be bothered."

Meyer's face flushed red and he rose to his feet. He was a good three inches taller than McCall, fifty pounds heavier, and he was angry. But McCall didn't care. As far as he was concerned, the man in front of him was a two hundred and thirty-pound sack of manure.

"Think what you want, McCall...but I care about my boys."

The reporter badgered the coach a bit more. "All you care about is what they can do for you. You use them, abuse them, then you're through with them."

"I think you'd better get out of my office."

"I'm on my way, coach, but not because you frighten me. It stinks in here. I was hoping you'd help me, but I guess you get your jollies trying to scare the dickens out of teenagers."

The fresh fall air did nothing to improve McCall's mood. He hated the facade of phony concern about Andy's and Scott's deaths that he was encountering. People seemed to have their heads buried in the sand. He hoped Andy's girlfriend, Melanie Richards, would be more helpful.

He drove back to the phone he had used earlier to call Bates and called Arnold. He went through a couple of voices before he was greeted with, "What are you up to, McCall?"

"Up to my eyeballs in a cover-up."

"You're investigating Scott Tyler's death?"

"Yeah...and Andy Tyler's. I could use some help."

Arnold was one of the first people McCall contacted when he

DEATH ANGEL

heard that Scott Tyler was dead. The Ol' Man's aide said, "You know we don't get involved in domestic situations. But what, short of sending a division of Marines, can I do for you?"

"I want some people checked out."

"You got it."

"They're all Putnam residents. Bob and Heather Mack, Jack Gregg, Joe Cherry, Jim Burt, Jay Sheldon, Barry Travis, Dade Decker, Jane and Dick Warrick, Alicia Stevens and Joe Caulder." He then filled Arnold in on what little he knew of each of the people mentioned.

"Sure you don't want us to check out everybody in town?"

He laughed. "Be great if you have the time."

"Do I call you...or do you call me?"

"I'll call you."

"I understand."

McCall drove back to the bank and picked up Alicia for lunch. They chose the barbecue place. As soon as he entered, his eyes picked up the blue uniforms of Joe Cherry and Jim Burt.

As they walked by the table the policemen were occupying, McCall said, "Don't guess this place has ever been robbed. You guys must give it around-the-clock protection."

Neither Cherry nor Burt responded. But McCall read in their eyes that he wouldn't be invited to either of their homes for Christmas dinner.

Alicia had been stifling a laugh. Once they were seated, she released it, softly. "Nice bit of agitation, Matt."

He grinned. "They don't know what agitation is...yet."

"I'm sure that's true. Did you learn anything today?"

"Yeah...a lot. I learned some of the people over at your school are like a lot of other people in education...wimps who can't see past their noses."

She laughed again. "My...aren't we in a good mood?"

He smiled. "I'm not in a bad mood. I ran into about what I expected. I was just hoping for more."

They ordered, made small talk, then the waitress brought their food. They washed it down with glasses of iced tea.

"Who's the bank's largest depositor?" McCall asked in a whisper.

Alicia glanced furtively around to make sure no one could hear,

Seventeen

then whispered back, "You know I'm not supposed to give out that kind of information. And what makes you think I know anyway?"

"I imagine you know plenty," McCall said.

"What if I told you Jack Gregg is the biggest depositor?"

"I'd believe it and ask you who was number two."

"I think you already know."

"Bob Mack."

"Like I said...you already know."

"I'll bet Bob Mack has more than one safe deposit box, too."

"Like I said...you already know."

"Does Heather have access to his safe deposit boxes?"

"No...he's the only one with access."

"Do you think he's dirty?" McCall asked.

"If you mean do I think he got all his money legitimately, the answer is no."

"Any way you could get me his bank records?"

"My gosh, Matt," she said, uneasily, "you're trying to make me a criminal."

He shrugged and laughed. "I'd call it a justifiable criminal act."

"I don't care what you'd call it...I would be the guilty party."

"I just thought I'd ask."

"I'll have to think about it."

"There you go. I didn't think I'd get that far."

She shook her head in mock resignation. "You're something else, you know that? Now I'll ask a question. What are your plans for tomorrow night?"

"Who knows? That's a long way into my future."

"Well, would you like to take me to the game?"

"Sure...if I'm not dead by then."

"I wish you wouldn't talk like that...even if you're kidding."

"Around here...I'm not sure I am."

They agreed that he would pick her up about seven-fifteen. She said she already had the tickets.

"Pretty sure of yourself, aren't you?"

She smiled. "Not really. They're free tickets I got from the bank. If I was sure of myself, I'd ask you to come over to the house for dinner tonight."

DEATH ANGEL

"I'll make it easy for you. I'll accept before you invite me."

"Great...around six-thirty."

McCall drove Alicia back to the bank, then went to the police station. It was one of the more modern buildings in Putnam and was adjacent to the fire station. Putnam's fire department was a volunteer one, giving every blue collar in town a chance to put a flashing light and siren on his pickup.

To get to the chief's office McCall had to get by a female police officer who looked like nine miles of bad road. In all his dealings with police in major cities, he had only seen a couple of female officers who came close to looking as good as actresses who played cops on TV.

Chief Dade Decker was a heavyset man who was about six-feet tall. He wore thick glasses, had a mustache that needed trimming, puffy lips and strange blue eyes that were magnified by his glasses. His cheeks had a permanent redness to them and his thinning hair was streaked gray and brown. There was a fixed frown on the man's face, though McCall figured his presence wouldn't do much to alleviate it.

"I don't really understand what you're doing here, Mr. McCall. But from what I hear, you don't care for anything we've done."

"Well, chief, I don't know what you've done."

"We've thoroughly investigated the deaths of Andy Tyler and his father."

"And you don't have any questions about their deaths?"

"None at all. Despite what you probably think, we know how to conduct an investigation."

McCall was sitting across the desk from Decker, who was slumped in an oversized chair, an oversized cigar protruding from his mouth. The fire on the end of the cigar had burned out, leaving only gray ashes. The big and expensive desk was too clean for that of a working police officer. Its surface was empty of the normal stacks of papers and file folders.

"Mind if I see your files on the investigations?"

"Sorry...that's not possible."

"You know I can get access to your files. It'll just take a little longer. There is a Freedom of Information Act, you know."

Decker said, smugly, "I ain't worried about your time. You ain't going to find us all that cooperative, Mr. McCall. You see, I don't care

Seventeen

what you write about us in that paper of yours."

The reporter had already checked the wood and glass barrister bookcases and wooden file cabinets in the office, the plush carpeting and Oriental rug on the floor, and the expensive lamps on mahogany side tables next to the expensive leather couch. He was sitting in one of two expensive leather chairs in front of the chief's desk.

Decker had the aura of a powerful man, but small town or international power didn't impress McCall. The reporter was the kind of man who wouldn't hesitate to tell the President of the United States off. And more than one person in the covert community had described him as the most dangerous man in the world.

"I came here friendly like, Decker. With a little cooperation from you, I'd leave here the same way."

"If you want to be real friendly, McCall...get out of town. Ain't nobody wants you here."

"I'm not here to win a popularity contest," the reporter said. "But I might have a pretty good shot against you."

Decker chewed his cigar and tried to look mean. "Let me make it real clear to you, Mr. McCall. If you're bound and determined to come in here and stir things up, my boys and me are going to be watching you real close."

"That's certainly reassuring. And since you won't give me the files on Andy and Scott Tyler, I don't guess you'd be willing to give me the file on Dick Warrick either, would you?"

"Warrick?"

"That's right...Warrick. I know how to turn over a few rocks to check for slithery things...and I don't think you're going to like what I find when I check into Dick Warrick's death."

"I heard you thought you were about half smart."

"That's one of the nicer things that has been said about me. Anyway, I'll go through due process and get the files...even though I figure they'll be altered."

"Are you saying we're crooked?"

McCall feigned surprise. "The police here...crooked?"

"Go through your due process, McCall. You ain't getting nothing from me."

"Thanks. Everybody else in this town has been giving me noth-

DEATH ANGEL

ing but pure fiction."

McCall went to the county courthouse to see if Barry Travis was in his office. He was. And this time Thelma Turner was more cordial, more like a rattlesnake in a cage with a rat sizing up its prey.

"Surprised to see you again so soon," the DA said. "You making any headway?"

"Depends on what you call headway. How about taking a drive with me?"

"Why not? I'm bored to death with this paperwork."

When the DA saw McCall's car he whistled and said, "Wow, maybe I should've been a reporter."

McCall laughed. "Being a lawyer's low enough. Why sink any further?"

He cranked the car, then asked Travis to direct him to Joe Cherry's home. The DA gave him the directions, then asked, "Why do you want to go there?"

"I like to know all I can about my enemies. And there's no doubt Cherry, Burt and Decker are my enemies. I want to see where all of them live."

Travis laughed. "If I was going to pick enemies, I wouldn't pick the ones who carried guns. Now you're going to be surprised at the houses these guys live in, but remember that real estate isn't as expensive here as in San Antonio."

Cherry's house was on a tree-studded ridge in what would have passed for the beginning of a small suburban development in San Antonio. There were six houses in the little community, each of which McCall was sure was in the six-figure range. Land on which to build was certainly cheaper in Putnam than in a major city, but he figured actual building costs weren't all that much more economical. One would not expect a small town police officer to be able to afford such a house.

The house was a big custom-made brick with an ample yard that was well kept. There was a new Cadillac in the driveway that ran into a three-car garage. The garage door was open, revealing an expensive boat and a new Ford pickup.

"What's Cherry's annual salary from the police department?" McCall asked.

Seventeen

Travis grinned and told him.

"His house had to cost ten times that. Does his wife work?"

"Nope."

"Well, where does Cherry get his money?"

Travis shrugged. "Don't ask me. And I don't have the resources to find out. Like I told you...I'm sort of the black sheep where law enforcement is concerned. But I've been asking myself the same question you're asking about Cherry, Decker and Burt."

"You mean Decker and Burt have homes like this, too?"

"You be the judge."

The DA directed him to where Decker and Burt lived. They did, indeed, have houses that were as nice as Cherry's. Decker's was even larger.

"What about the rest of the police department?" McCall asked.

"There's only four other officers...and one of them is a woman."

"Yeah...I met her," McCall said. "She looked like nine miles of bad road."

"She's my wife."

McCall's breath caught in his throat. "She's what?"

The DA laughed. "Just kidding."

McCall exhaled slowly and grinned. "Thank goodness."

"The other officers live in very modest homes," Travis said. "Their houses are about what you'd expect for someone living on a small town policeman's salary."

"What kind of house did Dick Warrick live in?"

"Modest...very modest. It was a rent house, a little white frame job. Dick was a local boy...grew up here."

"What about Cherry, Decker and Burt?"

"They're imports. The other officers are locals."

"So when did the three musketeers come to town?"

"A few years back...when Bob Mack took control of the city council. Bob owns the mayor, Joe Caulder. Joe fired the local guy who was police chief and brought in Decker."

"What kind of mansion does Caulder live in?"

"Funny you should say that. He used to live in a modest house, but he built one on par with Decker's the same year the chief did. You want to see it."

DEATH ANGEL

"No...I'll take your word for it," McCall said. "But I would like to see your house."

Travis gave him an incredulous look, then chuckled a bit nervously. "You don't trust anyone, do you?"

The reporter laughed. "Distrust and cynicism has done a lot to keep me alive over the years. But you may be misreading the reason I want to see your house."

"I doubt it...and you're going to be surprised."

Travis gave McCall directions and the reporter herded the Cadillac to where he lived. It was an older structure, nice enough, but definitely not in the same class as the houses owned by the policemen. It looked a lot like Alicia's mother's house.

"I know what you're thinking...that Cherry, Decker and Burt are involved in drug dealing. Now I ask you, does this look like the house of a dope dealer?"

McCall shrugged. "If I were you, Barry...I wouldn't try to guess what I'm thinking. But I'm not accusing you of anything. Don't get so sensitive on me. I just like to know where things are. I might need to get in touch with you when you're not in your office. And as for where drug dealers live, I've seen wealthy ones in crummy surroundings. They have different tastes...different uses for their blood money."

"You're a piece of work, McCall...you know that?"

"So I've been told. What I haven't told you is that I had some visitors last night."

"Visitors?"

"Yeah. Three guys tried to take batting practice on my head."

"What happened?"

"I bloodied a couple of them pretty bad...so bad they needed medical attention. I think they went to the local hospital, but Cherry and Burt beat me there. They intercepted me and told me no accident victims had been admitted. They wouldn't let me talk to any of the nurses."

"Wouldn't let you?"

"Well, I didn't push it. I didn't think the time was right to assault two police officers."

Travis laughed. "I don't believe there is a right time for that."

"I can't guarantee it won't happen...if those clowns get in my

Seventeen

way."

"My office can't protect you if something like that happens."

"I don't need protection. They do."

McCall and the DA spent some more time driving around and talking. Travis showed him where Jane Warrick's parents lived, where she now had to live with her kids. It was an ordinary white frame house, certainly nothing special. And it looked too small for two families.

"You want to see *the* house?" Travis asked.

"I've been to Jack Gregg's place."

Travis laughed. "I'm talking about Bob Mack's place."

"I was going to have you show me where he lived, but I didn't know it was *the* house."

"It is in Putnam."

Following the DA's directions, McCall drove out the highway leading to Beaumont until Travis told him to pull over on a shoulder. The mansion set on the crest of a hill, surrounded by huge oaks that looked as though they had been planted to perfectly accentuate its beauty. They hadn't been, of course, because they were probably a century old. The house was relatively new.

On each side of the winding road leading to the house was a lake of a minimum five acres. An artesian spring flowed in the middle of each.

"If you're a fisherman, McCall, those lakes are the best places to fish in this part of the state. Bob Mack stocks 'em with Florida bass. He even put some ten pounders in there a few years ago. No telling what they weigh now."

"I like to wet a line now and then. And you're right, Barry...about this being *the* house."

The place was every bit as stately as an English manor, the kind of structure where one would expect a nobleman to live. Even the fence around the property seemed appropriate, a mixture of stone and concrete with wiring all along the top that was obviously charged with electricity. The big gate that kept the curious from driving up the winding road was electronically controlled.

"Mack has household help that he brought here with him," Travis said. "Four to six armed guards live on the premises."

DEATH ANGEL

"How do you know that?"

"I listen. I've never been invited to the house, but I know a few local people who've been to parties there."

"How big is it?"

"Around thirty thousand square feet. Most of the contractors who built it were brought in from out of town, but I know one of the local guys who worked on it. That's what he says."

McCall laughed. "The restaurant business must be better than I thought."

"Oh, yeah," Travis said, sarcastically. "The restaurant business must be dynamite."

McCall put the idling car in gear, wheeled it around and headed back to town. He had an appointment with a young lady.

He parked in a space near the courthouse, fed the meter and bid farewell to Travis. He then headed across the street to the drugstore where he had arranged to meet Melanie Richards.

She was already in a booth when he got there, a soft brown-eyed girl with hair to match. The hair was long, the way McCall liked it, and she didn't have on too much makeup. He liked that, too. She was dressed in a coral colored sweater and skirt, wearing nice shoes with short heels.

They exchanged greetings and he asked what she wanted to drink. She chose a plain Coke and he opted for a frosted one. Rosie was not there so he gave the order to a kid he guessed to be around sixteen. The kid was having a serious battle with acne, and losing.

After they had their drinks the conversation got serious. "I can't tell you how sorry I am, Melanie...about Andy."

Tears crept into her eyes, but she controlled them. She nodded in appreciation for his expression of sympathy.

"Do you know why I'm here, Melanie?"

"I've heard some things."

"What things?"

"That you think Andy and his daddy were murdered."

"What do you think?"

"I...I don't know. My parents...they didn't want me to talk to you. I think they're scared. I didn't tell them I was going to see you."

He shrugged. "There's nothing to be afraid of. I'm not the bogey

Seventeen

man."

"I don't think it's you they're afraid of."

"Who then?"

"I don't know."

"Before Andy's death...was he despondent, anything like that?"

"No...not at all. I don't remember him ever being happier. We were planning to go out after the game, but we weren't going to stay out too late. He was going fishing with his dad the next morning."

"Do you think he felt any pressure from his dad?"

"Andy was committed to being the best football player he could be, but his dad never put any pressure on him. He told me that more than once. He might have felt some pressure...trying to live up to what his dad had done."

"But not enough to commit suicide?"

"Oh, no. And Andy hated drugs. He hated the people who sold them...even those who used them. I couldn't believe it when they said he died from drugs."

"Can you think of anyone who would want to kill him?"

The tears welled up in her eyes again. "No...no, I can't. Everybody liked Andy."

"Someone didn't."

McCall understood Melanie's confusion. She hadn't been able to accept Andy's death as a suicide, but had been forced to swallow the party line. Whoever the killer was, he had taken an emotional chunk out of her life, one she would never be able to replace or forget. It wasn't a matter of possibly loving Andy. It was a matter of trusting one's surroundings.

"How did Andy feel about his stepfather?"

It was obvious the question troubled her and she didn't want to respond. "Well, he didn't feel the same way about Mr. Mack that he felt about his real father, if that's what you mean."

"You know I mean more than that, Melanie."

She looked down at the table and said, timidly, "I...I don't think he liked Mr. Mack all that much. I don't think he felt comfortable around him."

"Did he tell you why?"

"I don't think he liked the house and some of Mr. Mack's friends.

DEATH ANGEL

And Andy wasn't into servants and guards...all that kind of stuff."

"You've been to the house?"

"Yes...a few times."

"Were you uncomfortable?"

"Mr. McCall, my father owns a hardware store. He provides a good life for my mother, brother and me. We have a nice house, but compared to Mr. Mack's it's a shack. Yes, the Mack house makes me feel uncomfortable. It's like everything there is expensive just for the sake of being expensive...like there's no end to the money. And Andy...he didn't care about money. Mr. Mack gave him a new Mercedes convertible, but Andy wouldn't drive it. He said it made him feel stupid...that no kid should have something like that. He drove the old Mustang that his dad gave him. He wanted to live with his dad, but Mr. Tyler said it wouldn't be fair to his mother to even ask about it."

"How did Andy feel about his mother?" McCall asked.

She shrugged. "He cared about her, but he didn't feel the same way about her that he felt about his dad. She can be cold and moody."

"How do you feel about Mrs. Mack?"

"I don't really know her."

"You said she was cold and moody."

"That's what Andy said."

"Well, you've talked to her, haven't you?"

"Yes...and she's always been very cordial to me. I just always felt uncomfortable around her."

"Why's that?"

"It's like when she talks to you it's just an obligation...like she does it because it's expected. Do you know what I mean?"

"I think so. Did Andy ever mention how his stepfather got his wealth?"

She hesitated before replying. "He didn't know...exactly. But I think he suspected Mr. Mack was dishonest. He didn't understand some of the people Mr. Mack associated with...or why they needed someone to guard the house."

"What kind of people did he say Mr. Mack associated with?"

"He said they were too slick...like some of the gangsters you see on TV or at the movies."

"How many guards are there...did Andy say?"

Seventeen

"Six. Mr. Mack even had one following Andy for a while...to supposedly protect him. Andy threw a fit about it and I think Mr. Mack quit having him followed. I heard a guard follows Mrs. Mack everywhere she goes."

Great, McCall thought. He said, "The principal and coach at your high school don't think there's much of a drug problem in Putnam. What do you think?"

She gave him a look of disbelief. "The stuff's everywhere...and they know it."

"So, if Andy wanted some crack it wouldn't be hard to find."

"No...it wouldn't. But like I told you, Andy hated drugs...and the people who sold them and used them."

"Maybe he just told you that."

Her eyes showed hurt. "I thought you wanted to..."

"I don't believe he used drugs either, Melanie. But I have to consider every possibility. Do you know kids in your school who use drugs?"

"Yes...I think so."

"Would you mind giving me their names?"

"I can't do that, Mr. McCall. For one thing, I'm not sure. I don't run in that crowd."

"Just give me the names of those you suspect...and I'll keep your name out of it, Melanie. One of that crowd is probably responsible for Andy's death...or they can point me in the direction of the person who is. I need to find out where high-school students here get their drugs."

He had put her in a tight spot and knew it. But he also knew the only way to find Andy's and Scott's killer was to penetrate the town's veneer of hypocrisy. She could give him the names to do just that.

"I can give you a few names," she said, reluctantly. "But please don't use my name, Mr. McCall."

He handed her a small notebook and pen. "I promise. Just jot the names down for me."

She did so, quickly, and handed the pen and notebook back to him. He didn't bother to look, just put the notebook in his inside jacket pocket. "I promise you something," he said. "I'll get Andy's killer."

"I know you will," she said.

EIGHTEEN

When Bates had taken McCall's telephone call early Thursday morning, the TV reporter was hung over from a night of partying with some Houston media people who were in Dallas covering a story. He was a man who liked fast cars and plenty of money in his pocket to live the good life. His problem was that working for the TV station he didn't make enough to support his preferred lifestyle. So he depended on freelance assignments from other news agencies and networks to keep his cash flow in line with the way he lived. It's why he also welcomed any assignment from McCall. He was willing to do anything for McCall gratis, but knew there would be a good check in the mail. The San Antonio reporter tended to be generous.

At first Bates had argued with McCall about paying him for what he considered a courtesy for another reporter. But McCall had assured him the money was not coming out of his pocket.

He had, of course, heard all the rumors about the San Antonio

Eighteen

reporter's alleged connection with the CIA, but McCall had never said anything about it. He had reason to believe some of the rumors were true, but figured that if they were it was no skin off his nose. He just knew that when it came to McCall's perceived idea of justice, the reporter could be one mean man.

Bates had a problem being opinionated, but figured he was a piker compared to McCall. He was also a little more reluctant to circumvent the law to achieve justice. McCall tended to be judge, jury and sometimes, he guessed, executioner. But the thing he was most sure of was that if McCall asked for information, it was not for some trumped-up story. He was not like as assignments editor trying to justify his position with busy work stories. If McCall was working on something, chances were it was big. It would be the kind of thing the networks would buy.

It stuck in Bates' craw that the assignment editor at his station was always asking, *How many stories have you got today?* It was that age-old problem of quantity versus quality, which he thought was the downfall of so many newsrooms. But it was the norm more than the exception. Maybe it was because stockholders wanted more dividends per share, and news departments were favorite whipping boys when it came to management cutting costs.

McCall was a guy, Bates knew, who worked on exclusives, but he wasn't greedy. He had let him break the story in the electronic media. Thinking about McCall, Bates couldn't help but laugh to himself. His reporter friend was the kind of guy who figured that if someone didn't get his news from the paper he didn't deserve to know.

In checking around Bates discovered that Bob Mack did, indeed, own three restaurants in the greater Dallas area. His flagship establishment, The Ripcord, was in Addison, which prompted Bates to call the police chief there. He knew the head cop well, knew he was a straight shooter.

They bantered back and forth for a couple of minutes, but when Bates mentioned the restaurant, the line went dead for a few seconds. "What do you know about the place, Paul?" the chief asked.

"I don't know anything about it...except it's a private membership deal or something like that."

"I know you're not calling me as a reference so you can join."

DEATH ANGEL

"Nah...just want to know something about the restaurant's owner, Bob Mack."

"We know Bob Mack pretty well," the chief said. "But anything I say about him has to be off the record."

"You know I'm a citadel of secrecy."

The chief laughed. "Yeah, right."

Bates joined him in laughing, then said, "Are you going to tell me what you know, or not?"

"Bob Mack's dirty, no doubt about it. We haven't been able to pin anything on him yet, but the slimeball is into drugs, prostitution...you name it. The Ripcord's just another of his so-called legitimate businesses where he launders dirty money."

The chief told Bates the restaurant and bar was a hangout for a few pro football and basketball players who liked nose candy. The place, he said, was under constant surveillance by the Addison Police Department, and his initial concern about the reporter's inquiry was because he had a couple of cops working undercover in an attempt to get something on Bob Mack.

"The scumbag is even into gun-running," the cop said.

"You might be getting some help on this one," Bates said. "I'll be glad to help, of course, but a friend of mine named Matt McCall has taken a serious interest in Mack."

"You talking about the reporter from San Antonio?"

"You know him?"

"Sure, every cop in the country knows of him. He sure ain't the usual media type. If he ever runs over a politician with his car, we know not to look for any skid marks. When it comes to a politician, the man can't find his brake."

Bates laughed and the chief continued, "Paul, you're a lot like McCall...maybe not as much a vigilante, but a lot like him."

"I'll take that as a compliment."

"It's meant to be."

"By the way...when I heard from McCall he was down in a little town called Putnam."

"Yeah...that slimeball Mack lives there now, has a big mansion. And he's got the local cops in his pocket. When you talk to McCall, warn him."

Eighteen

"I will. Anyone else keeping tabs on Mack?"

"Just about everybody. The DEA, ATF and FBI. Everybody wants a piece of him, but he's pretty well connected. He's got a lot of political clout."

"Funny, I hadn't heard anything about him before."

The chief grunted. "Everybody's trying to keep the lid on until they have something. Mack's not his real name, either...don't know what it is. He seemed to come out of nowhere, but we think he's from one of the families back East. While he was living here, he kept a low profile...still does. He's smart and he's got a big organization behind him. We haven't been able to nail him with a parking ticket."

"Think the DEA, FBI or ATF have anything on him?"

"They don't have anything," the chief said. "What we've got here is a drug lord...more than that. He's a crime lord, and he's virtually untouchable. Someone close to him gets ready to talk...they disappear. Those close to him are either loyal or dead."

"Is he in Dallas much?"

"He comes and goes. We think he's here now. His plane's here...over at Addison Airport."

"I'm sure you put a tail on him when he arrived."

"Sure we did. A limo picked him up and took him to the restaurant, but we don't know if he's still there. Maybe he switched cars and went somewhere else. We don't have the manpower to watch him twenty-four hours a day."

"If all of you were working together, the DEA, FBI and..."

The chief laughed. "I didn't know you were such an idealist. Personally, I don't care who busts the slimeball, but you know the competition between those federal boys."

"Yeah, I'm afraid I do."

"Mack's got a big townhouse here, but we can only guess when he's in it and what's going on there. He lets us tail him sometimes, but when he wants to get rid of us cars cut us off. We've got some pros when it comes to tailing a suspect, but his people spot them. They always know where we are, which is why I worry about my undercover guys. The man knows we want him and what we have to do to get him."

"So Mack...or whatever his name is...is not your average hood?"

DEATH ANGEL

The chief laughed. "Average? While the feds and my boys are busting their rears to nail the slimeball, his cash register is ringing up at least twenty million dollars a day."

"Whew!" Bates exclaimed. "Looks like a guy dealing in that kind of illegal cash would make a lot of mistakes."

"We're the ones who've made the mistakes...supporting a legal system that protects scum like Mack. Plus, we got our law-enforcement bureaucracy...agencies stumbling over each other and letting jealousy get in the way of justice."

"I'm sure McCall would agree with you. And you already know I do."

After talking to the chief, Bates was excited, the juices flowing. His mind shouted, *Thank you, McCall, for putting me on one like this.* When he and McCall wrapped it up, it would be the kind of piece that would stand on its own, without all the fanfare a producer insisted on giving a story.

Producers. He didn't care much for them. There were a few at the networks who knew what they were doing, but most where he worked were former P.M. Magazine sweater wearers who tried to make the evening news look like an episode of *Geraldo.* They insisted on slick musical openings and scene setting graphics that insulted the intelligence of most educated people. They catered to yuppies because the sales department convinced clients these were the people who would buy their products.

A female producer had once told him to turn an interview with a beauty queen into a great piece by making it sing. He wasn't sure what that meant. He also hadn't been able to determine which woman had the most air between her ears, the bimbo with the crown on her head or the one with a stopwatch in her hand and a sweater draped around her neck.

No matter how intense he was when working on a story, Bates always took time to mentally lament the idiocy of some TV sales people, producers and assignments editors. He wanted a pure newscast with no frills, one using stories that didn't require a pretty face to keep viewer interest.

What McCall had dropped in his lap had the makings of such a story. Now there were only allegations by a cop about a crime lord that

Eighteen

was virtually untouchable. But with some work and luck, maybe he could get inside the guy's operation and nail a lid on the story.

Just how involved he became, he figured, was up to McCall. After all, it was McCall's story. And knowing McCall as he did, he was willing to bet that his friend was up to his rear in alligators. McCall, he knew, liked to play Lone Ranger, but this one had more tentacles than an octopus. So maybe McCall would welcome his help.

Of late, Bates had been a little fuzzy about whether he wanted to stay in the news business. He often got in a funk like that, wondering if the job was worth it. It usually took a good investigative piece to pull him out of the doldrums, like the one on Bob Mack. *Who in the heck was Bob Mack anyway?* he wondered.

One of Bates' problems was that when he got a sniff of a potentially good story, it was like pouring gasoline on a raging fire. He couldn't stand it until he knew the ending. The story itself was never enough. He always looked beyond the surface to all the people involved. In the case of Bob Mack, his mind was on the people the gangster had and would continue to kill with all his poison. Though he liked money as well as the next guy, Bates had decided it truly was the root of all evil. It was what kept people like Bob Mack in business.

Bates spent the rest of the day digging up information on Mack. It wasn't easy. Very few people, including federal agents, were willing to talk. The more he looked into the affairs of the mysterious Bob Mack, the more convinced he became that the man had friends in high places.

Some of Mack's money, Bates decided, was greasing the palms of politicians in Austin and Washington, DC.

NINETEEN

After his visit with Melanie Richards, McCall had to fulfill a dreaded obligation that he knew wouldn't produce anything in the way of a lead. He had to see Scott's parents.

He had stated his sympathies at the funerals of Scott and Andy, which was the only time he had ever been in contact with them. Yet, because Scott had told him so much about his folks, McCall felt he knew them pretty well.

The senior Tyler was a retired sawmill worker. Scott's mother had always been a housewife. They were decent God-fearing people who didn't deserve the recent sorrow they had been forced to endure. But, who did?

After getting out of the prison camp, Scott had put a lot of emotional distance between his folks and himself. He hadn't been able to go to them with his problems because everything was black and white to them. Scott's father was one of those pull yourself up by your boot-

Nineteen

straps kind of guys with a low tolerance for what he considered weakness and sin. McCall figured that Scott, though he wouldn't admit it, was a lot like his father.

The Tylers had owned their house in Putnam for more than thirty years. Scott's dad had worked overtime at the mill every day for four years to earn the money for the down payment. It was a simple home, just a white frame structure with a nice yard and a vegetable garden in back.

Visiting the Tylers was a nostalgic experience for McCall, the house a reminder of the man who had grown up there. It was a comfortable place, one where a man could kick back, relax after a hard day's work and be sure that there would be something appetizing on the table.

He took the cup of coffee Mrs. Tyler offered him, but turned down a fresh baked cinnamon roll with the explanation that he would soon be having dinner. Scott's mother then insisted on packaging a couple of cinnamon rolls for him to take with him.

While he was relatively sure his talk with the Tylers would provide no leads regarding Andy's and Scott's deaths, he left nothing to chance. He asked all the right questions, understood when the couple knew none of the answers. They were much more interested in relating memories, recalling both Scott's and Andy's past triumphs. They expressed gratitude to McCall for the role he had played in their son's life.

They didn't believe Scott or Andy had committed suicide and harbored bitterness toward the local police for reaching such a conclusion. It was the normal reaction of grieving parents or grandparents, but McCall knew that in his case it was justified. He promised them he would find those responsible for the deaths of their son and grandson.

Back at the motel McCall didn't go immediately to his room. He went to the office to see if Jay Sheldon was on duty. He figured it was a good possibility since the man lived on the premises. Sure enough, Sheldon was behind the desk.

"I seem to have misplaced my key," McCall said.

Sheldon reached under the counter, brought out another and tried to hand it to McCall. "I'd appreciate it, Jay, if you'd just come down and unlock my door. I'm sure I just left my key inside."

DEATH ANGEL

"You can bring the key back. I'm kind of busy."

McCall reached out, grabbed the front of Sheldon's shirt and brought him up hard against the counter. "You don't look very busy to me."

Sheldon could have taken a swing at McCall, but thought better of it. Instead, he whimpered, "What the heck is this all about?"

"It's about selling a key to my room to someone else."

"She used to be your friend's wife. I didn't think you'd mind."

"How do I know you haven't sold a key to someone else?"

"I wouldn't do that."

"You'd sell your mother for a buck. Now get out from behind the counter and go open my door."

McCall loosened his grip on Sheldon's shirt and Sheldon looked in the reporter's eyes and decided it might be best to do what he asked. He came from behind the counter, fretting and grumbling under his breath. He was not a happy camper.

They walked to the door of McCall's room. He stayed back at a safe distance while Sheldon opened the door. "There," the man said, sarcastically, "are you satisfied?"

McCall smiled. "Yeah...thanks. I thought there might be an explosive device attached to the door."

Sheldon's face turned ashen. "Explosive device?"

"Yeah, Jay...some of your friends play rough."

"You...you let me open the door because you thought there might be a bomb?" It was a cool day, but beads of perspiration were standing on Sheldon's forehead.

"Don't take it personal. But since I may have you open my door pretty often...you might want to keep a close eye on my room, make sure that no one other than the maid goes in it."

McCall entered the room and Sheldon went back to the office, shaken and muttering. With the maid coming in to clean the room in his absence, the reporter hadn't been able to secure the room so that he would know if an unwanted visitor had entered.

Once inside, he did a quick check, then noticed that the red light on the phone was flashing. He did a careful check of the instrument, then dialed the office. "Jay...why didn't you tell me I had a message?"

The clerk grunted. "You didn't let me."

Nineteen

"Okay...okay. Who's the message from?"

"Bill Haloran wants you to call."

McCall decided he would call Haloran from the pay phone, so as not to tempt Sheldon's rabbit ears. He showered, shaved again, brushed his teeth, put on the good smelling stuff and dressed for dinner. He wanted to make a good impression on Alicia's mother. He figured he had already made a pretty good impression on Alicia.

He then secured the room and left. If anyone entered by the door or window, he would know it.

Haloran was at the police station, working late as usual. He was not a man who watched the clock. "You called?"

"McCall, you jerk, I called this morning about nine o'clock."

The reporter laughed. "If I'd known you were going to call, I'd have waited in my room."

"Sure you would," the detective said, chuckling. "Listen, the reason I called is because I heard from Dacus."

The reference was to Dacus Davis, a black San Antonio pimp who was one of McCall's informants. He had an MBA from Harvard, but found pimping more lucrative than working for IBM. "What's on Dacus' mind?"

"He's been trying to reach you because the word on the street is there's a contract out on you."

McCall's interest was piqued. "Does it have anything to do with what's going on here?"

"He doesn't know, but doesn't think so. The money's supposedly coming from some source in the San Antonio area."

"Does he have a line on the hit man?"

"No, but he's working on it."

"Does he think the guy contracted knows where I am?"

"I don't think there's anybody who doesn't know where you are," Haloran said, his voice unable to hide the worry. "Your trip to Putnam...and reason for it...isn't exactly a secret. Anyway, Celeste is really worried about you."

"You shouldn't have told her."

"Get on Dacus' case. He told her...not me."

McCall joked, "How about you...you worried about me?"

"I'm just concerned that if someone snuffs you I'm going to lose

DEATH ANGEL

a lot of free meals."

"Your concern is overwhelming."

"Just watch your back, pal."

"I was going to do that anyway, but thanks for the warning. Thank Dacus, too...okay?"

"I will. And Celeste and I are coming down Saturday morning...don't care if you want us there or not. Just be alive when we get there."

"I have every intention of being up and kicking."

"We're coming in my big ol' nasty Plymouth. It needs some road miles."

"It needs to be in a junkyard. I wish Celeste wouldn't come...in case something goes down."

"The woman's got a mind of her own. I don't know what she sees in you, but she would go to the wall for you."

"Yeah...I know. How long are y'all staying?"

"Just the weekend."

"As long as Celeste is coming, I want her to drive the Cadillac back to San Antonio."

"What are you going to do for wheels?"

"I'll get some wheels that aren't so obvious."

"Look, McCall...talking to you is like talking to a tree stump. But dang it, watch your back until I can get there and watch it for you."

A little later Alicia answered his knock and he could only hope dinner was as appetizing as she looked. She was wearing soft colored green slacks and a matching V-neck sweater that showed off some delicious looking cleavage. She kissed him lightly on the lips, then escorted him into the kitchen where her mother was putting the finishing touches on dinner.

He liked that. No pretense. She just took him into their home like he was part of the family.

He liked Mrs. Stevens, too. There was a warmth and genuineness to her that was as natural and unassuming as the streaks of gray in her brown hair. He guessed she was in her late fifties, but she had a figure that would be envied by women in their twenties.

"Smells good," McCall said.

"I hope you like pot roast," Mrs. Stevens said.

Nineteen

"One of my favorites. You shouldn't have gone to all this trouble, Mrs. Stevens."

"Millie...call me Millie. And it's no trouble. It's nice to cook for a man again...especially a handsome one."

McCall laughed. "If you were wearing glasses, I'd be concerned about them being steamed over. Maybe your contacts are steamed."

She laughed, too, and said, "Alicia...why don't you get Matt something to drink. I'm afraid we don't have anything alcoholic. We have sugar-free lemonade and Diet Coke."

"Lemonade's fine. Believe it or not, I'm one of those newspaper types who doesn't like booze."

"That's refreshing," Millie said. "A former editor of our paper drank himself to death."

"Mother!"

"Well, it's true."

"I'm not surprised," McCall said. "Some of my colleagues think it's honorable to die with a bottle in their hand."

The lemonade tasted good to McCall. Sitting in the kitchen drinking it, talking to Alicia and her mother, also felt good. There was a nice feeling to the kitchen. It was as warm and forgiving as the woman who cooked in it.

The dining room was not large and the furniture had been around the block. In spite of its age, it was quality stuff; the kind yuppies paid big bucks for at an antique store. McCall knew the Stevens' hadn't bought the stuff at an antique store. It had been handed down, from one generation to the next.

The pot roast was as good as it smelled. McCall stuffed himself, then downed a piece of real homemade apple pie with his coffee. The coffee wasn't as good as Rosita's boiled brew, but it was close, and definitely better than what Jay Sheldon made at the motel.

After dinner they retired to the living room, which had a comfortable oversized couch and chairs to match. There was a fireplace with artificial logs and a big mirror above it. On each side of the fireplace were built-in bookcases that didn't fill the entire length of the wall. The books were a combination of old and new.

At one end of the room was a baby grand piano, its top covered with framed pictures of family and friends. There were a couple of

DEATH ANGEL

paintings in the room, which were as comfortable as the furniture. McCall figured Millie, or possibly a friend, was the artist. He asked and she was, indeed, the artist.

After another cup of coffee and light conversation, Millie announced that she would leave them alone and do the dishes. McCall wouldn't hear of it. He insisted on helping.

Once the task was done, Millie retired to her room. Alicia and McCall went outside to sit in the porch swing. It was a nice night, cool but nothing more severe than sweater weather. There were a lot of glittering stars and a bright moon peeped over the treetops.

"Mother likes you...I can tell."

"I like her, too," he said, smiling. "And when the occasion demands, I can make a decent impression."

She smiled back. "Do you think the occasion demanded?"

"I certainly do. What you have here...it's a nice way to live."

"It's good for me, but I doubt you'd be happy here. It's probably too quiet for you."

"I'm not so sure about that."

"I am. If it wasn't for the murders, you wouldn't be here."

"That's what brought me here, of course, but I do like the country. I have a ranch out in the boonies that I escape to every chance I get."

He spent some time telling her about the ranch, and about his cabin on the river near Wimberly.

"It's hard for me to see you relaxing at either place," she said. "I see you as someone who likes life in the fast lane."

"It's probably not as fast a lane as you think it is."

"You're a complex man, Matt McCall."

"Not really," he said. "I'm just a simple man who's been forced to live in a complex world."

She laughed. "You also have a great line. But I've got something that'll make your complex world a little easier. I have copies of Bob Mack's bank records."

TWENTY

Back in his motel room, McCall studied Bob Mack's bank records. Alicia hadn't wanted him to leave so early, but he was more than a little concerned about the direction she seemed to be steering their relationship. He liked being with her, but there was some discomfort, too.

As suspected, the records showed Bob Mack to be a very wealthy man. He had more than a million in certificates of deposits, plus healthy personal and business bank accounts. McCall could only imagine what was in the safe deposit boxes, and figured Gregg's bank was just one of many where Mack did business.

McCall was sure Mack was dirty. Jack Gregg had to suspect it. Heather had to know it.

There was nothing in the bank records, however, that would tie Mack to organized crime. Big money, whether in deposits or CDs, came under scrutiny of the feds. So the money he was showing had been cleaned and scrubbed before being folded into the accounts.

DEATH ANGEL

But what did Mack have in his safe deposit boxes? Better still, what did he have at home? A man with a half dozen guards was hiding or protecting something other than his antiques, wife and body.

He really has more than six guards, McCall thought. *He has the police department, probably the sheriff's office and the mayor. Add it up and the man has one heck of a private army.*

The more the reporter thought about it, the more he wanted to explore Mack's house. The guards were the first problem. The second would be the security system, which McCall figured was at least the equivalent of the one at Fort Knox. That didn't particularly bother him. A man willing to pay the price for the solution could solve any problem.

McCall wasn't a cat burglar and had never had training in the CIA's black-bag operations. He didn't even have an outfit to play the part. The closest he came to dress-for-success as a burglar was some camouflage gear. He changed to it about midnight, after he made up his mind to visit the Mack mansion.

Once over the property's fence, he figured he had the advantage of decent cover from the trees and vegetation. But the grounds would probably have sensors for an alarm system, which he would have to neutralize.

He knew, of course, that even if he made the sensors inoperable the chances were good that reinforcements would be called to the estate. He was sure Sergeant Cherry and Officer Burt would roar to the rescue of their master. That meant there was no safe place to park the Cadillac near the Mack house. It meant he would have to go on foot, a distance of some five miles. He smiled at the prospect, figuring that if Bill Haloran faced five miles to a place and five miles back he would probably croak before getting out the door.

McCall assumed that Cherry, Burt and others were checking on his whereabouts regularly. He also assumed that the porky cops would believe he was still in his room if his car was in the motel parking lot. So after making sure the coast was clear, he glided cautiously and silently out the door of his room, secured it, then maneuvered quickly through the dim lighting surrounding the motel, using what cover was available. Once clear, he knew he had the ditch along the highway and the nearby woods for cover. He chose to run along the edge of the trees

Twenty

and brush, which would afford quick entry to deeper cover at the sight of approaching headlights.

The ground was still soggy from recent rains, so the mud sucked at the soles of his boots and forced extra effort on the part of his strong thighs and not-so-strong knees. The knees had suffered severe damage from college football, wounds and age. The pain from his old wounds intensified with each jarring, sloshing jolt of the boots hitting the ground. What he was doing was tougher than normal jogging.

It was a good night for what he had in mind. The moon was pale and yellow, with a fine white mist of clouds constantly passing across it. The terrain was dark, as if there were no moon at all. Ghostly shapes of objects seemed to leap up all around him as his boots pounded against the soft earth. Occasionally, headlights from a distant car forced him into the wooded cover, but the run to the Mack estate was without incident.

He located the transformer that directed city power into the Mack estate. McCall believed Mack was too cunning to depend only on the power company. There would be an alternative generator inside the grounds. McCall knew that most backup power sources took up to thirty seconds to kick in and restore full operations.

McCall cut the power into the transformer and leaped over the fence within a few seconds. The people monitoring the security system would have no reason to believe that whatever was happening was anything other than a happenstance power failure. At least for a few minutes.

All lights from the house and on the grounds were out briefly, then flared back to life. The power surge also kicked on powerful spotlights to supplement the regular lighting. McCall had expected that the switch to on-site power would trigger escalation in some parts of the security system. Escalating the system still didn't mean that the security people would yet be alarmed.

His eyes picked up the cameras -- most of them inconspicuously nestled in the branches of trees. He made mental note of the scan pattern and speed of movement. It was a good bet that he could avoid the stare of the electronic eyes, but the dogs were another matter. Two swift and silent Dobermans bounded toward him.

He hated doing it, but there was no choice. He put a nine-mil-

DEATH ANGEL

limeter slug between the eyes of each dog. There was little noise from the gun, only the muffled hiss from the silencer. The dogs immediately collapsed and didn't seem to feel any pain. McCall sighed.

The Animal Rights League won't be asking me for an autographed picture anytime soon, he thought.

The dead dogs would negate any idea that the temporary power failure might be the work of uncertain nature or an incompetent utility company. The absence of the dogs would alert Mack's troops, who would soon be combing the grounds. When that happened, it would be tough to hide.

He heard sirens in the distance and knew Putnam's finest were riding to the rescue, probably Cherry and Burt. It bothered him that he had had to kill the dogs, but snuffing a couple of cops was something else. If he had to shoot a cop, he would be in a world of hurt, even if the cop were dirty.

He moved swiftly toward the house, using available cover and avoiding the camera sweeps as best he could. Everything was happening quickly, in seconds and fractions of a second. It was like a runaway roller coaster in a dream.

As he approached the house he saw four men emerge from it, each carrying an Uzi. He recognized three of them, two of whom had bandaged faces. This was the batting practice crew from the motel.

McCall had the ability to blend into his surroundings like a chameleon, something he had been trained to do. Two of the men passed by on either side of him, completely unaware of his presence. They were concentrating their attention on the area near the fence, believing the lights and cameras would keep the intruder pinned down near the fence, which was more than a hundred yards from the house.

McCall watched the four men fan out and move forward. Their body English told him they weren't certain there was an intruder on the grounds. They had to be thinking that what had happened still could flow from a brief power failure. The men appeared to be going through motions they had gone through before, without result.

That laxity would end when they found the dead dogs.

Two police cars, lights flashing, were now at the gate, their sirens suddenly silent. Someone inside the house obviously remained to control an electronic device to open the substantial metal gate, which

Twenty

swung open. The police cars raced up the long driveway and bumped to a halt near two of Mack's henchmen, who were in earshot of McCall.

As McCall expected, Cherry and Burt got out of the first car, their guns drawn. Two officers also alighted from the second car, but they looked bored. Their guns remained holstered.

"What's the problem?" Cherry asked.

"Don't know," said one of the men McCall had smashed in the face with a bat. "We either had a power failure or somebody tried to break in."

Burt grunted. "I'll bet it was McCall."

McCall smiled. Burt was smarter than he had thought.

"Thought you told me his car was at the motel," Cherry said.

"I did," Burt said. "Don't mean somebody couldn't have brought him here."

The gunman with the bandaged face growled, "If the jerk's on the grounds, he's a dead man."

McCall noticed that the two officers with holstered guns looked at each other nervously. It was obvious that they weren't comfortable with the situation.

Cherry said, "Okay, let's spread out and see what we can find."

"You're not in charge here, Cherry...I am," the gunman said. "And you guys better stick with us because the dogs are out. They don't know the difference between tearing out the throat of a fat cop and a smart aleck reporter."

"Don't get your bowels in an uproar," Cherry said. "We're just here to help. Tell us what you want us to do."

The guy with the bandaged mug ordered them to do just what Cherry had suggested. McCall smiled. It was good to know there was no love lost between Mack's troops.

They were soon beyond him, between him and the fence. They would check the lakes; figuring the possible intruder might have taken refuge in the tall weeds that grew in the shallows. And it shouldn't take them long to find the dogs.

Four men had come out of the house. McCall figured one of them was supposed to be watching the monitors for the cameras, but had gotten so excited at the prospect of shooting someone that he had deserted his post. Mack supposedly had six guards, two of whom were

DEATH ANGEL

with him in Dallas. Of course, for all McCall knew Mack might be back from Dallas, waiting in the house with the other guards. For that matter, Mack might have more than six guards.

Oh, well...nothing ventured, nothing gained, he thought.

McCall heard a keening yell from one of the men on the grounds. He had found the dogs. They now knew that this was no false alarm, that someone had penetrated their security.

Getting inside the house wasn't difficult. Mack had concentrated on outside electronic and canine security and manpower. McCall hadn't expected any steel curtains. The question remained: *Was Mack in the house with his other two bodyguards?*

If it were like in the movies, McCall thought, Mack would have a safe behind a picture in his study. That, of course, would be too easy. Before looking for a safe, though, he needed to thoroughly scout out the house, to be sure of the location of all the players. Death would be the penalty for any miscalculation or foul-up.

The furnishings in Mack's mansion were about what he expected. He figured a high-dollar interior decorator had been called in to work his or her magic. The place was so spacious it had taken a furniture store full of stuff to fill it.

After checking out the downstairs area, McCall worked his way up the wide staircase to the second level. There he located what he guessed was the master bedroom suite. The door was locked, but it took him only seconds to open it.

In the semi-darkness, the only light coming from the outside flood lamps, he recognized Heather. She was standing at one of the suite's large windows, obviously trying to see what was going on. One of the guards, McCall guessed, had told her to turn out all the lights and to stand back from the window so she wouldn't be silhouetted. She was so intent on the drama unfolding outside that she was completely unaware of his presence.

"Heather," he whispered.

She turned, a pistol in her hand, and for a split second he thought she was going to fire. "Matt...is that you?"

"One and the same."

"What...what are you doing here?"

"Maybe I just wanted to see you."

Twenty

She laughed, softly. "If I'd known you wanted to see me enough to create this kind of ruckus, I'd have come to you."

He smiled. "Well, I wasn't sure you could. And I couldn't just come driving up to the front door, could I?"

"Really, you could have. I'm not a prisoner here."

"Well three of the boys down there are the ones that paid me a visit last night. I don't think they like me."

She tossed the gun on the bed and came across the room to him. They met halfway, hugged, and she said. "I really didn't know they were the ones who attacked you...not until I saw Jack and Bevo today."

He laughed. "Bevo?"

"He's the big one."

"He's the one whose face I crushed with a baseball bat."

"I guess I should have suspected," she said. "Marty...he's the ugly one...usually never lets me out of his sight when Bob's away. But last night he told me he had to go somewhere...asked if I was going to stay home. I told him I was. I guess he went down to the hospital to check on the others."

"Which allowed you to come to my room."

"That's right. If he had been here, I couldn't have come. And if Bob finds out Marty left me here alone, he'll be out of a job."

"I hate that," McCall said, sarcastically. "Guys like Marty being unemployed is of great concern to me."

She laughed. "You're a devil, Matt McCall. You'd better lock the door."

"Don't worry, I locked it when I came in."

Fire was licking at logs in the fireplace, casting irregular shadows throughout the room. Their whispers meshed with the crackling of burning wood and the soft ticking of a grandfather clock featured against a wall of the elaborately furnished room.

Then there was a knock at the door, bringing a sense of reality to the serenity. "Mrs. Mack...it's me...Marty."

Heather walked to the door. "What do you want, Marty?"

"Just wanted you to know that whoever tried to break in is gone."

She smiled. "That's good, Marty."

"If you want to turn your light on or anything, it's okay. I don't think he'll be back."

DEATH ANGEL

Heather came back and did a stage stare at the nine-millimeter pistol in McCall's hand. Then she laughed softly. "Did you think I was going to let him in?"

"I'm not able to predict you...yet."

"I'm not all that hard to predict."

"I hope that's true."

"It is," she said. "And for a man who just broke into Bob Mack's house, you look relaxed even with that pistol in your hand."

"That's because I am."

"Well, would you like to relax even more?"

"It depends on what you have in mind."

She laughed. "Do you know what we have in the bathroom?"

"If you're like most folks you have a john, tub and shower," he said, jokingly.

She laughed more. "We have those, but we also have a hot tub and sauna. Does that interest you?"

"The hot tub...yeah. The sauna...no."

"Well, why don't you go in and make yourself comfortable and I'll fix us a drink. I don't have any buttermilk, but I can offer you a Diet Coke."

"Fine. But I don't think a hot tub is a good idea right now."

"Oh, c'mon. I promise not to molest you."

"It's not you I'm worried about."

"I'm flattered."

"I'm just not as nice as you think I am."

"I wouldn't complain."

"Yeah...but neither of us would feel right about it tomorrow."

"The funny thing is...in the past my attitude toward you was pretty bad. Of course, I didn't know you."

"And now?"

She laughed. "Let's just say you're sort of growing on me. I think you're a very nice man. Strange, but nice."

"That's good. There are some people I like to grow on. Others...I don't care about."

"You do have that I don't care attitude," she said.

"That's wrong. I care about lots of stuff...important stuff."

"Are you interested in being honest?" she asked.

Twenty

"Not particularly. Of course, I guess it really depends on what you want me to be honest about."

"I'd like to know why you really came here tonight."

"I doubt it."

"Really...I'd like a little honesty."

"I can see why. It's an endangered species in this town."

"I can't argue that. But I would like to know why you came here...please."

"Heather, you're sure not a naive woman. In fact, I'd say you're smart, so you have to suspect your husband's restaurant business doesn't provide all this. How many restaurant guys need six bodyguards?"

"You think Bob's a gangster?" she asked, matter-of-factly.

"In a word...yes. And I have to believe he's the worse kind...that he's a drug dealer. My gosh, Heather...Andy and Scott were killed because of drugs."

"Matt, I can assure you Bob had nothing to do with Andy's or Scott's deaths."

"How can you assure me of that?"

"I just know...that's all. Bob's not a killer."

"What is he then?"

"You're right in saying I'm not stupid. I know Bob does illegal things, but he wouldn't have harmed a hair on Andy's head. He loved Andy...just like he loves me."

McCall wanted to tell her that Mack didn't love her, that like most drug lords he just loved possessing things, including people. And maybe Andy wasn't willing to be a possession, so he had to be killed. He didn't say it. Expressing the thoughts would serve no worthwhile purpose.

"What do you really know about your husband?" he asked.

"I know he's not a killer. Of course, he might kill you if he found you here."

"He might try. Lots of people have."

She laughed, nervously. "Oh, he wouldn't pull the trigger. He would have it done."

"Is that why you say he's not a killer, that he doesn't pull the trigger himself...that he has it done?"

"Can't we talk about something else?"

DEATH ANGEL

"You're the one who wanted to talk about why I came here."

"And so far you haven't told me."

"I came here to try to find some evidence about Andy's and Scott's deaths."

"What did you hope to find here?"

"I don't know. I'm looking for any kind of lead. It's like looking for a needle in a haystack. But I'll know when I find something."

"There's nothing here."

"Are you sure?"

"Yes...I am."

"What's in Bob's safe?"

"I don't know. I can't open it."

"I can."

"And you want me to help you?"

"All you have to do is point me in the right direction."

"You're long on gall, Matt McCall."

He laughed. "Sounds like one of those gosh-awful rap songs. But I can't argue the point, Heather. And if Bob doesn't have something to hide, why did he send the three goons to crack my skull?"

She hadn't given a thought to the bodyguards. Now she was thinking about it, and the reporter could tell it bothered her. "I...I don't know."

McCall figured the truth was that she didn't want to know. She didn't want to know where her husband's money came from or what he did for it. She just wanted to live in a safe world where all her wishes were granted, and Mack certainly had the bucks to make all her material dreams come true. She was an exciting and beautiful woman, but spoiled rotten. She had never wanted for anything and had never matured. McCall's eyes swept over her beauty. Her character weaknesses didn't make her physically less attractive.

He sighed with resignation. "Look, Heather...I'm going to find out who murdered Andy and Scott. And I don't care who I have to step on to get the truth. Maybe you didn't care about Scott. I can understand that after all he put you through...but I have to believe you loved Andy. I think you want to see his killer pay, no matter who he is."

Tears welled up in her eyes. "I do owe it to Andy, Matt. But Bob...I'm afraid of him and his friends."

Twenty

She had put it out on the table now. She was no longer trying to protect the husband she knew was dirty. He knew he had recruited an accomplice, no matter how unwilling, and didn't feel badly about involving her in what he wanted to do. "That's a poor way to live...being afraid."

She continued to cry, which McCall found touching and depressing. He was tough but not insensitive. And the tears of a woman touched a nerve. He pulled her close and held her, stroking her hair.

"I could fall in love with you, Matt McCall," she said.

"Up to now you haven't made any mistakes," he said. "That would be a big one."

TWENTY ONE

Getting off the grounds of the Mack estate was much easier than getting on. Heather woke Marty and told him to go to an all-night convenience store to pick up a quart of strawberry ice cream. McCall was in the trunk of the car, slipping out when Marty went into the store.

McCall thought it fortunate that the store was on the way to the motel. He knew the Putnam police would be on the prowl for the estate intruder and the territory between the estate and motel would be the prime hunting ground. He knew that getting into his room unseen would be difficult. The police would be watching the room and his car.

He hid until Marty got the ice cream and left, then used the pay phone to call Alicia Stevens. She answered on the ninth ring.
"Matt...it's four o'clock in the morning."

"Well, I couldn't sleep. Would you mind picking me up?"

"Where are you...and why?"

Twenty One

He explained that he was at the convenience store and needed her to lie for him. She indicated only a minor reluctance, which intensified his appreciation for her.

McCall stayed in the shadows of the store until Alicia's arrival, then quickly got in her car. "How did you get so dirty, Matt?"

He grinned. "Crawling around on the ground."

"Should I ask why you're wearing camouflage clothing and crawling around on the ground?"

"Probably not."

"What's going on, Matt?"

"I paid a visit to Bob Mack's house."

"You what?"

"It was the only way I could find out what I wanted to know."

"I can't believe you broke in there."

McCall mocked the painful delivery of a television minister. "Oh ye of little faith."

She shook her head as she giggled.

She was driving aimlessly, not in the direction of the motel. "So you think the police are watching your room?"

"Probably the only time they weren't watching was when I was at the Mack estate. They rushed out there to his rescue."

"How in the world did you get in...and out? I know he has dogs and all kinds of security."

"That's not important," he said. "The film in this camera is."

"That's the smallest camera I've ever seen," she said.

"Well, it's not small enough. I have to ask you to hide the camera and my gun, because I know the police are going to search me."

"Where am I going to hide them?"

"I'd say somewhere safe at your house. I'll pick them up tonight when we go to the game."

She drove to her house, took the gun and camera inside while he waited in the car. He hadn't wanted to involve her, but there had been no choice. He had to trust someone. She was as good a candidate as any.

When they got to the motel, Cherry and Burt were waiting in a patrol car parked beside McCall's Cadillac. The cops got out of their car when McCall exited Alicia's vehicle. The reporter acted like he did-

DEATH ANGEL

n't see the cops, came around to the driver's side of Alicia's car and gave her a light kiss on the cheek.

Cherry's voice stopped him as he started toward his room, "Hold on just a minute, McCall."

"Well, Sergeant Cherry...what brings you out this early in the morning?"

Burt asked, "Where you been?"

McCall laughed. "Not that it's any of your business, but I went for my morning jog."

"Yeah," Cherry said. "And where did you jog to?"

"Obviously to Alicia's house. I got tired and she was kind enough to bring me back to my room."

"You always jog in a camouflage outfit and boots?" Cherry asked.

"Sometimes I just wear the boots," McCall said, flashing an ironic grin.

Alicia was still sitting in her car, observing and listening. Cherry turned to her and asked, "You backing him up on this little tale, Alicia?"

"Why shouldn't I?" she said.

"Because it might get you in a world of trouble," the policeman said.

"I could see where telling the truth would cause some problems in this town," McCall said.

"Shut up!" Burt ordered.

That triggered McCall's boiling point. "Why don't you try to shut me up?"

"Enough," Cherry said. "You know the routine, McCall. Assume the position."

"I don't know what you're talking about."

Cherry said, "Get your hands on the top of the car and spread 'em."

McCall followed instructions, but said, "I don't know the sexual orientation of either of you clowns, so don't like you behind me. And please, don't get fresh while you're doing this little search."

Burt uttered a few expletives and Cherry did the search. "Nothing," he said. "No gun. Just a motel key and wallet."

"Maybe the gun's in Alicia's car," Burt said.

Twenty One

"What about it, Alicia?" Cherry asked. "Did he hide the gun in your car?"

"Why would someone need a gun to jog?" she asked.

Cherry smirked. "Don't be a smart aleck. Just remember this guy will be leaving Putnam in a day or two, but you still have to live here."

"No she doesn't," McCall said.

"Put a lid on it," Cherry said. "Get out of your car, Alicia. We're going to search it."

"Whoa!" McCall said. "Do you have probable cause?"

"I told you to zip your lip," Cherry said, "and I meant it. How about it? You going to let us search your car...or are you going to play bad like your friend here?"

"Search all you want," she said, getting out of the car. She stood by McCall while the officers searched. They found nothing, putting both in a fouler mood.

Cherry said, "You may think you're smart, McCall, but we know where you were tonight."

"You should. I know you guys have been watching over me."

"Very funny, smart aleck," Cherry said. "How about letting us take a look at your room. And don't give me any crap about probable cause, because we got plenty."

"Help yourself. You'll find I live a very austere life. You do know what austere means, don't you?"

The sergeant handed McCall his wallet and motel key, which had been on the hood of Alicia's car. "Okay...show us."

They all walked to the door, but before inserting the key McCall asked, "Cherry, haven't some of your people already been in my room?"

"What are you talking about?"

"Someone's been in my room."

"So...open the dang door," Burt said.

"No thanks."

"What do you mean, no thanks?" Burt asked, aggravated.

"I mean I'm not opening the door because someone's been in my room."

"How do you know that?" Burt asked. "You're just stalling."

"You open it," McCall said, offering the key.

Burt snatched the key from his hand and McCall said, "I would-

DEATH ANGEL

n't if I were you."

"And why not?"

"A lot of people don't like me. The room may be booby trapped."

"You're full of it," Burt said, going to the door.

McCall started backing away and to the right of the door, pushing Alicia with him. He noticed that Cherry was moving with them. Burt, muttering expletives, jammed the key in the lock and turned it, which was the last thing he ever did.

The explosion disintegrated the door. Parts of it mingled with the mangled body of the police officer. His fractured body was hurled backward, blood and pieces of flesh flying through the early morning air.

McCall, Alicia and Cherry were knocked down by the explosion, but escaped injury from door splinters and flying glass. McCall recognized the device both from its pattern and outcome. It was a controlled directional blast; one designed to take out only a person standing at the door. It was the handiwork of a high-grade professional hit man.

They got to their feet slowly, Alicia crying and Cherry looking with horror at what was left of his partner. "My god," he kept saying over and over. "My god."

McCall held Alicia in his arms, her eyes away from Burt's body. "Can you drive?" he asked.

She nodded and he said, "Then get in your car and go home."

Other motel guests were milling about, curious and frightened about what had happened.

After Alicia was gone, McCall suggested to Cherry, "Don't you think you might want to call someone?" He figured Jay Sheldon was probably already on the line, but thought he should say something to Cherry.

The stupefied sergeant followed McCall's suggestion almost robotically. He went to his car and used the police radio to call for help. While he was doing it, McCall stepped into what had been his room.

He found that the explosion had disturbed none of his possessions. His suitcase was still intact and his clothing hung in the closet next to the bathroom. The windows had shattered but the drapes had been drawn and there was very little broken glass in the room.

"McCall...what are you doing here?" Cherry asked.

Twenty One

The reporter looked at the policeman, who seemingly had gotten better control of himself, and replied, "This is my room, Cherry. I'm just checking my stuff."

"Right now it's a crime scene...so get out of here."

McCall saw Jay Sheldon standing outside the door, his face drawn with fear. "What about it, Jay...you got another room for me?"

"It doesn't matter if he has a room or not," Cherry said. "You're coming down to the jail with me. You got some explaining to do."

"About what?"

"About how you knew there was going to be an explosion."

"Look, you idiot, I didn't know there was going to be an explosion. I just knew someone had been in my room and I didn't want to take any chances. Your pal was too stupid to listen."

Cherry, obviously angry, dropped his hand to his gun, growling, "Why you..."

"Don't even think about drawing it, Cherry...or I may make you eat it."

They locked eyes for a second and Cherry shivered, then dropped his hand to his side. "You can't intimidate me, McCall."

McCall's smile was like that of a coiled rattlesnake ready to strike. "Oh, I'd never think anything like that, Cherry. If you want to check my stuff...do it, because I want it moved to another room."

"Do yourself a favor, McCall. Check out and leave town."

"I thought you were taking me down to the station."

"I am. But I'd say you ought to give your statement and get out of town."

"Nothing I'd rather do, but I'm not going for a while. Now...you want to check my stuff or do you want me to describe it to you?"

Cherry uttered a few expletives, then entered the room to go through McCall's possessions. Sirens that seemed to be coming from every direction were piercing the morning air. Onlookers were milling about, shuddering at the sight of what was left of Burt. "Give me a blanket," McCall told Cherry. "We can at least cover the body."

The policeman obliged and McCall took the opportunity to also talk to Jay Sheldon. "Did you see anyone messing around my room?"

Sheldon, his voice quavering and his eyes fixed on Burt's body, said, "No...no, I didn't see anybody."

DEATH ANGEL

"Fine, Jay...I believe you."

"You do."

"Sure. If you'd seen the guy who did this, he would have iced you."

The motel clerk shuddered. "I...I...I can't believe this happened."

"I don't care what you believe. Just get me the key to another room...pronto."

Sheldon scurried off and Cherry came out of McCall's room. "Find anything interesting?" the reporter asked.

"No...nothing. No gun."

"Why did you think I had a gun? And why were you and Burt hassling me?"

"We'll tell you what you need to know."

"You may. Burt's not going to be telling anyone anything."

McCall's statement seemed to awaken Cherry to the fact that his partner was really dead. McCall could see that the cop was still suffering from shock.

The sirens were getting louder and moments later a police car and ambulance were on the scene. Dade Decker, the police chief, showed up moments later in an unmarked car.

McCall stood aside and watched Decker, Cherry and two other cops screw up the crime scene. One of the officers took a few pictures of Burt, and then the two ambulance guys put what was left of the body in a bag. It was not a pretty sight.

The cops continued sifting through the debris for evidence, but McCall could have told them they wouldn't find anything. What had happened was the work of a pro. Maybe the guy was on Mack's payroll and he had just failed to tell his cop friends what he was going to do. Or maybe it was the work of the hit man Bill Haloran had told him about. That was most likely. He thought, *Well, it's not the first time and it sure won't be the last that someone tries to nail me.*

"What do you know about this?" Decker asked McCall.

"All I know is that if I'd opened the door, I'd be the one in the body bag."

"That's the way it ought to have been," Cherry said.

McCall laughed. "Sorry to disappoint you, Cherry. All I can tell you, Decker, is that I've been turning over rocks and must have some-

Twenty One

body squirming."

"Cherry here tells me you wouldn't open your door...that you suspected something was wrong. Maybe you rigged the explosion yourself."

"Yeah, maybe I did. And maybe Abe Lincoln committed suicide. Hooking a bomb to my own door wouldn't be a real bright move on my part. Why would I do something like that?"

"To keep people out of your room."

"It would darn sure keep me out," McCall said. "But why would I think people were trying to get in my room. Do you know something that I don't, chief?"

Decker didn't have a good answer. "You still haven't told us how you knew somebody had been in your room."

"Let's just say I have some strange habits. When I'm in hostile territory, I always fix my doors and windows to alert me to unauthorized entry."

"Sounds a little paranoid to me," Decker said.

"Maybe, but it's helped keep me alive over the years. When you deal with the kind of people I do...dirty cops and all...you can't be too careful."

Decker's face reddened. "You insinuating something, McCall?"

"Now why would I do that? But you know the people around here better than I do. You know who's capable of rigging an explosion like that, don't you?"

"I want you to come on down to the station to make a statement," Decker said.

"Okay...I'll drive down. It'll save one of your boys the trouble of driving me back out here."

"Fine. You can follow my car."

"I need to stop by the motel office first and get a key to a new room."

"You can do that when you get back."

"Is there a chance I might not get back?"

"Of course not. Go ahead and get your key."

McCall checked out the Cadillac and was satisfied no one had tampered with it. He drove the short distance to the motel office, finding Sheldon behind the counter. When the man saw him he started

DEATH ANGEL

rummaging through keys and said, fearfully, "I was on my way out...to bring you a key."

"Hold on to it, Jay. We'll pick a room when I get back. And guess what? You get to open the door. Now...I want you to do two things for me. First, call Barry Travis and tell him I'm going down to the police station. Second...get my stuff out of what's left of my old room and hold it here. And Jay...do what I tell you because I will be back."

"You can count on me."

"I think you know you can count on me, too, Jay."

McCall followed Decker to the police station. The chief led him to what McCall guessed was used for an interrogation room. The place looked like it came straight out of a B movie, complete with bright lights.

Cherry and another cop were there, along with a tape recorder. McCall sat down at a table and Cherry switched on lights directed right at the reporter's face. He reached over the table and turned them off. Cherry, angrily said, "What the..."

"I'm here of my own free will. Treat me nice, Cherry, or I'll shove those lights down your throat."

The cop who hadn't been introduced grinned. Decker wasn't amused. "You're in a world of trouble, McCall."

"I'm in your world, Decker, so I guess I have to agree..."

McCall saw the blow coming, but not in time to avoid it completely. Decker's fist struck him a glancing blow on the side of the head, causing McCall to topple backward out of the chair. He landed on his backsides, his back to the wall. "Body punches," Decker yelled. "Nothing to the head."

If that's the game they want to play, McCall thought, I may as well join in.

As Cherry approached him, McCall caught the policeman flush in the groin with his boot. The blow, landed with violent force, caused Cherry to drop to his knees in agony, groaning out expletives through the pain. "Get the jerk, Caldwell," Decker screamed at the other cop.

But McCall was now on his feet. A karate chop to Cherry's nose brought blood and another scream. The reporter had broken enough noses to know that Cherry's had joined the club.

Decker had retreated to a corner, but away from the only door.

Twenty One

Caldwell was trying to position himself to take McCall from behind and Decker was continuing to scream at him for not charging the reporter.

McCall wasn't worried about Caldwell. He was angry, fire in his eyes. He wanted a piece of Decker and wasn't about to be denied. He charged, launched himself and put both boots on Decker's chest. The chief crumpled to the floor and McCall quickly got up to face Caldwell, who had worked up the gumption to charge him.

He used Caldwell's momentum to slam him into the wall, then again turned his attention to Decker. He figured there was no point in injuring his hands on the jerk, so he kicked him in the face. Blood spurted from the chief's mouth and he tried to play possum, but McCall wasn't buying it. He pulled Decker to his feet, kneed him in the groin and then leveled a combination of punches to the man's stomach.

His obsession with Decker cost him. Caldwell had gotten off the floor and made a bull-like rush that rammed McCall against the wall. He buckled McCall's knees with a couple of blows to the head.

McCall suddenly had a new appreciation for Caldwell. The guy was young, strong and powerful. His fists hurt like the devil. But the young hulk of a man hadn't been trained in the dirty and deadly fighting techniques that were second nature to the reporter.

From his knees, McCall launched an uppercut that caught Caldwell between the legs. Before the man's knees buckled, McCall used his groin for a punching bag. Caldwell fell to his knees with a moan and McCall gave him a vicious head butt to the face. Caldwell went out like a light.

McCall rose to his feet shakily. He saw that Cherry's body still was moving and delivered a kick in the ribs. A stream of officers cascaded into the room. McCall tried to fight back but was slammed into the wall. His fists were no match for their clubs and metal flashlights. He broke the nose of one khaki-clad sheriff's deputy before the lights went out.

McCall regained consciousness in a hard straight-backed chair, his hands cuffed behind him. The harsh lights were in his face and blurred figures were standing behind them. Decker said, "So, you're coming out of it, huh?"

DEATH ANGEL

Then the chief punched him hard in the stomach. The chair would have turned over if someone hadn't been bracing it from behind.

McCall could feel the taste of blood in his mouth when he spoke. "You're a real bad one, Decker...real tough when you've got someone cuffed. But all these guys know you're nothing but a wimp when the odds are a little more equal."

Decker buried his fist in McCall's stomach again, and his breath oozed out. But he wouldn't give Decker the satisfaction of even the slightest groan of pain. McCall knew what real torture was, not just a few fists to the face and body. He knew how to mentally disassociate himself from his surroundings. It had been part of his training, and he had been a good pupil.

"Wimp," he said, "is that the best you can do?"

The police chief slapped him across the face, a stinging blow but one that made him more alert. It cleared some of the cobwebs from his brain.

Decker shouted, "Where were you last night, McCall?"

"None of your business, maggot."

Decker hit him again and Caldwell said, "You'd better watch it, chief."

"I know what I'm doing," Decker growled.

"You'd better hope you do," said Barry Travis, who had just walked into the room.

"How did you get in here?" Decker asked, angrily.

"Walked," the DA answered. "I guess you forgot to lock the door. If you're going to beat prisoners, you should lock the door. Even people in this town won't tolerate their police chief beating prisoners."

McCall couldn't see Travis because of the harsh light in his face. But he was grateful that Sheldon had made the call to the district attorney, even if he had done it out of fear. He had to remember to give the motel clerk a little something extra.

"Barry, I'd suggest you get out of here," Decker said.

"Glad to...but I'm taking McCall with me."

"He assaulted three police officers."

"Was that before or after you started beating him? You know darn well you don't have a leg to stand on, Dade. You can file charges if you want to, but you know they're going to be tossed. You got your tail in

Twenty One

a crack...and you'd better hope McCall doesn't file charges against you."

"Get out of here, Travis," Decker said.

"When I go, McCall's going with me. Or do you want to beat up on me, too?"

Decker wasn't in the mood to let McCall go, but saner heads prevailed. He eventually realized that he could be in a world of legal hurt. "Okay...get out of here, McCall. If you're smart, you'll leave town and won't come back."

McCall laughed. "You don't help the tourism people much, do you? I'll bet you're the pride and joy of the chamber of commerce."

Decker started to move toward McCall, but by then the cuffs had been removed. Seeing McCall's hands were free froze his feet, but not his mouth. "Just get out."

McCall and the DA walked outside. Travis said, "McCall...you look a mess."

"It's kind of a natural look when you're beat up by a bevy of cops. But I clean up pretty good. I'm just glad Jay Sheldon got my message to you."

"He didn't call me. Alicia's the one who called."

McCall decided right then that he was going to have a serious conversation with Jay Sheldon.

TWENTY TWO

Battered and bruised, McCall drove back to the motel where he planned to have that serious talk with Jay Sheldon. He, however, could not be found. It was the day clerk, a nice lady, who set McCall up in a new room.

The reporter had a first-aid kit in his car. He treated his cuts and got a couple of buckets of ice for his bruises. Then he showered and changed out of his camouflage gear.

McCall hadn't slept since early Thursday morning and his body told him to crash. But his mind was in overdrive. There were still things he wanted to check out.

He drove to the convenience store and called Paul Bates. A sleep-laden, heavy-throated voice answered the phone. "Hey, Bates, do you sleep all the time?"

The TV newsman laughed. "I can't. You keep waking me up."

"Find out anything interesting about Bob Mack?"

"Only that he has as much money as you do."

Twenty Two

It was McCall's turn to chuckle. "I'm sure he has a little more than I do."

"A police chief here says Mack's operation probably runs twenty million or more a day."

"Yeah, I'd have to say he has me bested by a dollar or two," McCall said, sarcastically. "Of course, I don't have any restaurants."

Bates laughed. "Nice fronts, huh? By the way, the chief says Mack's not the guy's real name."

"I'm not surprised. You been able to put a name on him?"

"No...sure haven't. But I found out there are a lot of people checking him out...DEA, FBI and ATF. The guy just appeared out of nowhere a few years ago. He has to have friends in high places."

"He does," McCall said. "Last night I got a list of some of them...and records on some of the payoffs they've received."

"Sounds like you've just about got this thing nailed down."

"Not even close. I'm a couple of miles from the finish line."

Bates figured McCall was just being modest, or secretive. He suspected the latter. "Well, my police chief friend here told me to tell you to watch your step. He says Mack has the cops in Putnam in his back pocket."

McCall laughed. "I learned that the hard way."

Concerned, Bates asked, "You in trouble?"

"Not just trouble, Paul."

"Want me to come down there?"

"I don't know what you'd do. I don't even know what I'm going to do."

Bates was intrigued by the story and wanted a piece of it, yet his friendship with McCall was stronger than a chunk of news, no matter how important. "You need any help, just holler and I'll come running. You know that, don't you?"

"Yeah...I know. But I can handle this end. Thanks, though."

McCall then called Arnold. "Listen, I can't believe you acted like you didn't know who Mack was when I called before."

"You know the routine, McCall. I had to get permission from the Ol' Man before I could say anything. Of course, he says you would have known about Mack if you had spend more time working for the Agency and less time messing with the newspaper."

DEATH ANGEL

McCall laughed. "He never gives up, does he?"

"We need you, McCall. We have a lot of Mickey Mouse legislators giving us the dickens about Central America and the Middle East. You could make a difference."

"You know how I feel about everything south of the Texas border. The whole culture down there is a cesspool. I feel about the same about the Middle East. What I can't understand, though, is why you guys haven't done something about Bob Mack."

Arnold laughed. "You know we're not supposed to mess in anything domestic."

"Yeah...sure."

"Besides, Mack's a pretty small fish."

"I heard his operation is doing twenty million a day or more."

"You know that's small potatoes in the drug game...and a lot of that money goes to people above him. Mack's a small fish in a really big organization. He has a little rank, of course, but there are several people over him. He does green the wallets of a few legislators, though."

"Yeah...I know. I went through the papers in his safe last night."

Arnold laughed again. "That figures. I guess you did a little photography work."

"Yeah...a little."

"Are you going to share the film with us?"

"Glad to...especially if it'll help get the jerk out of circulation."

"Tell you what, McCall...nobody's going to complain if you take him out."

"Well...yeah, I'm sure that's true. Taking him out, though, won't solve the problem. Getting rid of Congress and untying the hands of the Agency might do a lot to solve the problem."

Arnold laughed. "Hey, we're not going to complain if you want to take out the Congress, too. Right now some of those toads are accusing us of running drugs. You know that's a crock."

"Well, you know how everyone who gets his tail in a crack claims to have been working for the CIA," McCall said. "And a lot of people claim to be CIA to get people to do stuff for them. If you counted up everybody who said they worked for the Agency, you'd have more names than have ever gone through Marine boot camp. Then, too, you have some people in the Congress who just want to believe everyone

Twenty Two

who says that they're part of the Agency."

Arnold sighed. "Yeah...that's for sure. For your information, Bob Mack's real name is Roberto Petralli. He's from one of the families in the New Jersey area. He's suspected of killing at least a half dozen people when he was in his teens. The cops were about to nail him back then, but he just sort of disappeared for twenty years or so. When he reappeared, it was as Bob Mack, complete with a new face and no fingerprints.

"He spent those years in Europe and Brazil, doing a little on-the-job training. He's responsible for a lot of unsolved murders in Europe and Brazil."

"So he's earned the opportunity to be respectable...to pay off lawmakers and run drugs," McCall said.

"That's about the size of it," Arnold said. "The others you asked about...Cherry, Decker, Burt...those are all aliases. Cherry's real name is Tony Antonelli. Decker is Nick DeMarco and Burt is Bernie Cisco. They've been Mack's...Petralli's boys for several years."

"Burt's dead."

"What happened?"

"Someone tried to blow me up again...got him instead."

"Who do you think tried to nail you?"

"Darned if I know. The guy was a pro, though. I got word from San Antonio that there's a contract out on me."

"Want me to check into it?"

"I'd be obliged. If it's not too domestic for you."

Arnold laughed. "The other people you asked about...they're clean as far as we can tell. Barry Travis doesn't ring true. I'd watch him. But, of course, I'd watch anyone who went to law school."

"I hear you," McCall said, laughing.

"You need some help down there, McCall? I can send someone, but you know what the Ol' Man expects...a favor for a favor."

"Thanks, Arnold...but for the moment, no thanks. If I need help, I'll let you know."

Bill Haloran got the next telephone call. "What are you doing?" McCall asked.

"Trying to shinny my way over a mountain of paperwork," the detective grumbled.

DEATH ANGEL

"I don't guess you've tried to talk Celeste out of coming down here?"

"Sure haven't. I catch enough verbal abuse at home."

"Well, I sure wish she wouldn't come. Someone tried to blow me to kingdom come early this morning."

"What happened?"

McCall recounted the events of the morning. "I'll be darned! I was afraid you'd get into a war down there...or start one," Haloran said.

"Can't believe you'd say that, Bill. Most folks consider me a peacemaker."

"Yeah, right."

"Has Dacus come up with anything on the contract killer?"

"If he has...he hasn't told me anything."

"See if you can get in touch with him...tell him I need him down here."

"What do you need him for?"

"I need to have him talk to some of the brothers. If I talk to everyone I need to talk to...I'll be here forever."

"I know he'll be thrilled to get to go to East Texas. So you're not making much progress, huh?"

"Oh, I'm finding all kinds of snakes in the grass, but I'm not sure I'm any closer to Andy's or Scott's killer."

"You said you wanted Celeste to drive your car back to San Antonio. What are you going to do for wheels?"

"Tell Dacus to bring his Yukon."

Haloran laughed. "He's going to love that. He already claims you've put more miles on it than he has."

"I may use it some, but I'm going to buy a new car, too."

"What are you going to do with another car?"

"I'll use it here...then maybe I'll give it to you."

"That's just dandy," the detective said. "The chief already thinks I'm on your payroll."

"Give the chief my love."

"Anything else...besides messing with the chief that is?"

"Yeah...bring me another gun."

"What happened to your piece."

"I used it."

Twenty Two

"I was afraid you were going to say that."

"Don't get bent out of shape. I just iced a couple of dogs, but I don't want the local cops checking my gun and running ballistics. I wasn't where I should have been when I shot the dogs."

Haloran grunted. "Any other good news?"

"Well, they weren't bird dogs."

After the conversation with Haloran, McCall went back to the motel to get some sleep. His mind was still running at breakneck speed, but his body was aching from pain and loss of sleep. He needed some time to recuperate.

Just a routine twenty-four hours, he thought, smiling. The cops and Mack's bodyguards were out to nail him. And there was a contract killer in town trying to earn his fee. Other than that, everything was normal.

McCall turned the air conditioner up full tilt, undressed and crawled under the covers. But although his body was tired, sleep did not come quickly. His mind was roiling with the tangle of events and people.

Along with everything else, there was Heather Mack, who had to be more than a cardboard figure in the scenario. And there was Alicia Stevens, someone who would possibly demand more than he was willing to give.

More important, of course, were the papers that had been in Bob Mack's safe. And one name in particular. That name was Bob Bright, congressman from McCall's own district. There was a connection between Mack and Bright, one that did not bode well in McCall's eyes. He had always figured Bright was dirty, but hadn't known he was drug dirty.

Everything was speeding out of control. He had come to Putnam to find Scott's and Andy's killer, and had, in the process, uncovered a world of trouble that might not be connected to their deaths in any way. He was, however, willing to bet there was some connection.

The needs of his battered body finally conquered his consciousness and he slept. But it was an uneasy voyage through a maze of dreams. His mind was still a whirlwind even as his body tossed in fitful slow motion.

TWENTY THREE

He awoke late in the afternoon. He was still groggy and his body felt the effects of the beating administered by Dade Decker and other members of Putnam's finest. He grimaced when he breathed, but smiled at the recollection that he had put some heavy hurt on Decker and Cherry. As for what had been done to him, he had taken worse licks in his lifetime and suspected he might take more in the future.

It occurred to McCall that there had been something strange about the first part of his encounter with Cherry and Burt. They hadn't tried to search his car. For that matter, if he had been in Decker's place he would have made certain he got to search Alicia's house.

The whole deal was strange, including the fact that he was not now in jail. It seemed that Decker just wanted to beat on him a while, then send him out of town. The way he interpreted it, Decker and Cherry didn't even want him sitting in their jail. Maybe they figured that even there he posed a threat, so the idea was to get him out of

Twenty Three

town or get him dead. He figured both probably liked the latter idea best.

McCall opted for a bath rather than a shower. He wanted to soak his aching joints in a hot tub, which was made even more pleasurable with a cold glass of buttermilk. Sitting in the tub sipping the buttermilk gave him more time to think about the characters with whom he was dealing.

He kept thinking about the strangeness of Heather. There had to be more depth to her than he had seen thus far. From what Scott had told him, she was a wonderful woman. Of course, that was coming from a man who was crazy in love with her. He was convinced she knew more about Mack's business than she let on. She had helped him when he was trapped in the house; even showed him Mack's safe, but he still didn't trust her.

And what about Mack, or Roberto Petralli? Just how much did he know about Scott's and Andy's deaths? And what about the connection between Mack and Congressman Bob Bright?

Soaking in the hot tub and sipping the buttermilk, McCall's mind revved up again. He was certain it was Mack who had told Putnam's finest to put the squeeze on him, to try to run him out of town. Mack had even used his own boys to try to get the point across. But who had put a contract out on him?

It seemed obvious that the order for the hit didn't come from Mack. *He's capable of doing it himself,* McCall thought. No, the news about the hit was on the streets in San Antonio, so whoever ordered it was probably there. There were just so many people who wanted to see him dead that he had trouble pinpointing just one in his mind.

Arnold had told him he hadn't been able to find any significant information on Jack Gregg. That didn't bother McCall. The man had been a small town banker all his life and was concerned with appearances. Legally, he was probably pure as mountain snow. The only thing that bothered him was that Jack and Louise Gregg were just too nice and too rich. And they had to know more about Bob Mack than the banker had thus far revealed.

Melanie Richards, who had been Andy's steady girlfriend, had given him some names of high school students whom he planned to check over the weekend. Talking to them on a Saturday and Sunday would cause less commotion than trying to visit with them at school.

Thinking about Melanie, McCall suddenly realized he would see her later at the football game. She would be leading cheers for Putnam. *To be young again and a football hero*, he thought. Well, being with Alicia made him feel young. But then, so did being with Celeste. He was anxious to see Celeste, but with a hit man stalking him worried that both women were in danger.

His thoughts turned to Mack, Decker and Cherry, and he was determined to find out what the three knew about Scott's and Andy's deaths. Was what they knew about the deaths the reason they wanted him out of town? Or was it because they were afraid he might look into Dick Warrick's death?

He did plan to talk to Jane Warrick, to find out if Scott had told her anything before he died. Of course, if in the process he found out something about her late husband's death that would just be icing on the cake.

He still had difficulty thinking in terms of Jane and Scott dating. She was so different from Heather. Maybe he was just talking to her about Dick Warrick's death. Maybe one of the companies he represented wrote a life insurance policy on the late police officer.

McCall still had some questions about Barry Travis, questions that couldn't be answered by the simple explanation that the district attorney had defied the controlling political party. There had to be more to Travis than that. And as DA, he had the power to do something other than wring his hands.

It was six when McCall got out of the tub. Game time was eight, but he was going to pick Alicia up at six-thirty for dinner. He would have been content with PTA-made chilidogs, but figured Alicia would prefer something served on a plate.

At Alicia's house he picked up the gun and camera and hid them in a special place in the Cadillac. About the only way anyone could find them would be to tear the car completely apart.

He felt naked not having a gun handy, especially with a hit man on his trail. That problem would be remedied on Saturday when Haloran, Celeste and, possibly, Dacus Davis showed up. Haloran had told him that he and Celeste would arrive about ten-thirty in the morning.

Twenty Three

Alicia looked delicious. She was wearing beige slacks, a light yellow sweater and a green jacket. En route to the barbecue restaurant, she said, "I can't believe what the police did to you."

He laughed. "Do I look that bad? Maybe you'd prefer not to be seen with me."

"Don't be silly. It's just hard for me to believe this kind of thing going on in Putnam. It's always been such a quiet town."

"Well, I guess I'm a little on the noisy side."

"I'd say more on the nosy side," she said, laughing, "which is why all this happened."

"Scott and Andy being murdered is why it all happened. Probably Dick Merrick, too. The good people of Putnam have let scum take over the town. That's the reason for the murders. That's the reason this place is becoming a sewer."

"Most of the people around here...they just want to live their lives in peace," she said.

"That's the story all over the world. Most people want to live in peace...but if you don't stand up to the bullies, it isn't possible."

"Someone has to lead," she said, "and we just don't have any leaders."

"Why don't the ministers do something...at least speak out? They have to know about the drugs and corruption. Maybe it's because the drug dealers and corrupters drop a ton into the collection plate."

"I don't think you're being fair, Matt."

"Probably not. Of course, life isn't fair."

There wasn't a police car at the barbecue place, nor had anyone been following him. *With Burt dead and Cherry recuperating, maybe Decker doesn't have enough dishonest cops to keep an eye on me*, he thought. He figured Decker was also doing a little recuperating on his own.

They found a table, ordered, and McCall asked, "What do you know about a cop named Caldwell?"

"Tommy Caldwell," she replied. "We were in high school together."

"What kind of guy is he...or should I ask?"

"Tommy's okay. He's no rocket scientist, but he's smart enough."

"How about honest enough?"

DEATH ANGEL

"A few days ago I would have said he was honest, but now you have me doubting everyone, Matt."

"Good...you might end up a journalist yet."

"I'm not sure I like distrusting everyone," she said, laughing.

"Granted, it's a poor way to look at world. But I've lived that way so long I'm not sure I can adjust to thinking any other way. I guess I don't have a high regard for my fellow man."

"We're all different," she said. "You're just being you."

"I was trained to be this way."

The waitress interrupted when she brought them bottles of strawberry soda pop. Alicia touched his bottle with hers and toasted, "To us."

McCall looked into the young woman's eyes and knew he didn't want to do anything to hurt her. She was good people, the kind of woman for whom many a man had gone to war. She was worth fighting for, and he felt a twinge of regret that he was not going to be the man with whom she shared her life. But it just wasn't in the cards.

"To a Putnam victory," he said.

"That's a strange response to my toast."

"Don't you want the home team to win?"

"Of course."

"Then what's strange about it?"

She shrugged. "Nothing...I guess. You know, you really haven't told me all that happened last night. Since I'm somewhat of an accomplice, don't you think I ought to know?"

"Probably not. It can't help you...and it could hurt you. I shouldn't tell you everything so that you can be truthful to the police."

She took a sip of the pop and said, "I feel a strong sense of dread. Some terrible things have happened, but I'm afraid even more terrible things are about to happen."

"Premonition? Women's intuition?"

"I guess you could call it that."

"I can't say you're wrong, Alicia. You start turning over rocks and what you find isn't always pleasant. But hey, I'd like to forget all this for the evening. I'm with a beautiful woman...going to a high school football game. It's a little like I'm reliving my youth."

She laughed. "In your so-called youth, I'm sure you'd be playing

Twenty Three

in the game as well as going to it."

"That's true. And afterward, I'd be trying to steal a kiss from Cindy Cheerleader."

"Well, I'm no cheerleader, but you can at least try that after the game."

The sparks had been jumping between them since they met. And Alicia kept adding fuel to what could become an out-of-control fire. There was no doubt that there was some magic between them. She knew it and kept sending him invitations. But he kept thinking about Celeste.

He changed the subject with what passed for a question. "You told me Scott dated Jane Warrick?"

"That's right."

"Do you know if Dick Warrick had an insurance policy with Scott?"

"No...but that's a good possibility."

"Well, the reason I ask is that I just can't see Scott with Jane."

"Why not?"

"Scott was a pretty good looking guy and Jane..."

She laughed. "I can't believe what you're saying. You think Scott was too good looking for Jane? That shows what you know."

"What do you mean?"

"I mean...I never thought Scott was all that good looking. Jane, on the other hand, is a beautiful woman...especially when she fixes up."

"I can't see it."

"You've only seen her in the restaurant...and she's been under a tremendous strain. Her husband gets killed and accused of dealing drugs...then when she finally starts dating again the man she chooses supposedly hangs himself. Give the woman a break."

He polished off his soda pop and said, "Yeah...I see what you mean. And I have a feeling she may know something about Scott's death. She can't be comfortable carrying that burden around."

"I guess you're planning to talk to her."

"Yeah...sometime this weekend. I have to fit her in with everyone else."

"Who else?"

"Several people. I haven't made out a list."

DEATH ANGEL

She laughed. "Matt McCall...you don't even trust me. You're impossible."

He smiled. "Okay...so I'm impossible. I'm still going to buy you another soda...no matter what you think."

They had another pop with their dinner, made small talk, and then it was time to go to the game. They arrived at the stadium at seven-forty and had trouble finding a parking spot. They finally found one on a side street, a two hundred-yard walk from the entrance. A band was playing; its brass section and drums drowning out the other instruments.

"Putnam's band or Newton's?" McCall asked.

Alicia laughed. "Hopefully, Newton's."

They found their seats in a special section that was also occupied by Jack and Louise Gregg. "The game's being dedicated to Andy," the banker said in a semi-whisper. "I had to come."

McCall nodded understanding, but really thought it was typical of the jock mentality to be expected from a coach. It was the team's first home game since Andy's death, and the coach was using the kid's memory to try to get the other players emotionally high. It was the kind of stuff that made McCall want to puke.

Alicia and McCall had been seated only a couple of minutes when Bob and Heather Mack showed up accompanied by two goons. They also had seats in the same section. The two bodyguards gave McCall hard stares, but Mack was cautiously cordial.

"I see you've discovered Putnam's most beautiful young woman, Mr. McCall," Heather said, coyly.

McCall nodded and a look of understanding passed between him and Heather. "She's obviously not too particular," he said, jokingly. "Or she likes father images."

Alicia laughed. "A little gray keeps the doctor away."

Heather smiled, but her piercing eyes told another story. They took Alicia apart, looking for flaws. McCall could readily see that neither woman liked the other, which he figured was fairly normal for two beauties in the same small pond.

Heather was wearing emerald green slacks and a sweater to match. She had an ample supply of gold jewelry; fingers loaded with diamonds and a short white mink jacket. Her mother, Louise Gregg,

Twenty Three

was wearing a short mink coat, too.

It was cool, but McCall figured it was a little warm for mink. He guessed status was important in Putnam, even if it made you sweat.

Despite his cynicism about most coaches, McCall found himself caught up in the excitement of the game. The crowd, he guessed, numbered five thousand or more, and they were a noisy bunch. The stands were full, with fans also standing behind the cable that separated the field from the track that circled it.

The teams came running onto the field led by their cheerleaders, each enjoying the cheers of their fans and the strains of their fight songs. Newton's band and fans were on the opposite side of the field.

The crowd stood while each band played its school song and while the Putnam High band played the Star Spangled Banner. They remained standing while the Putnam High principal used the public address system to announce the game was being dedicated to the memory of Andy Tyler.

Reverend Raymond Fuller then gave a lengthy prayer about the real purpose of the game, how it built character and so on. It was, McCall thought, an extension of the coach's jock mentality. And despite what Fuller said, he just couldn't picture Jesus in a football uniform. He wondered if the preacher had ever played the game.

While everything was going on, the principal's tribute in particular, McCall was observing. Heather's mouth was closed tight and her eyes were cold. Louise Gregg could not hold back the tears.

McCall noticed that while he was watching Heather, Bob Mack was watching him. The man had killer eyes, but McCall wasn't afraid to look right into them. He wanted the bum to know what he was and what he had been. He figured his own eyes conveyed the message pretty clearly, and was pretty sure Bob Mack was a good reader.

Melanie Richards in a cheerleader outfit was not a disappointment. The young woman reminded McCall of some cheerleaders he had known and loved when he was younger.

Putnam won the toss and elected to receive. The kick was fielded by a slender black youth at the ten-yard line and returned to the thirty-three. From there, Putnam punched out a couple of first downs before being forced to kick. McCall had Chuck Meyer figured as a conservative coach, one committed to the basics. He would have his boys play defense and wait for the other team to make a mistake.

The problem was that Newton's head coach was a lot like Meyer, content to use safe running plays and then punt. The first quarter was played between the thirty-yard lines.

In the second quarter a big kid from Newton burst up the middle and went fifty-two yards for a touchdown. The point after was good. Down seven to zip, McCall figured Meyer would loosen up his offense a bit, but Putnam kept playing *blah* football.

At the half, McCall felt the need to stretch. He asked Alicia, the Macks and the Greggs if any of them wanted a chilidog. They all declined, but Gregg decided to walk with him to the concession stand operated by the PTA. McCall figured the banker was probably curious about what he had been doing.

It was after McCall bit into his chilidog that Gregg said, "I couldn't help but notice the bruises on your face, Matt. Barry Travis told me what happened."

McCall shrugged. "I've been in tougher scrapes. Decker's a wimp compared to some of the people I've dealt with."

Gregg laughed. "I'm sure that's true, but what happened is not the kind of thing that ought to be going on in Putnam. The decent people here won't tolerate it."

"Talk's cheap, Jack. The truth is that Decker belongs to your son-in-law. The same's true of Cherry...and was true of the late Jim Burt. From what Travis tells me, Mack owns the mayor, too."

Gregg's eyes flashed sadness. "I'm afraid you're right. Too many people here belong to Bob Mack...including my daughter."

So now it was even more out in the open, further evidence that Gregg wasn't enamored of his son-in-law. McCall said, "Mack's dirty...you know that, don't you?"

"I guess I'd prefer not to know," the banker said.

McCall figured it was an honest answer, and he respected Gregg for the candor. It was the banker's way of letting him know that he knew things were fouled up, but that he couldn't, or wouldn't, do anything about it. He doubted there was much Gregg could do anyway. Mack was a hoodlum and there was only one way to deal with such people. He just wondered if Heather was afraid to leave Mack, or if she enjoyed the power he wielded over the town.

Twenty Three

"I think Bob Mack's responsible for your grandson's and Scott's deaths. Maybe he didn't give Andy the stuff that killed him, and maybe he didn't put the noose around Scott's neck, but he's the reason it happened."

"Matt, I...never mind."

"I know you have a real problem, Jack. The man's your daughter's husband. But she has to know the slimeball's the reason her son is dead."

Gregg sighed. "Sometimes I don't know about Heather. She's hard to understand."

"Well, here's something everyone needs to understand," McCall said. "I'm going to nail the maggot...or maggots...who killed Andy and Scott. If that means pulling the rug out from under everyone in town who kisses up to Bob Mack, so be it."

"There are a lot of good people in this town...a lot of honest people," Gregg said.

"I believe that. I just tend to move in the wrong circles."

"What are you going to do next?"

"For one thing, I'm going to talk to Jane Warrick. Don't ask me why, but for some reason I think Dick Warrick's death is tied to Andy's and Scott's."

"I don't understand," the banker said.

"To tell you the truth, neither do I. But right now I'm looking for anything. Did Dick Warrick have an insurance policy with Scott?"

"I don't know."

"I thought he might have mentioned it, since you had coffee with him almost every day."

"Scott was pretty close-mouthed."

That was true. From what McCall knew of Scott, he was certainly no blabbermouth. "Give it some thought, Jack. If you can think of anything Scott said about Dick Warrick, or anyone else, let me know."

Gregg said he would, then went back to his seat to catch the performance of the Putnam High band. McCall ordered another chilidog and some coffee to wash it down. He was busy ingesting the culinary delight when Melanie Richards approached him.

"Mr. McCall...I've been asking around, and a couple of the foot-

DEATH ANGEL

ball players want to talk to you."

"I appreciate that, Melanie. Who are they?"

"Charley Booth...he was Andy's best friend...and Dan Thompson. I've written their phone numbers down for you."

She offered him a small piece of paper. He handed her his coffee cup, took it and put it in his jacket pocket. He then retrieved the coffee from her. "Can I buy you a chili dog and Coke?"

"Yuck...I don't know how you can eat those things."

"Just one of my many vices."

"Are you enjoying the game?"

"Sort of. Is the team always this boring?"

She laughed. "It wasn't...not when Andy was playing."

"Well, I've enjoyed watching you," he said. "You look very good in that cheerleader outfit."

She blushed. "Thanks. You look good, too."

McCall finished the hog dog and coffee and returned to his seat. Mack's watchdogs glowered at him, so he flashed them a thanks-for-caring smile. Heather was tight-lipped. She refused to look his way. He figured Mack had said something about her friendliness to him, or that she was angry because he was with Alicia. He suspected the latter.

The coach, obviously, had lit a fire under the Putnam team. In the second half, they scored thirty-five unanswered points, running the same type plays they had run in the first half. The difference was that the bigger Putnam offensive linemen were tearing gaping holes in Newton's defensive line, allowing the team's big backs to run wild. McCall couldn't help but notice that Putnam outweighed the opposition by more than forty pounds per man.

Steroid City, he thought.

TWENTY FOUR

It was close to eleven o'clock when Celeste, Haloran and Dacus Davis arrived at the motel. The detective was driving his old Plymouth, which McCall thought should be put in mothballs. Dacus was driving his new Yukon, which was equipped with all the bells and whistles available.

As always, seeing Celeste stirred McCall. She was so beautiful that he again mentally cursed himself for his lack of commitment. He kissed her while Haloran and Dacus looked on.

Celeste was dressed casually in a designer sweatshirt and jeans. Haloran wore baggy brown slacks and a tan sports coat. Dacus, as usual, was dressed in bright colors that reminded McCall of the plastic and neon in Las Vegas. There were times, he was certain, when Dacus dressed outlandishly just to elicit some kind of reaction from him.

Dacus' mind was even brighter than his clothing. Haloran claimed a severe dislike for him, though McCall thought some of his so-called distaste was simply the party line. Dacus was really a likable guy, one who would do practically anything, including putting his life on the line, for a friend.

He was protective of the girls who worked for him, provided them health insurance and a savings plan. He encouraged all his girls to find a better way of life. As for caring, McCall would have put him up against a lot of preachers and other religious folks. The man put out a lot of contrived jive, but he wouldn't lie to his friends. And outside of promoting prostitution, something McCall certainly did not condone, Dacus had the morals of a Papal candidate.

Dacus lived two lives in San Antonio. He had a huge house in a suburb that was the abode for his wife and their well-scrubbed kids. Dacus' children went to private schools. To and from his home Dacus wore a three-piece suit and on weekends cranked up the outdoor barbecue by his big swimming pool. He even attended PTA meetings and was looked on by his neighbors as the consummate family man.

But he also had a townhouse near the business district, where he changed into his working clothes. He knew the streets, knew what was going down and often provided McCall with vital information. "I hope you didn't have me come down here just so you could tear up my Yukon, McCall."

"Dacus...are you more worried about a vehicle than a pal?"

"Oh, you're a pal all right, McCall...always getting me involved in some heavy stuff that might get me killed. Who's going to take care of my wife and kids if I get wasted?"

"Don't tell me you haven't made arrangements. Besides, I just have a few simple things for you to do...nothing dangerous."

"That's what you always say."

McCall put Celeste's stuff in the room that he had reserved for her, then told Haloran and Dacus, "I got you guys a room together...figured the two of you would have a lot to talk about."

"You've got to be kidding," Haloran said. "You expect me to stay in the same room as this sleazebag?"

"I'm sure not staying in the same room with fatboy here," Dacus said.

McCall laughed. "I was just joking. I got you clowns separate rooms. You guys get settled, we'll get a little lunch, then I'll run by a

Twenty Four

dealer here and buy a vehicle."

"Just like that, huh?" Haloran said.

"Buying a car isn't exactly hard," McCall said.

The detective laughed. "Not for you, moneybags."

Dacus, seeing McCall's former room, asked, "Someone trying to blow this place up?"

"Just some renovation going on," the reporter said.

Dacus shook his head in resignation. "Yeah, McCall...yeah."

Haloran wanted to return to the barbecue restaurant, so they ended up there, all having ribs and bottles of red pop. "It doesn't get any better than this," Haloran said.

"You're very original," Dacus said.

The quartet got a lot of stares from other patrons. McCall figured it wouldn't take long for the word to get out that he had formed a posse. He filled his companions in on all that had happened, including his problems with local law enforcement. Dacus asked, "You think the guy who tried to blow you up was local, or do you think it was related to the hit I heard about in San Antonio?"

"I don't think it was a local."

"Oh, great," Dacus said. "I was afraid we might just have to watch for your enemies from one direction...wouldn't have been much of a challenge."

"So where do you want to go from here?" Haloran asked.

"I want you to talk to a few high-school students who might be dopers...do some general nosing around."

"Just so my nose doesn't end up like yours," Haloran said.

"I'm hardly scratched," McCall said, laughing.

Celeste said, "You look a little bruised to me."

"Celeste...you've hurt me more than those guys did."

She blushed and they all laughed. "You may get hurt worse a little later on," she said.

Dacus said, "I guess you want me to go see what I can find out from the brothers?"

"Yeah...anything you can pick up on the drug trafficking here, who's dirty and who's not. We're probably talking small potatoes, of course. Mack's real business has to be in the major cities, but you might find something interesting."

DEATH ANGEL

"Anything you're involved in is going to be interesting...deadly interesting," Dacus said.

After lunch, Haloran went to check out some of the students on the list Melanie Richards had given McCall, and Dacus went to see if he could get any leads in the black community. Celeste and McCall went to see the local GM dealer, where McCall picked out a fully equipped Yukon. He gave the salesman a check and told him he could call Jack Gregg to verify that it was good. He had already told Gregg what he was going to do.

"We can have it ready for you about noon Monday," the salesman said.

"I want it by six o'clock this evening. If you can't have it ready by then, I don't want it."

The salesman complained, but said the vehicle would be ready.

"What do we do now?" Celeste asked.

"We're not going to do anything. I'm taking you back to the motel. You can watch TV or read. I have to see a few people."

"You're crazy as a loon, Matt McCall, if you think I came here to be cooped up in a motel room."

"If you'll recall, I tried to talk you out of coming."

"But you didn't. I'm here...and I'm going with you."

He figured he would have as much success talking a signpost out of going with him, and figured her presence would not do any harm. He was going to try to get Jane Warrick to talk. Celeste, he decided, might actually be an asset.

McCall had checked on Jane the day before and discovered she didn't work at the Elite on weekends. He guessed it was so she could spend more time with her kids. Whatever the reason, he thought seeing her at home would make her more receptive to questions.

When he herded the Cadillac around a corner, he saw a police car parked in front of Jane Warrick's parents' home. Given the circumstances of the previous day, some men would have avoided contact with the police. Not McCall. He parked behind the police car, then he and Celeste walked to a fence gate about fifty feet from the front porch. He was about to open the gate when Tommy Caldwell came out the front door. Their eyes locked for a few seconds, and then the police officer dropped his gaze rather sheepishly.

Twenty Four

"What are you doing here, McCall?" the policeman asked.

"I could ask you the same question."

"You don't know then?"

"Know what?"

"Jane Warrick...she's dead."

"How? When?"

"Murdered," Caldwell said. "Pure and simple murder. But let's not talk here. There's a little café a couple of miles from here. Follow me over there and we'll talk."

McCall drove behind Caldwell to the black section of town. They parked in front of a small white frame building with Coca-Cola sign in front. Scrawled across the front of the place in poorly done hand lettering was the name *Elmer's Place*.

Celeste and McCall followed Caldwell into the café. There was a screen door on the front of the place, but it didn't keep any flies out. There were too many holes in it. The ceiling was low and there was the kind of pale lighting usually attributable to dirty light fixtures.

They sat at a wooden table that had seen better days in chairs that were a good match. The entire place was so decrepit that McCall was pretty sure Bill Haloran wouldn't be interested in eating there, which was the real test of how a place looked. It did smell of Lysol, though, and the floors and tables appeared clean, if less than spotless.

A heavy dark woman who looked to be in her sixties moved toward them, a big smile on her face. "What y'all want, Mr. Tommy?"

"Just coffee, Bessie. How about you, McCall? And you, Miss..."

"Celeste," McCall said. "Celeste Grigg. And we'll both have a Diet Coke. Don't bother to bring glasses, ma'am...we like drinking out of the can."

Bessie's big feet took her in the direction of the coffee and cold drinks. Then Caldwell said, "Sorry about yesterday, McCall. I can't believe what's going on here."

McCall smiled and rubbed his chin. "I believe you did hit me a couple of times."

"I didn't want to. I didn't even know what was going on."

Caldwell was big and muscular. He looked like he could take care of himself in a fight. McCall figured he could take him, but that it wouldn't be easy. "Jane Warrick...tell me what happened," McCall said.

DEATH ANGEL

The police officer bit his lip and reflected for a moment. "She didn't come home from the restaurant last night. Her parents called early this morning and we started looking. We found her car about eleven this morning. She had been shot in the head."

Bessie brought their order, quieting the conversation momentarily. McCall took a sip of Diet Coke and asked, "Where did you find the car?"

"On a dirt road down by the creek."

"The one that runs through town?"

"Yeah."

"That's the creek Scott said he would use if he ever decided to take himself out."

Puzzled, Caldwell questioned, "Take himself out?"

McCall saw no reason not to tell Caldwell about Scott's suicide plan, so he told it all. He was especially interested in watching Caldwell's expression while he talked.

"I was never satisfied with the ruling that Scott's death was a suicide," the policeman said, "but I wasn't allowed to work on the case. Everything was handled by Decker, Cherry and Burt."

"I take it you're not that fond of Decker and Cherry?"

"The more I know about them, the more I know what a policeman shouldn't be," he answered, sarcastically. "Burt was a pig, too. Excuse me, ma'am...I didn't mean to say that."

Celeste laughed. "I don't care what you say, just don't call me ma'am."

Caldwell smiled. "Sorry...it's the way I was raised."

McCall figured Caldwell had been brought up pretty well, but that he had gotten caught up in a situation he couldn't control. There were obviously some limitations to living in a town like Putnam and trying to get a job you liked. "Have any suspects?" McCall asked.

"We don't have doodley squat...ain't likely to, either."

"Why's that?"

"Decker and Cherry are handling the investigation. They just recruited me to give Jane's folks the bad news."

"Did you know Jane pretty well?"

"Yeah...I did. She had it rough, Dick being killed and all."

"Do you know if Dick had an insurance policy with one of the

Twenty Four

companies Scott represented?"

"Can't say," Caldwell replied. "Jane didn't get anything from the department, Dick being killed the way he was."

"Did the way he died bother you?"

"Yeah...sure did. I'd known Dick all my life...couldn't believe he was messed up in something illegal, especially drugs. You know he and Scott were friends, don't you? Maybe they weren't close friends, but they had coffee together sometimes."

"How well did you know Scott?"

"I knew him," Caldwell said. "We weren't close or anything...the age difference and all. But he was always nice to me. We had coffee together sometimes, too."

McCall said, "I'm a little surprised that you're talking to me. Aren't you afraid you'll get your tail in a crack with Decker and Cherry?"

"I thought about that," the policeman said. "I guess I just don't care anymore. Maybe I'll regret it tomorrow, but Jane being killed and all...I know something's bad wrong. I figure you might know what's going on."

McCall laughed. "Tommy, it doesn't take a rocket scientist to know that Decker and Cherry are dirty...that they belong to Bob Mack."

Caldwell sighed. "Yeah...I know. Like a lot of people, I guess I just wanted to turn my back on what's going on...what's been going on since Bob Mack moved here. But all these people dying...I just didn't know whether to leave or to try to do something. I guess you can call me a coward, but I just didn't have the nerve to take them on alone."

McCall appreciated the man's candor. It took a brave man to admit he was afraid. One man against half a police department, a number of city officials and Mack's boys. It was too much. "You're just showing good common sense," the reporter said. "Anyone who wasn't afraid of the odds...who thought he could play Lone Ranger...would be stupid."

"You don't seem to be afraid," Caldwell said.

Celeste laughed. "Matt's never been accused of having good common sense...or of not being stupid."

McCall ignored her and Caldwell said, "I don't know what to do,

DEATH ANGEL

but I'm willing to do something. I think there's another guy on the police force that'll back me. We just need some direction."

"I can't ask you or anyone else to risk his life," McCall said. "That has to be a personal decision."

"I guess I'm making that decision," Caldwell said. "If there's anything I can do to help you...I will."

"What do you know about Mack and his operation?"

"Not much. I know he pulls a lot of strings. He supports all the worthwhile projects in town...and his money provides jobs. People around here are willing to look the other way because of his money."

"Dirty money," McCall said, sarcastically.

"That's true," Caldwell said. "But you're on the outside looking in. You don't really know what it's like living here."

"I guess I have a few things to be grateful for," the reporter said.

"I don't guess I have to warn you that Decker and Cherry aren't nice enemies. They want you out of town, and if you don't leave they might kill you."

McCall's eyes turned icy. "They might try."

They left the café, Caldwell to return to the police station and Celeste and McCall to return to the home of Jane Warrick's parents. He didn't enjoy the prospect of talking to the murdered woman's folks, but it was necessary.

En route, Celeste asked, "Do you trust him?"

"You know better. I want to, but I really don't trust anyone in this town."

She laughed. "Some things never change."

While McCall was preoccupied with the murders that had happened in Putnam, he was also vigilant to the fact that a hired killer was on his trail. He knew better than to let his guard down for a single moment.

Jim and Clara Donaldson, Jane's parents, were about what McCall expected. They were down home, salt of the earth type people who had experienced more than their share of sorrow in a relatively short period of time. They were typically small town, bewildered that what they had always considered as big city crime had invaded their domicile.

McCall was good with grieving people. He let them talk. He lis-

Twenty Four

tened. He wasn't sure why, but it had been his experience that people who had lost a loved one were anxious to talk about it, especially when that loved one was a murder victim. McCall had spent a lot of time talking to such people.

Neither parent could give him much information about their daughter's activities outside the house. Jane had worked hard, they said, had been a good mother and had been subjected to more than her share of heartbreak. It was the kind of eulogy McCall expected the Donaldsons to give their daughter, but he had no quarrel with it.

"How many guys was she dating?" McCall asked.

"She hadn't dated anyone except Scott since Dick died," Mrs. Donaldson said.

"Do you know if Dick had an insurance policy with Scott?"

"Yes," Jim Donaldson said, "but nothing has ever been paid on it. The delay has had something to do with the way Dick died. Scott had been working on getting the money for Jane for a long time. She needed it...the kids and all. She just kind of gave up after Scott died."

McCall figured he owed it to Scott to try to get the money for Jane's kids. Being raised by grandparents, theirs wouldn't be an easy life. But there were a lot of kids living under worse conditions than the love of grandparents. It would probably be harder on the Donaldsons than on the kids.

While the reporter left the Donaldson home with no real leads about the recent epidemic of unusual deaths in Putnam, he did have the satisfaction of having his suspicions about an insurance policy on Dick Warrick confirmed. He figured that knowledge and a dollar would get him a cup of coffee and change in a few places. He thought the information might prove important somewhere down the line.

McCall drove to the pay phone outside the convenience store and called Charley Booth, one of the two football players with whom Melanie Richards had suggested he talk. Charley was watching a game on the tube, but agreed to meet McCall at the drugstore and to bring Dan Thompson, the other player, with him.

They met about thirty minutes later. It was obvious the youngsters were quite taken with Celeste. McCall could understand why, since he was quite taken with her himself.

He ordered milk shakes for Charley and Dan, a cherry Coke for

DEATH ANGEL

Celeste and coffee for himself. It was easy enough to secure a private booth because the drugstore was almost empty of customers. A couple of women were in the rear browsing through hair products and a man was waiting at the drug counter for a prescription.

Charley Booth was a slender but well built kid, standing slightly over six-feet and weighing in at a little less than one hundred and seventy pounds. His sandy colored hair was cut short and his nose had a slight bend to it. McCall figured it had been whacked a few times on the football field. Charley also had blue eyes, good teeth and a ready smile.

Dan Thompson was a good two inches taller and forty pounds heavier than Charley. He had big hands and a muscular frame, which seemed to fit his short-cropped hair and dark eyes. He also had heavy eyebrows, sleepy eyes and a generally laid-back look that went well with his prominent nose, chin and forehead. McCall figured Dan was destined for major college football. He had that look about him, tough and sure.

McCall didn't waste any time. "Melanie Richards tells me you guys might help me with my investigation into Andy's death."

The two young men looked at each other, then Charley, who Melanie had said was Andy's best friend, spoke. "I...I'm not sure that we know anything, but we do know Andy wouldn't take drugs. We know he didn't kill himself."

"I agree," McCall said. "But if he didn't, who did...and why?"

Charley, who obviously was going to be the spokesman for the two, replied. "We don't know, but we do know Andy was going to speak out about a problem we have on the football team."

"What kind of problem?"

The two youths looked at each other, nervously, before Charley responded. "Steroids...a lot of the players are using them."

Such a revelation didn't surprise McCall. He had been impressed with the size of the Putnam team and suspected that some of the bigger players might be taking steroids. A lot of high school, college and pro players, he knew, were willing to accept the hazards of steroid use in trade for more bulk, strength, speed and endurance. Medical research had proven those hazards for men included greater risk of liver, prostrate and testicular cancer. An injured user might also not heal

Twenty Four

properly. Steroids could distort the immune system, which could result in a tumor.

"It's a little far-fetched to think someone would kill Andy because he was going to tell that they used steroids," McCall said. "Now if he was going to tell who's supplying them, well..."

"That's exactly what he was going to do...tell who's supplying them," Charley said.

"And who's that?"

"Coach Meyer."

TWENTY FIVE

Learning that Chuck Meyer was supplying steroids didn't surprise McCall. He had known a lot of guys like Meyer, coaches who were eaten up with the win at any cost syndrome. That a man like Meyer might be capable of murder certainly wasn't out of the question, especially if someone was about to upset his apple cart.

But he doubted it.

As to possibly being Scott's and Andy's killer, Meyer was at the bottom of McCall's suspect list. Why would he kill Jane Warrick? Of course, there was the possibility her death wasn't related to Scott's and Andy's.

But he doubted that, too.

Maybe Scott had stumbled onto something that linked Meyer to Andy's death. Maybe he had told Jane. Or, maybe even if he hadn't Meyer might have thought he had.

No, McCall thought, there were just too many maybes. The key,

Twenty Five

the reporter decided, might just be Meyer's source for steroids. *Or maybe I just want to tie Bob Mack into these murders so badly that I can't see the nose on my face.* He was quite aware that his subjective judgment often got in the way of the truth. *Well, not everyone can be as objective as Sherlock Holmes*, he thought.

Charley Booth and Dan Thompson claimed they had never used steroids, but peer pressure had been put on them to do so. They said Andy had refused to use steroids, too.

It was strange, McCall thought, that Scott Tyler had never mentioned that Andy was under such pressure. Surely, Andy would have told him. And why, under the circumstances, would Scott have failed to share that information? A father might have some blind spots where his only son was concerned, but Scott would have been proud that Andy had spurned the use of steroids. *He would have told me*, McCall thought.

There was, of course, the possibility Andy would have been afraid to tell his dad. Scott did have a temper. Maybe Andy was afraid his dad would do a little vigilante work on his own, maybe even kill Meyer. Scott had been capable of killing, though it wasn't something he had set out to do.

It's a possibility, McCall thought. *Andy didn't tell Scott, but Scott finds out after Andy's killed. He confronts Meyer and Meyer kills him. Nice bit of speculation, but probably no cigar. Well, it's nice to have the puke as a suspect. Even if he's not guilty of murder, I'll nail him for what he's doing to these kids.*

With what he knew, McCall figured he could push Meyer for some truth, whether it related to the murders or not. He wondered what he would do if Meyer told him Andy did use steroids, that he was hooked on them. That would, of course, explain Andy ingesting the crack and Novocain. There was some evidence that persons addicted to androgen anabolic steroids could not stop using them without experiencing withdrawal symptoms, depression and disabling fatigue. Steroid use could cause a person to become uncontrollably violent, paranoid and suicidal.

McCall had been told that Andy played football with reckless abandon. He preferred to think such motivation came from an attempt to emulate his father, not a drug. Steroids could, he knew, foster reck-

DEATH ANGEL

lessness. There were plenty of football coaches who preferred their players be uncontrollably violent, paranoid and suicidal. And that's the impression he had of Meyer, one that was substantiated by Charley Booth and Don Thompson.

Steroids usage was common, McCall understood, because it had become the macho thing to do, not just in high school, college and the pros, but in junior high as well. Kids saw steroids as an aid to being big man on campus, a college scholarship and eventually a big money pro career. Unlike high-profile drugs, steroids had become a quiet disease affecting more than a million athletes at all levels of competition.

I can't stop all the coaches in the country from dispensing steroids, he thought, *but I can darn sure make life a living hell for those who I know are doing it*. Meyer didn't know that his next meal in life was going to be a knuckle sandwich. And if he was Andy's and Scott's murderer, he might just have to digest it in the cemetery.

A little before six o'clock McCall drove to the GM dealership and took delivery on the Yukon. Celeste drove the Cadillac back to the motel and McCall followed in the new vehicle. Haloran and Dacus had returned from their afternoon of snooping, so they gathered in McCall's room to discuss what they had learned.

Dacus said, "Before we get started, I just want you to know how happy I am that you got yourself a four-wheel drive vehicle, McCall. Now maybe mine will get some peace."

Haloran laughed. "With what's going on here, I wouldn't get too happy just yet, Dacus. By the time this thing is over, there may not be anything left of McCall's new wheels."

"Okay, you clowns," McCall said, "let's not get emotional about machinery. I want to know what you learned today."

They all laughed and Haloran said, "You start, McCall. Let Dacus and me fill in."

It sounded like a right way to handle things, so the reporter gave a play-by-play of what he and Celeste had learned that afternoon. After he finished, the detective said, "Tough to get people around here to talk, but I've been around the block enough to know there's a real problem here. The kids you wanted me to talk to...well, they're not talking. After what you just said, I can see why. But I think it goes way beyond steroids.

Twenty Five

"I just started talking to anybody who would give me a listen and picked up pretty much what we already know. None of the cops, even the good ol' boys, are really trusted because Decker and Cherry are on the take...and everybody knows who's providing the take. The people know Mack's dirty, but that he controls the police and city government. Most people are willing to look the other way because of what his money does for the community. He's the fountainhead of charitable contributions in Putnam.

"I think just about everybody knows he's a dope dealer, but they don't want to admit it. They prefer to think he's involved in decent crime, something that doesn't offend their delicate sensibilities."

McCall laughed, then somberly asked, "What about Andy and Scott? Did the people you talked to believe they were suicides?"

"My impression is that they don't want to think about it."

"What about Dick Warrick...Jane?"

"The cop's death shook a few people up," the detective said, "but again...I don't think most of them wanted it brought to their attention. Some of the people I talked to hadn't even heard about Jane Warrick's death. Fact is...I heard about it kind of accidentally. But I will say you're going to have trouble making people here believe the coach is anything less than a saint. He puts a winner on the field and that's all the people care about."

Dacus agreed. "That's the impression I got, too. The coach kisses up to the black mamas so they're willing to provide their sons as cannon fodder. Scott Tyler...he was pretty popular in the black community, but most people have good things to say about Bob Mack, too. The man's been a supporter of minority businesses, so people tend to forgive him his other sins."

McCall sighed. "Mack's smart." He spreads money around pretty freely, but we're talking pennies compared to what he's taking in."

"These pennies you talk about are a lot to these people," Celeste said. "In fact, what Bob Mack considers pennies would be a lot to most of us."

The reporter knew she was making a good point, but he didn't have to like it. Mack had feathered his nest well, and it was going to be hard to bring him down. McCall had told himself that his primary focus was to find Scott's and Andy's killer, but even if Mack was not involved, he wanted to bring him down. That would be frosting on the cake.

Dacus, as was often the case, splashed him with reality. "McCall, all we picked up...Bill and me...are moods, attitudes, the way we perceive things to be. But we got squat for evidence about who killed Scott and Andy. And all you have are a couple of accusations against the coach that are probably going to be hard to prove. And even if the man is handing out steroids, that doesn't make him a killer."

"Sure, Dacus...I know we're thin on hard evidence," McCall said. "But maybe with a little luck I can scare Meyer into some kind of admission. He may not have killed Scott and Andy, but the clown knows more than he's telling."

Haloran warned, "You need to go easy, McCall. I think it's obvious that Decker and Cherry...and God knows who else around here...want you dead."

Dacus said, "And somebody from San Antonio. Probably Bob Mack, too."

"Be nice to be dealing with just one problem," the reporter said."

Haloran laughed. "You'd be bored stiff."

The Elite was suggested as a place for the evening meal, but Haloran squawked so much about it that they returned to the barbecue restaurant. They ate slowly, changed from red soda pop to Coke and speculated on all those who might have been involved in Scott's and Andy's deaths.

McCall was anxious to talk to Heather again, to ask her if Andy had talked to her about the coach. He kind of doubted it. Still, there was a mystery about the woman that he hadn't been able to solve and that bothered him. He wanted to understand what made her tick. But with Bob Mack back in town and a bodyguard shadowing her, it was going to be tough.

Returning to the motel, McCall parked the car then went to the office to confront Jay Sheldon. He wasn't there. A new clerk, a portly woman, told him Sheldon was dead. "When did it happen?" he asked.

The woman shrugged her shoulders. "I don't know...just heard about it myself. By the way, Tommy Caldwell wants you to call him at this number." She handed him a piece of paper with the number scrawled on it.

Twenty Five

McCall made the call from his room. He was past caring whether someone was listening in or not. Caldwell answered on the first ring. "Thanks for returning my call," the cop said.

"Where are you?"

"I'm at home. I didn't want to call you from the station."

"I can't guarantee this phone line isn't tapped."

"It doesn't matter," Caldwell said. "I'm fed up with what's going down around here...ready to help you clean it up if you'll take my help. Did you hear about Jay Sheldon being murdered."

"Just heard he was dead...figured it was murder. What's the story?"

"Identical with what happened to Jane Warrick...shot in the head, probably with a twenty-two."

"Favorite weapon of a hit man," McCall said.

"Who in the heck would put a contract out on Jane...and Jay? It doesn't make sense."

"No...it doesn't. But your guess on the contractor is as good as mine...probably better."

"McCall...tell me what to do. I'm ready to follow your lead."

"Just hang loose. How long can I reach you at this number."

"I'll be here until I go to work in the morning. But call anytime. I have an answering machine and I'll be checking in."

After McCall hung up, Celeste asked, "What was that all about?"

"I'm not sure."

"I take it you're suspicious of Tommy Caldwell."

He laughed. "I'm even suspicious of you."

They were sitting on the bed and she playfully whacked him with a pillow. That led to a wrestling match, which ended with some kissing. Then there was a knock at the door.

McCall asked, loudly, "Who is it?"

Haloran replied, "It's me...and Dacus."

Celeste straightened herself up and McCall went to the door. Haloran and Dacus stepped inside. Haloran offered an explanation. "It's still early and we're thirsty."

"You guys are experts when it comes to bad timing," McCall said.

"Sorry about that," Dacus said. This time he broke out the clean glasses, filled them with ice and poured them all a Diet Coke.

DEATH ANGEL

McCall laughed. "You do that well, homeboy."

"We know you're not settling in for the night. What's the game plan?"

"I don't know what you're talking about."

Haloran said, "I know that mind of yours. You're planning on going out again, aren't you?"

McCall shrugged. "I was considering going to a store to pick up some cookies...maybe some ice cream."

Haloran grinned. "And you were probably going to ask us to keep an eye on Celeste while you were gone. Am I right?"

"What's going on?" Celeste asked.

"Ask your friend here," the detective replied. "Do you think I didn't see the gray Ford tailing us, McCall? Who do you think it was...the hit man or the police?"

Celeste questioned, "You saw the hit man?"

"Can't be sure...but maybe," Dacus replied. "There was a guy in a gray Ford tailing us. We figured McCall here would be going out to check on the guy."

"You guys talk too much," McCall said. He hadn't wanted Celeste to know about the tail. He was going to pretend he was making a trip to the store, take care of business and come back. There was no reason for her to know.

Haloran grunted. "What were we supposed to do...tell Celeste about it after you got yourself killed?"

"Whoever it is...I can handle him," McCall said.

"Maybe," the detective said. "But with our help I know you can. What were you going to do, McCall, put on your Superman outfit and let the bullets bounce off your chest?"

McCall sipped his Coke, smiled and said, "Well, to tell you the truth...I was planning to lead the guy out of town, then spring a trap on him. The car's been following us all day. It's so plain it called attention to itself."

Haloran grumbled, "So, what were you going to do when you got the guy in this so-called trap of yours?"

"Reason with him," McCall said. "Heck, Bill, I've got the forty-five you brought me."

"I don't imagine he's carrying a water pistol," the detective said.

Twenty Five

"Now why don't you tell us about this plan of yours? If you really have one."

"I do. I've scouted the area...know a dead-end road that goes out into the woods just north of town. I plan to lead him down that road."

"What makes you think he'll follow?" Dacus asked.

"He's been following me everywhere else. He'll figure I'm going to meet someone...maybe want to know whom. Most likely, though...if he's the hit guy...he'll welcome the opportunity to get me in the woods where he can waste me with no witnesses."

"Okay, so he follows you down the road," Haloran said. "What then?"

"I get out of my car, double back and get behind him. The road's narrow. He'll have to back out."

"He could still run you down," Dacus said.

"I'm not planning on impersonating a speed bump. I'll take cover behind a tree. You've seen me shoot, Bill. What kind of chance do you think the clown has?"

Celeste, who had been listening intently, broke into the conversation. "All of you...you're making it sound like a game. You could be killed, Matt."

"No way."

Tears welled up in her eyes. "You can't say that for sure."

"He's apt to say anything," Haloran said. "But don't worry, Celeste...he'll have backup whether he wants it or not."

"It isn't your fight," McCall said.

Haloran laughed. "Why in the dickens are we here? Besides, I'm in fights almost every day that aren't of my making. Dacus and me are backing you and that's final. Now show us what you have in mind."

"Not just you and Dacus," Celeste said. "Me, too."

McCall argued, but it was three against one. Finally, he said, "Better if I just draw you a map."

After they had thoroughly discussed the plan, McCall said, "Give me a five minute head start. I'll stop at the convenience store, make like I'm calling someone, then head north. Tell you what...you guys just wait here and I'll call you."

"Sorry, McCall, but that little ploy ain't going to work with me," Haloran said. "Just fake your phone call. We're going to be where we

DEATH ANGEL

can see the puke in the gray car."

It was about nine o'clock when McCall got in the Yukon and drove away from the motel. He went directly to the convenience store and used the outside phone. He didn't, however, fake a call. He called Alicia, but Millie Stevens said she didn't expect her daughter home until the next day. The information troubled McCall, but he had too much on his mind to worry about it. He could see the gray car parked in the distance.

McCall was soon in the Yukon and rolling, the gray Ford in the distance. He didn't see the vehicle carrying Haloran, Celeste and Dacus, but that didn't surprise him. The detective was an expert in the fine art of tailing another car.

McCall figured that if it was the hit man in the gray car, he was probably a big city guy, unfamiliar with the country. That kind of guy couldn't be tricked into following him down a dead-end alley in a city, but he might not understand country roads. There was one way to find out.

A couple of miles out of town McCall turned right onto a dirt, sparsely graveled road that led past a country church on the left and a cemetery on the right. Then he doused his lights.

While on the highway he had kept tabs on the gray car's headlights in his rear view mirror. The driver was hanging back at a safe distance, probably unaware that he had been detected. *The guy might not know my background*, McCall thought. *Or, he might think I'm just another newspaper reporter, one who doesn't know much about setting someone up. Well, he's going to find out I know as much about that as he does. Maybe more.*

When the driver of the gray car turned onto the dirt road, he killed his lights, too. There was no problem driving without lights. A pale moon provided adequate lighting.

The road was really only wide enough for one car, with tall pines rising on each side of it. To let another car pass, coming from either direction, a driver would have to pull his vehicle off the road and onto what passed for a shoulder. The shoulder quickly became a shallow ditch, which was still slick and muddy from recent rains. With four-wheel drive, McCall knew he would have no trouble, but figured if the gray Ford got off the main tracks the driver would be in a world of

Twenty Five

trouble.

When doing his scouting, McCall had found there was a turnaround by a creek. He didn't plan to lead his quarry that far.

The man in the gray car was staying back at a safe distance, to the point where McCall couldn't see the vehicle by the light of the moon. It would have been difficult to see even if the car had been close, given the irregular shadows caused by the tall trees.

After taking a curve in the road, McCall cut the engine of the Yukon and let it glide to a stop. He didn't use the brakes, because the brake lights would have alerted the person following him. He had earlier fixed the vehicle's interior lighting so it wouldn't come on when he opened the door.

McCall exited the Yukon, hurried off the road, into the trees, and headed back in the direction from which he had come. He traveled only a short distance, taking cover where he could still see his vehicle.

He felt a bit uncomfortable in street clothes. He hadn't changed to his boots and camo gear because he thought it might give the wrong signal to whoever was following him.

Ever so slowly, the gray car eased passed him. Once it was past his hiding place he stalked it, moving behind it in a crouching manner.

Then the driver saw the Yukon blocking the road and knew he had been had. He braked to a stop and put the car in reverse, activating the backup lights. That's when he first saw McCall standing in the middle of the road, the forty-five at the ready position.

There was panic in the way the man accelerated in reverse. Maybe he was trying to hit McCall, and maybe it was from suddenly seeing another vehicle's headlights coming up behind him. Whatever the reason, the gray car careened backward until a rear and front wheel ended up in a ditch.

In the mud.

The driver slammed the accelerator to the floor and the engine unleashed all its horses. The wheels whined and the car lurched out of the ditch, now going forward. But it simply rammed into the ditch on the opposite side of the road.

The driver had no alternative but to get out. The door opened on the driver's side, but that was a diversion. He crawled out on the passenger side, firing wildly in McCall's direction, did a roll and disappeared into the darkness of the timber.

McCall didn't shoot. He wanted the man alive, wanted to know who sent him. Dacus had pulled his Yukon to a stop and cut the lights. Then he, Haloran and Celeste got out, using the vehicle as cover.

"I'm going after him," McCall said. "The three of you wait here...and be careful."

"One of us better go with you," Haloran said.

"No...stay here. Things can get hairy out there in the dark. I don't want to shoot the wrong person."

The detective grumbled, "I wouldn't want you to."

"I'd like to take him alive."

"I wish you wouldn't go after him alone," Celeste said.

"Believe me...it's best if I do."

She didn't argue. She seemed confident he could handle the situation. She had seen him in action before. When she had been held captive by terrorists, he had rescued her when the odds were seemingly all against him. That's how her mind was working, even though there was deep worry. Chances were good that the man in the dark was a trained assassin, and no one was exempt from a bullet.

McCall had his big Bowie knife, an awesome weapon and the forty-five. He handed his sport coat to Celeste and disappeared into the darkness.

Everything had happened in seconds, so McCall knew the hit man hadn't gone far. He figured the man would take cover and wait, since he didn't know the terrain.

The woods were quiet, as still and peaceful as some of those beautiful but deadly nights he had spent in various jungles. Peacefulness and beauty had never deceived him. He knew in a split second it could all erupt into violence. He knew death could come as quickly as a twig or leaf making the slightest noise beneath his shoe.

There was a way to move in the woods, a way to be as one with nature. It was something McCall had been taught from youth, a knowledge that had served him well in the jungle. So he moved with that kind of deadly precision, his ears attuned to the quiet, hearing even the descent of a leaf from a tree.

His movement came to an abrupt halt at the sound of breathing. It was nothing more than normal breathing, but he could hear it, sense

Twenty Five

it, even feel it. The enemy was close, and in a second he had him located.

The man was unaware of McCall's presence. He had his gun at the ready, waiting for his pursuer. *City guy*, McCall thought. *He might be great in an asphalt alley, but doesn't know a thing about the woods.*

Though he wanted the man alive, McCall wasn't about to jeopardize his own life to achieve that end. He could have jumped the man, tried to wrestle the gun away from him, but decided on a different approach. He became as one with the ground.

The assassin never saw McCall until he seemed to explode from the wet leaves and brush, the big knife slashing the wrist of the man's gun hand and sending the weapon flying into the underbrush. The hit man fell backward, his scream of pain resounding through the timber.

In an attempt to follow up on his advantage, McCall's feet slipped and he fell. He rolled defensively, his trained eyes piercing the darkness and shadows to pick up the assassin reaching for a gun in an ankle holster.

There was no choice. He couldn't risk trying to reach the man before he got his gun working. So, before the man could get off a shot McCall's forty-five bellowed twice. One slug got the would-be assassin in the chest. He caught the other in his forehead.

TWENTY SIX

By late Saturday night McCall had a fix on the dead hit man and was relatively sure he knew who had sent him. The ID in the man's wallet was phony, of course, but he was carrying a motel key. He was staying at the same motel as McCall.

A search of his room revealed an interesting phone number, which was scrawled on a piece of paper in a hidden compartment of his luggage. Haloran checked the number and discovered it belonged to Reggie Smith, the public relations flak for Congressman Bob Bright.

"I have an article about Bright in the paper tomorrow morning that's not very complimentary, but I can't believe he had have me hit for it," McCall said.

"How would he know it's not complimentary until it comes out?" Celeste asked.

McCall chuckled. "Are you kidding? Turnip and Katie probably gave him a copy the minute I turned it in...after doing their best to get

Twenty Six

it changed."

"What I can't believe is the dumb brother Bright's got working for him," Dacus said. "Why would he be stupid enough to arrange the hit...and to give the man his phone number?"

"It's got to be a lot of things...not just one article," Haloran said. "And there may be some other reason for the guy to have Reggie's phone number."

"I agree," McCall said. "It's hard for me to figure that weenie Reggie as the hit man's contact. And Bright could have arranged something like this without it being traceable to anyone around him, especially a lamebrain like Reggie. He could have had Bob Mack handle it for him. From what I saw in Mack's safe, they're connected."

"Maybe the congressman didn't know you were going to be in Putnam when he had the hit arranged," Celeste said. "But maybe he wouldn't have asked Mack's help anyway. That would be something else Mack could hold over his head."

McCall nodded. "Good point."

"When are we going to be able to see what you photographed in Mack's safe?" Haloran asked.

"I developed the film last night. I always carry my little enlarger and some chemicals in the car. I'll black out the bathroom and do some prints in a little while."

"There's something about the hit man we haven't discussed," Haloran said.

Dacus asked, "What's that?"

"Where's the guy from?" Haloran asked. "From the phony ID to the other stuff we found in his room, what nationality do you think the guy was?"

"My guess is Nicaraguan, which is also strange," McCall replied. "Why would Bright...or Reggie for that matter...choose a Nicaraguan? I figured the hitter would be some big city guy."

Haloran laughed. "Hey, I'm just a dumb detective. You're supposed to be the great investigative journalist."

McCall grinned. "Well, flat foot, just give me a chance to investigate."

It was after midnight early Sunday morning before McCall had prints of the documents he had photographed in Bob Mack's house.

DEATH ANGEL

Haloran, Dacus and Celeste were too intrigued by what had and was happening to even think about sleep. Dacus and Haloran alternated in going to the motel office to bring back steaming cups of coffee.

The prints revealed a lot. Bright and several other congressmen and senators were regular recipients of payments from Bob Mack and the organization of which he was a part. The prints weren't pretty pictures, but were indicators of how American taxpayers were being sold out by some of their elected officials.

After they had reviewed the pictures, McCall called Arnold and told him to get to Putnam. The Ol' Man's aide didn't even complain about being roused from a sound slumber. He just agreed to be in Putnam as fast as a company plane could get him there from Virginia. Fortunately, because of Mack, the local airport could accommodate a Falcon jet.

By eight on Sunday morning, Arnold was in McCall's room. Dacus picked him and two operatives up at the airport. Dacus, Haloran and the two operatives drove to the wooded area where the hit man's body was located. The two operatives bagged it. They then had Dacus drive them to the plane and they loaded it aboard. Arnold wanted to take the body back to Virginia.

Dacus drove back to the motel and gave the keys to his Yukon to one of the operatives. The two men, along with the pilot and copilot, wanted to get some breakfast.

"No need in reporting what happened to the local authorities," Arnold told McCall. "We'll take care of everything."

That bothered Haloran, but he didn't say anything. Maybe it was best, he thought, and it was not in his jurisdiction. Still, when dealing with some of the people with whom McCall worked, he often had questions. He figured, of course, that they were CIA, but he had difficulty understanding the way that they operated.

After Arnold reviewed the pictures, he suggested they all go to breakfast. They went in McCall's new vehicle and found a place that served biscuits and gravy. That, for Haloran, made up for a lot of things.

It was quiet in the restaurant, only a few patrons. McCall figured most people were at church, or getting ready to go. Whatever the reason for the dearth of customers, McCall was grateful. It gave them a

Twenty Six

chance to talk seriously, stopping only when the waitress came by regularly to refill their coffee cups.

Arnold said, "McCall, these prints of the contents of Bob Mack's safe...you've come up with stuff we've been needing for a long time. The Ol' Man's going to be grateful."

"What we have here...if I'm reading it right," McCall said, "are a dozen congressmen and senators on Bob Mack's payroll. These guys have been sympathetic to leftists in Central America and every group of terrorists in the world.

"But Bob's kind of like me...he's apolitical. His only interest is money. He exports weapons and imports drugs...and he doesn't care who he deals with...U.S. friends or foes...as long as he makes a buck. And you know what? That makes me think Bob's a heckuva lot more honest than any of these politicians. You at least know where he's coming from.

"Now the funny thing is that these politicians on his payroll are the ones who holler loudest that the CIA is running guns and importing dope."

Arnold laughed. "I won't deny that we support forces friendly to this country. But we don't smuggle dope."

"You don't have to convince me," McCall said. "I know how the Ol' Man feels about drugs. He used to think there was a Communist conspiracy to get every American hooked. Then the liberals would have been able to let the Communists waltz in and take over the country without firing a shot. Now about the only place you can find a Communist is on a college campus, which again proves that education is about twenty years behind the times."

"Don't you think that's a little simplistic?" Celeste asked.

McCall laughed. "The Ol' Man's that way at times. I remember when he talked about shipping cigarettes to this country's enemies free of charge...as many as they would take. He figured it might take longer, but that cigarettes could kill more people than an army."

They all laughed and Celeste said, "It's hard to argue with that kind of logic. And there's no doubt that drugs have weakened our country...a lot."

"Yeah," McCall said, "but we can't blame the Communists. We have ourselves to blame for letting scum like Bob Mack and other drug

DEATH ANGEL

dealers walk around free as birds."

Arnold changed the conversation's flow. "What happened here, I think, is that McCall caused Bob Bright to panic for some reason. I doubt Bob Mack knew, or would have approved, of a hit on McCall. I sure don't think he would have wanted him hit in the town where he's chosen to live. I think that if Bob Mack even hears about the attempted hit on McCall, without his approval, Bob Bright's going to have some tough questions to answer."

"I can't be absolutely sure Bright ordered the hit," McCall said. "There are quite a few people who would like to see me dead."

Haloran laughed. "Oh, really. That's real hard to believe, you being the sweet guy that you are."

Celeste asked, "With what you have on Bob Bright and Bob Mack, won't they be going to jail?"

"I wish it was that simple," Arnold replied. "The evidence McCall got was obtained illegally. The court won't allow us to use it to convict these clowns, but we can use it in a different way. We know who to watch...what they're doing. With a little manipulation we can work things to where these people end up working for us without even knowing it."

"Yeah," McCall said, "or you've got enough info on each of them to get them killed if they don't cooperate."

Arnold shrugged. "That's true. What I'd like, though, is a pledge of secrecy from each of you regarding this information. I can't demand it, but it's important."

The reporter looked at his companions and they nodded agreement. It was not, after all, the kind of information you shared with a neighbor. It was the kind of stuff most people wouldn't believe anyway.

"As for you, McCall...I hope you'll back off Bob Bright and Bob Mack and let the Agency handle things."

"Sorry, Arnold, but I'm not in the habit of letting people who try to kill me off the hook. Bob Mack...he's slime. But I agree with you that he doesn't want me killed in his adopted hometown. But Bright...I have to deal with that. If he sent this last guy, he'll probably send someone else."

Arnold nodded understanding. "Well, if you can see your way clear to leaving him alone...we sure can use him."

Twenty Six

"I'll think about it."

Arnold left shortly after breakfast, taking McCall's prints with him. The reporter kept the negatives. Celeste, Haloran and Dacus left about one in the afternoon. She wanted to stay, say to heck with her job, but he insisted she drive the Cadillac back to San Antonio.

"You've done all you can do here," Celeste said.

"I haven't caught Andy's and Scott's killer. When I do, I'll be heading back. It won't be much longer."

"If Reggie Smith's in San Antonio, you want me to look him up?" Dacus asked.

"I'll take care of Reggie...whether he's in San Antonio or Washington. He'll keep."

When they left, Celeste and the Cadillac were sandwiched between his trusted friends. Dacus was leading in his Yukon and Haloran following in his old car. McCall had suggested the convoy be set up that way for Celeste's protection, but hadn't told her. She didn't like his mothering.

After a few minutes he called Alicia, but her mother said she was still gone. "I don't mean to pry, Millie, but would you mind telling me where she is?"

"She went to Beaumont...to visit a friend. I expect her back late tonight."

He thought it strange that she hadn't told him about any plans to leave town. Well, he decided, she was a woman and he had yet to find one who was predictable.

There was a lot he could have done, but he was tired. It had been another long night without sleep, but at least one worry had been put to rest. Maybe another hit man would be hired to take him out, but for the moment he was relatively sure no one knew he had taken out the first guy. There was, of course, the possibility that the dead man had a partner. It was not something he wanted to think about for the moment.

He tuned the TV to an NFL game, took off his clothes and laid down to watch with his head resting on a couple of stacked pillows. The AC was on high. He loved to watch pro football, but unless the game was exciting, it often put him to sleep. He was hoping for a boring game.

DEATH ANGEL

Lying there in the semi-darkness, the drapes drawn, it occurred to him that his friends had caught only snatches of sleep during the night. He worried about Celeste, but decided Haloran would make enough coffee stops that everyone would be okay.

The game was truly boring, but his mind wouldn't rest. He had to corner Coach Chuck Meyer, find out if he was responsible for Andy's and Scott's deaths. And how were the murders of Jane and Dick Warrick connected to Andy's and Scott's?

Why was Alicia in Beaumont? And why was Heather such a cardboard figure in the entire scenario, a woman seemingly devoid of feelings in some areas? At times she seemed like a cold fish, selfish and uncaring. The closest thing to genuine emotion he had witnessed on her part was the obvious jealousy she felt toward Alicia.

Could Tommy Caldwell be trusted? And where did Barry Travis, the district attorney, really fit in the total scheme of things? For that matter, where did Bob Mack fit?

He was pretty sure Bob Mack didn't want him killed in Putnam. Did that mean Mack didn't want others killed in his adopted hometown? What about Jane and her husband? Maybe Mack killed people in Putnam only when it was absolutely necessary.

Mack pulled the strings on Decker and Cherry, and McCall knew they could have tried to kill him at any time. But they hadn't. They had opted to try to run him out of town even when he was sure they would have preferred to kill him. That had to be Bob Mack's doing.

McCall finally fell asleep, but not for long. At a little after six, the phone started ringing. He answered and a voice said, "McCall, this is Bob Mack. I need to see you."

TWENTY SEVEN

Mack wanted McCall to come to his house, but the reporter figured that would put him at too much of a disadvantage. He agreed, instead, to meet Mack at the Elite, which he thought, was disadvantage enough.

Their meeting was scheduled for seven p.m., which gave McCall a chance to shower, shave and get into some fresh threads. He decided not to wear a tie.

Mack was already at the restaurant when McCall arrived; sitting at what the reporter guessed was his special table. A couple of his bozo bodyguards were occupying a nearby table.

"Sit, McCall," Mack said in what passed for a commanding voice. It made the reporter hesitate before taking a chair. Mack tried to cover his earlier tone of voice with a laugh. "Hey, lighten up, McCall. This is a friendly meeting. You had dinner yet?"

"No...I haven't."

"The lemon veal and pasta...it's great. Take my word for it."

DEATH ANGEL

McCall didn't respond immediately. He checked the menu that was already on the table and a waitress suddenly appeared. She reminded him of Jane Warrick. The last time he had seen her was at the restaurant. "I'll have a porterhouse steak, medium, baked potato and green salad."

A momentary frown crossed Mack's face. "I took the liberty of ordering a bottle of wine, McCall. I hope you like it."

"Thanks, but I'll have a Diet Coke. I don't drink."

When the waitress was out of earshot, Mack said, "You should've taken my advice on the veal."

"I don't take advice very well."

Mack laughed. "I've noticed that."

McCall noticed that Mack's accent was different than it had been on previous encounters. He was speaking with a clipped accent, like an actor trying to emulate an East Coast gangster. So the reporter asked, "Where did your slow, down home accent go?"

Mack shrugged and laughed again. "There's no point in me trying to jive you, McCall. I know you've had me checked out from here to Sunday."

"You've got that right. You prefer I call you Bob or Roberto?"

"Bob's fine."

"Well, Bob...let's dispense with the courtesies and get on with what you have on your mind. Why did you want to see me?"

Mack sipped some wine, then his face clouded with seriousness. "You know who I am...what I am, so you might have trouble believing anything I say. But on my mother's grave, I didn't have anything to do with Andy's or Scott's deaths."

"Why are you trying to convince me?"

"'Because you're so tenacious, jerk...a man who never gives up. I've had you checked out, too, McCall. And hey, I admire a man who bites down on something and won't let go."

"Bob, I don't care if you admire me or not. There's not one thing about you that I admire."

Mack's lips curved slightly in what passed for a smile and his head bobbed up and down in what passed for agreement. McCall thought he looked like a rattlesnake ready to strike. "Okay...so we're not going to be buddies," Mack said. "But I don't like all this stuff that's going

Twenty Seven

down in my backyard. You can believe it or not, but I really cared about Andy."

"Is that why you had the cops here rule his death a suicide? You're not the Hallmark card type, Bob?"

"I'll find out who killed Andy...and I'll take care of him."

"You should have told Scott that. If you had, he might still be alive."

"You think I cared a lick about Scott Tyler? Good riddance as far as I'm concerned. But I figure the same guy did both of them."

"You're suggesting then that I go back to San Antonio and leave Scott's and Andy's killer to you?"

"Be best for all concerned."

"Forget it, Bob."

Mack's face crimsoned. "I don't know why..."

"I said...forget it."

"I've killed men that didn't do what I asked them to do. And I've asked you real nice."

"I'm not interested in niceties, Bob. And threats don't set too well with me, either. But if you get too stupid and call on your goons to help carry out your little threat, I've got a forty-five loaded with hollow points aimed at your guts. That is...if you have any. And I'd like nothing better than blowing you away. I don't care for drug dealers...never have."

The waitress temporarily defused the situation when she brought McCall's Diet Coke. The reporter raised his glass in toast fashion, with his left hand, and said, "Here's to me catching Scott's and Andy's killer."

Mack chuckled, uneasily. "I was told you were crazy, McCall."

"You had a good source, Bob."

"CIA, weren't you...Southeast Asia, Middle East, Central and South America?"

McCall shrugged. "Ask your source."

"Why did you go into the newspaper game?"

"Ask the guy who told you the other stuff about me...the one who told you I was crazy."

"Just curious. I know you don't need money."

"Everybody needs money, Bob. But money's not everything."

"That's where you're wrong. There's nothing money can't buy."

DEATH ANGEL

"You're looking across the table at someone money can't buy."

"Maybe not. But I can hire someone to put your lights out...permanently."

"How about you trying it, Bob? I heard you used to be pretty good. Or did you tie up your victims and shoot them in the head?"

Mack responded, angrily, "I'm still good."

"If you're so good, Bob," McCall taunted, "why did you send your three stooges after me with baseball bats? Why didn't you come yourself?"

"I admit, that was a mistake. That was before I knew who you were. I thought the boys could scare you...make you leave town."

"And then you had your police chief and his cronies lean on me," McCall said.

"That's where you're wrong. You must have just made them mad. They knew I wanted you out of town, sure...but I didn't give them any direct orders to beat up on you. They know I wanted you out of town alive. That's why I'm curious about the bomb...about Burt being blown to pieces."

McCall laughed. "The bomb was probably compliments of your pal...Congressman Bob Bright."

Mack's eyes couldn't hide his surprise, the fact that McCall knew about his connection with the congressman. "What makes you think I know this guy Bright?"

"C'mon, Bob...he's on your payroll...along with eleven other legislators."

"I don't know where you would get that kind of information, McCall...but it's wrong. I don't have any congressmen and senators on my payroll."

The reporter realized he was playing a dangerous game, but counted on it working to his advantage. He knew Arnold would be ready for any moves by the legislators and their benefactor. He also liked that Mack was a bit shaken that he knew so much about his clandestine business. Mack would figure there was a mole, an informant in his organization. There would be a purge and someone would die, but McCall wasn't going to get teary-eyed about one gangster killing another.

He wasn't worried about Heather. She had showed him the loca-

Twenty Seven

tion of husband's safe, but didn't know how to open it. Mack wouldn't suspect her.

"Okay, Bob...let's say you don't know Bright. If that's the way you want to play it, fine with me. But I figure he's the one who sent a hit man to kill me."

"Why would he do that?"

Mack, McCall knew, didn't like what he was hearing. If Bright were responsible for the hit man, Mack would be on him like ugly on an ape. He would be angry that the congressman had bypassed him, especially in his town.

"You probably won't believe this, but I probably get on the congressman's nerves more than I get on yours."

Mack chuckled, again nervously. "You're a cocky jerk...I'll give you that. So what happened to this hit man?"

"Accident. A shame, too. I don't think he had been in the country all that long...probably hadn't had time to taste the good life. He was from Central America. I figure he might have had something to do with your drug connections down there."

"What makes you think I have drug connections down there?"

"Bob, Bob...a lot of people know you run guns down there, drugs from there to here."

"If these people know so much, why don't they arrest me?"

"Oh, I don't think you'll ever be arrested Bob. I think you'll have an accident. The people I'm talking about...they don't want to waste taxpayer money on a trial."

Mack's face paled. "The CIA...you're talking about the CIA."

"Am I?"

"You're full of it, McCall...if you think you can scare me. If I've got these congressmen in my pocket like you say, what makes you think I don't have the head honchos from the CIA?"

McCall laughed. "You may have some people in your pocket who say they're with the CIA. Many people claim to be...few are. Liberal scumbags all over the place conspire to discredit the CIA, but if you're putting bucks into people who claim to be inside the real Agency, you're wasting your money. You're a little like the guy who paid a billion for a Stealth Bomber and figured he got his money's worth because he couldn't see it."

DEATH ANGEL

He could tell the conversation was bothering Mack. "Like I said, you can't scare me, McCall."

"I didn't think I could, slimeball. But then, I haven't been trying. You're the one who's been trying to scare me, which you have to admit is pretty childish."

"Okay, I can't scare you and you can't scare me. Where does that leave us, McCall?"

The waitress showed up with their salads and McCall said, "It leaves me hungry. I'm going to have my salad and steak."

After the waitress was out of earshot, Mack said, "We can work this out, McCall. We're both after the same thing."

The reporter gave his adversary his best incredulous look. "After the same thing? Who do you think you're kidding, Bob? You're embarrassed that people have been murdered without your blessing in what you think is your town. My interest is in bringing Scott's and Andy's killer to justice. And, if opportunity presents, I'll blow up your little empire in the process. I'd just as soon swim in a sewer as work with people who deal drugs."

Mack grunted. "You're a self-righteous jerk, a real Boy Scout...and I think you're trying to provoke me. Just remember that my guys can nail you in a split-second if I give the word."

"Just remember what I have under my napkin. And what I promised."

"I think you're bluffing."

"Are you willing to call my hand?"

The waitress brought their entrees and removed the salad plates. Mack quipped, "How you going to cut your steak and keep a finger on the trigger, McCall?"

The reporter laughed. "What makes you think I need a finger? Your source told you I was formerly with the CIA. You must know the Agency has all kinds of strange weapons to kill a man with."

"You're crazy...you know that? You're just liable to end up hanging on a meat hook."

"I'll be careful. And you might want to heed your own advice. I happen to know there are people in your organization that wouldn't grieve if you were to have an accident. Bon appétit, Bob."

McCall, of course, personally knew of no one in Mack's organi-

Twenty Seven

zation that wanted him dead. But he knew the gangster mentality, was sure there were at least a few guys associated with Mack who liked the idea. Mack knew it, too, and didn't appreciate the reminder. He learned over dinner that playing mind games with McCall wasn't any fun.

TWENTY EIGHT

It was about nine o'clock when McCall left the restaurant and drove back to the motel. Alicia was waiting in her car. "Been waiting long?"

"About thirty minutes."

"Sorry...I would have called you."

"Mother said you had. She said you seemed to be worried about me."

"I guess I was. With all that's been happening, there's reason to worry."

"I was in Beaumont."

"That's what your mother said."

"Aren't you going to ask me why?" she asked.

"Why what?"

"Why I was in Beaumont."

McCall shrugged. "I don't figure it's any of my business...unless you want to tell me."

Twenty Eight

She laughed a bit nervously. "I'll bet a lot of people wish you weren't curious about them."

"I didn't say I wasn't curious. It's just that people I care about...well, I cut them more slack than I would a suspect."

"I'm relieved that I'm not a suspect...and I'm glad you care about me. I'd just like to know how much you care."

He didn't like the question, knew where it might be leading. "I can't answer that. I don't know what kind of measurement I'm supposed to use."

"Do you love me?"

Now it was his turn to laugh nervously. "Love? That's always been a tough word for me. I'm not sure I understand the meaning, though I did think I was in love once."

"What happened?"

"She was murdered...with a bomb meant for me."

"I'm sorry."

He shrugged and she continued. "And you think you loved her?"

"To tell the truth, I've thought more about it since she was killed than before. Maybe it's guilt, not love. I don't know."

"Would I have to be killed for you to know whether you love me or not?"

"That's an unanswerable question?"

"You're right...it is. But in the short time I've known you, you've played havoc with my emotions, Matt McCall."

"You're right about it being a short time, which is probably why we shouldn't be having this conversation. And my emotional state has never been all that steady."

"What does time have to do with anything? And you not being steady...I'm not buying it. I think you're capable of turning your emotions on and off like a faucet."

"Where's all this leading, Alicia?"

"You won't ask me why I went to Beaumont, but I'm going to tell you anyway. There's a man there who says he loves me. He's been saying it for a long time. After meeting you, I had to go there to try to understand how I feel about you."

Well I'll be, McCall thought. Here he had been comparing Alicia with Celeste and Heather, and she had been out comparing him with

DEATH ANGEL

another guy.

"So, did you come to some sort of understanding with yourself?"

"I think I'm in love with you...and it scares the dickens out of me."

"It should. I'm really not worthy of your love, Alicia."

"That's a crock...and you know it."

"Whatever...I don't think it's a good idea for anyone to be in love with me. That is, if they're sure they know what love is. Alicia, we've only known each other a few days."

"I know. But like I tried to say earlier in this stupid conversation, what does time have to do with it? I guess I'm romantic enough to believe in love at first sight. Maybe I'm wrong, but I think you're just afraid to reveal your real feelings and emotions."

He shrugged. "You're probably right."

"You don't have to agree with me."

He laughed, though there was no humor in it. "Look, Alicia, you're a beautiful and desirable woman. And any man who wasn't a tad off center would tell you any lie you wanted to hear. I just happen to be one of those off center guys. I'm not going to lie to you. There are things I just can't say now. Maybe I'll never be able to say them."

She said nothing as tears welled up in her eyes. When she did speak her voice was almost a whisper and, he thought, a little over-dramatic, as if she had been rehearsing. "You may not love me tomorrow, but will you please make love to me tonight?"

"You're going to really think I'm more than a tad off center, but I can't."

TWENTY NINE

At ten o'clock Monday morning, Congressman Bob Bright was in Clark Ramsey's office. It was an unscheduled visit. After the usual greetings, and after Ramsey's secretary had brought them coffee, the district attorney said, "I'm surprised, Bob. I thought you were in Washington."

"I flew in this morning. Something came up that I thought I should talk to you about."

The visit and statement made Ramsey nervous. He was still fearful that the party might bypass support of him as a gubernatorial candidate, and Bright would probably be the bearer of such bad tidings. "What's so important that you'd make such as early flight from Washington?"

"You remember our recent talk about Matt McCall, Clark?"

"Yes...of course. I thought the article he wrote about you that was in yesterday's paper was garbage."

Bright sighed. "I'll survive it. But it's not the article I want to talk

DEATH ANGEL

about."

"Well, you know you'll always have my support, Bob."

"Yes...and I'm appreciative. Is your office clean? No bugs?"

"My security people swept it this morning."

"Well, you can't be too careful, Clark."

"I agree."

"What I wanted to tell you was that a man tried to kill Matt McCall Saturday night."

A chill ran up Ramsey's spine. He recalled the recent conversation with the congressman, how Bright had said it would be necessary to take care of McCall. " You said tried."

"McCall's alive. The would-be assassin's dead."

"I could call the police department in Putnam to find out what happened."

"They don't know anything," Bright said. "A friend of mine called, told me he had already checked with the police. My guess is that some of McCall's CIA friends were involved in protecting him. Or maybe that local cop."

"Bill Haloran?"

"Yeah...he's the one."

"Interesting," the district attorney said, "but it shouldn't create any problems for you, Bob. After all, it wasn't you who tried to kill McCall."

The congressman's eyes locked with Ramsey's and a look of understanding passed between them. "That's right, Clark...it wasn't me. It may have been someone close to me, though...someone who thought they were helping me. But I'm afraid McCall might think it was me."

"You're right to be a little nervous about it, Bob. The man tends to go off half-cocked. But who do you think who's close to you might have been involved?"

Bright sighed. "Maybe Reggie. He's so loyal to me he might have hired someone to kill McCall."

"Well, I know you appreciate that kind of loyalty...but it can be dangerous."

"I agree. This friend in Putnam, the one who told me about someone trying to kill McCall...he tells me I need to get rid of Reggie.

Twenty Nine

But I really hate to fire him."

"Sure you do, but sometimes you don't have a choice in matters like this. Besides, Reggie being black and all...we can find a good spot for him. There are lots of people in the party looking for a black public relations person."

"You're right, Clark. I don't see a problem at all on that score. And by the way, this friend in Putnam...I want you to meet him, get to know him. He can be a big financial help when you're running for governor."

"Who is he?"

"Bob Mack. He's a businessman...owns restaurants, makes investments."

"I'd like to meet him."

"It'll be arranged."

"About this McCall thing, though. What can I do to help?"

"I'm not sure," Bright said. "I just wanted to come down here for a couple of days...maybe talk to you about your plans. I left Reggie in Washington."

"You might want to tell him to stay clear of here, especially when McCall comes back to town."

"I don't think he's safe in Washington, either. I'm beginning to believe all those stories about McCall."

Ramsey had no trouble understanding Bright's paranoia. He had suffered McCall phobia for a long time. "Any chance of Reggie taking a long trip until things cool down?"

"Bob Mack suggested that. It's probably a good idea. I'm sure Bob Mack can arrange it."

Ramsey nodded and Bright continued. "Let's spend some time together the next couple of days, Clark. I think I can give you some insights that'll help you politically."

"I'm sure you can, Bob. I'll clear my calendar...make myself available for as long as you want my ear."

"I guarantee you...our time together will be beneficial. Let's call Turner Sipe and Katie Hussey...see if they can have lunch with us. They can give us some media input for your run as governor."

"Good idea."

"Tell me, Clark...honestly now, have you ever had any sort of

DEATH ANGEL

relationship with Katie?"

The district attorney laughed. "No...I honestly haven't. Why do you ask?"

Bright grinned. "Well, I was just wondering. I was thinking about inviting her out tonight, getting to know her more intimately. I already have a young woman in Washington who's costing me plenty, but it wouldn't hurt to have one staked out here. I don't figure Katie would cost me anything."

Ramsey couldn't understand anyone being interested in Katie, but figured to each his own. "I don't figure you'll have to spend a dime that you don't want to, Bob. Katie likes power...and you've got that."

"I heard she's been seeing Ed Parkham," Bright said, forgetting he had already discussed the situation with Ramsey. "Turner told me that."

"She had to...to get where she is at the paper. But I don't think she'll turn you down. I'm sure of it."

"Good. I'm not used to being turned down."

They met Katie and Sipe at a Mexican restaurant on the River Walk at eleven forty-five. Being close to the congressman and district attorney, Katie was in hog heaven. Ramsey again wondered what Bright saw in her.

He knew the congressman had a large home on the outskirts of San Antonio and another in Virginia where his wife was currently residing. He also kept a hotel suite in downtown San Antonio, which is where Ramsey figured the congressman would take Katie. From what Bright had told him, he figured he was also paying for an apartment in Washington for a young mistress. Ramsey didn't even question where Bright got the money for such extravagance. He figured it was the way an important legislator was supposed to live – money, power and women. As for himself, he had plenty of money and would get more as he climbed the party ladder. It was power he craved, more power than being district attorney offered.

There was no doubt in Ramsey's mind that Bright had orchestrated the failed hit on McCall, but he tried to purge that kind of thinking. It had to be Reggie Smith. *Besides,* he thought, *what's the harm in sacrificing a nigger or two?*

THIRTY

Coach Chuck Meyer was an early riser, but one who did more than simply drink coffee and take his daily constitutional. He got up at five a.m., drove to the high school and then began his regimen by running three miles on the track that circled the football field. He allowed himself twenty minutes for the run, though it never took that long. He didn't time himself because he saw no need to run against the clock. It was just part of his routine to stay in good shape.

Meyer then spent thirty minutes in the school's weight room, utilizing the equipment most beneficial for upper body strength and keeping his gut in check. He figured he had a pretty good body.

After his exercise program, Meyer normally went to a small restaurant near the school for breakfast. It was a freebie because the owner was a rabid supporter of the school's football program.

Monday started like any typical weekday for the coach. He got up at the usual time, went to the track and did his running, then went

DEATH ANGEL

to the fieldhouse where the weight room was located. Matt McCall was blocking the door, leaning against it and drinking coffee from a Styrofoam cup.

"What are you doing here, Mr. McCall? How did you know I was here?"

"A lot of people know your routine, coach, which could cause you a world of problems if someone was after you."

"Well, nobody is...so what do you want? I need to finish my workout, shower and go to breakfast."

"Maybe I'll join you. For breakfast...not a shower."

"Maybe you're not invited."

McCall laughed. "You've got an attitude problem, coachie pooh."

Meyer grumbled, "Well, I didn't like some of the stuff you said when you were in my office the other day. The more I've thought about it, the madder it's made me."

"Anger's not good for the heart."

"I don't have to take anything from you, McCall. You may've been a stud football player in your day...I'll give you that. But now you're not anything."

"Chuck, I was hoping we could be friends...that you would be someone I could talk to. You've got to be the most articulate person in Putnam."

Meyer snarled and inserted a key in the door. His intention was to enter quickly and slam the door on McCall, but the reporter pushed in right behind him. His quick move frustrated and angered the coach. "Get out of here, McCall."

"Or what?"

"Or I may just kick you out."

"You're welcome to try."

Meyer sized up his opponent. He figured he was much stronger than the reporter. He knew he was younger and bigger. So why was this guy challenging him? "I don't want to hurt you, McCall."

The reporter laughed. "You've already hurt my feelings, Chuck...by saying you don't want me to join you for breakfast."

"That's it," Meyer said, launching a roundhouse right as the words tumbled from his mouth.

McCall easily ducked Meyer's fist and popped him in the nose

Thirty

with a left jab. Blood spurted and Meyer looked dazed and surprised. Then he became a raging bull, charging McCall with the intention of pinning him against the wall. The reporter avoided the charge, ended up behind his adversary, and placed a karate kick to a kidney area. Meyer slammed against the wall and crumpled to the floor.

The coach got to his feet slowly, blood covering the front of his gray sweatshirt and still running from his nose. McCall felt no remorse in taking advantage of the lumbering jerk in front of him.

Expletives flying, Meyer again charged. He moved like a wounded rhino, but to McCall, he was a sitting duck. He placed a strategic kick to the man's groin that made him sink to his knees. The coach's eyes started watering and McCall knew it was over. Meyer had a massive body and talked big, but he was a wimp.

"Ready for a little serious conversation, Chuck?"

Meyer didn't say anything, just stared at his adversary with a pained expression. McCall continued, "I want to know about the steroids. Was Andy Tyler going to blow the whistle on you? Is that why you killed him?"

The coach was still on his knees, gasping for breath. "I...I didn't kill him. And I don't know nothing about steroids."

"C'mon, Chuck...you know what I'm talking about. Don't lie to me. You've been supplying your boys with steroids."

"Honest to god, McCall...I don't know anything about any steroids or about Andy's death."

McCall slapped Meyer across the face with the back of his hand, causing the man to tumble backward. The coach whined, "What do you want, McCall? I'm telling the truth."

The reporter had dealt with beaten men before, knew how to put the pressure on them to tell the truth. The stakes for Meyer, he understood, were about as high as they could be. He was being asked to admit to murder. "The way I see it, coach...you've been providing your players steroids and Andy wouldn't take them. He was going to blow the whistle...mess up your little playhouse. That's why you had to kill him."

Meyer denied the murder accusation and McCall believed him, though he didn't want the coach to know that. He figured a cowardly wimp like Meyer would kill to keep what he had, but he didn't have a strong feeling about the man's guilt. And if Meyer was the killer, attacking him, alerting him was a dumb move. *A dumb move...that's something I'm good at,* he thought.

McCall realized he needed to talk to some players other than Charley Booth and Dan Thompson about the coach. However, since he had alerted Meyer, McCall spent another fifteen minutes grilling him, banging him around and trying to get answers. All he got were animal-like whines of fright and self-pity.

When McCall finally left, the coach was in a fetal position, still groaning. The reporter figured he really hadn't done the man much harm, other than to bruise his ego. It might be a while before Meyer acted or talked tough again, but his obnoxious attitude would eventually return.

The nose was going to take some explaining on the coach's part, but bruises from McCall's other blows wouldn't show. A little ice on the nose would help, and after a shower, Meyer would probably be able to go eat his free breakfast. McCall wished he could hear Meyer's explanation for the nose.

As for what he had actually accomplished, the reporter felt a bit disgusted with himself. Mentally justifying his actions was a tough sell. The truth was, he had acted stupidly. *In this entire scenario I haven't used good judgment or proper investigative procedures,* he thought. He told himself that he was going to bring to a halt his shotgun approach, but wasn't really sure he could. He realized he was too emotionally involved in the investigation.

If the coach was guilty, McCall's hope was that the man would come after him, try to quiet him as he had quieted Andy and Scott.

Though he hadn't worked up a sweat pounding Meyer, the fisticuffs had activated McCall's appetite. He didn't want to eat alone, so called the county district attorney, Barry Travis, and suggested they meet for breakfast at the barbecue place.

Though he had given Arnold's phone number to Travis to call in case of serious trouble, he still wasn't sure whether he trusted the district attorney. After all, the man was a lawyer. He figured there wasn't much percentage in trusting any lawyer, even if the one in question was allegedly one of the good guys.

Travis did get some points from McCall for being on time. He

Thirty

hated to be kept waiting, or to keep anyone waiting. Time and schedules were to him like deadlines, to be respected.

After the waitress had poured them coffee and they'd ordered, McCall asked, "What do you know about Chuck Meyer giving steroids to the athletes at the high school?"

"What? I don't know anything about it."

"Don't kid me, Barry. Ever since I came to this town I feel like I've been drowning in excrement. People open their mouths here and it just oozes out."

Travis laughed. "What got your dander up this morning?"

"I've already had a little talk with Chuck Meyer. If he feels the urge, I guess he could file assault charges against me. I don't think he will, though, because I don't think he would want anyone knowing I whipped up on him.

"You whipped Chuck?"

McCall shrugged. "Yeah. Pretty badly, I guess. His nose isn't pretty."

"Chuck's a big guy."

"Chuck's a wimp. And you still haven't answered my question...not really."

"About the steroids? Oh, I guess there's been a little talk. I didn't put much stock in it...knew there wasn't much I could do about it."

"I'm sick of that, Barry. It makes me want to puke."

"Sick of what?"

"Your excuses...that you can't do anything. You're the district attorney. Start acting like it."

Travis' face turned crimson. He wasn't used to anyone talking to him the way McCall did. "McCall, I..."

"Not another excuse for not doing anything, Barry. That's all I've heard from you since I've been here. You're either incompetent or a coward. Which is it?"

The district attorney started to get up and leave, but McCall uttered an authoritative command. "Sit down, Barry. It's time someone talked to you the way I'm talking to you now."

McCall could be frightening, especially to someone like Travis. After all, he wasn't as big and strong as Chuck Meyer. He was, in fact, soft. Whatever the reason, he hunkered back in his chair. "McCall, you don't have enough friends in this town to treat the ones you do have this way."

"I'd rather see a little backbone in you than have you as a friend. If your delicate psyche has been hurt...tough. I'm tired of treading lightly. If I have to smash a few heads to get some answers, I'm going to do it. Now...do you trust Tommy Caldwell?"

Still shaken by McCall's verbal barrage, Travis pondered the question for several seconds. "Yeah...Tommy's all right."

"He's been making a few overtures...like he wants to do something about the stuff that's happening here."

"What can he do?"

McCall sighed. "I have no idea, Barry. But maybe the two of you...together...could do something. People are being killed like flies around here and no one seems to care. The people elected you to do something and I'd think you'd feel an obligation to try."

Breakfast was not pleasant for Travis. McCall, on the other hand, had begun to feel pretty good about whipping up on Chuck Meyer. He was feeling very strong, combative, ready to take on the entire town if it became necessary.

By the time McCall finished having breakfast with Travis, it was about time for Jack Gregg to be having coffee at the drugstore. He decided to join him. He didn't want to visit with him in the bank because of Alicia. He didn't like to be pressured about his feelings. Also, Celeste had called him just after he and Alicia had talked. Just talking to her after having been propositioned by another woman made him feel strange. He had been close to giving in and that made him feel guilty. Celeste made things even tougher by giving him more slack than most women would give a man.

Gregg seemed subdued, but acted as though he was glad to see him. McCall figured the banker didn't like all that was going down in his town. He wondered if Gregg blamed him in any way for the murders of Jane Warrick and Jay Sheldon. If he did, McCall couldn't blame him. Maybe his prying had caused their deaths.

Settled in a booth with steaming cups of coffee in front of them, Gregg asked, "Anything new on Andy's or Scott's deaths?"

"A little. What do you know about Chuck Meyer giving his players steroids?"

Thirty

Gregg's face gave McCall his answer. The banker probably didn't know the difference between a steroid and an aspirin. He had probably read about steroids, of course, but they were alien to him. "I'd be surprised to hear that Chuck was giving the boys something that would hurt them."

"Why?"

Gregg sipped his coffee before replying. "I've got no reason to believe anything else, Matt. Chuck's never given me any reason to doubt him."

"What if I told you a couple of the football players told me Meyer was providing steroids...and that Andy was going to blow the whistle on him?"

The banker was shocked and showed it. "They...they say Chuck killed Andy?"

"They have some suspicions. They didn't go so far as to make an accusation, but they find it strange that Andy died right after threatening to expose Meyer."

"I'm having trouble believing what you're telling me."

"That's understandable. I'm not sure I believe it myself. I'm going to talk to other boys on the football team."

"If Chuck's been passing out steroids...I can't believe it's been such a secret," Gregg said. "Kids tend to talk."

"Yeah...they do. But I'm sure he's been very selective. And some kids have an almost godlike reverence for their coach. He could convince those kids that the things would help them. And they will...temporarily. They make you stronger...faster. But they can kill you in the long run."

McCall realized Gregg's doubt was well founded. Who, other than a stone blank idiot, would be fool enough to believe that a group of teenagers could keep a secret about steroid use? He wanted to believe Meyer was such an idiot, but his mind told him something else.

"Matt, I want Andy's and Scott's killer punished, but I can't believe Chuck Meyer is a killer. If he is, though...I want him to pay."

McCall shrugged. "Frankly, I'd rather the killer be your son-in-law than Meyer, but he told me last night he had nothing to do with it. Of course, he was probably lying. Everyone around here seems to be into denial."

DEATH ANGEL

"Bob talked to you?"

"Yeah. We had dinner together."

"I'm surprised."

"So was I."

"Why did you tell me about Chuck, Matt?"

"What do you mean?"

"I think you're the kind of man who has a reason for everything he does. That's how you strike me."

"You see me differently than I see myself. Jack, I go off on tangents...push and pull...shake trees...rustle through bushes...all in the hope that something will fall out. I'm not as logical as people give me credit for being."

"What you told me about Chuck...even if it's not true...the accusation could ruin a man's life. And if it's not true, I have great concern for his wife and children. I hope you'll be very sure about his guilt before saying anything to someone else."

Gregg was a good man, McCall decided, but he figured he needed to feed the fire to get it blazing. He didn't want to hurt an innocent man, either, but sometimes people tended to get too close to the fire and they got burned.

Gregg asked, "Did you tell Bob Mack about Chuck?"

"No. He claims he's looking for Andy's killer and that he'll deal with him. I don't have to tell you what that means."

"No...no you don't," Gregg said, deliberately. "I've known what Bob Mack is for a long time. I haven't wanted to admit it...even to myself. I guess I'm a coward. And, of course, there's my daughter to consider."

McCall felt sympathetic. Gregg was truly a man caught in the middle. "Whether he's the killer or not, I think he's responsible for what this town has become. And I'd lay odds he had Jane Warrick and Jay Sheldon killed."

Gregg sighed. "I hope you're wrong about Bob being involved. But you're right about what the town has become...and I guess he's responsible for some of it. I blame myself, too...for letting it happen."

The reporter didn't respond. There was nothing to say.

"What are your lunch plans, Matt?"

"I don't have any."

Thirty

"Would you consider coming to my house for lunch? I might have something for you."

"Sure. Be a nice change from restaurant food."

While McCall figured Gregg was an honest man, his mind wouldn't discount the possibility that he was being set up. After his previous evening's conversation with Bob Mack, he wasn't sure what the drug lord might do. His CIA connections, he figured, made Mack a tad nervous. After all, a lot of people had suggested that the CIA be more involved in the war against drugs, even to the point of executing drug lords. That certainly wasn't a pleasant thought to people like Mack.

From a pay phone McCall called the police department and asked to speak to Tommy Caldwell. When Caldwell came on the line the reporter said, "Meet me," then told the policeman where the meeting was to take place and at what time.

Fifteen minutes later McCall's Yukon was parked on the same road he had led the hit man down on Saturday night. He, however, was not in the vehicle. He had taken a position amid some tall oaks off the side of the road.

Minutes later a police car came to a stop behind the Yukon. Caldwell got out and looked around. He was, obviously, confused that McCall was not in his vehicle. He called out his name, but McCall didn't immediately show himself. The policeman seemed to be alone, but McCall wanted to be sure.

Caldwell didn't know McCall was around until the cold steel of the reporter's forty-five barrel touched his neck. He jumped with fright. "Dang it, McCall...you scared the dickens out of me."

"Slowly, with your left hand, take your gun out of its holster and hand it to me butt first."

Caldwell emitted a nervous laugh. "What's up, McCall. I came out here as a friend."

"Maybe you did...maybe you didn't. I haven't known you long enough to call you a friend."

Caldwell did as he was told. Then McCall said, "Now the boot gun...your throwaway piece."

"I don't have one."

"Pull your pant legs up. I want to see."

Again, Caldwell followed instructions. McCall couldn't see a hidden piece, but checked the policeman out thoroughly before saying, "Let's walk."

"I don't like this, McCall."

"Sorry about that. But we walk into the woods. If someone followed you, it makes it tougher for them to get a shot at me."

"You'd have heard the car if anyone followed me."

"If they were smart, they'd come in on foot."

"You don't trust anyone, do you?"

"Good observation, Tommy. Not trusting is what's kept me alive all these years."

They walked into the woods for about five minutes, until McCall reached a spot where he felt comfortable. It was a place with good cover, but one that would be difficult for an enemy to approach without being seen and heard.

"All right, Tommy...convince me you're not one of them."

"How can I do that?"

McCall took a mini recorder from his jacket pocket. "First off, spill your guts...tell me what you know."

"You're asking a heckuva lot, McCall. The tape could fall into the wrong hands."

"It's more likely to fall into the right hands."

"Like I told you before...I don't know much. I just suspect certain things."

McCall laughed without mirth. "You're going to be like everyone else around here...talk a good game, but when it comes down to it you'll have temporary amnesia. Is that the way it is?"

Caldwell's face flushed. "Okay...okay. What do you want to know?"

"First off, what about Chuck Meyer? Is he giving steroids to some of the kids on the football team?"

"If he is...it's news to me. Now I've heard some of them were taking steroids, but I don't know where they get them."

"And you haven't bothered to find out."

"C'mon, McCall...my hands have been tied."

"That's something you have in common with your district attorney."

"I don't have anything in common with that jerk."

Thirty

McCall was surprised. He figured the policeman would be a Travis fan. "Seems to me you do. Both of you are quick to make excuses for not doing anything."

"Well, I'm ready to do something now. And I hope you don't think Travis is on your side."

"I don't think anyone's on my side. But what's your beef with Travis?"

"I don't trust him."

"Why?"

Caldwell semi laughed. "I think the man would sell out his grandmother. There's a political reason for everything he does."

"He connected with Bob Mack in any way?"

"I don't think so, but I think he would like to be Bob Mack. I can't prove it, but I think he deals a little dope."

The allegation surprised McCall. "You're kidding?"

"No...I'm not. Travis hangs around with some high school kids more than what I'd consider normal, especially some of the athletes."

"Maybe they hang around him."

"Maybe so. But why? I'd come closer to believing he was providing steroids than Meyer."

"You like Meyer, huh?"

"Hey, it's not a matter of liking the guy. I happen to think he's an arrogant pain in the neck, but I don't think he deals drugs...even steroids."

McCall pondered what Caldwell had told him. The check on Travis had come up blank. That didn't mean he wasn't a drug dealer. The nation's law-enforcement computers weren't infallible. After all, who and what he had been had been erased off all the government's computers.

He was about to ask Caldwell for the names of the athletes who hung around Travis when he noticed a slight movement in brush about fifty yards away. He tackled the big policeman, knocking him sprawling. The familiar whine of a bullet passed overhead and thumped into a tree.

"You maggot, you set me up," he yelled, pushing the barrel of his forty-five under Caldwell's chin.

"No, McCall," the policeman said, fearfully. "That bullet was

DEATH ANGEL

meant for me."

The reporter quickly assessed the situation. Maybe Caldwell was telling the truth. They both hugged the ground as more bullets whined overhead. McCall was more angry than scared, and determined to get the shooter in his sights. And he wouldn't miss.

There was something about the morning, bullets plunking into trees and cutting through leaves and brush, that reminded McCall of years past in Southeast Asia. He felt very alone and very deadly, the same way he had felt when surrounded by another enemy.

"Please, McCall...give me my gun. They're trying to kill me, too."

He wasn't ready to trust Caldwell completely, but it did seem that whoever was out there was trying to kill both of them. He handed the man his gun and said, "One wrong move, Tommy, and you're a dead man."

"It looks like we're both dead men. They have automatic weapons."

Like Caldwell, McCall had already determined there was more than one shooter. He figured at least two, but numbers and firepower didn't daunt him. He had always been able to maintain a deadly calm when under fire; an attitude that whatever happened had been predetermined.

McCall struggled out of his jacket and said, "I hope you can shoot, Tommy. I want you to return their fire while I get behind them."

"That's crazy, McCall. They'll see you."

"Staying here is what's crazy. We have good cover but they'll get us eventually...if we don't do something."

"Don't worry about my shooting, McCall. I can at least make them duck."

Strangely, McCall found himself worrying about the mud on the jacket he had just shed. *Funny, the things that concern a man when death is closing in*, he thought.

He hated mud, yet the soft spongy earth would prove beneficial. After removing his shirt, he painted his upper body and slacks with the earth, a natural camouflage.

Bursts of fire from the automatic weapons were sporadic, punctuated by shots from Caldwell's weapon. The sounds of the guns were somewhat muffled by the trees and hillsides, rhythmic beats harmo-

Thirty

nious with nature.

McCall figured the shooters were Decker and Cherry, or some of Mack's boys. He thought there might be a combination.

Slithering along with the silence of a snake, McCall first found Cherry peering toward Caldwell's location from the cover of a large fallen tree. Only a small part of his head was visible.

Once Cherry was located, he set out in search of his accomplices. It was important to know the direction from which other danger might come.

The other shooter, he discovered, was Dade Decker. He was confident he could sneak up on Decker and take him alive, though there was some risk involved. The risk negated any positive factors.

Still, there was a bit of cowboy in McCall, a kind of code of the Old West. Though he had often shot his country's enemies from ambush, the situation was different. The code demanded that he give Decker a chance.

Given McCall's skill with a handgun, it wasn't much of a chance. But there was the slim possibility Decker would get off a lucky shot. So McCall showed himself, appearing to Decker's right. The man whirled with an Uzi and a slug from McCall's forty-five tore between his eyes.

"Dade...you okay?" Cherry called out.

McCall answered, "Sorry, Cherry, but your pal's never going to be okay again."

The voice froze Cherry for a moment. Then he responded with wild bursts from his Uzi in McCall's direction. But he heard no cries of pain. Only silence.

For at least a minute, which seemed like an hour to Cherry, he cowered behind the fallen tree. Then panic set in and he tried to retreat. He was, however, disoriented by fear.

McCall appeared to his left and he fired wildly. Then McCall appeared to his right and he fired wildly again. McCall then seemed to pop up everywhere, all around him. He was pulling the Uzi's trigger instinctively, the woods alive with the spitting sound of the automatic weapon. Finally, all his spare clips were expended and McCall was standing in front of him.

"I'm out," Cherry said, dropping his weapon.

"I'm not," McCall said, pulling the trigger of the forty-five. The

DEATH ANGEL

hollowpoint took out Cherry's heart.

McCall might have felt some remorse had Cherry been a noble enemy, but for the kind of scum he represented there was no sorrow. For his kind of filth there was no point in wasting taxpayer money on a prolonged trial.

Caldwell yelled out, "McCall...you okay?"

"Yeah, Tommy," he yelled back. "It's all clear. You can come out now."

McCall watched Caldwell emerge from the trees, his pistol still in his hand. He thought, maybe, just maybe, the guy could be trusted. "You can holster it, Tommy. These guys aren't going to hurt anyone...ever again."

The policeman holstered his gun and came to where McCall was standing. He immediately saw Cherry's body, the empty eyes looking heavenward and a large splotch of blood on his chest.

"I heard Cherry call Decker's name."

"Neither of them will be calling each other's names anymore."

"What now, McCall? How do you explain shooting two cops?"

"Tommy, I'm going to take a chance that you're an honest man. I want to keep these bodies on ice a while, then you can call whomever you please. I'm going to give you a guy's name to call. He'll tell you exactly what to do. You can trust him."

McCall gave Caldwell Arnold's number, which he jotted down in his notebook. "What are you going to do now?" the policeman asked.

"I'm going to retrieve my shirt and jacket, clean up and go to lunch."

"Lunch?"

"Yeah...lunch. Who knows, it might be an important lunch. It might put me a step closer to the guy who killed Andy and Scott."

"You don't think it was Decker and Cherry?"

"Might have been, but I doubt they orchestrated the murders. I'll know more this afternoon and then I'll get in touch with you."

"Before I forget it, McCall...thanks."

"For what?"

"For saving my life."

McCall shrugged. "If you hadn't been talking to me, it probably wouldn't have been necessary. Call Arnold."

Thirty

He left Caldwell to take care of the shooting scene; drove back to the motel, showered and got ready for lunch. He arrived at the Gregg mansion on time.

McCall was surprised when Jack Gregg answered the doorbell chimes. He invited the reporter to follow him to an area just off the kitchen where a large black woman was tending pots on a stove. There was bubbling from the pots that created a delicious aroma.

Gregg asked, "You like purple hull peas and boiled okra, Matt. Louise...she doesn't care for peas, but I love them."

"I've been known to eat a few peas in my time...blackeyes, purple hulls and crowders."

"They tell me people up North won't eat peas...that they feed them to the cows."

McCall laughed. "Then the cows are eating better than the people up North."

"Matt, I didn't want to tell you this morning because I thought you might object, but I've invited Chuck Meyer to have lunch with us. I thought we ought to talk."

"If Chuck's in a talking mood, it's okay with me. After this morning, I don't figure he's too anxious to see me again. Not that he was the first time."

"Chuck and I discussed that," the banker said, "and he admits he started the entire thing. I think he's anxious to talk...to clear the air."

McCall shrugged. "Well, he may be taking blame for a little too much on that score."

The doorbell rang and Gregg went to answer it. McCall joined the woman in the kitchen, introduced himself and discovered her name was Sophie. "I've had a rough day, Sophie. Could I trouble you for a cup of coffee?"

"'Course you can," she replied, laughing and showing pearly white teeth. "Word around town is that you done caused lots of trouble. If half what's being said about you is right, you got a right to be tired."

"I didn't know I was so well known around here."

"Believe me, Mr. McCall...right now you are about the best known man in this town."

He took the mug of coffee she poured him, doctored it and

DEATH ANGEL

asked, "Is what's being said good or bad?"

"It depends on who's doing the talking."

They laughed together and Gregg came back into the room, Chuck Meyer in tow. McCall ignored the coach's offer of a handshake, so they all sat at the table and Sophie put the food on it. In addition to the peas and okra there was macaroni and cheese, cornbread, fried pork chops, turnip greens and iced tea. Gregg excused Sophie and they all began filling their plates.

"McCall, I'm sorry about this morning," Meyer said. "What you said took me by surprise...made me mad, too."

The reporter noted that the coach's nose didn't look too bad. It was red and puffed up, but it could have been worse. "Some kids came to me and told me you were dispensing steroids. Now why would they have done that if it isn't true?"

"You've got me," Meyer said. "I'm opposed to steroids...preach against them. I'm sure some of the kids take them, but they don't get them from me. I admit I took them in college...so I know what they can do for you and to you. But I was ignorant back then. Like most of the guys who played in my day, I didn't know about the after effects."

The coach's confession wasn't winning McCall over and Gregg knew it. "I thought if I could get you two together," he said, "that we might find some explanation for these accusations against Chuck. Would you be willing to tell us the names of the boys who made the accusation, Matt?"

"You know I won't do that, Jack. I wouldn't even if I was convinced Chuck isn't guilty, which I'm not."

Gregg sipped his iced tea, smiled and said, "That's what I figured you'd say."

"If you're so all-fired anxious to prove your innocence, Chuck, give me the names of some of the drug dealers who work the high school."

"I don't know any."

"Bull."

Meyer sighed. "Okay, McCall, okay. Like everyone else there are people I suspect, but I'm not sure."

"All I need is one good suspect. I'll take care of it from there."

"There's a kid named Damon Carter," Meyer said. "I think he

Thirty

may be peddling a little stuff."

"The kid's from the wrong side of the tracks," Gregg said, "been in and out of trouble all his life. His dad's a sawmill worker and they live just across a railroad spur from the black community. I think his folks try, but they can't control him."

"He sounds like just the kind of guy who can give me some information," McCall said.

"He's a tough kid," Meyer said.

McCall laughed. "As tough as you?"

"Well...no."

"Then I'm not worried."

THIRTY ONE

Damon Carter, Meyer had told McCall, might or might not be in class that afternoon. Carter, it seemed, just kind of came and went as he chose. He usually went to classes in the morning, but in the afternoons could often be found hanging out behind the building that housed the Future Farmers of America.

Meyer said Carter was not enrolled in FFA, that the only farming he was probably interested in was growing marijuana in some of the clearcuts near town. He said he figured Damon spent his afternoons smoking.

The Ag building was a red brick structure with white trim. The main campus was on a hill, but the FFA's building was at the foot of it, a small creek running behind it. Large oaks stood like soldiers on the banks of the shallow and winding stream.

As with most schools, there was considerable segregation. Groups of students of varying persuasion and color chose certain

Thirty One

locales for their free periods, such as the lunch hour. An area behind the Ag building was, from what McCall had learned, a preferred gathering spot for a group that felt society had betrayed them. Thus, they vented their anger by wearing strange clothing, hairstyles and earrings, refused to adhere to accepted practices of personal hygiene, and used drugs. Such losers were not a new phenomenon to McCall.

He made a couple of inquiries as to Carter's identity and found him leaning up against a tree, sharing a joint with a couple of his cronies. "You Damon Carter?"

"Who wants to know?"

Carter had yellow-colored stringy hair that hung to his shoulders and looked as if it was wet. If it was, it wasn't because it had been recently washed. The hair was matted and dirty.

"My name's McCall."

"So?"

"So I want to talk to you."

The kid had blue eyes streaked with red, but there was nothing patriotic about them. He needed a shave, had a strong chin and a Roman nose. McCall figured that if he were cleaned up he would be a good-looking kid.

Carter had an earring dangling from his left ear. McCall knew an earring in the left ear meant one thing, one in the right ear another. But with him, it didn't matter. He might as well have had earrings in both ears and one in his nose. McCall thought earrings were for women.

"So maybe I don't want to talk to you, man."

Carter's companions took delight in the way he responded to an adult. Of course, the young men didn't understand whom they were dealing with. McCall, obviously, didn't wear an earring, but he wore a very short fuse.

"Look...I just want to ask you a few questions."

Carter was wearing faded and tattered jeans, which McCall figured had been soaked in Clorox and beaten with rocks. The kid's jeans jacket was in the same shape and his shirt hadn't been within one room of an ironing board. The look was, allegedly, fashionable.

The other kids were clones, except that they were scrawny. They each looked to be five inches short of six-feet, and neither would push the scales to a hundred and thirty-five. Carter, though, was more than

DEATH ANGEL

six-feet tall and weighed better than two hundred. He was muscular, too, and McCall immediately thought he might be taking steroids. He remembered Meyer telling him that from a physical standpoint he would like to have had Carter on the football team, but didn't want the problems the kid brought with him.

"Hey, man...I'm not into answering questions...for you or anybody like you."

The clones smiled approval and Carter smirked. McCall put a hand on the kid's chest, shoved him against a tree, and with the other hand grabbed his earring and tore it from his ear. Carter screamed with pain. "Hey, man, what the heck...?"

One of the kid's hands had gone to his ear. With the other, he took a wild swing at the reporter. McCall deflected it and rammed a knee into Carter's groin. The fight went out of him immediately. His back slid down the tree until he was sitting on the ground, groaning.

McCall had used up all his nice for the day. So he said to the clones, who had their mouths agape, "You little weirdoes make yourselves scarce." They didn't have to be told twice.

Carter choked out in a whimper, "Who are you?"

"To paraphrase a line in an old movie, I'm your worst nightmare...if you don't answer my questions."

"I don't know anything."

"I haven't asked you anything yet."

McCall pulled Carter to his feet and shoved him against the tree. "I want you to try something, because I'd like to give you the kind of whipping you deserve."

"I ain't going to try nothing. And I know who you are. You're the guy looking for whoever killed Andy Tyler."

"So you know it was murder, huh?"

"Yeah, man. Everybody who isn't stupid knows Andy was murdered."

"You got any idea who killed him?"

"Got no idea, man...really."

"How well did you know Andy?"

"I wouldn't say we were friends or anything like that, but he was an okay dude. He always spoke to me...was friendly to me. He wasn't like some of those stuck-up people he ran around with."

Thirty One

"I've been told you sell a little dope, Damon...that maybe you provided the stuff that killed Andy."

"No way, man. People talks about me selling dope don't know what they're talking about. I do a little grass now and then, but I don't sell the stuff."

"I'm supposed to believe you, huh?"

"Hey, man, I'm telling the truth. Why does everyone want to make me the heavy?"

Blood was trickling down from Carter's ear and there was fear in his eyes. Most adults, including his parents, didn't know how to handle the youth, but McCall did. "Maybe people treat you the way they do because of the way you dress and act...like you want to be the heavy. You're so busy trying to be different that all you can be is stupid."

"Hey, man, I..."

"Cut it, Damon. From now on, you address me as Mr. McCall. If you don't, I'm going to do to you what some people think is a physical impossibility."

"You can't get away with this kind of stuff."

McCall grasped the youth's jacket collar and slammed him against the tree again. "Wrong. I can get away with it. Besides, if someone tried to stop me...which they won't...by the time I get through working you over you'll look like cow patty soufflé."

Carter was brighter than he appeared. He was quick to analyze his situation. "Look, Mr. McCall...I'm telling you the truth. I don't sell dope. I smoke it, but I don't sell it."

"Who does?"

"Maybe you ought to ask some of Andy's friends."

"Do I have to interpret everything you say, Damon?"

"I'm saying I don't sell it, but maybe some of Andy's friends do."

"Maybe?"

"It's more than a possibility."

"You telling me Andy was into drugs?"

"I ain't saying nothing about Andy. From what I know, he was straight arrow. But some of his friends...they're into a lot of stuff. The problem, Mr. McCall, is that everybody wants to blame poor kids. Heck, it's hard for me to come up with enough change to buy a little grass. But the rich kids here...heck, it's easy for them."

DEATH ANGEL

"Damon, I'm sorry for you...sorry your parents don't have more money so you could buy more drugs."

The youth grinned. "That didn't come out the way I wanted it to."

"It probably came out closer to the truth than anything I've heard from you so far. But I warn you, if I don't get the truth I'm going to cut your ears off so you'll never be able to wear another earring."

"You wouldn't do that."

"You want to try me?"

"Hey, Mr. McCall...do you push people around all the time?"

"No, Damon...sometimes I sleep. Now don't try to con me and talk straight. Are you the punk providing steroids to the football team."

Carter laughed. "If I was, my pockets wouldn't be empty right now."

"Okay...who is? For that matter, who's selling you grass?"

"You're asking a lot, Mr. McCall. I could get killed for giving you that kind of information."

"You're going to get leveled if you don't." He took a money clip filled with bills from his pocket and handed Carter two hundred-dollar bills.

"What's this for?"

"Call it good faith."

Carter shoved the bills into a back pocket of his jeans. "Now you might not believe me, Mr. McCall, but the way I hear it two guys on the football team are selling the steroids."

"And who are these two guys?"

"Charley Booth and Dan Thompson. But I can't see them having anything to do with killing Andy. They were his buddies."

McCall was a bit surprised by Carter's revelation, but didn't let it show. "What about Coach Meyer...he ever give steroids to the players."

"You kidding. The man's like a holy-roller preacher when it comes to drugs. There's no fun in him. Charley and Dan, though...I hear they like to get a buzz. And they got plenty of money for inventory."

Dan's dad, McCall knew, owned a construction company. And Charley's dad was a dentist, which meant the youth might have fairly easy access to Novocain.

Thirty One

"You thinking what I think you're thinking, Mr. McCall."

"Tough question, Damon, since I don't know what you're thinking I'm thinking."

"Well, I was thinking that you might be thinking Charley and Dan killed Andy."

What McCall was thinking was that Booth and Thompson, both unsophisticated in the art of murder, had possibly tried to incriminate the coach in an effort to get him off their trail. In so doing, they had gotten him on their trail. Amateurs tended to complicate things.

"What I'm thinking is probably too complicated for someone whose mind is screwed up by dope," McCall said.

"Like I told you, Mr. McCall...I do a little marijuana, nothing heavier."

"I guess you're going to tell me you've never taken steroids, either."

"Well, yeah...I took them for a while, but I quit. They made me feel kind of funny, but I bulked up quite a bit. Steroids are probably the reason Charley and Dan look the way they do. I can't believe they're killers, though."

"Just keep your mouth shut about our conversation."

"Hey, no problem. My lips are sealed. Charley and Dan...I don't want them doing me."

"I can't believe you're that worried about it, Damon. What I'm going to have to do is try to verify what you've told me. Your word's not something I'd feel comfortable taking to the bank."

"I'm telling the truth, Mr. McCall. Funny, too. Maybe I knew Charley and Dan did Andy. Maybe it was just resting there in my subconscious, waiting to pop out."

McCall rolled his eyes. "Keep smoking marijuana and experimenting with other drugs and you're not going to have a subconscious."

"Swear to god, Mr. McCall...I been thinking about quitting."

"It takes a little more than thinking, Damon. By the way, what do you know about Barry Travis, the district attorney?"

"Just that Charley and Dan...they hang around his house a lot."

THIRTY TWO

With Tommy Caldwell's help, McCall spent the afternoon trying to verify whether Carter was telling the truth. This involved interviewing a number of high school students. It was no easy task, but by the end of the school day the policeman and reporter had gleaned enough information to be fairly certain that Charley Booth and Dan Thompson operated a profitable little business dealing steroids and recreational drugs.

Caldwell was feeling upbeat. He had contacted Arnold and had been told how to proceed; also that federal help was on the way. Mack, of course, wouldn't be nailed until the Ol' Man was ready to slam the door on a number of government officials. And that wouldn't be done as long as he could use them.

McCall figured Bob Mack might come after him when things got hairy. He was looking forward to it, planning to save the taxpayers the expense of a trial and taking care of the slimeball for years. Drug dealers, McCall thought, ought to be dead, not wards of the state.

Thirty Two

"Well, we didn't get anything really solid," Caldwell said, "but it looks as though your boy was telling the truth."

McCall laughed. "My boy? A subconscious fear of having a kid like Damon Carter is probably why I've never married."

Caldwell grinned. "What now? Do you want me to arrest Charley and Dan?"

"Not yet. They'll be at football practice now. If I were you, I'd get search warrants for their homes and cars. They've got their drug stash somewhere. I'd also be on the lookout for a twenty-two...rifle or pistol."

The policeman gave him an incredulous look. "Do you think they might have killed Jane Warrick and Jay Sheldon, too."

McCall shrugged. "Maybe they thought Jane and Jay knew something that they were going to tell me. I'm not dead bang sure they killed Andy and Scott, but if they did...well, they might have done Jane and Jay, too."

"It's hard enough to believe Charley and Dan gave Andy the drugs that killed him," Caldwell said, "and I sure don't know how they could have overpowered Scott and hanged him."

"We tend to think of Dan and Charley as kids because they're in high school. But they're young men who are physically powerful. Still, I find it hard to believe they overpowered Scott. They had to have taken him by surprise."

"Maybe they drugged him. The autopsy on Scott was a sham."

"I suspected as much. I've never seen any of the police department's records on Andy's and Scott's deaths."

Caldwell snorted. "Neither had I...until today. They're open to you now, McCall...anytime you want to look at them."

"While you and your people are searching Charley's and Dan's cars and homes, I'll take a peek."

McCall followed Caldwell, parked the Yukon and went inside the station with the officer. Caldwell left him with the ugly woman cop while he and another officer went for search warrants.

McCall was busy checking the files on Andy's and Scott's deaths when Bob Mack came into the room. "Heard you were here, McCall. Heard about Decker and Cherry, too. I had nothing to do with them trying to take you out."

"Oh, that'll help me sleep better tonight."

DEATH ANGEL

"I can do without your sarcasm. I just haven't decided what to do about you yet."

"Too bad, Bob...because I have decided what to do about you."

"Yeah...what?"

"Worry about it."

"You don't scare me, McCall. No one has anything on me. What are you looking for in those files?"

"None of your business."

"I heard you might have a line on Andy's killer...that you were talking to some kids at the school today. What did you find out?"

"Go ask them."

"I can't get away with questioning a bunch of kids. You can get away with that kind of stuff, McCall, but I can't."

"I thought this was your town...that you could get away with anything."

"Okay...so maybe I could. But there are a few unwritten rules."

McCall laughed. "Gangster ethics. Please, Bob...don't make me puke. As for sharing information with you, when I know something you'll be the last to know."

The reporter realized he and Caldwell would have to work fast. Mack still had most of the town in his hip pocket, and would soon learn about the search warrants.

"With Decker and Burt gone, I guess you think you have the run of things," Mack said. "But there'll be another police chief soon and you'll be right back where you started."

"You picked your man yet?"

"Now that's none of your business."

"Maybe the mayor will pick Tommy Caldwell."

Mack smirked. "The mayor will pick whoever I say. If he picks Caldwell, it'll be because I own Caldwell."

"There are some people coming to town tomorrow. The mayor might be more afraid of them than he is of you."

"Let them come. I told you before, McCall...money can buy anybody except an idiot."

McCall realized those willing to sell out outnumbered those willing to take a stand. That's why he wanted to pull the forty-five from his waistband and put a slug between Mack's eyes. But with a touch of

Thirty Two

bravado he said, "Even you don't have enough money to buy everyone, Bob."

Mack grinned. "You're right, McCall...but we do."

The drug lord's reference was to the organization of which he was a part. "I told you, McCall...I want Andy's killer. Why don't you make things easy for both of us and work with me?"

"If you got Andy's and Scott's killer, it wouldn't be the same. You want the killer to cover your rear...to make sure he's not connected to you in some way. With me, it's pure vengeance. He killed my friend and my friend's kid. He has to pay."

"What difference does it make who gets him?"

"You wouldn't understand."

"What I can't understand is you caring about some wimpy coward like Scott Tyler."

McCall came out of his chair and over the table. His right fist caught the big man flush in the nose, knocking him backward and into the far wall. By the time Mack's back hit the wall McCall was all over him, his fists pounding the pudgy flesh around the man's middle.

As the drug lord doubled over in pain, McCall caught him with a series of uppercuts to the face. The soft flesh tore easily; blood with cuts mixing with blood from the nose. It was not enough just to make Mack's nose bleed. McCall wanted to break it. So he stood the gangster up and kept smashing him, feeling the bone buckle against his fist.

Mack fell to the floor and McCall stomped and kicked him.

The one-sided battle lasted little more than a minute. Attracted to the noise, the ugly female cop entered the room. "My god," she gasped.

She made an almost-reflexive move to the handcuffs dangling from her belt. "Don't even think about it."

She averted his glance.

McCall walked angrily out of the police station; out to where two of Mack's goons were leaning against his big car and smoking cigarettes. He jerked a cigarette out of one guy's mouth and crushed the burning end on his forehead. Before the other could act, McCall smashed him across the face with the forty-five, causing him to go staggering backward against the hood of the car. He put a knee in the groin of the man whose forehead he had burned, then smashed the side of his head with

DEATH ANGEL

the gun.

Both hoodlums lay heaped in the street in a semi-conscious state, groaning. McCall took their guns and said, "If either of you pukes can hear, pick up what's left of your boss when you're able to get to your feet."

He then got in the Yukon, backed it, put it in drive and headed for his next destination. It had been one heck of a Monday, and it wasn't over yet.

THIRTY THREE

Events of the day, some of which were hearsay, had made Barry Travis antsy and irascible. In mid afternoon he had learned Dade Decker and Joe Cherry were dead. He had tried, without success, to get in touch with Tommy Caldwell. Still later, he had learned about the search warrants.

Travis had hoped McCall would keep him informed of his activities, but from the first had feared the man was a lone wolf. Now he didn't know what to do, or what his role should be. He did know he was treading on thin ice, and that he might be forced into making some unpleasant decisions.

The day had been bright, sunny and cool, but the first shadows of darkness brought a light rain that threatened to turn to sleet. Travis drove home with his windshield wipers swishing a rhythmic refrain that tortured his mind. He was distraught and angry. He realized that if he had made a right move here and there, he wouldn't be in the predicament in which he now found himself.

DEATH ANGEL

Travis parked the car in the garage, which was not attached to his large frame house. He tugged the collar of his coat up to better protect his neck, hunched his shoulders upward and got out of the car. He used his briefcase as an umbrella and sprinted for the back door.

The back door opened to a small utility room, which opened to the kitchen. Once he was in the warmth of the kitchen, Travis turned on one of the burners on the gas range. He filled a kettle with water and put it on the burner, hoping a cup of hot instant coffee would eliminate the constriction that seemed to be rising in his throat. It was like a floating ball.

While waiting for the water to heat, he walked through the house, down the long hallway that led to the front door. He opened the door and stepped out on the big covered porch to check the mailbox, which was just outside the door and attached to the wall. Grasping a handful of mail he went back inside, closed and locked the door, then returned to the kitchen. Though it was warm inside the house, his brief check of the mailbox had caused shivers to course through his body.

Travis didn't particularly care for instant coffee, but didn't want to wait for a pot to brew. He put a heaping spoonful of crystals in a mug, poured in boiling water and stirred. After adding sugar and cream, he stirred again.

He sipped the hot liquid and it felt good to his throat, but it didn't take away what seemed like a large wad that was stuck there. He wasn't sure anything could take it away. He didn't want to admit to himself that it was a lump of fear.

The district attorney usually ate out, but on this night there was more reason than the weather to stay inside his house. Though not hungry, there was a gnawing in his stomach. So he searched the cupboard for something to eat, something to keep himself busy and to, hopefully, quiet the fear that kept getting louder and louder in his mind.

Soup? Chili? He had both. It was an appropriate night for chili, but he figured it would be harder to keep down than the soup. He reached for a can of soup, had it in his hand when a voice said, "I don't like vegetable."

The can hit the floor and Travis shook with fright, a chill running up his spine. "What's the matter, Barry...weren't you expecting me?"

Thirty Three

"What...what are you doing here, McCall? How did you get in?"

"You know why I'm here...and your locks are child's play."

Travis seemed frozen. McCall, calmly and deliberately, walked to a kitchen cabinet, opened it and got a coffee mug. He spooned instant coffee from the jar and put it in the cup, then added hot water from the kettle. He added sweetener and stirred.

"Let's go to the living room, Barry...maybe get a fire going in the fireplace. There are some things I want to talk to you about and I think we'll be more comfortable there."

The district attorney wanted to run, but knew it wouldn't do any good. He knew escape from this man who had upset the lives of so many was impossible. So he did as he was told.

Travis realized McCall was giving him ample opportunity to make some foolish move, including grabbing the fireplace poker and using it as a club. He figured the reporter would welcome such a response from him. He refused to be tricked. But then he remembered the pistol behind a cushion in his recliner.

"Mind...mind if I sit down?" he asked.

McCall laughed. "It's your house."

Travis sat, rather timidly, in the big chair, watching McCall all the while. The reporter turned his back and stoked the fire, giving the district attorney a chance to grasp the cold steel behind the cushion. When McCall turned to face him, Travis was pointing the gun in his direction.

"Darn," McCall said, smiling. "You're full of surprises, Barry."

"I'll bet this is a surprise, you jerk," Travis said, his bravado betrayed by a cracking voice.

"You're not being very friendly. What's your problem?"

"Can it, McCall. I know why you're here."

"You do, huh?"

"It's about the boys and me."

"Oh, you mean you think I know you're the source for the drugs Charley Booth and Dan Thompson have been selling."

It bothered Travis that McCall could look down the barrel of a gun and be so calm and collected. "How long have you known?"

"Not long. To tell the truth, I didn't even suspect for a long time. You're good, Barry. You had me fooled."

DEATH ANGEL

The district attorney managed a weak smile. "More than fooled, McCall. You didn't know until one of the kids broke."

"You kind of jumped the gun there, Barry. Neither of the kids broke. I haven't talked to them. Neither has Tommy Caldwell."

Travis frowned. "Then how did you find out?"

"C'mon now, Barry. You know I have to protect my sources."

"It doesn't really matter. You're a dead man."

"That being the case, mind telling me why you killed Andy and Scott?"

"I didn't. The boys did it."

"You orchestrated it."

Travis smiled. "Let's just say they take my advice on most matters. It's been very profitable for them. Andy...he found out I was dealing and threatened to tell. His only problem was that he didn't want to involve his friends. He, obviously, didn't imagine his friends would kill him."

"They may have killed him, McCall said, "but you put them up to it."

The district attorney shrugged. "None of us had a choice."

McCall hated the man in front of him, the way he had used two kids to do his dirty work. However, he figured the two youths were old enough and smart enough to know better. They had been too easily led.

"What about Scott?" McCall asked, seeing that Travis was enjoying telling him about his ability to manipulate the youths.

"Dan knocked Scott out with a club...then they hanged him."

"But why?"

"Call it tying up loose ends. Scott was asking lots of questions and the boys were getting nervous. So I figured, why not? If Scott were dead, they wouldn't have to worry. Of course, I wasn't counting on you showing up."

"Okay, so why Jane Warrick and Jay Sheldon?" McCall asked.

"Blame yourself for both of them. I wasn't sure what Jane knew...if anything. And Jay...well, you got him all stirred up and he started asking questions all over town. He was the kind of creep who would have taken anything he learned to Bob Mack. I couldn't have that."

Thirty Three

"I don't guess you could," McCall said. "I don't imagine Mack wants even a little competition."

"I don't think we have a lot more to talk about, do we, McCall?"

The reporter laughed. "No...I don't guess we do, Barry."

McCall's attitude unnerved Travis. "For someone who's about to die, you're a cool cucumber."

"I'm sure not worried about you killing me. You get kids to do your killing. Excuse me a minute, I'm going to the kitchen to get another cup of coffee."

"Don't even think about it, McCall. I mean it."

The reporter laughed, opened a hand and showed Travis the bullets from his gun. "I got here early...took the liberty of unloading your gun."

The district attorney's knees almost buckled. The lump of fear crawled back into his throat. "What...what are you...?"

"Take it easy, Barry. I'm not going to do anything," McCall said. He took a miniature tape recorder from his shirt pocket. "I taped our conversation...all of it. Now you may think that I'll give this tape to the police, but I won't. I think I'll give it to Bob Mack. Sort of a get-well gift."

Fear choked the air from Travis' lungs. "You can't do that, McCall. For god's sake, you can't do that."

"Oh, I can do it okay," the reporter said. "I don't want you getting away with just a prison sentence. Mack and his people will probably come up with something special for you."

McCall left, knowing Travis would wait a few minutes before rushing to his car in a vain attempt to escape. While the district attorney had been putting the kettle on to boil, the reporter had been fixing his car.

THIRTY FOUR

McCall contacted Tommy Caldwell from his usual pay phone. The policeman said a twenty-two-caliber pistol had been found in Charley Booth's car. "We're having a ballistics check done," Caldwell said.

"I'd lay odds it's the gun used to kill Jane Warrick and Jay Sheldon," McCall said, "but I think you can get both boys to confess if you use a little pressure."

Caldwell laughed. "I'm not allowed to use your kind of pressure, McCall."

The reporter laughed. "I'm sure you have someone keeping an eye on the boys."

"Yeah...they're not going anywhere."

"Tell you what, Tommy...pick the boys up and bring them down to the station. I've got a tape I'll play for them that will encourage them to confess. But first I need to play the tape for Bob Mack."

"McCall...I've got to say you're crazy. I heard what you did to

Thirty Four

Mack and a couple of his goons. I'm guessing he has some of his people out looking for you."

"I'm real easy to find. I don't think any of Mack's boys are that anxious to find me."

Caldwell laughed. "You're probably right."

"Just to ensure my rear end is protected, though...call Mack and tell him I'm on my way out there, to have the gate open for me. Tell him you would come, too, but that some of my fed friends are here asking you all kinds of questions."

The policeman laughed again. "You love to rub salt in a wound, don't you?"

"Just have the boys, their parents and their lawyers at the police station in an hour. It won't take us long to wrap this thing up."

"I'll do it, but I don't understand why you want to play this tape you're talking about for Bob Mack."

"You will."

As long as he was at the pay phone, McCall decided to call Bill Haloran. He had to go through a couple of husky voices before reaching the detective. "What are up to, clown?"

"Paperwork...as usual. Glad you called because I've got some news for you."

"Good or bad."

"Kind of neutral. Reggie Smith's dead."

"How?"

Haloran laughed. "Another of those alleged suicides. He hanged himself in his Washington apartment. There was a note."

"What did it say?"

"It was addressed to his mama. He was repenting of his homosexuality."

"Bright had him killed," McCall said. "He was the only link to the hit man...and Bright knew if I got hold of Reggie I'd get the truth."

"I hate to admit we're on the same wave-length, but that's the way I read it, too."

"Where's Bright now?"

"Way I understand it...he's here in San Antonio. Been here meeting with your old pal, Clark Ramsey. Convenient, huh?"

"Very."

DEATH ANGEL

"Reggie's being shipped back here for burial. He's from some podunk town around here."

"Bright will hang around then, go to the funeral and shed a few tears for the media. Do me a favor and have Dacus keep an eye on him. I want to know where he is at all times."

"Dacus? Sometimes I worry about the kind of people you run with."

"You should be concerned. I run with you more than anyone else."

Haloran laughed. "That's supposed to reassure me? I forgot to ask how things are going there."

"It's a wrap. I should be coming home tomorrow."

"You found Scott's killer?"

"Yeah."

"Is he still alive?"

"Yeah."

"Will wonders never cease?"

McCall gave Haloran a brief summary of the day's events, then drove to the Mack estate. He braked at the big gate leading to the house, but within seconds, it opened electronically. He drove onto the grounds and was soon parked in front of the house's massive columns. Heather's bodyguard, Marty, escorted him to the library.

The reporter didn't discount Mack's street smarts, but figured the man didn't read many books. The library and all it contained was just the work of an interior decorator.

Mack was sitting behind a large oak desk, a dim lamp to his right. What showed of his face was red and puffy, even in the low light. His nose was swollen and some stitches had been taken to mend the cuts in his face. Bandages covered them, but McCall knew they were there.

The drug lord didn't rise to greet him. He hadn't expected such courtesy anyway, but figured Mack was having trouble standing.

"What do you want, McCall?"

The reporter didn't wait for an invitation to sit. He just flopped down in a chair across from the desk. "You wanted to know who killed Andy. I'm here to tell you."

Suspicious, Mack asked, "Why?"

"I thought you wanted to know."

Thirty Four

"There's got a be more to it than that, McCall. I'm not stupid enough to think you want to do me any favors."

Taking the tape recorder from his pocket, he said, "You're right about that, Bob. I just want you to hear this tape. After that, do whatever you want to do."

"What I want to do is blow you away, but the time's not right...not with all the feds in town."

McCall pushed the play button on the recorder and his conversation with Barry Travis came through loud and clear. The bandages and dim light kept him from seeing much in the way of changes of expression on Mack's face.

When McCall clicked off the recorder, Mack said, "Those kids...Charley and Dan...they've been here lots of times. It's hard to believe they killed Andy."

McCall shrugged. "You don't have to believe anything. The boys are at the police station now...and I think they'll confess to the murders. There's a lot more evidence than this tape."

Mack snarled, "And what about Barry Travis? He's more guilty than the kids."

"As far as I know, he's still at home."

"He hasn't been arrested?"

"Not yet. He won't be until the boys implicate him...or until I play this tape for the police."

"Tommy Caldwell hasn't heard the tape yet?"

"Not yet?"

"What do you think will happen to Barry Travis...if the police arrest him?"

"He'll do some time, but not as much as the boys."

"That's what I figure," Mack said. "When are you going to play your tape for the cops?"

"Oh, I don't know. I think you've got at least an hour or so before I play it."

"You're a cold, calculating man, McCall. You're a lot more like me than you'll admit."

"Like you, Bob? Not in your wildest dreams."

THIRTY FIVE

McCall left for San Antonio the next morning. He had been tempted to stay in Putnam to dig up more on Bob Mack, but decided to let Arnold and other federal agencies deal with the drug lord. He knew if he stayed around he might end up killing the man, and figured it would be better if Mack's own people did it. That would definitely happen if Arnold and the feds played their cards just right.

The previous evening Charley Booth and Dan Thompson had confessed to four counts of murder. They had blamed Barry Travis for sending them down the road to ruin. McCall figured they were old enough to be accountable for their own actions. He did feel sorry for their parents. They had seemed to be good, honest people who had done their best to make a good home for their sons. Sometimes that just wasn't enough.

The boys broke after hearing the tape. The lawyers for both wanted to strike a deal. Since the district attorney was himself being

Thirty Five

sought for murder, the situation was more than a little muddled.

Tommy Caldwell and another officer went to arrest Barry Travis. They found him hanged on the front porch of his house, an apparent suicide. McCall knew better. He suspected Caldwell did, too. But, what the heck? Justice had been served. The taxpayers had been spared the expense of a costly trial and the long-term cost of incarcerating him. And in due time Bob Mack would get some of the same kind of justice he had dispensed.

McCall wrote the story and called it in to the *Tribune*. He also shared it with Paul Bates in Dallas. He had suggested Bates come to Putnam and do some interviews, which the newsman said he planned to do.

The reporter had been tired from the long and eventful day, but Alicia had left word for him to call no matter what the time. He did and she insisted on coming to the motel. They had a Diet Coke and she talked about their future together. She knew there wasn't one, but wanted to believe. He didn't encourage her.

McCall had telephoned Jack Gregg the morning he left town and suggested they get together for a cup of coffee at the drugstore. He found Gregg in a booth waiting for him, got a cup of coffee from Rosie and sat down.

"Well, I guess it's all over," the banker said.

"Not quite. There's still your son-in-law. However, I don't think he'll be a problem all that much longer. You might want to tell Heather to get out of that situation...and fast."

"Heather quit listening to me a long time ago."

"If Heather stays around Mack, her life's going to be in danger."

"Tell her that. She'll be here in a few minutes."

"Here?"

"She wanted to see you before you left. I told her I was going to meet you and she insisted on coming. But before she gets here, I want to thank you for what you did here...finding Andy's and Scott's killers. If there's anything I can ever do for..."

"There is."

"Name it."

"I've already talked to Tommy Caldwell about it, but you have more power than Tommy. I want to make sure Jane Warrick's kids get

DEATH ANGEL

the insurance money for the wrongful death of their father...the city's policy and the one from the company Scott was representing. And the city needs to make a settlement on the wrongful death. Jane's parents need the money to raise the kids...to send them to college."

"I can assure you...that's not going to be a problem, Matt."

"If it gets to be...I'm going to personally pay a high-powered attorney to come in here and sue the daylights out of the city on behalf of the kids."

Gregg laughed. "The mayor and city council won't fight the settlement. I'll personally handle it."

"Tell the mayor something else for me, Jack."

"What?"

"Tell him to appoint Tommy Caldwell police chief. If he chooses someone Mack has in his pocket, I'll be back."

Gregg laughed again. "I'm backing Tommy. The rest of the city council will, too. But I'll see the mayor gets your message. I don't think any of our elected officials want you back. They're afraid you'll dig up something on them. If anything, you've proven that one man can make a difference, Matt."

"I had lots of help. That kid, Damon Carter, for one. I'm going to write you a check for a college scholarship, which I want you to present to the kid if he straightens up his act. I don't want him to know the scholarship's from me. Just tell him he's got a scholarship if he makes his grades and quits smoking dope."

"That's very generous. I don't know why you wouldn't want to take credit for it."

McCall smiled. "I don't want Damon to ever think I'm anything short of the meanest man he ever met."

Heather showed up just after they worked out the details of Carter's scholarship. Her bodyguard, Marty, stationed himself near the entrance.

McCall got Heather a cup of coffee and a refill for himself. Gregg said his good-byes and left.

"I see you still need to lose two hundred pounds of surly fat," McCall said, referring to Marty.

She smiled. "I'm afraid so."

"To what do I owe this honor, Heather?"

Thirty Five

"I didn't even know you had come to the house last night. Bob told me early this morning. He also told me who killed Andy. It's hard to believe his friends did it."

"That's what drugs will do. When it comes to choosing between a friend and a profitable drug deal, the friend usually gets the short end of the stick."

"I don't like the way it turned out," she said, tearfully, "but I appreciate what you did. I'm glad Andy's killers...Scott's, too...are going to pay for what they did."

"Heather, please listen to me and try to understand...it's not over yet. There's going to be more killing. You have to get away from Bob Mack...far away."

Her eyes showed surprise. "Is someone trying to kill Bob?"

"Yeah. I don't know who and I don't know when, but it's a lock. The killer probably will be someone from Bob's own organization...and he may not be satisfied just to kill him."

"Matt...I just can't believe what you're telling me."

"Please believe it, Heather."

"I'm scared," she said, her voice choking with emotion. "I'm scared all the time. But I'm afraid of Bob. I'm afraid of what he might do if I try to leave him."

"I can arrange it...get you away from him where you don't have to be worried anymore."

"I...I don't know."

"It's your decision...your life. But if you decide you want my help, just tell your dad to get in touch with me. I'll arrange everything."

They talked a while longer and he reiterated the danger she was in, again offering his help. He could understand her confusion, her inability to think clearly. But such confusion could mean her death.

Finally, she said, "I'd better go. Bob agreed to let Marty bring me here to meet you and dad...to let me tell you how much I appreciate what you did. But I also wanted to tell you how much I enjoyed our time together. I wish we could..."

"It wouldn't work, Heather. There are too many ghosts between us...especially Scott's."

"It wouldn't be a problem for me," she said.

"Maybe not...but it would for me."

DEATH ANGEL

She left with Marty and McCall finished his coffee. Gregg had paid for it, but he tipped Rosie an Andrew Jackson. She couldn't believe it. "So you won't forget me, Rosie."

He walked out of the drugstore and saw Bob Mack's limo parked beside the Yukon. Two of his goons were sitting in the front seat of the stretch car. Then the dark back window rolled down and he saw Mack's face.

"McCall."

"Fancy seeing you here, Bob."

"Understand you're leaving town."

"That's right. Any objections?"

"None at all. Between you and me, though, just wanted you to know...it's not over."

"Hey, I wouldn't have it any other way. Remember that I'm from San Antonio. That's the home of Dan Cook, the guy who brought us the words *it ain't over 'til the fat lady sings*."

"Just want you to know I might come after you any time, McCall. Know it and worry."

"I'll be waiting, Bob...but I'll lay money you won't be coming after me. You don't have the intestinal fortitude for it. You'll send someone else."

"Don't be so sure, McCall. Don't be so sure."

"But I am, Bob. I am."

Mack was still flapping his gums when McCall drove away. He figured it was important to get away from the drug lord quickly, because he was feeling a real temptation to smash his nose again.

By the time McCall stopped at the police station and had a discussion with Tommy Caldwell, it was noon. He turned down Caldwell's invitation to lunch and drove to the high school. He found Damon Carter behind the ag building, leaning against the same tree where he had first seen him. When Carter's two companions saw him, they scurried away.

A cigarette was dangling from Carter's lips. He removed it and said, "Hey, Mr. McCall...you kind of turned things upside down around here."

"I couldn't have done it without your help."

"Hey, don't be saying stuff like that around here. I didn't do any-

Thirty Five

thing."

McCall laughed. "Don't worry. Your name wasn't mentioned. At least, it wasn't mentioned to anyone who would find fault with what you did."

Carter gave him a suspicious look. "What does that mean?"

"It means, Damon, that your secret is safe."

The youth took a drag from the cigarette, then flipped the butt on the ground. "Mr. McCall...guys like you...well, you worry me."

The reporter laughed again. "Sorry, but I'm afraid I can't help that. But listen, there's a reason I stopped by. You're a senior, right?"

"Yeah, I'll be blowing this place next May."

"Any plans?"

The youth shrugged. "Maybe I'll join the Army or something. May's a long ways off."

"I just wondered if you might be interested in a job?"

"What kind of job?"

"Well, I own a ranch west of San Antonio. I could use a hand. The work's hard and the food's good. The pay's decent, too...enough in the summer to see you through a year of college."

"Why are you making this offer?"

"I'm not sure. I just figure you're halfway bright and might like to take a shot at college."

"I never gave it much thought...didn't figure there was much reason to."

McCall handed Carter one of his business cards. "Think about it. If you want the job, call me. I can even get you enrolled at a junior college near the ranch. You can live there and work part-time while you're going to school."

The reporter figured Rosita, Juan and the isolation of the ranch would do a lot to straighten the kid out. Maybe all he needed was a chance.

"Yeah, Mr. McCall...I'll think about it. I sure will."

"You do that, Damon. By the way, I see you're not wearing an earring."

Carter grinned. "I figured I'd retire it until you left town."

The kid was smart, McCall thought. Very smart.

THIRTY SIX

Congressman Bob Bright was a cautious man. He didn't mind certain colleagues knowing about his indiscretions, but only if he held the trump card with those colleagues. He could, for example, say and do anything around Clark Ramsey. He knew more dirt on the district attorney than Ramsey knew on him. Ramsey was also dependent on Bright's political power in the party to help him get the nod to run for governor.

So Bright hadn't hesitated to tell Ramsey he was going to make a play for Katie Hussey. And the district attorney figured a relationship between the two, no matter how shallow, would make them greater allies of his political aspirations.

The congressman, of course, couldn't be seen romancing Katie in public. Having lunch was one thing. Intimacy was something else. So Ramsey had made his home available. He hosted a quiet dinner for the three of them, then made himself scarce.

Katie reveled in the kind of power Bright wielded. Therefore, at

Thirty Six

his command she had no aversion to sneaking up to his hotel suite. That's where she was the night McCall arrived back in San Antonio.

"I don't know what either one of them sees in the other," Dacus told McCall when reporting on the congressman's whereabouts. "They're both ugly as homemade soap."

"Ugly attracts ugly, Dacus. And it's not just physical with those two. They have ugly souls."

"McCall, there are times when your logic scares me."

"You find fault with my logic?"

"To the contrary, what you say makes perfect sense. It's ridiculous, but true."

McCall joked, "Maybe I ought to run for public office."

"No point in getting that ridiculous."

■ ■ ■

Katie had dinner with Bright in his hotel suite. The congressman had a New York strip and she had fillet of sole. Along with the meal, they shared a bottle of the hotel's most expensive wine. Bright always went first class.

He seemed anxious to finish the meal. She didn't know why he was so amorous toward her. She liked it, though.

Lately, there had been coldness to the relationship she had with Ed Parkham. She suspected it was because the managing editor's wife was giving him trouble about staying away from home so much.

Katie liked being with Parkham because of the power he wielded at the newspaper, but his power was small potatoes compared to that of a congressman. She had begun to think that Bright might consider taking her to Washington to take Reggie Smith's place. She liked the idea.

"Awful about Reggie," she said.

"Yes...awful. It's hard to know what goes on in a man's mind."

Katie sipped her wine, then asked, "You had no idea Reggie was thinking about something like this? Had you noticed if he was depressed or anything?"

Bright shook his head in resignation. "No...I had no inkling anything was wrong. He was one of the finest colored men I've ever been associated with."

Katie's and the congressman's professed concern for minorities

DEATH ANGEL

was well known. It was as phony as they were, but they even felt obligated to play the game with each other. "Being black and all, I know Reggie was a big help to you...reaching a constituency that's sometimes hard to reach."

"That's so true. I don't know how I'm going to replace him."

"When you do replace him, will it be with another minority person?"

Bright laughed. "You wouldn't be applying for the job now, would you?"

"You could do worse than have a woman in the position."

Bright said, chuckling. "My political instincts tell me you're a natural for the job, but you're so valuable to me where you are. We'll talk about it again, my dear...after we bury Reggie."

Katie figured if she did all the right things, maybe she wouldn't have to ask again. Maybe Bright would want her closer to him all the time. She leaned forward and gave him a light kiss on the lips. "Why don't we retire to the bedroom and get comfortable," she suggested.

They went into the darkness of the bedroom and began kissing. Then a voice from the darkness said, "Hey, Bob...Katie. How are y'all doing?"

Bright and Katie separated with weak cries of fear. Chills ran up their spines. A bedside lamp suddenly brightened the room. Four terror-stricken eyes saw Matt McCall calmly sitting in a chair beside the bed.

"Sorry to barge in like this, congressman, but I really needed to talk to you."

Katie was stunned, speechless. Bright, his voice quavering, was able to choke out, "What are you doing here, McCall?" He thought he was a dead man. McCall could see it in his eyes.

"I'm not going to hurt you, Bob."

"Call the police, Bob," Katie said, her voice also quavering. "McCall can't get away with this kind of thing."

"Fine with me if you want to call the cops," McCall said. "I just wanted to talk to you about Reggie. But go ahead, Bob...call the police."

Bright's heart rate had, he thought, doubled from the fear he felt. Now McCall's willingness to have the police called created more fear.

Thirty Six

What did the reporter know? "You're not above the law, McCall."

The reporter threw up his hands in a signal of desperation. "God forbid that I should think something like that. Only congressmen and senators are above the law."

"You've gone too far this time," Katie said.

"Not as far as you, Katie. But then...I never want to go that far."

Bright, attempting to regain his composure said, angrily, "Get out, McCall...or I'm going to call the police."

The reporter reached over to the nightstand, picked up the phone and handed it to the congressman. "Go ahead, Bob...call them. In fact, let's call the TV stations, too. You've always wanted to be a star, haven't you, Katie?"

Bright slammed the receiver back in its cradle. "What do you want, McCall?"

"Maybe it would be better if your bimbo here didn't hear, but that's up to you, Bob."

"There's nothing you have to say that Bob's afraid for me to hear," Katie said, hissing.

McCall laughed. "Your call, Bob."

Bright looked into the reporter's eyes and didn't like what he saw. "Maybe you'd better go to the other room, Katie."

She started to object, but the congressman said, "Please, Katie. It's best."

Katie wanted to defy McCall, but not Bright. So she left.

"Okay, McCall...what do you want?"

"I want to talk about the hit man you sent after me."

"I didn't..."

"Oh, yes you did, Bob. But that's immaterial now. If you send another one, though, I'm going to personally come after you...and not to give you a kiss."

"You can't scare me."

"I already have, Bob. There's no place you can go...no place you can hide...where I can't get to you. There's no lock on any door that can keep me from getting you. Even if you sleep with a dozen bodyguards, I can still come in and slit your throat."

Bright's face turned ashen. He knew what McCall said was true. "Men in my position can't be bullied," he said.

DEATH ANGEL

"Men in your position don't know anything but bullying and being bullied. But when you yanked my string, congressman, you got the cat's meow. And by the way, I've got some really good intimate pictures of you and Katie. I've had some of my people taking them for the past few days. And, of course, you know who my people are, don't you, congressman?"

Bright looked like he might be choking. For a few seconds McCall thought he was having a heart attack. The reporter stood and said, "You can call your honey back in now, Bob. If you want to tell her about the pictures, it's fine with me. You see, if something happens to me all the major publications in the country will get a set of the pictures. So will your wife and kids."

Bright choked out; "You're bluffing. You don't have any pictures."

"Do you want to take the chance that I don't? I'll be glad to send you a set of prints for your family album.

"Another thing, Bob...your old pal, Bob Mack, is threatening to kill me. You might want to tell him it would be bad for your career if he did. You might even want to consider resigning your congressional seat."

Bright, sitting on the bed with his face in his hands, seemed to be in a trance. He couldn't believe what had happened to him, couldn't believe it had all happened so fast.

McCall walked out of the bedroom and passed Katie, who was sitting on a couch in the other room. "He's all yours, Katie."

Riding an elevator to the hotel lobby, McCall decided it had been a pretty good day. He figured a good way to top it off would be to call Celeste and Haloran and have them meet him at the diner. Messing with the greasy mind of a congressman always made him hungry for chilidogs.